# SONG
## of the Turtle

BOOKS BY PAULA GUNN ALLEN

*Shadow Country*

*The Woman Who Owned the Shadows*

*The Sacred Hoop: Recovering the Feminine in
American Indian Traditions*

*Skin and Bones*

*Spider Woman's Granddaughters:
Traditional Tales and Contemporary Writing
by Native American Women*

*Grandmothers of the Light:
A Medicine Woman's Sourcebook*

*Voice of the Turtle:
American Indian Literature, 1900–1970*

*Song of the Turtle:
American Indian Literature, 1974–1994*

# SONG
## of the Turtle

---

American Indian
Literature
1974–1994

---

Edited and with an Introduction by

# Paula Gunn
# Allen

ONE WORLD
BALLANTINE BOOKS • NEW YORK

A One World Book
Published by Ballantine Books

Copyright © 1996 by Paula Gunn Allen

Illustration copyright © 1994 by Don Davis

All rights reserved under International and Pan-American
Copyright Conventions. Published in the United States by Ballantine
Books, a division of Random House, Inc., and simultaneously
in Canada by Random House of Canada, Toronto.

http://www.randomhouse.com

Permission acknowledgments can be found on pages 351–353,
which constitute an extension of the copyright page.

LIBRARY OF CONGRESS CATALOGING-IN-PUBLICATION DATA
Song of the turtle : American Indian Literature, 1974–1994 / edited with
an introduction by Paula Gunn Allen.
p.   cm.
ISBN 0-345-37525-4
1. American fiction—Indian authors.   2. Indians of North America—
Fiction.   I. Allen, Paula Gunn.
PS508.I5S62   1995
813'.54080897—dc20                                                95-39251
CIP

Text design by Holly Johnson

Manufactured in the United States of America

First Edition: August 1996

10   9   8   7   6   5   4   3   2   1

In Memory of

Mary Randle TallMountain
and
Ralph Waldo Ellison


*There is no word for goodbye.*
—MARY TALLMOUNTAIN

# Contents

# CONTENTS

# CONTENTS

# BUFFALO POEM #1

## (or)

ON HEARING THAT A SMALL HERD OF BUFFALO
HAS "BROKEN LOOSE" AND IS "RUNNING WILD"
AT THE ALBUQUERQUE AIRPORT—SEPTEMBER 26, 1975


—roam on, brothers . . .

—GEARY HOBSON

# SONG
## of the Turtle

American Indian
Literature
1974–1994

Acoma Pueblo in New Mexico, Pine Ridge in South Dakota, or the Cherokee Nation in Oklahoma, pauperized.

But there is a difference between being caught in destructive circumstances that must be met, creatively, powerfully, or disastrously, and being allowed visibility only when acting within a prescribed role. The role assigned to Native peoples is Victim, and Native attempts to play the hand history dealt them successfully and well are generally perceived negatively by non-Native interests. Unfortunately such attempts, particularly when effective, are all too often met with equal negativity by Native people as well. The "indians" who rebel, who are seen as politically activist, subversive, leftist, or revolutionary—that is, who conform to the assigned role of renegade—are valorized. They attain truly heroic dimensions when they suffer severe consequences for their rebellion. But they are seldom granted celebrity status when they are powerful, healthy, and successful. Perhaps Squanto, Senator Ben Nighthorse Campbell, the Olympic runner Jim Thorpe, or Pocahontas can be said to have attained a measure of celebrity despite their success; but their stature as heroes hardly matches that of Pontiac, Sitting Bull, Crazy Horse, Cochise, or Geronimo. The thing about "indians" is that they must be peaceful, noble, nature-loving, pure, dysfunctional, or dead, victims of a world they never made. But the contemporary situation for Native peoples is rapidly undergoing major transformation, and as it does, literary and, eventually, one hopes, popular notions of what constitutes "indianness" are changing as well. The movement from "lo! the poor Indian!" to a person who belongs to a foreign, albeit domestic, nation, is being chronicled by Native writers, and it is in terms of this transformational process that contemporary Native narrative and fiction can best be understood.

As the United States has moved from a fundamentally industrial society to a "high-tech," service, art, travel, and leisure-based economy, the fortunes of Native communities have noticeably improved. The bumper sticker that jokes "Indian Affairs Are the Best" suggests our increasingly upbeat frame of mind. Native-generated and -implemented efforts are continuing to improve the quality of Native life in the United States and Canada.

The development of gaming and other resort facilities on Native Nation land has significantly improved the economic picture for those Nations that have built casinos, hotels, and the like. In combination with diversified economic development and sophisticated political activity, economic stability is slowly transforming Native communities from exotic bone yards to thriving "domestic-dependent nations" as Chief Justice Marshall defined them early in the life of the white nation. Continuing economic development enables a growing number of First Nations members to live in their homelands if they wish. It also provides funds for the improvements in educational, medical, and other programs designed to enhance Native life.

The old traditions increasingly inform the many aspects of Native life and thought, reversing the trend toward thoroughgoing assimilation that characterized the first two-thirds of this century. Crowded powwows with as many as fifteen drums—complete with between ten and twenty singers per drum—are held all over the country with regularity. Traditional dances such as the Corn dance, the Buffalo dance, Feast Day dances, and the like have regained their popularity among Pueblos. It is expected that a hundred or more dancers, from gray-haired elders to toddlers, will participate in the ancient ceremonial dances, accompanied by a satisfying throng of men singing the traditional songs to the beat of the hand-held Pueblo drum.

The Indian Rodeo is gaining national attention, the Haudenoshonee hockey team plays in international meets, and the American Indian Museum, to be located on the Mall just next to the Capitol Building in Washington, D.C., gathers funds to build. A major Native casino donated 10 million dollars to the fund raising in the fall of 1994, bringing our dream much closer to realization. In New Mexico, Alaska, Minnesota, and parts of California, I see Native people wherever I go—hotels, shopping malls, at the movies, fast-food outlets, upscale restaurants, and coffeebars, working in white-collar jobs in corporate offices, and in numerous government facilities.

Of more moment, there is a growing presence of Native American journalists, celebrities, producers, and directors in electronic and print media on all fronts. The works of Native writers fill more and more shelves, and the audience for media centering on contemporary Native arts, music, literature, and film is growing.

First Nations people are resilient; our survival under centuries of devastation bears witness to the enduring strength of the human spirit. However slow and painful the recovery, Native economic, educational, social, and governmental destinies will continue to come under Native community control, while images of Native people come increasingly under the control of Native writers.

Consigned to cultural and physical extinction by sympathizers and enemies alike, the Native world is rising to face every new challenge with increased determination, clarity, and indefatigable humor. If Native American history over the past five centuries demonstrates anything, it demonstrates the miraculous strength of the human spirit. As we approach the next century and the next millennium (in Christian time), we can borrow a (somewhat amended) comment from Mark Twain: "Reports of our demise have been greatly exaggerated."

In the spring of 1994, the U.S. government removed the gray whale and the American bald eagle from the endangered species list, and that summer, an albino buffalo calf was born to a herd in Wisconsin, in accordance with the prophecy given to the Sioux centuries ago. According to

Lakota tradition, the birth of this white female calf, an event that has not occurred in centuries, signals the beginning of reconciliation between the nations. Perhaps it is that to which Black Elk referred when his vision told him of the restoration of the sacred hoops of all the nations in his memoir, rendered by John G. Neihardt, *Black Elk Speaks*.

The first wave of Native fiction spanned the first seventy years of the twentieth century. The narratives from that period dealt entirely with issues of recovery and identity engendered during the long war and ensuing Reservation Era. For the most part, first wave Native writers referred to the period that stretches from the 1870s to the 1970s, during which time Native nations were dispossessed by the alien nation that conquered them.

The process that culminated in the decimation of Native nations had begun by the end of the eighteenth century, when the United States was expanding rapidly. A combination of northeastern urbanization and industrialization and southeastern agriculture provided a firm economic foundation for the new country, while continuing growth made westward expansion necessary. The transfer of major food production from the South to the Prairie generated a need for land and for improved and extended transportation. The mounting, competing pressures caused turmoil that resulted not only in the Civil War, but, in its aftermath, the almost complete annihilation of Native nations from the Mississippi to the Pacific.

With the end of hostilities between North and South, large numbers of unemployed, traumatized, armed soldiers and dispossessed civilians—black and white—were thrust into a world that no longer had a place for them. Their homes were destroyed; their families lost, scattered, or dead; their fortunes even more uncertain than they were before the war. The displacement of these people compelled a vast and far-reaching transformation in American identity. For Americans of African descent, the upheaval brought the additional burden of sudden change in status from slave to free in a nation that had no desire for citizens not of Anglo-European extraction. Once a small nation plagued by ancient wars imported from England and Europe, the United States emerged from the Civil War a nation in its own right, flexing newly developed military muscles.

Throughout the eighteenth and nineteenth centuries most of the depredations, devastations, and vicissitudes experienced by the infant nation were blamed on Indians. Death, murder, loss of status, failure, and social and physical ills of all kinds were laid at the door of the "Injuns," who more and more came to signify the poverty, disease, homelessness, and degradation the immigrants from across the Atlantic were desperate to escape. This special role of scapegoat, filled by Native peoples until very late in the nineteenth century, expanded to include African Americans as the Native population's threat to Anglo-European dominance waned along with its self-determination and sovereignty. Simultaneously, African and Native peoples intermingled, to an even greater extent than did Anglo-Europeans and Natives, creating a new base of Native population and identity, Native nation by Native nation.

First wave Native fiction did not noticeably center on what popularly became "authentic" Indianness. First wave fiction often involved characters, themes, and settings drawn from mainstream America and Europe. A number of first wave Native writers had been to Europe and England, as well as to New York City, Boston, and San Francisco. A sort of "touring the Western world" convention was tenuously established during that period, connected to boarding school and a host of other assimilationist experiences Native people underwent.

Writers E. Pauline Johnson, D'Arcy McNickle, John Oskison, John Joseph Mathews, and celebrities such as Black Elk, Sitting Bull, and Will Rogers, traveled extensively abroad. Several were educated at Oxford University. Others, like E. Pauline Johnson, niece of the famed American critic William Dean Howells, were closely related to luminaries on the global literary scene.

*Voice of the Turtle: American Indian Literature 1900–1970* is largely devoted to first wave Native narrative, and includes short stories, novel excerpts, autobiographical and biographical narratives, and narratives collected from the oral—or, more properly, the ceremonial—tradition of a wide variety of First Nations. The greater amount of that material had been, of course, collected, translated, and edited for academic journals by non-Native ethnographers and folklorists, though numerous stories were collected by Indian agents working for the United States government, priests and preachers, mountain men, cowboys, and women missionaries, educators, housewives, ranchers, health workers, and artists. Even merchants and soldiers stationed throughout Indian Country contributed to this enormous body of literature. A number were written by native collectors such as Samual Parker and Mourning Dove (Cristal Quintasket).

The second wave, began roughly in 1974, with the publication of Kenneth Rosen's anthology *The Man to Send Rain Clouds*, which concentrated on the work of Southwestern Native American writers. Rosen's anthology features a few themes and approaches that characterized the first wave, but adds what over the ensuing fifteen or twenty years (1974–1989/94) became the defining characteristics of second wave fiction: a sense of renewal and hope; reasserted often deeply angry, Native identity; and incorporation of ritual elements in both structure and content drawn from the ceremonial traditions.

Some selections drawn from Rosen's collection, "Tony's Story" and "Zuma Chowt's Cave," introduce this collection, and the themes they set will be developed in the fiction produced over the next two decades. By and large, second wave stories center on cultural conflict facing the protagonist and/or the community; often the protagonist is mixed-blood, though he/she might also be bicultural. In either case the internal conflict is devastating. The characters, if Native, are usually drawn as innocent, simple folk, who strive to maintain or return to traditional ways. By contrast, the white world surrounding the main Native characters is portrayed negatively; the inhabitants of that world are thoughtless, careless, ignorant, cruel, mendacious, and greedy. There are occasional "good white" characters, but they tend to be portrayed as powerless to comprehend or ameliorate the dreadfulness brought about by their very presence on this continent. The protagonist rebels against whiteness; refusing to assimilate, defiant, and victimized, he (or less often, she) is a proud, angry renegade who attempts to come to terms with oppression that is as much spiritual as economic. In a word, the sympathetic protagonist is always "off the reservation."

Whatever the case, the "drums and feathers" school of indianness in fiction and personal narrative assumed a powerful presence on the American popular, progressive, and literary scene of the 1970s and early 1980s, although, as Native writer and editor Geary Hobson once quipped, "We don't molt!"

Its major popular draw was its near-caricaturing of Native life and thought. For the most part, the second wave of Native fiction depicted Native life as exotic and alien. It was portrayed as marginal, and the catchall term "Indian" unfailingly evoked images of Native people as a variety of fauna, as profoundly spiritual, and as dreadfully victimized—sometimes all at the same time. "Real Indians" were identified by feathers, buckskins, tipis, sweat lodges, pipes, vision quests, psychedelic-induced shamanic experiences, or "medicine power," as well as by a belief system that included the idea that buffalo, coyote, bear, and eagle were possessed of supernatural powers to which the good guys of all races could gain access. The proper situation for authentic Native protagonists was dispossession, anger, and internal conflict brought on by the opposing demands of polarized cultures. The second wave Native protagonist was portrayed by Native writers as a classic victim whose reaction to victimization was sixties civil rights–type protest, with feathers, drums, and sweats added for flavor, deep and ineradicable spiritual conflict with the dominant society, and an aggressive pursuit of traditional spiritual practice—in short, a protagonist modeled on the constructed Native character in works created or heavily edited by Anglo-Americans.

Within this construct, the vast numbers of rural, reservation, and urban Native Americans who are Christian, Republican, conservative, or labor-related Democrat, and bound by all the constraints and conventions of modern American life, were dismissed as "apples"—that is, Native people who are "red on the outside, white on the inside"—or portrayed as ignorant, unlettered victims of white oppression, if they appeared at all within the pages of Native work recognized and lauded by establishment intellectuals, critics, and publishers.

This popular view of "authentic" Indian experience orginated in the work of first wave Native writers and their editors, collaborators, or translators. It was largely a reflection of the Euro-American intellectual's construction of the Indian. From the late 1930s until the late 1960s the characterization of native peoples as both noble and doomed was reinforced by Anglo-American novelists such as Oliver La Farge *(Laughing Boy)* and Frank Waters *(The Man Who Killed the Deer* and *Book of the Hopi)*, as well as by rediscovered classics of Native life such as *Black Elk Speaks.* Their characterization of Native people as inexorably doomed was reinforced by the many films portraying Natives as befeathered, tragic, and conquered—oppressed by nefarious white smugglers, rumrunners, traders, officers in the U.S. military, or local sheriffs. Although it is tempting to excoriate these white predecessors, it is important to remember that their writing generated an audience and provided a template for the second wave of Native writers.

In many second wave works of fiction the Native protagonist was also required to "fall between cultural chairs" and die a noble, tragic death. An alternative outcome, one that gained in popularity as the second wave matured during the seventies and eighties, portrayed a protagonist falling between two chairs, but although all but destroyed, survives, laughs, and walks away, as were the nameless narrator in James Welch's *Winter in the Blood* and Tayo in Leslie Marmon Silko's *Ceremony.* A third option in second wave fiction awaited Abel in N. Scott Momaday's *House Made of Dawn;* Jim Loney, in James Welch's *The Death of Jim Loney* and Ephanie Atencio in my novel, *The Woman Who Owned the Shadows.* In each of these works the protagonist survives, most notably in the ritual made central to their particular traditions. They all accept and thus *become* the tradition-dictated role within the true—that is, the ritual—life of their tribe. Each transcends mundane reality as prescribed by "white-think," and rejoins consciousness in its entirety, the stream of being, the "sacred path," as it might be termed, that defines his or her people's collective identity. The fragmentation of their consciousness is a symptom of coming reintegration or "enwholement." Their redemptive transformations bespeak the inner truth that the oral tradition as well as most of the old tribal lifeways were designed to symbolize. Each of these novels, though largely characteristic of second wave preoccupations, suggest a return of the native narrative to its originating tradition.

In fact, Momaday's Pulitzer Prize–winning novel not only resulted in the development of fiction that would satisfy white readers while responding to the imperatives of traditional life and thought, but also reestablished the position of the old ritual-centered worldview of Native consciousness in Native narrative. In many respects, Momaday is the first writer of the third wave. In first wave fiction the ritual way was portrayed as dying; but beginning with Momaday it began to reassert itself as the center of the narrative in modern fiction, as it is in the old tradition. In much second wave fiction, ritual was stereotyped; however, despite the clichés, it was also reestablishing its central place in the Native narrative. The new narrative was fashioned from a fusion of the west's phonetic alphabet and narrative conventions with tribal modes of inscription and narration. The merger (or marriage, as elders might style it) signaled a new era in both native and American literature.

This major literary event was formally inaugurated at the end of the 1960s with both Momaday's *House Made of Dawn* and stories like Simon J. Ortiz's "Woman Singing," Grey Cohoe's "The Promised Visit," and Ronald Rogers' "The Angry Truck," all included in *Voice of the Turtle*. But it had been signaled within First Nations communities a decade or so earlier. For example, the Hopi, known over the world for their kachina dolls, developed a Mickey Mouse kachina in the fifties. Viewed perhaps quizzically by other Americans, Mickey Mouse kachina implied what the clowns and chorus at feast day dances dressed as Anglo ranchers, bankers, insurance salesmen, and turquoise-laden *touristas* also signified: We are ritual, sacred-centered peoples who reside equally in the modern and the ancient worlds. Liminality is our chronic state, and transformation is our daily enterprise.

Liminality, literally a state of being on the threshold, is the most common theme in the native narrative tradition, present long before Momaday but revitalized by him and addressed by most Native writers of the second and third wave. The preponderance of stories from the ritual tradition are concerned with liminal states. It is while one is on the threshold that sacred things happen. The threshold or the doorway implied in the anthropological term "liminal" (from limen, which means threshold), pertains to the process of initiation or transformation. According to *The Random House Dictionary*, liminality is the transitional period or phase of a rite of passage, during which the participant lacks social status or rank, remains anonymous, shows obedience and humility, and follows prescribed forms of conduct, dress, etc. Associated terms that clarify the concept of liminality include limit, which is defined as "the final, utmost, or furthest boundary or point . . . ," and limbic, an adjective that pertains "to or of the limbus or border; marginal." Limbus, a related word used in anatomy and zoology, is defined as "a border, edge, or limb."

Ritual is concerned with liminality; a ritual is invariably occasioned when a person, a community, a region, a season, a wildlife cycle, or any other significant feature concerned with or impinging upon human life is in flux. Of such great consequence in the tribal world is liminality that the entire narrative tradition deals with the many circumstances, effects, and consequences that mark and might result from the liminal phase or passage. It is ritual—that is, a structuring of liminality and the forces that shape it to effect the best results—that informs native narrative as it informs native life.

The period of conquest and colonization led to a massive displacement of ritual from the center of Native life to its margins. But this in itself is in accordance with Native thought, for marginality is in itself sacred, that is, liminal. Even the very forces that whites identify as history, politics, economics, deculturation, and genocide are sacred because they signify the presence of ritual on a virtually cosmic scale. The period between 1492 and 1992 was a liminal state, characterized by the marginalization of the old ways, of native languages, religions, and modes of consciousness. During that time the First Nations were pushed to the "final, utmost, or furthest boundaries" of their existence and they spent five hundred years on the boundaries of consciousness where they were, in old sacred terms, "re-made."

As this great change in consciousness reached its final stage in the twentieth century, native writers and raconteurs, taking their cue from the changes in the oral-ceremonial tradition, from the altered rituals, dances, visions, and dreams, chronicled the movements of the tribal peoples from the utmost boundaries where the natural and the supernatural interact in unpredictable ways to what the Mexican (Aztec) people identify as Sexto Sol, and the Pueblos identify as the Fifth World. During this terrible time the world was transformed; it became something quite other from what it had been. The great change was not confined to the First Nations of the Americas. It included everything. By the end of the century the movement was complete, and second and third wave fiction emerged.

For many native writers adjustment to this startling transformation in the narrative tradition took some time. In their work they chronicled a series of images of Native people and tribal life largely derived from the Euro-American construction of "indian." Native writers, alienated from their home traditions and reservations one way or another, began to explore this strange, new, albeit ancient, Fifth World that had so unexpectedly reappeared, like a mythic phoenix arising from the ashes.

The adjustment was difficult for a number of reasons—the most obvious being the very strangeness of a ritual point of view to modernized, assimilated Native writers. Another was the complexity of the emotional responses to recent events: grief, rage, and despair resulting from the perceived near death of the old ways collided with renewed hope. The results in the narrative were equally complex. One of the prominent early responses in Native fiction was the development of the doomed political activist as protagonist. It was not a far leap from D'Arcy McNickle's Archilde Leon

*(The Surrounded)* or John Joseph Mathews' Challenge Windzer *(Sundown)* to Ortiz's Clyde ("Woman Singing") or Silko's Tony ("Tony's Story"). Even Abel and the events surrounding his rite of passage in *House Made of Dawn* can be read as a further development of the firmly established theme of the renegade who must perish.

But the protagonists in second wave fiction don't perish so much as transcend. This departure from first wave treatments constitutes a recontextualization of the Native world's historic position. The Native protagonist is transformed from white-inspired genocided victim-cum-romantic martyr to the more traditional one who is remade so that he or she can take up the particular ceremonial role to which he or she is suited. In all the stories of this period the unformed, often unnamed, certainly fragmented and virtually anonymous, ancestorless victim/protagonist establishes a secure identity that, often as not, restores the ritual life of the community in some way.

As the second wave gained momentum, stories that flooded from Native pens, typewriters, and word processors began to forge a literary presence apart from the older, white-inspired one. By the late eighties Native fiction was exuberantly exploring every facet of contemporary Native life. Employing a diversity of themes, characters, and settings in kinds of fiction that included serious, fantasy, espionage, mystery, popular, avant-garde, and postmodern, Native writers became an influential presence on the American literary scene.


By the 1990s a new wave of Native fiction, first suggested in the work of second wave writers such as David Seals, James Welch, Leslie Marmon Silko, and Robert J. Conley, began to emerge. New work by writers such as Martin Cruz Smith, Louise Erdrich, and Sherman Alexie was articulating authentic Native American experience. Native identity was being shaped more and more strongly by Native writers who were as comfortable in literary circles as back home on the Res or traveling the powwow highway.

By the closing years of the twentieth century Native histories, stories, narratives, art, and thought were readily accessible in film and on television in dramas, documentaries, and sitcoms. More truly representative Native voices were abroad in the land. Native protagonists might be identified by their drumming or feather ornaments, but just as often they moved in settings that featured jet planes; international wars and intrigue; paramilitary, almost surreal adventures; UFO investigations; and hyperspace starships replete with cappuccino and plates of pasta with pesto. The third wave of Native fiction, developing out of both streams preceding it—mainstream American and international fiction and traditionally "Indian" (drums, feathers, molting seasons, and all)—is following the oldest First Nations traditions. Inclusion, incorporation, and transformation of alien elements into elements of ceremonial significance mark the work of major writers such as Sherman Alexie and emerging talents such as Esther Belin, D. Renville, and Dan Crank, whose stories are among the later entries in this volume. It should be noted that while third wave fiction is a current development in the area of Native fiction, both first and second wave stories continue to be published. It is those works that are most likely to be taught, and on the whole they are the works that gain the widest readership. The three kinds of fiction contained in *Voice of the Turtle* and *Song of the Turtle* are not confined by the calendar; rather they are stories arising from Indian Country that take significantly different approaches to the field.

The works included in *Song of the Turtle* examine the manifold ways in which spirituality and its system of values, attitudes, customs, and manners define the Native world. Each explores some of the consequences of living within a particular paradigm. Essentially, that paradigm assumes that human social and physical well-being requires an openly acknowledged relationship to all varieties of consciousness—human, animal, plant, meteorological, geographic, astronomical. It also assumes that national sovereignty and self-determination, coupled with the renewal of religious traditions, Native languages and knowledge, and economic independence, are equally imperative. These assumptions inform Native texts in particular ways, lending a characteristic stance, structure, and treatment to Native fiction, regardless of the subject, the setting, and the cultural identity of the characters. Stories by third wave writers add a new premise to these assumptions. Their focus shifts from history and traditional culture unalterably opposed to Anglo-European culture to urbanity and a more comprehensive, global perspective.

Ritual or ceremonial understanding of every aspect of human experience is a central preoccupation of Native literature, and even though, increasingly, allusions to the ritual tradition are absent, every work reflects the embedded presence of ritual understandings in Native life and thought. In various ways, every third wave work responds to old traditions by employing devices and themes drawn from them—like the trickster or war—and marrying them to devices and images drawn from modern American life.

Irony, punning, and quirky or wacky points of view are modeled on the trickster tradition that lurks within every traditional narrative and ritual cycle. Some trickster stories center on gambling; some on religion; and some on white laws, social institutions, and beliefs, and their oftentimes ridiculous consequences.

Abduction narratives and rituals often underlie contemporary stories about boarding school, army life, college, marriage, urban life, rape, and growing up Indian. In many ways the abduction story is the Native form of the loss-of-innocence motif that informs much of Western literature. It is most often a primary form for Native women's fiction, as it is a major part of women's traditional narrative.

Similarly, the traditional theme of war plays a central role in Native men's fiction—although there are as many short stories featuring women warriors and soldiers as there are abduction stories that feature male protagonists. Both motifs may have received more Native attention than other equally ancient ones because our recent history of conflict and engulfment made abduction and war stories the most reflective of Native life in the past two to five centuries. Whether or not a similar situation obtained prior to contact is historically unclear. Perhaps much depended on movement and expansion as populations grew or declined, as in the pre–European contact American Southwest, when Athabascan migrations into the region led to at least sporadic warfare between the newcomers and those they would designate *anasazi*, or enemy, the present-day Pueblo and o-o-tam nations.

Partly because of this history, which as with all things had been ritualized when it was incorporated into Native life, and partly because America's need for soldiers as well as for acculturated Native people gave rise to a boarding school system that regimented Native children under strict rules of military discipline, war has long been a major subject of Native fiction. First wave writers addressed the still raging or only recently ended wars between Native nations and the United States, as well as World War I, in which many of those writers fought. Second wave writers took up later world conflicts, using World War II, the Korean War, and the war in Vietnam to further the warrior-writer tradition.

More Native men per capita served in World War II than men of any other group, though at the time many were still officially held as prisoners of war, POWs, by the United States. As many served in Korea, although by then the government's terrorization had lightened sufficiently for one draftee to protest the draft on the grounds that, as a POW, he was prohibited from carrying firearms. His bold act had the result of the "freeing" of Native populations from the tyrannical, all-encompassing grip of government control.

The Vietnam conflict saw even more Native men in the field, although their contribution has not been officially acknowledged as that of African Americans and Hispanic Americans has. Like women in war, Natives are dismissed, though the Pima hero Ira Hayes was honored in statuary for his participation in planting the American flag at Iwo Jima. Whatever post-traumatic stress syndrome returning Native Vietnam vets suffered must have merged with the post-traumatic stress that had already affected their lives, and the lives of the Native community nationwide. While service in Vietnam undoubtedly rendered a number violent, abusive, alcoholic, and drug-addicted, it also freed the vets from the last vestiges of Reservation Era psychology.

Because of the impact of centuries of war on generations of Native people, much of second wave fiction is bound up with the mysteries and horrors, the surprises and transformations that war, when placed within a ritual framework, necessarily involves. And because of Native people's powerful tendency to perceive events as inextricably bound up in the Great Mystery, conquest, enforced change, assimilation, acculturation, and reeducation all become vehicles for transformation, and at the same time function as engines of devastation, itself a profoundly sacred process.

The questions of identity and of the boundaries of consciousness and race permeate all First Nations texts, relating them securely both to the tribal tradition from which they spring, and to the larger American world in which they exist. But the narrative of loss and recovery of identity, a process which informs much of both contemporary Native and contemporary American fiction, is giving way to a cynical, ironic, complex assertion of identity.

In Native oral, ritual, and narrative traditions, identity loss, identity development, and more than one transformation in identity over a given character's lifetime play a major role. Often, the identity of several characters shifts from one category to another, in the course of one narrative or "dance," instructing us that permanency of identity is neither basic nor even necessary to orderly human existence. This fluidity can be perplexing or threatening, but its presence in a story signals and defines the transformational nature of human experience. In the Native narrative tradition everything, including personal identity, is a complex, strange yet familiar series of shifts and transitions; a green corn dance, spring renewal, or autumn hunt dance.

As it happens, Native fiction based on identity issues holds particular appeal for American readers because identity is a major preoccupation of American literature. In this country the rigid sense of self demanded by Anglo-European values is difficult to achieve. The United States is a society based on a multiplicity of cultures, languages, and traditions. It is still in a formative stage. Fluidity of identity implies fluidity of every kind of boundary, an attractive notion for Americans. And while boundary crossing is fraught with dangers, Native narratives often highlight the even greater danger of fixing those boundaries. The interplay among forces that characterize one side of the boundary or the other is a major source of humor in Native stories, where it contrasts Native views to the rigidity required in mainstream American society.

Transformation is a miraculous thing: At present, First Nations are transformed into recreational vehicles that cruise the freeways of life forever. Sometimes splendid Winnebagos meet Cherokees that have miraculously become sturdy all-purpose vehicles built to roam the wilderness untroubled by anything but fences, like great Native leaders who not so long ago threatened the burgeoning white nation, or are overtaken on superhighways by rotary-engined Navajos. During the Reservation Era, Chief Pontiac's sculpted profile, mounted triumphantly on sleek, polished hoods, headed courageously into the winds of change, and a stylized "Indian head" and a buffalo adorned a nickel that was still of worth.

Lately, items of clothing bear names taken from Native nations. They are sold in shopping centers named Sacajewea Square and Kachina Mall. Gigantic investment combines support and promote athletic teams called Chiefs, Redskins, and Braves. The Gambler, one of the more shadowy supernaturals that people Native life and legend, takes over where Coyote left off: Bingo, electronic poker, roulette—good times on the brink of pouring in glitter temptingly across reservation lands. The old ways—counting coup, settling grievances with a certain kind of dance, *waltis* (that incredibly diverting Micmac game), the moccasin game, and footraces against the sun—change into court battles, barricades, black-hatted rifle-armed New World warriors holding out against time, radioactive land and water, and livestock, game, and human beings that glow in the dark. It's transformation time. Amazing.

Third wave fiction is a powerful sign of the spring winds that blow over urban Indian neighborhoods, rural communities, and reservations. This wind arises out of the colliding weather fronts of despair, rage, laughter, and celebration, the intense meeting of the ancient and the not-yet-come, and the words of the writers who formed the waves that came before. Out of it a distinctively American fiction first crafted by Native writers exerts its growing influence on the American literary scene.

Aho!

# OPAL LEE POPKES

## Zuma Chowt's Cave (1974)

*Opal Lee Popkes' story, "Zuma Chowt's Cave," appeared in* The Man to Send Rain Clouds, *the earliest fiction anthology devoted to work by Native writers. In her perceptive and rollicking tale, Popkes institutes an approach to Native fiction that for the most part will lie dormant for twenty years. The story takes place over the course of the Reservation Era, and reveals Native possibilities that far outreach those prescribed by conventional wisdom. A popular tale, "Zuma Chowt's Cave" has been republished numerous times in the United States and in other countries.*

*In the autobiographical note included in the anthology, Popkes recalls her mother's response when she asked why they didn't have any oil property like some in their family. "My relatives were smart," the eighty-four-year-old woman replied. "They married rich Indians. I married an illiterate Irishman who gave my oil rights away." No doubt her family's atypical experience had real bearing on her wonderful, atypical work.*

In 1903 an Indian named Chowt followed a pack of rats through Dume Canyon, north of Santa Monica. To Chowt, the wind-scarred canyon was not Dume Canyon (a white-man name) but was called Huyat, something white people would have laughed at had they known its meaning.

But the white man chasing Chowt was less interested in the terrain than in proving his superiority to a fleeing Indian. Chowt had learned devious methods of avoiding capture. He tried to tell them the truth. He was following a rat, which was the truth. The white man stopped chasing, and sat down to laugh so long and hard that Chowt escaped and continued to follow the trail of the rat.

Chowt did not particularly care for his diet of small animals unless he was near starvation, but at that moment he was. He was also thirsty.

Nineteen hundred and three was a dry year, when rats in prolific numbers left their haunts in search of water. In fact, the year was so dry they said that even a rat with an itch could start a fire with the shine of his eyes. Rubbing two blades of grass sparked a conflagration.

The rats searched for water. Chowt hungered for the fresh coolness of spring water. So he followed the rats through Dume Canyon, along the split-rock cliffs beside the Pacific Ocean. There was plenty of ocean to drink, but the rats knew as well as Chowt to scamper down the ocean edge, to other places, darting back and forth. Chowt sat down on a rock and waited for them to make up their minds. The little water wands didn't seem to be in any great hurry.

Chowt was a little man, small even as Indians go, and appeared to be a large bird poised on the rock, with his tiny legs drawn up under him.

The rats angled up a burned slope. Chowt followed. They ignored him. He was too far away to be attacked, but close enough to see the hundreds of gray bits of coarse fur, slipping in and out among the rocks, clinging with long tails and claw feet, always upward on the smooth slope, bypassing the boulders, going around the steep upward crags, speckling the side of the hill. They angled back and forth, but their general direction was to the north, from where even Chowt could smell water.

It took them two days to reach the top of the hill. They drank the meager dew at night, ate the same wild oats Chowt ate, and chewed on the same berry bushes. Chowt's body craved meat, but he waited patiently for them to find water before he would devour the water wands.

Chowt could see higher hills, even a few mountains to the north, but the rats seemed to prefer this particular hill, which climbed abruptly toward the ocean, ending in a sharp, high cliff facing the Pacific. Chowt knew the hill also ended in an abrupt cliff on the north side. The south slope was covered with gray vegetation, burned by wind, salt, and sun. Toward the east, the hills meandered into other, taller hills. But the rats went north, where a five-hundred-foot drop awaited them.

They continued onto a rock jutting out ten feet or so above the northeast canyon floor and disappeared. Others traveled over the top until all the rats had disappeared. None fell into the canyon, therefore Chowt knew they had found their gold.

Chowt waited patiently, in case the rats came out. During the night he heard them scurrying about, eating grass seeds, and then hiding again before the sun lightened the sky.

Chowt waited for the sun to come up, to evaporate any dew that might make the rocks slick. Then he walked casually to the top of the boulder, squatted, leaned over to see a small cave entrance large enough for any midget Indian named Zuma Chowt.

Slowly he swung himself down, with nothing but a half thousand feet of air below him, and clung to the rock with lichen tenacity, hanging by the sweat of his fingers. His feet swung blindly toward the rocky lip below the cave entrance. With a mighty swing he heaved himself feet first into the cave.

He crawled backward, listening, hearing the gush of liquid echoing in the silent cave. Every few feet he swept his short arms above him, judging the ever-increasing height of the cave ceiling. Then he stood erect in the damp stillness.

Dark encircled him completely as he felt along the side of the cave until water splashed onto his hand. He smelled the water before he drank, then felt with his feet to find where the spring splashed from the cave wall; he stood under the cold water and murmured pleasures. On hands and knees he followed the stream to its outlet in the rocks.

The next few weeks Chowt spent trying to get out of the cave. He made the inside of the mountain into a molehill in his desperate struggle for survival. He pounded the walls, listening for the dull, flat sound that said dirt instead of rock, a place to dig for an opening, an escape.

Using his strong, thin fingers, he clawed and dug at the dirt that faced the ocean, because a deep cleft in the rock floor indicated that at one time the water had emptied into the ocean through a waterfall which had been shunted aside during some past earthquake. Somewhere in that rocky cliff there must still be an opening.

When hunger gnawed at him, he sat quietly, waiting for the rats to attack. Then he pounced and came out the victorious diner. But the supply of rats was rapidly becoming exhausted, and still he had not found an exit.

Then one day Chowt's raw and bleeding hands dug into dirt and returned filled with nothing but salty ocean air. He peeked through the hole to see the sun setting on a brilliant ocean. He ripped his clothing apart, made a rope, and swung down.

In the months that followed, Chowt decided that the better part of valor—eluding the white man—would be to make the cave his home. He stole ropes and spades from nearby villages and returned to the cave.

He would sit on the top of the hill and contemplate his home and stare for long hours at the ocean which crashed against the cliff below. Then one day he shoved a few stones here and there, placing them carefully at the top of the hill where the cracked stone layered beneath the thin vegetation. Then he swung down to the bottom of the cliff and stood in the surf, looking upward. Carefully he shoved stones here and about. Though the rocks appeared to be shoved at random, he had a plan.

When he went topside again, he broke small stones loose from beside and beneath the larger ones, and suddenly it seemed that the whole cliff was tumbling into the ocean.

He waited until the dust had subsided, then looked down at the debris he had created. The top of the hill was now reasonably flat, and as the stones and boulders had fallen they had crashed into the smaller ones he'd placed so carefully, thus changing the course of the stones so they landed in a haphazard V in the ocean.

He sat for a long time in the cliff opening, waiting for the tide to come in, and when it did the water roared into his inlet with a vengeance. He tossed out a long piece of twine with a fishhook on the end.

But along with the man-made fishing hole came an unexpected problem. The tide rushed into the V-shaped inlet and, with nowhere else to go, rose with a roar, splashing water halfway up the cliff. During storms the waves would expend themselves, with a mighty heave, into the cave itself.

Luckily, however, storms were infrequent, and with his stolen spade he dug dirt from inside his new home, moved rocks, chiseled, and finally fashioned a commodious place which, though dark and cool, was periodically washed by ocean storms.

He dug out the other veins of the cave. He stopped fighting the white man long enough to settle peaceably in Dume Canyon.

Once or twice a year he walked to Oxnard to earn or steal oddments of clothing. He was past the time when the pecking between races excited him, and, too, the white man had become bored and embarrassed by the continual harassment of the remnants of Indian bands.

His female Indian acquaintances wanted nothing to do with itinerant Indians. They had jobs as servants, or returned to the reservations.

During the hot California summers he walked throughout the state, wherever he pleased, looking not unlike a tiny Mexican—except for the fold of skin across his eyelids and his thin mouth—dressed in a pair of boy's overalls. In winter he improved his quarters.

Dume Canyon, squatting halfway between Santa Monica and Oxnard, improved with the help of Chowt. He trimmed dead branches for firewood, used the dead brush for bedding, trapped the wild animals that harassed the ranchers, cleaned the cliffs of dangerous rocks that might fall on him, or unsuspecting cowboys, and developed the water source in the cave. He learned to harness the black gold which dripped and disappeared between the rocks inside his cave—and in the discovery, made quite by accident, he almost buried himself alive.

Few people knew that Chowt lived in a cave in Dume Canyon. After two white men fell off the cliff trying to get to him, they decided he was a monument to the judiciousness of the new laws that said Indians hurt nobody.

A few years after Chowt arrived, the state built a road along the ocean, cutting through the rocks at the foot of his cliff home. The builders never realized Chowt was watching them from behind the dead branches that camouflaged his cave opening.

Civilization closed in on Chowt after that first road was built. It hurt him to see a wagon and team of mules, then eventually a car or two, drive past, filled with people. Though he mellowed and became like a bonsai—tiny, pruned, seeming to live forever as an unseen gray ghost—civilization hurt him. When there had been no one, it had been easier; now he felt an ache, like a missing leg, a missing arm; he longed for human laughter, a human voice.

One day he returned to the cave with a friend, a fellow Indian, but after a year or two the friend couldn't stand the solitude and loneliness, and left. Chowt tried bringing a squaw to live with him, but she couldn't stand him. So he built, and struggled on, until loneliness overwhelmed him again.

One day when Chowt was seventy-five, he raided the home of an Oxnard banker, kidnapped the Indian servant girl, and took her for a wife. The older people in Oxnard remembered him then and laughed at the romance of such an old codger. Newspaper people searched old files and reprinted the old stories about him. A master's thesis was written about the one remaining Indian in the area, the goat of the hills. One doctor's dissertation was begun, but when the doctor-to-be tried to climb up to Chowt's cave for an interview, he fell off, after which people decided to leave Chowt alone. Indians were no longer being punished for white men's clumsiness.

And much to everyone's surprise, including Chowt's, the Indian girl stayed with him.

By 1944 he was completely forgotten by the younger generation. He was ninety years old, but still active and well. He had learned a few English phrases from his wife and still made a few trips into Oxnard, but most of his time was spent happily with his wife and daughter, whom he taught to survive in the best way he knew how—through his old Indian ways. His fortress was inaccessible, his life was secure, and he saw no reason to change his ways for himself or his little family. His cave was situated on public land, so no person harassed him about it.

Once a scoutmaster shepherding his troop through the area thought he saw a gray ghost of a woman swinging across the cliffs on a rope, but he refused to admit it to his scouts, and instead told them about Tarzan. A motorist swore he heard a mermaid singing off key, but the motorist had liquor on his breath. An intrepid teen-age rock hound told people how he caught his foot in a trap and a dark woman with a hairy body opened the trap and set him free. But the teen-ager gave up rock collecting and did not return for a second look.

A man named Leo Carrillo offered to finance a public park out of the area, but nobody wanted useless rocks and a cruel surf.

Also in 1944, Chowt's daughter turned fifteen. Her brown skin blackened from the sun, she was a thin shadow climbing over rocks and through bushes, with wild, uncombed black hair and a bloodcurdling scream that practiced peculiar English to the Pacific Ocean. She would swing on a wet seaweed rope firmly anchored inside the cave, or use one Chowt had stolen at Oxnard. Any person seeing her thus move over the face of the rocky cliffs would have sworn he had seen a mountain goat skipping nimbly. And with good reason. She wore garments of fur or skins, having made them according to Chowt's instructions. She balanced herself with the agility of a mountain goat, having learned that from her father, too. He taught her how to squat high up in the rocks in the sun, like a gray wildcat, to watch the ocean for food. He taught her everything he knew, and her mother taught her pidgin English.

The Indian girl squatted on a rock far up on the cliff to watch what appeared to her to be a log drifting in to shore. She spread her leather skirt about her legs, dug her toes against the rock, and pondered what she could do with that log.

It wasn't the same kind of log one chopped down green or picked up from a dead tree. Driftwood was hard and light.

"I want that log." In her mind she devised various uses for it. She could cut it in half and make two stools. She could burn out the center and make a dugout canoe. She could split it, burn it, make fence posts, a seat, or even a ladder out of it. No, it wasn't a scrubby pine or a limber sapling. It would be pretty, too. She could even float on it out into the ocean and catch fish.

She swung down the cliff on her rope, ran across the rutted road to the beach, and dived into the breakers, her leather skirt clinging to her body like a second skin. As she swam closer she saw a person clinging to the driftwood and as she came up to him he smiled wanly, thinking help was arriving. The girl slapped him across the side of the head, sending him tumbling into the breakers. With one hand grasping the log, she swiftly outdistanced the weary man.

He pleaded, but she was already nearing the beach. Salt water filled his mouth. He sputtered. He turned on his back to float, letting the surf carry him toward the beach, until finally he lay like a half-drowned rat amid the litter of rusty cans, half-buried old fire holes, broken bottles, soggy paper cartons. All with a stench to match.

"Fuckin' bastard!" He lay there shivering, the sand filtering over him in the strong wind, as he waited for his breath to return. He looked about for a place to hide in case the military was searching for him. Down the coastline, shrouded in September heat, he could see the outlines of a military post. He judged the distance to be about five or ten miles. "Goddamn! I didn't desert just to be shot for a deserter!"

The entire beach was as silent as the day Chowt had first stepped upon it. Seagulls perched or stood at the water's edge, backing away when the surf nibbled at their feet. Then they followed the water as it went out again, leaving bits of smelly sewage. They clustered in groups that flew upward to avoid the incoming water, searching to find fish, because they had already picked the rusty cans clean or eaten the last bit of discarded meat. No sunbathers came to this beach any more, because of the garbage and also because its surf dumped clumps of oil and tar from a sunken tanker a few miles offshore.

Sand whirled and dribbled over the rocks, only to be captured by the water as the surf pounded forward. There was a smell of tar and oil everywhere.

When the man finally staggered to an upright position, the seagulls fled. "I wonder where that damn dame came from," he said aloud, but his words drifted into the wind and smashed on the red-rock canyon walls leaning in layers for miles down the deserted shoreline.

He could see the road clinging to the edge of the ocean. But there was no car in sight. "Gas rationing," he said, glad no civilian was about to intrude on his freedom. The eroded stone peaks stood defiantly against the ocean, with only the ribbon of road hanging between.

He stared at the cliffs. No vegetation except bunches of dead bushes dotting the cliffs. Nothing but broken rock—pocked, burned black by wind and sun, or bleached red. No life. To the south, through the haze, he could see what he thought was Santa Monica.

He crossed the road and stood beneath the canyon cliff, where the wind was less fierce. Breakers followed him obediently to the road, fell back. Huge boulders lay to either side of him.

He saw a car coming so he hid among the coarse rocks. There, warm, resting in a pocket of sun, he moaned, laid his head on a bunch of dry grass, and waited for the car to pass. Then he sighed, leaned more comfortably into the warm afternoon sun, closed his eyes, and went to sleep.

Several jeeps full of military police drove slowly back and forth, and had Private Nelson Winks been awake he would have heard them say, "Probably sharks got him." And, "Don't see how he had the strength to make it. Probably drowned."

The girl hid above in the cave, and when Private Winks awoke, the beach once more seemed vacant and captured in silence. He rummaged in his pockets for food, found nothing but a chewed wad of gum and a wet cigarette package. He laid the package of cigarettes on the rocks to dry and popped the gum into his mouth, chewing lint and gum together. The gum still contained its spearmint flavor.

He climbed up onto one of the boulders. Just as he reached the top he fell back, but not before he had seen a service station down the road. "Coupla miles. And I don't see no MPs." His intention was to walk to the service station, but he changed his mind when he heard a jeep nearing from the north.

"Damn, they ain't gonna find me!" He hid behind a boulder. "Thousand miles of water in front of me, and rocks behind me. No better than a cornered rat."

But the jeep drove by, and his confidence returned. He said aloud, "I can make it to the service station before dark."

Seagulls once more perched around him. Then he heard a noise above. Thinking it was a seagull, he looked up, preparing to duck, but he saw the figure of a girl dressed from head to foot in skins.

"Rat's ass!" he exclaimed, sheltering his head from the shower of rocks. "I know that's a girl," he muttered, "but she don't look like no broad I ever seen." He moved aside as a large rock bounced where his head had been a moment before. "That's the same priss that tried to bash my head in and stole my log. How the hell did she get way up there? She must be half mountain goat!"

She was brushing rocks off the ledge, and they fell like bullets around Winks. He clasped his hands together over his head. "Damn you, you she-ass. I ain't gonna take that!" He reached for a rock and slung it upward. She plucked a rock out of a crevice and threw it at him. He ducked. The rock missed his head but slammed into his leg, knocking him sideways, so that he hit his head against the cliff and crumpled down, unconscious, on a jagged seat.

She sat on the ledge, dangling her feet over the side, now and then nonchalantly peering down at his prone figure. She was very dark, and her long black hair was plaited into a pigtail that coiled like a snake beside her on the ledge.

She heard a call from above, and the face of a woman appeared out of the cave. Her mother said something in her native tongue to the girl and it was ignored as the girl casually swung her feet back and forth. The woman repeated her demand and the girl said, in English, defiantly, "I won't!" It wasn't the kind of flat, angry "won't" a white girl might have uttered, in that there was no stubbornness to her tone of speech. Rather, her voice was coarse and untrained, oddly singsong, as though she'd learned English that had been tuned in to the wind, moving up and down as though the notes had been blown across the top of a bottle. Actually, that was indeed why she spoke English that way—because it had come to her from across the cave entrance.

"You will!" said the older woman, in a softer English than the girl, for the mother had learned her English from people accustomed to speaking it.

"I won't!" said the girl. "Kill him." She picked up another rock, aimed it down at Winks.

The mother said patiently, "I tell you it is a man. A man like your father. It is a man like a husband. It is not an animal to be slaughtered for food. It is a man. A man!"

"White man?" she asked, and the words were strangely harsh against the cliff.

"White man," said the mother.

"Kill, kill, kill, kill," she singsonged. "Kill, kill, kill, kill."

The mother reverted to her native tongue. *"Ubayi na Chowt, na Chowt."* Then she lowered a rope.

The girl pouted, muttered angrily, but climbed down the rope, barely touching the rocks as she swung in and out, shoving with her toes like a ballet dancer. Then she stood beside Winks, looked down at his limp figure, picked up a rock, and pulled back her arm for a good hard aim.

The woman let loose a blistering string of words, clearly condemning the girl. She kept scolding her, chattering like an angry bird, while the reluctant girl tied the rope about Winks. Then the woman began pulling him up the side of the cliff to the cave above.

The girl made no attempt to move the soldier's limp, unconscious body out of the way of the sharp rocks which ripped into his flesh; his blood marked his ascent up the wall.

Then the girl shoved him into the mouth of the cave, tossed the rope in, and went away to sulk on the ledge hewn out of the wall inside the cave. She watched her mother take long thin leaves from a plant and lay them on Winks's bleeding back, on the open wounds the rocks had cut into his shoulders, and where his head had banged against the cliff. She tied the leaves on with green seaweed strings around his head, waist, and chest. She tied his hands together and his feet; then she, too, went to the ledge and sat down beside her daughter.

They argued, jabbered, chattered—first in their native tongue, then in sprinkles of Spanish, English, whatever language the woman had picked up in the kitchens of her past. There was even a *"mais oui."* However, English came more easily.

The old woman said, "When I came here there were no soldiers, no roads, nothing but water and rock and Henry's tree. Now we got dirty beach and rocks. Trash on beach."

"Trash on beach," echoed the girl. "Trash on beach."

"I sen' you to Mrs. Eli. She teach you white ways of white man," said the mother, not knowing the woman called Eli had been dead for ten years.

"But Dowdy says stay here where Henry only kill," argued the girl. "Henry" was the name they had deciphered from a cross Chowt had once stolen from a church. The cross now occupied a revered niche next to the drops of oil that fell continually onto a rock where, once lit, they burned steadily like a candle might—a spot where the family did its cooking and odd worshiping.

Winks opened his eyes, rolling them in an arc that took in the whole room with a quick glance. On seeing the two women, he yelled. They answered coolly, in quiet words that, even though spoken in English, had a wild quality, perhaps because they blended with the pounding surf. *"Pray to Henry,"* the old woman was saying.

They watched Winks struggle with his seaweed bonds, screaming at them. They did not stir, even when he wriggled across the stone floor to the cave entrance and looked down at the road below. He moaned, inched himself backward, sliding, dragging a seaweed mat they had placed under him.

For a long time he stared at them, the gloom of the cave broken by a single shaft of light from the cave opening, then he whispered in an agonized voice through his pain. "You ain't niggers. You ain't got them flat noses or wide lips, and they ain't got your kind of hair. I know now. I'm on Guadalcanal, and you're natives, and I'm about to be dumped in a stew pot." He began to whimper. The two women did not move.

"Who are you?" he pleaded. They ignored him but continued their jabbering to each other while he tried to add them up to something. "Let me see.... I was near Santa Monica when I dove overboard. I know I wasn't rescued. I couldn't have drifted down to Old Mexico because I never lost sight of that string of mountains. But you can't be Americans, because people like you don't live in the U.S.A."

His head hurt, and he wondered if they had smashed it. His hands were tied. They had even knotted the seaweed between his fingers, spreading them until they felt like crabs. The rough weeds with which the old woman had treated his wounds felt like spikes. He looked toward the little oil flame beside the cross. The slow drip would fall on the rocky niche, burn furiously, then almost go out before another drop ignited it again, and the smoke curled up to disappear mysteriously.

"This is a cave," he argued to himself. "I must be near Santa Monica. I remember. I looked up and something knocked me down. You—dressed in skins. Skins! Indians! You Indians? I'll be damned. Indians!"

The old woman looked steadily at him and nodded as she picked up a flat, hollowed-out rock.

He said, "Well, you ain't friendly Indians. How in the hell did people like you keep from gettin' civilized? Where you been? Don't you know there's a world out there?"

The girl picked up another rock, a long flat one shaped like a fence picket.

He ducked, expecting to be smashed. "Cut me loose?" he asked.

The old woman got up and went over to him, her long black cotton skirt swishing. She reached over him and untied a few of the knots that held his hands and arms.

"She understands, I think," he murmured. He picked some of the leaves from his head, smelled them, muttered, and threw them on the floor. "Wonder what kind of junk they doused me with? They must have beat me up."

He sat up and could see more clearly that the cave was fairly well lighted from the large entrance, beside which was set a cross of wood on which were tied bushes, with their roots sticking out into the cave: a removable camouflaging door.

The room extended backward into darkness, but there appeared to be another source of light where the rocks jutted out to semienclose this particular large room, which was about fifteen feet wide and barely tall enough for a man of Winks's size to stand up. He wished he could.

The floor of the cave was covered intermittently with seaweed mats, tightly woven. Here and there throughout this front area, and in the semidarkness beyond, rocks jutted up two or three feet from the floor; they were hewn flat across the top and crudely made articles were set upon them.

His head began to pain him again. "Damn if that junk didn't have some kind of medicine in it." He felt the side of his face, covered with dried blood. It hurt, so he reached for the leaf he'd thrown away and reinserted it under the seaweed strings.

Here and there on the floor he could see reflections of light playing, as though reflected from water, and he wondered if escape would be possible. As his eyes became more accustomed to the gloom, he saw other things—a crude loom made of tree branches that leaned against a wall near the cliff entrance, bearskins and woven mats hanging neatly from wooden pegs in the rock walls.

The old woman slipped up behind him, grabbed his hands, and looped the seaweed around them so quickly Winks could not protest.

"Damn you to hell. If I wasn't aching in every bone I'd bat you one."

The girl walked away into the depth of the cave. The old woman sat down and silently watched him.

Then Winks became aware of the light sounds of tinkling water falling, bubbling, gurgling, dripping. Yet he saw nothing.

The girl returned, having taken off her wet leather skirt, and was wearing a very short, ragged skirt and a sleeveless cotton shirt. As she moved around he saw she wore no underclothing at all, and there was not a hair on her body. The soles of her feet were white and the palms of her hands were white, in contrast to the deep brown of the rest of her.

I hope they ain't cannibals, he thought. Then, expecting no answer, he said, "How long you lived here?"

The girl said nothing, but the old woman said, in her strange singsong voice that flirted up and down like a flute, "Chowt came here fifty years ago."

"Forty, Mowma," said the girl. Winks could scarcely understand either of them because of the way they trilled and spilled their words like water.

"I'll be damned. What do you want to live here for?" He could smell the salt in the air. Ocean air. "How come your old man picked this place to hole up in?"

The old woman turned to the girl, and they threw his words back and forth, trying to translate them. Then the girl said, in a surly manner, "He followed the rats."

"Rats follow water," explained the old woman.

After having listened to their meager conversation, he was beginning to make out their language. They acted as though their oldest friends were the sun, the wind, the stars. There was no human touch about them. They were people in name only.

"How far to Santa Monica?" he asked. "Why don't you live there? I'd go on relief before I'd live here."

They seemed to tire of him suddenly, because the girl walked away to the place where the little pool of oil burned and returned with what appeared to him to be pieces of tiny tree limbs, which she shared with her mother.

"I'm hungry," he said. He might as well have been one of the rocks protruding from the floor of the cave. "I'm hungry!" he shouted. "Is that a stove? What you got cookin'? I want something to eat." His fear of the woman waned as his pain eased, so he shouted. "You goin' to let me lay here and starve? Gimme one of them sprouts to eat."

The woman bit them off, chewing slowly, ignoring him. "Chowt come and you eat," said the old woman.

Winks thought about her words. "Shout come and you eat?" But he'd been shouting and nothing had happened.

Then the woman went to the kitchen niche again and by the light of the burning oil he could see her pick dishes from between the rocks in the wall. She returned with a tray made of seaweed, on which were a few chipped dishes and some coarse spoons whittled from wood.

She set the tray on one of the protruding floor-rocks near him. He could identify pepper-tree twigs among the woven seaweed of the tray. She set her table.

"You goin' to untie me?" asked Winks.

She returned to the niche for more dishes, this time of metal. She plucked more dishes from a woven bag hanging from a peg between two rocks on the wall. These dishes had the appearance of tarnished, unpolished silver.

Winks turned his attention again to his wounds, which were completely covered by the long strips of leaves and bark. "Whatever medicine man you got, he's better than what they gave me at the dispensary. I'll bet these leaves would even cure the clap!" He looked closely for a long time at his bandages. Then suddenly he said, "You got a bathroom?"

Surely they understood *that* word. The girl looked at her mother, then sat down at the crude table and bit off a piece of stick. She began to chew.

"I gotta go to the john," he repeated. The girl glared, picked up a smooth round stone from a basket filled with rocks, and threw it at him. It missed only because he ducked.

"I gotta go," he said, wondering how Robinson Crusoe had managed. In all his reading about shipwrecks or people abandoned on desert islands this basic bodily function had never been a problem.

He could feel the salt caking on his body, the dried blood. He grunted, imitating a bodily function, hoping. In answer the girl picked up a handful of stones and slammed them at him.

"You are the throwinest female," he muttered.

"I kill him?" the girl asked her mother.

"No. Mrs. Eli had white husband. You have white husband, too, and I have grandbaby."

# LESLIE MARMON SILKO

## Tony's Story (1974)

*Leslie Marmon Silko was very young when Officer Nash Garcia was killed. "Tony's Story," her fictional treatment of that event, sets the tone for her later work and introduces many of the major themes that characterize it, particularly the underside of ritual power. The story chronicles a well-documented event in which materialist and traditional modes of consciousness collide. Silko's narrative thus serves as a commentary on the larger American community, where conflicts between differing modes of consciousness all too often result in disaster.*

*In the early 1950s a state police officer named Nash Garcia was transferred to western Valencia County (now Cibola County) after having been charged with numerous instances of brutality in the Santa Fe area, where he was originally stationed. His brutish habits moved with him and were now directed against Acoma, Laguna, and Navajo residents of that part of the state.*

*At that time there was a state law against selling alcoholic beverages to Native people. However, a number of Native men had returned from World War II accustomed to being treated like Americans. They did not easily accept the degraded status American law and American people extended to Native people across the country. About the time Garcia moved to western Valencia County, a couple of vets, the Filipe brothers from Acoma Pueblo, took exception to the law prohibiting the sale of alcoholic beverages to Indians, as well as to police brutality.*

*One afternoon Garcia observed the brothers making a purchase at the back door of a liquor store in the nearby Anglo town of Grants. Back-door sales to Native people were common at the time. But Garcia saw his chance to accost two men he particularly disliked. He pursued them east on*

*Highway 66 and onto the Acoma Reservation, although New Mexican law prohibited local police from entering the reservation in an official capacity. When he had chased the vets well into the hills, they shot him.*

*"Tony's Story" is not the only story about that pivotal event. It is featured in Acoma writer Simon Ortiz's "The Killing of a State Cop," published in* The Man to Send Rain Clouds, *and forms the basis for N. Scott Momaday's 1968 novel* House Made of Dawn.

## One

It happened one summer when the sky was wide and hot and the summer rains did not come; the sheep were thin, and the tumbleweeds turned brown and died. Leon came back from the army. I saw him standing by the Ferris wheel across from the people who came to sell melons and chili on San Lorenzo's Day. He yelled at me, "Hey Tony—over here!" I was embarrassed to hear him yell so loud, but then I saw the wine bottle with the brown-paper sack crushed around it.

"How's it going, buddy?"

He grabbed my hand and held it tight like a white man. He was smiling. "It's good to be home again. They asked me to dance tomorrow—it's only the Corn Dance, but I hope I haven't forgotten what to do."

"You'll remember—it will all come back to you when you hear the drum." I was happy, because I knew that Leon was once more a part of the pueblo. The sun was dusty and low in the west, and the procession passed by us, carrying San Lorenzo back to his niche in the church.

"Do you want to get something to eat?" I asked.

Leon laughed and patted the bottle. "No, you're the only one who needs to eat. Take this dollar—they're selling hamburgers over there." He pointed past the merry-go-round to a stand with cotton candy and a snow-cone machine.

It was then that I saw the cop pushing his way through the crowds of people gathered around the hamburger stand and bingo-game tent; he came steadily toward us. I remembered Leon's wine and looked to see if the cop was watching us; but he was wearing dark glasses and I couldn't see his eyes.

He never said anything before he hit Leon in the face with his fist. Leon collapsed into the dust, and the paper sack floated in the wine and pieces of glass. He didn't move and blood kept bubbling out of his mouth and nose. I could hear a siren. People crowded around Leon and kept pushing me away. The tribal policemen knelt over Leon, and one of them looked up at the state cop and asked what was going on. The big cop didn't answer. He was staring at the little patterns of blood in the dust near Leon's mouth. The dust soaked up the blood almost before it dripped to the ground—it had been a very dry summer. The cop didn't leave until they laid Leon in the back of the paddy wagon.

The moon was already high when we got to the hospital in Albuquerque. We waited a long time outside the emergency room with Leon propped between us. Siow and Gaisthea kept asking me, "What happened, what did Leon say to the cop?" and I told them how we were just standing there, ready to buy hamburgers—we'd never even seen him before. They put stitches around Leon's mouth and gave him a shot; he was lucky, they said—it could've been a broken jaw instead of broken teeth.

## Two

They dropped me off near my house. The moon had moved lower into the west and left the close rows of houses in long shadows. Stillness breathed around me, and I wanted to run from the feeling behind me in the dark; the stories about witches ran with me. That night I had a dream—the big cop was pointing a long bone at me—they always use human bones, and the whiteness flashed silver in the moonlight where he stood. He didn't have a human face—only little, round, white-rimmed eyes on a black ceremonial mask.

Leon was better in a few days. But he was bitter, and all he could talk about was the cop. "I'll kill the big bastard if he comes around here again," Leon kept saying.

With something like the cop it is better to forget, and I tried to make Leon understand. "It's over now. There's nothing you can do."

I wondered why men who came back from the army were troublemakers on the reservation. Leon even took it before the pueblo meeting. They discussed it, and the old men decided that Leon shouldn't have been drinking. The interpreter read a passage out of the revised pueblo law-and-order code about possessing intoxicants on the reservation, so we got up and left.

Then Leon asked me to go with him to Grants to buy a roll of barbed wire for his uncle. On the way we stopped at Cerritos for gas, and I went into the store for some pop. He was inside. I stopped in the doorway and turned around before he saw me, but if he really was what I feared, then he would not need to see me—he already knew we were there. Leon was waiting with the truck engine running almost like he knew what I would say.

"Let's go—the big cop's inside."

Leon gunned it and the pickup skidded back on the highway. He glanced back in the rear-view mirror. "I didn't see his car."

"Hidden," I said.

Leon shook his head. "He can't do it again. We are just as good as them."

The guys who came back always talked like that.

33

## Three

The sky was hot and empty. The half-grown tumbleweeds were dried-up flat and brown beside the highway, and across the valley heat shimmered above wilted fields of corn. Even the mountains high beyond the pale sand-rock mesas were dusty blue. I was afraid to fall asleep so I kept my eyes on the blue mountains—not letting them close—soaking in the heat; and then I knew why the drought had come that summer.

Leon shook me. "He's behind us—the cop's following us!"

I looked back and saw the red light on top of the car whirling around, and I could make out the dark image of a man, but where the face should have been there were only the silvery lenses of the dark glasses he wore.

"Stop, Leon! He wants us to stop!"

Leon pulled over and stopped on the narrow gravel shoulder.

"What in the hell does he want?" Leon's hands were shaking.

Suddenly the cop was standing beside the truck, gesturing for Leon to roll down his window. He pushed his head inside, grinding the gum in his mouth; the smell of Doublemint was all around us.

"Get out. Both of you."

I stood beside Leon in the dry weeds and tall yellow grass that broke through the asphalt and rattled in the wind. The cop studied Leon's driver's license. I avoided his face—I knew that I couldn't look at his eyes, so I stared at his black half-Wellingtons, with the black uniform cuffs pulled over them; but my eyes kept moving, upward past the black gun belt. My legs were quivering, and I tried to keep my eyes away from his. But it was like the time when I was very little and my parents warned me not to look into the masked dancers' eyes because they would grab me, and my eyes would not stop.

"What's your name?" His voice was high-pitched and it distracted me from the meaning of the words.

I remember Leon said, "He doesn't understand English so good," and finally I said that I was Antonio Sousea, while my eyes strained to look beyond the silver frosted glasses that he wore; but only my distorted face and squinting eyes reflected back.

And then the cop stared at us for a while, silent; finally he laughed and chewed his gum some more slowly. "Where were you going?"

"To Grants." Leon spoke English very clearly. "Can we go now?"

Leon was twisting the key chain around his fingers, and I felt the sun everywhere. Heat swelled up from the asphalt and when cars went by, hot air and motor smell rushed past us.

"I don't like smart guys, Indian. It's because of you bastards that I'm here. They transferred me here because of Indians. They thought there wouldn't be as many for me here. But I find them." He spit his gum into the weeds near my foot and walked back to the patrol car. It kicked up gravel and dust when he left.

We got back in the pickup, and I could taste sweat in my mouth, so I told Leon that we might as well go home since he would be waiting for us up ahead.

"He can't do this," Leon said. "We've got a right to be on this highway."

I couldn't understand why Leon kept talking about "rights," because it wasn't "rights" that he was after, but Leon didn't seem to understand; he couldn't remember the stories that old Teofilo told.

I didn't feel safe until we turned off the highway and I could see the pueblo and my own house. It was noon, and everybody was eating— the village seemed empty—even the dogs had crawled away from the heat. The door was open, but there was only silence, and I was afraid that something had happened to all of them. Then as soon as I opened the screen door the little kids started crying for more Kool-Aid, and my mother said "no," and it was noisy again like always. Grandfather commented that it had been a fast trip to Grants, and I said "yeah" and didn't explain because it would've only worried them.

"Leon goes looking for trouble—I wish you wouldn't hang around with him." My father didn't like trouble. But I knew that the cop was something terrible, and even to speak about it risked bringing it close to all of us; so I didn't say anything.

That afternoon Leon spoke with the Governor, and he promised to send letters to the Bureau of Indian Affairs and to the State Police Chief. Leon seemed satisfied with that. I reached into my pocket for the arrowhead on the piece of string.

"What's that for?"

I held it out to him. "Here, wear it around your neck—like mine. See? Just in case," I said, "for protection."

"You don't believe in *that*, do you?" He pointed to a .30–30 leaning against the wall. "I'll take this with me whenever I'm in the pickup."

"But you can't be sure that it will kill one of them."

Leon looked at me and laughed. "What's the matter," he said, "have they brainwashed you into believing that a .30–30 won't kill a white man?" He handed back the arrowhead. "Here, you wear two of them."


Four


Leon's uncle asked me if I wanted to stay at the sheep camp for a while. The lambs were big, and there wouldn't be much for me to do, so I told him I would. We left early, while the sun was still low and red in the sky. The highway was empty, and I sat there beside Leon imagining what it was like before there were highways or even horses. Leon turned off the highway onto the sheep-camp road that climbs around the sandstone mesas until suddenly all the trees are piñons.

Leon glanced in the rear-view mirror. "He's following us!"

My body began to shake and I wasn't sure if I would be able to speak. "There's no place left to hide. It follows us everywhere."

Leon looked at me like he didn't understand what I'd said. Then I looked past Leon and saw that the patrol car had pulled up beside us; the piñon branches were whipping and scraping the side of the truck as it tried to force us off the road. Leon kept driving with the two right wheels in the rut—bumping and scraping the trees. Leon never looked over at it so he couldn't have known how the reflections kept moving across the mirror-lenses of the dark glasses. We were in the narrow canyon with pale sandstone close on either side—the canyon that ended with a spring where willows and grass and tiny blue flowers grow.

"We've got to kill it, Leon. We must burn the body to be sure."

Leon didn't seem to be listening. I kept wishing that old Teofilo could have been there to chant the proper words while we did it. Leon stopped the truck and got out—he still didn't understand what it was. I sat in the pickup with the .30–30 across my lap, and my hands were slippery.

The big cop was standing in front of the pickup, facing Leon. "You made your mistake, Indian. I'm going to beat the shit out of you." He raised the billy club slowly. "I like to beat Indians with this."

He moved toward Leon with the stick raised high, and it was like the long bone in my dream when he pointed it at me—a human bone painted brown to look like wood, to hide what it really was; they'll do that, you know—carve the bone into a spoon and use it around the house until the victim comes within range.

The shot sounded far away and I couldn't remember aiming. But he was motionless on the ground and the bone wand lay near his feet. The tumbleweeds and tall yellow grass were sprayed with glossy, bright blood. He was on his back, and the sand between his legs and along his left side was soaking up the dark, heavy blood—it had not rained for a long time, and even the tumbleweeds were dying.

"Tony! You killed him—you killed the cop!"

"Help me! We'll set the car on fire."

Leon acted strange, and he kept looking at me like he wanted to run. The head wobbled and swung back and forth, and the left hand and the legs left individual trails in the sand. The face was the same. The dark glasses hadn't fallen off and they blinded me with their hot-sun reflections until I pushed the body into the front seat.

The gas tank exploded and the flames spread along the underbelly of the car. The tires filled the wide sky with spirals of thick black smoke.

"My God, Tony. What's wrong with you? That's a state cop you killed." Leon was pale and shaking.

I wiped my hands on my Levis. "Don't worry, everything is O.K. now, Leon. It's killed. They sometimes take on strange forms."

The tumbleweeds around the car caught fire, and little heatwaves shimmered up toward the sky; in the west, rain clouds were gathering.

# JAMES WELCH

## Yellow Calf (1974)

*In his first novel,* Winter in the Blood, *from which this story is excerpted, Welch chose transformation as his major theme. The narrator, unnamed throughout the book, has reached a liminal state; he is caught between childhood and manhood, unable to move either way. Though he is long past adolescence, he's stuck. His girlfriend has just left him, taking his rifle and his razor, and he spends much of the book trying to find her. He has a pronounced limp, caused by an accident that occurred just as he entered puberty. He lives with his mother, his grandmother, his mother's second husband, and Amos the duck.*

*His own father, along with his brother Mose, is dead, leaving the narrator hung up on death, entangled in it, as are his mother, Teresa, and grandmother and even the narrator's faithful horse, Bird. Lost in the folds of family, grief, and history, the narrator cannot find his identity and so cannot gain a name. In earlier times, before history came to the northern plains, he could have followed the practice of crying for a vision; he would have, because custom and ages-old wisdom prescribed exactly that course for adolescent males. It was a socially sanctioned and elder-directed method by which a boy could be brought safely through the dangerous liminal state of puberty, finding his sense of self and place in the community on the other side of his quest. The nameless protagonist is far too old to have remained nameless. The reason his adolescence, and thus his liminal state, has been so prolonged forms the axis of the story.*

*"Winter in the Blood" is a title that turns on the bitter seasonal conditions Montana suffers; on oral tradition references to winter, to supernaturals with powers that cause blizzards, subzero temperatures and lethal windchills, and death to all that hasn't a safe place to nest from the brutal*

cold; and on the condition placed upon the Blackfeet people in the previous century, from which they still suffer. "Blood," of course, refers to the narrator's race, "blood" being one of the informal names Native young people name themselves. "Blood" refers more subtly to "blood" quantum, to ancestry and definitiveness of identity, both of which are out of kilter in the nameless narrator. "Winter in the Blood" also signifies the time when nothing moves, when Earth herself is in a liminal state, a time that passes almost surreally, all familiar landmarks made strange or invisible beneath the deep snows.

Yellow Calf, a very old man whom the narrator visited a few times with his father and begins to visit again during his time of seeking, holds the key to the mystery of the narrator's identity, to their band's history, and to the narrator's grandmother's heart. The family secret is dreadful, alien to Indians in a modern American world—however rural—and fraught with a depth of shame that goes beyond the almost ordinary bounds of history straight to the heart of war, of old religion, and of devastation. In discovering the family secret the narrator finds himself at last able to move; and the first sign that he has passed through the danger to cross the threshold into maturity is his ability to laugh.

First old Bird tried to bite me; then he tried a kick as I reached under his belly for the cinch. His leg came up like a shot turkey's, throwing him off-balance, and he lurched away from me. He tried a second kick, this time more gingerly, and when his hoof struck the ground, I snaked the cinch up under his belly and tightened down. As soon as he felt the strap taut against his ribs, he puffed his belly up and stood like a bloated cow. He looked satisfied, chewing on the bit. He was very old. I rammed my elbow into his rib cage and the air came out with a whoosh, sending him skittering sideways in surprise. The calf stood tense and interested by the loading chute. Lame Bull cradled his chin on his arms on the top rail of the corral and smiled.

It was a hot morning and I was sweating as I grabbed the saddle horn, turned the stirrup forward and placed my foot in it to swing aboard. As soon as Bird felt my weight settle on his back, he backed up, stumbled and almost went down. Then we took off, crow-hopping around the corral, old Bird hunkering beneath me, jumping straight up and down, suddenly sunfishing, kicking his back legs straight out, and twisting, grunting. We circled the corral four times, each jolt jarring my teeth as I came down hard in the saddle. He started to run, racing stiff-legged at the corral posts, changing directions at the last instant to make another run. Each time we passed Lame Bull, I could see him out of the corner of my eye, head thrown back, roaring at the big white horse and the intent, terrified rider, both hands on the saddle horn, swaying in the wrong direction each time the horse swerved. The calf had started to run, staying just ahead of Bird, bucking and kicking and crapping and bawling for its mother, who was circling on the other side of the corral.

Finally Lame Bull opened the gate, ducking out of the way as calf, horse and rider shot by him out onto the sagebrush flat between the tool-shed and slough. I gave Bird his head as we pounded clouds of dust from the Milk River valley. The escaped calf had peeled off and pulled up short, swinging its head from side to side, not sure whether to follow us or return to its mother. We were beyond the big irrigation ditch by the time Bird slowed down and settled into a nervous trot. He panted and rumbled in-side, as though a thunderstorm were growing in his belly. We reached the first gate and he was walking, trying to graze the weeds on the side of the road. I got down and opened the gate, leading him through and shutting it. A garter snake slithered off through the long grass, but he didn't see it.

We followed the fence line to the west between a field of alfalfa and an-other of bluejoint. Through the willows that lined the banks of the irrigation ditch I could see our small white house and the shack in front where Mose and I used to stretch muskrat pelts. The old root cellar where Teresa had seen a puff adder was now a tiny mound off to the side of the granary. A crane flapped above the slough, a gray arrow bound for some distant target.

Bird snorted. He had caught his breath and now walked cautiously with his head high and his dark eyes trained on the horizon in front of us. I slapped a horsefly from his neck but he didn't shy, didn't seem to notice.

"Tired already?" I said. "But you're an old war pony, you're sup-posed to go all day—at least that's what you'd have us believe."

He flicked his ears as if in irritation but lumbered ahead.

My bad leg had begun to ache from the tenseness with which I had to ride out Bird's storm. I got down and loosened the cinch. He took a walk-ing crap as I led him down the fence line toward the main irrigation ditch. The wooden bridge was rotten. There were holes in the planks and one could see the slow cloudy water filled with bugs and snaky weeds. Bird balked at crossing. I coaxed him with soft words and threats, at last talking him across and down the bank on the other side.

Before us stood a log-and-mud shack set into the ground. The logs were cracked and bleached but the mud was dark, as though it had been freshly applied. There were no windows, only a door dug out of the earth which banked its walls. The weeds and brush stopped a hundred feet away on all sides, leaving only a caked white earth floor that did not give under one's feet. The river flowed through jagged banks some distance away. The old man stood at the edge. As we approached, he lifted his head with the dignity of an old dog sniffing the wind.

"Howdy," I said. The sun flared off the skin of earth between us. "Hello there, Yellow Calf."

He wore no shoes. His suit pants bagged at the knees and were stained on the thighs and crotch by dirt and meals, but his shirt, tan with pearl snaps, seemed clean, even ironed.

"How goes it?" I said.

He seemed confused.

"I'm First Raise's son—I came with him once."

"Ah, of course! You were just a squirt," he said.

"It was during a winter," I said.

"You were just a squirt."

I tied Bird to the pump and pumped a little water into the enamel basin under the spout. "My father called you Yellow Calf . . ." The water was brown. I loosened the bridle and took the bit out of Bird's mouth. It must have tasted strange after so many years. "And now Teresa says you are dead. I guess you died and didn't know it."

"How's that—dead?" He dug his hands into his pockets. "Sometimes I wish . . . but not likely."

"Then you're still called Yellow Calf."

"I'm called many things but that one will do. Some call me Bat Man because they think I drink the blood of their cattle during the night."

I laughed. "But you should be flattered. That means they are afraid of you."

"I have no need to be flattered. I am old and I live alone. One needs friends to appreciate flattery."

"Then you must be a wise man. You reject friends and flattery."

He made fists in his pants pockets and gestured with his head toward the shack. "I have some coffee."

It was only after he started walking, his feet seeming to move sideways as well as forward, that I realized he was completely blind. It was odd that I hadn't remembered, but maybe he hadn't been blind in those days.

He gripped the doorframe, then stood aside so that I could pass through first. He followed and closed the door, then reopened it. "You'll want some light."

The inside of the shack was clean and spare. It contained a cot, a kitchen table and two chairs. A small wood stove stood against the far wall. Beside the pipe a yellowed calendar hung from the wall. It said December 1936. A white cupboard made up the rest of the furniture in the room. Yellow Calf moved easily, at home with his furnishings. He took two cups, one porcelain, the other tin, from the cupboard and poured from a blackened pot that had been resting on the back of the stove. I coughed to let him know where I was, but he was already handing me a cup.

"Just the thing," I said.

"It's too strong. You're welcome." He eased himself down on the cot and leaned back against the wall.

It was cool, almost damp in the banked shack, and I thought of poor old Bird tied to the pump outside. He might get heatstroke.

"You're a good housekeeper, old man."

"I have many years' practice. It's easier to keep it sparse than to feel the sorrows of possessions."

"Possessions can be sorrowful," I agreed, thinking of my gun and electric razor.

"Only when they are not needed."

"Or when they are needed—when they are needed and a man doesn't have them."

"Take me—I don't have a car," he said.

"But you don't seem to need one. You get along."

"It would be easier with a car. Surely you have one."

"No."

"If you had a car you could take me to town."

I nodded.

"It would make life easier," he went on. "One wouldn't have to depend on others."

I wondered how the old man would drive a car. Perhaps he had radar and would drive only at night.

"You need a good pair of shoes to drive a car," I said.

"I have thought of that too." He tucked his feet under the cot as though they were embarrassed.

"There are probably laws against driving barefoot, anyway."

He sighed. "Yes, I suppose there are."

"You don't have to worry—not out here."

"I wouldn't say that."

"How so?"

"Irrigation man comes every so often to regulate the head gate—he keep his eye on me. I can hear him every so often down by that head gate."

I laughed. "You're too nervous, grandfather—besides, what have you got to hide, what have you done to be ashamed of?"

"Wouldn't you like to know . . ." His mouth dropped and his shoulders bobbed up and down.

"Come on, tell me. What have you got in those pants?"

"Wouldn't you like to know . . ." With that, his mouth dropped open another inch but no sound came out.

"I'll bet you have a woman around here. I know how you old buzzards operate."

His shoulders continued to shake, then he started coughing. He coughed and shook, holding his cup away from the cot, until the spasm of mirth or whatever it was had passed.

He stood and walked to the stove. When he reached for my cup, his hand struck my wrist. His fingers were slick, papery, like the belly of a rattlesnake. He poured to within half an inch of the cup's lip, to the tip of the finger he had placed inside.

"How is it you say you are only half dead, Yellow Calf, yet you move like a ghost. How can I be sure you aren't all the way dead and are only playing games?"

"Could I be a ghost and suck the blood of cattle at the same time?" He settled back on the cot, his lips thinned into what could have been a smile.

"No, I suppose not. But I can't help but feel there's something wrong with you. No man should live alone."

"Who's alone? The deer come—in the evenings—they come to feed on the other side of the ditch. I can hear them. When they whistle, I whistle back."

"And do they understand you?" I said this mockingly.

His eyes were hidden in the darkness.

"Mostly—I can understand most of them."

"What do they talk about?"

"It's difficult ... About ordinary things, but some of them are hard to understand."

"But do they talk about the weather?"

"No, no, not that. They leave that to men." He sucked on his lips. "No, they seem to talk mostly about ..."—he searched the room with a peculiar alertness—"well, about the days gone by. They talk a lot about that. They are not happy."

"Not happy? But surely to a deer one year is as good as the next. How do you mean?"

"Things change—things have changed. They are not happy."

"Ah, a matter of seasons! When their bellies are full, they remember when the feed was not so good—and when they are cold, they remember ..."

"No!" The sharpness of his own voice startled him. "I mean, it goes deeper than that. They are not happy with the way things are. They know what a bad time it is. They can tell by the moon when the world is cockeyed."

"But that's impossible."

"They understand the signs. This earth is cockeyed."

A breeze came up, rustling the leaves of the tall cottonwoods by the ditch. It was getting on in the afternoon.

I felt that I should let the subject die, but I was curious about Yellow Calf's mind.

"Other animals—do you understand them?"

"Some, some more than others."

"Hmmm," I said.

"This earth is cockeyed."

"Hmmm ..."

"Of course men are the last to know."

"And you?"

"Even with their machines."

"Hmmm . . ."

"I have my inclinations."

"The moon?"

"Among other things—sometimes it seems that one has to lean into the wind to stand straight."

"You're doing plenty of leaning right now, I would say," I said.

"You don't believe the deer." He was neither challenging nor hurt. It was a statement.

"I wouldn't say that."

"You do not believe me."

"It's not a question of belief. Don't you see? If I believe you, then the world is cockeyed."

"But you have no choice."

"You could be wrong—you could believe and still be wrong. The deer could be wrong."

"You do not want to believe them."

"I can't."

"It's no matter."

"I'm sorry."

"No need—we can't change anything. Even the deer can't change anything. They only see the signs."

A pheasant sounded to the east but the old man either did not pay attention or thought it a usual message. He leaned forward into the shadows of the shack, holding his cup with both hands, looking directly at me and through me. I shifted from one buttock to the other, then set my cup on the table.

"It's not very good," he said.

"No—that's not true. It's just that I have to leave; we're weaning a calf . . ."

"I'm old."

"Yes."

"You must say hello to Teresa for me. Tell her that I am living to the best of my ability."

"I'll tell her to come see for herself," I said.

"Say hello to First Raise."

"Yes, yes . . . he will be pleased." Didn't he know that First Raise had been dead for ten years?

We walked out into the glare of the afternoon sun.

Bird tried to kick me as I swung my leg over his back. "Next time I'll bring some wine," I said.

"It is not necessary," he said.

"For a treat."

I started to wave from the top of the bridge. Yellow Calf was facing off toward the river, listening to two magpies argue.

• • •

"Hello," he said. "You are welcome."

"There are clouds in the east," I said. I could not look at him.

"I feel it, rain tonight maybe, tomorrow for sure, cats and dogs."

The breeze had picked up so that the willows on the irrigation ditch were gesturing in our direction.

"I see you wear shoes now. What's the meaning of this?" I pointed to a pair of rubber boots. His pants were tucked inside them.

"Rattlesnakes. For protection. This time of year they don't always warn you."

"They don't hear you," I said. "You're so quiet you take them by surprise."

"I found a skin beside my door this morning. I'm not taking any chances."

"I thought animals were your friends."

"Rattlesnakes are best left alone."

"Like you," I said.

"Could be."

I pumped some water into the enamel basin for Bird, then I loosened his cinch.

"I brought some wine." I held out the bottle.

"You are kind—you didn't have to."

"It's French," I said. "Made out of roses."

"My thirst is not so great as it once was. There was a time . . ." A gust of wind ruffled his fine white hair. "Let's have it."

I pressed the bottle into his hand. He held his head high, resting one hand on his chest, and drank greedily, his Adam's apple sliding up and down his throat as though it were attached to a piece of rubber. "And now, you," he said.

Yellow Calf squatted on the white skin of earth. I sat down on the platform on which the pump stood. Behind me, Bird sucked in the cool water.

"My grandmother died," I said. "We're going to bury her tomorrow."

He ran his paper fingers over the smooth rubber boots. He glanced in my direction, perhaps because he heard Bird's guts rumble. A small white cloud passed through the sun but he said nothing.

"She just stopped working. It was easy."

His knees cracked as he shifted his weight.

"We're going to bury her tomorrow. Maybe the priest from Harlem. He's a friend . . ."

He wasn't listening. Instead, his eyes were wandering beyond the irrigation ditch to the hills and the muscled clouds above them.

Something about those eyes had prevented me from looking at him.

It had seemed a violation of something personal and deep, as one feels when he comes upon a cow licking her newborn calf. But now, something else, his distance, made it all right to study his face, to see for the first time the black dots on his temples and the bridge of his nose, the ear lobes which sagged on either side of his head, and the bristles which grew on the edges of his jaw. Beneath his humped nose and above his chin, creases as well defined as cutbanks between prairie hills emptied into his mouth. Between his half-parted lips hung one snag, yellow and brown and worn-down, like that of an old horse. But it was his eyes, narrow beneath the loose skin of his lids, deep behind his cheekbones, that made one realize the old man's distance was permanent. It was behind those misty white eyes that gave off no light that he lived, a world as clean as the rustling willows, the bark of a fox or the odor of musk during mating season.

I wondered why First Raise had come so often to see him. Had he found a way to narrow that distance? I tried to remember that one snowy day he had brought me with him. I remembered Teresa and the old lady commenting on my father's judgment for taking me out on such a day; then riding behind him on the horse, laughing at the wet, falling snow. But I couldn't remember Yellow Calf or what the two men talked about.

"Did you know her at all?" I said.

Without turning his head, he said, "She was a young woman; I was just a youth."

"Then you did know her then."

"She was the youngest wife of Standing Bear."

I was reaching for the wine bottle. My hand stopped.

"He was a chief, a wise man—not like these conniving devils who run the agency today."

"How could you know Standing Bear? He was Blackfeet."

"We came from the mountains," he said.

"You're Blackfeet?"

"My people starved that winter; we all starved but they died. It was the cruelest winter. My folks died, one by one." He seemed to recollect this without emotion.

"But I thought you were Gros Ventre. I thought you were from around here."

"Many people starved that winter. We had to travel light—we were running from the soldiers—so we had few provisions. I remember, the day we entered this valley it began to snow and blizzard. We tried to hunt but the game refused to move. All winter long we looked for deer sign. I think we killed one deer. It was rare that we even jumped a porcupine. We snared a few rabbits but not enough . . ."

"You survived," I said.

"Yes, I was strong in those days." His voice was calm and monotonous.

"How about my grandmother? How did she survive?"

He pressed down on the toe of his rubber boot. It sprang back into shape.

"She said Standing Bear got killed that winter," I said.

"He led a party against the Gros Ventres. They had meat. I was too young. I remember the men when they returned to camp—it was dark but you could see the white air from their horses' nostrils. We all stood waiting, for we were sure they would bring meat. But they brought Standing Bear's body instead. It was a bad time."

I tapped Yellow Calf's knee with the bottle. He drank, then wiped his lips on his shirt sleeve.

"It was then that we knew our medicine had gone bad. We had wintered some hard times before, winters were always hard, but seeing Standing Bear's body made us realize that we were being punished for having left our home. The people resolved that as soon as spring came we would go home, soldiers or not."

"But you stayed," I said. "Why?"

He drew an arc with his hand, palm down, taking in the bend of the river behind his house. It was filled with tall cottonwoods, most of them dead, with tangles of brush and wild rose around their trunks. The land sloped down from where we were sitting so that the bend was not much higher than the river itself.

"This was where we camped. It was not grown over then, only the cottonwoods were standing. But the willows were thick then, all around to provide a shelter. We camped very close together to take advantage of this situation. Sometimes in winter, when the wind has packed the snow and blown the clouds away, I can still hear the muttering of the people in their tepees. It was a very bad time."

"And your family starved . . ."

"My father died of something else, a sickness, pneumonia maybe. I had four sisters. They were among the first to go. My mother hung on for a little while but soon she went. Many starved."

"But if the people went back in the spring, why did you stay?"

"My people were here."

"And the old—my grandmother stayed too," I said.

"Yes. Being a widow is not easy work, especially when your husband had other wives. She was the youngest. She was considered quite beautiful in those days."

"But why did she stay?"

He did not answer right away. He busied himself scraping a star in the tough skin of earth. He drew a circle around it and made marks around it as a child draws the sun. Then he scraped it away with the end of his stick and raised his face into the thickening wind. "You must understand how people think in desperate times. When their bellies are full, they

47

can afford to be happy and generous with each other—the meat is shared, the women work and gossip, men gamble—it's a good time and you do not see things clearly. There is no need. But when the pot is empty and your guts are tight in your belly, you begin to look around. The hunger sharpens your eye."

"But why her?"

"She had not been with us more than a month or two, maybe three. You must understand the thinking. In that time the soldiers came, the people had to leave their home up near the mountains, then the starvation and the death of their leader. She had brought them bad medicine."

"But you—you don't think that."

"It was apparent," he said.

"It was bad luck; the people grew angry because their luck was bad," I said.

"It was medicine."

I looked at his eyes. "She said it was because of her beauty."

"I believe it was that too. When Standing Bear was alive, they had to accept her. In fact, they were proud to have such beauty—you know how it is, even if it isn't yours." His lips trembled into what could have been a smile.

"But when he died, her beauty worked against her," I said.

"That's true, but it was more than that. When you are starving, you look for signs. Each event becomes big in your mind. His death was the final proof that they were cursed. The medicine man, Fish, interpreted the signs. They looked at your grandmother and realized that she had brought despair and death. And her beauty—it was as if her beauty made a mockery of their situation."

"They can't have believed this . . ."

"It wasn't a question of belief, it was the way things were," he said. "The day Standing Bear was laid to rest, the women walked away. Even his other wives gave her the silent treatment. It took the men longer—men are not sensitive. They considered her the widow of a chief and treated her with respect. But soon, as it must be, they began to notice the hatred in their women's eyes, the coolness with which they were treated if they brought your grandmother a rabbit leg or a piece of fire in the morning. And they became ashamed of themselves for associating with the young widow and left her to herself."

I was staring at the bottle on the ground before me. I tried to understand the medicine, the power that directed the people to single out a young woman, to leave her to fend for herself in the middle of a cruel winter. I tried to understand the thinking, the hatred of the women, the shame of the men. Starvation. I didn't know it. I couldn't understand the medicine, her beauty.

"What happened to her?"

"She lived the rest of the winter by herself."

"How could she survive alone?"

He shifted his weight and dug his stick into the earth. He seemed uncomfortable. Perhaps he was recalling things he didn't want to or he felt that he had gone too far. He seemed to have lost his distance, but he went on: "She didn't really leave. It was the dead of winter. To leave the camp would have meant a sure death, but there were tepees on the edge, empty—many were empty then."

"What did she do for food?"

"What did any of us do? We waited for spring. Spring came, we hunted—the deer were weak and easy to kill."

"But she couldn't hunt, could she?" It seemed important for me to know what she did for food. No woman, no man could live a winter like that alone without something.

As I watched Yellow Calf dig at the earth I remembered how the old lady had ended her story of the journey of Standing Bear's band.

There had been great confusion that spring. Should the people stay in this land of the Gros Ventres, should they go directly south to the nearest buffalo herd, or should they go back to the country west of here, their home up near the mountains? The few old people left were in favor of this last direction because they wanted to die in familiar surroundings, but the younger ones were divided as to whether they should stay put until they got stronger or head for the buffalo ranges to the south. They rejected the idea of going home because the soldiers were there. Many of them had encountered the Long Knives before, and they knew that in their condition they wouldn't have a chance. There was much confusion, many decisions and indecisions, hostility.

Finally it was the soldiers from Fort Assiniboine who took the choice away from the people. They rode down one late-spring day, gathered up the survivors and drove them west to the newly created Blackfeet Reservation. Because they didn't care to take her with them, the people apparently didn't mention her to the soldiers, and because she had left the band when the weather warmed and lived a distance away, the soldiers didn't question her. They assumed she was a Gros Ventre.

A gust of wind rattled the willows. The clouds towered white against the sky, but I could see their black underbellies as they floated toward us.

The old lady had ended her story with the image of the people being driven "like cows" to their reservation. It was a strange triumph and I understood it. But why hadn't she spoken of Yellow Calf? Why hadn't she mentioned that he was a member of that band of Blackfeet and had, like herself, stayed behind?

A swirl of dust skittered across the earth's skin.

"You say you were just a youth that winter—how old?" I said.

He stopped digging. "That first winter, my folks all died then."

But I was not to be put off. "How old?"

"It slips my mind," he said. "When one is blind and old he loses track of the years."

"You must have some idea."

"When one is blind . . ."

"Ten? Twelve? Fifteen?"

". . . and old, he no longer follows the cycles of the years. He knows each season in its place because he can feel it, but time becomes a procession. Time feeds upon itself and grows fat." A mosquito took shelter in the hollow of his cheek, but he didn't notice. He had attained that distance. "To an old dog like myself, the only cycle begins with birth and ends in death. This is the only cycle I know."

I thought of the calendar I had seen in his shack on my previous visit. It was dated 1936. He must have been able to see then. He had been blind for over thirty years, but if he was as old as I thought, he had lived out a lifetime before. He had lived a life without being blind. He had followed the calendar, the years, time—

I thought for a moment.

Bird farted.

And it came to me, as though it were riding one moment of the gusting wind, as though Bird had had it in him all the time and had passed it to me in that one instant of corruption.

"Listen, old man," I said. "It was you—you were old enough to hunt!"

But his white eyes were kneading the clouds.

I began to laugh, at first quietly, with neither bitterness nor humor. It was the laughter of one who understands a moment in his life, of one who has been let in on the secret through luck and circumstance. "You . . . you're the one." I laughed, as the secret unfolded itself. "The only one . . . you, her hunter . . ." And the wave behind my eyes broke.

Yellow Calf still looked off toward the east as though the wind could wash the wrinkles from his face. But the corners of his eyes wrinkled even more as his mouth fell open. Through my tears I could see his Adam's apple jerk.

"The only one," I whispered, and the old man's head dropped between his knees. His back shook, the bony shoulders squared and hunched like the folded wings of a hawk.

"And the half-breed, Doagie!" But the laughter again racked my throat. *He wasn't Teresa's father; it was you, Yellow Calf, the hunter!*

He turned to the sound of my laughter. His face was distorted so that the single snag seemed the only recognizable feature of the man I had come to visit. His eyes hid themselves behind the high cheekbones. His mouth had become the rubbery sneer of a jack-o'-lantern.

And so we shared this secret in the presence of ghosts, in wind that called forth the muttering tepees, the blowing snow, the white air of the horses' nostrils. The cottonwoods behind us, their dead white branches angling to the threatening clouds, sheltered these ghosts as they had sheltered the camp that winter. But there were others, so many others.

Yellow Calf stood, his hands in his pockets, suddenly withdrawn and polite. I pressed what remained of the bottle of wine into his hand. "Thank you," he said.

"You must come visit me sometime," I said.

"You are kind."

I tightened the cinch around Bird's belly. "I'll think about you," I said.

"You'd better hurry," he said. "It's coming."

I picked up the reins and led Bird to the rotting plank bridge across the irrigation ditch.

He lifted his hand.

# ROBERT J. CONLEY

## Wili Woyi (1979)

*Robert J. Conley's story appeared in 1979 in* The Remembered Earth, *Geary Hobson's seminal anthology, which also included "The Witch of Goingsnake," the title story in Conley's 1988 collection of short fiction.*

*"Wili Woyi" is a contemporary trickster story of the Cherokee, for whom Rabbit, rather than Coyote, plays that creative, comedic, liminal role. In "Wili Woyi" the Trickster is a politically savvy, gifted conjurer, able to avoid detection and detention while demonstrating the injustice of Anglo-American laws.*

*Wili Woyi's response to his persecution is uniquely Native traditional; he does not write letters, file petitions, or organize marches and rallies—all of which are Anglo-American modes and failed the Cherokee Nation miserably in their fight against removal from their homelands in the American Southeast in the 1820s and 1830s. Instead, he calls on the Spirit people by means of a traditional Cherokee charm, invoking ancient law to aid him in his dispute with the white man's legal system. One can all but see Brer Rabbit, the Trickster of the Tsalagee, winking at us in this splendid Cherokee story: "There is a way," his insouciant expression seems to say. "There is always a way."*

### Illinois District, Cherokee Nation, summer, 1886

Wili Woyi sat in the small clearing behind his cabin. The great rocks rose sharply just behind, and above and beyond the rocks, the hills, covered with woods. In the small clearing Wili Woyi sat, and he burned tobacco. *Tso laga yun li.* And as the smoke from the burning *tso laga yun li* rose upward toward the rocks, toward the hills, toward the clouds rolling overhead, Wili Woyi repeated in Cherokee seven times the following charm.

> Listen.
> They will speak well of me today
> there at Illinois.
> Those who would do me harm
> will be wandering about.
> Today I will ride back home again.
> Ha.

Later that same morning Wili Woyi rode toward the Illinois Court House in the Illinois District of the Cherokee Nation where he was to stand trial for having killed a man. He was going in alone. He had given his word that he would appear, and his word had been accepted. He was known as a man of honor. Wili Woyi was not only a man of honor, he knew that he had nothing to fear, for the killing had been done in self defense and, as such, was provided for in the Cherokee National Constitution. Wili Woyi knew that the Cherokee courts were fair, and he knew that Benge, the judge for the Illinois district, was a fair, honorable and intelligent judge. The trial would be brief, and he would be on his way back home soon. He rode with confidence.

Then from ahead on the road he heard the noise of fast hoofbeats. He could not see the rider for the bend in the road, but as he rounded the bend he recognized his friend, Turtle Brashears. When Turtle saw Wili Woyi he called out to him in Cherokee and reined in his mount.

"Wili Woyi. Wili Woyi. Go back."

Wili Woyi, too, stopped his horse.

"What is it, Turtle? Why should I go back? You know that I have given my word to appear in court today because of that man I killed. I cannot go back now."

"It is because of that man that I ask you to go back, Wili Woyi. You will be hanged if you do not go back."

"I am no murderer, Turtle, and our courts are just. They will not hang me. Come. Ride in with me."

"No. Wait. There will not be a trial. Not today and not in Illinois Court House. That is why I have ridden out here to meet you and to stop you from going into court. Judge Benge knows that I have come out here to meet you, though he must keep that a secret."

"Perhaps you should tell me what is going on at Illinois Court House, Turtle."

"Yes. There is a United States marshal waiting there to take you to Fort Smith for trial. There is nothing that Benge can do anymore. That man you killed—he was not of our Nation."

"Ai," said Wili Woyi, smacking himself on the forehead, "then you are right. I will not be taken to Fort Smith to the hanging judge, Parker. It is part of his divine purpose, it seems, to hang Indians in order to bring the law of the *yoneg*, the white man, to our country. He would hang me for sure. I will not go in now."

"What will you do, Wili Woyi?"

Wili Woyi looked up at the sky.

"*U-lo-gi-la,*" he said. "It's cloudy. Come in, Turtle, let's go to my house."

"*Uh, inena,*" Turtle said.


At Illinois Court House a crowd had gathered. There were a number of Cherokees standing about, not waiting to see if Wili Woyi would show up for they knew that once Turtle had intercepted him on the road and told him the news he would not, but to see what the white law man from Fort Smith would do when he had realized that Billy Pigeon was not going to arrive. The white law man was pacing about nervously in front of Illinois Court House. The Cherokee were standing calmly with crossed arms leaning against the side of the court house or sitting idly about under the great walnut trees and cottonwoods which stood nearby. Benge stood in the doorway to the court house. Then the white law man, who was called Glenn Colvert, took a watch from his vest pocket and looked at it.

"He's forty minutes late, now, God damn it. I knew he wouldn't come in here by hisself like you said he would. I never heard of such God-damn foolishness."

"You have no patience, Mr. Colvert," said Benge. "We Cherokee have a different way of looking at time than do you whites. If a Cherokee promises he will be somewhere then he will be there. He may not be there on time, for we have never lived our lives according to clocks as you do. But Wili Woyi—uh, excuse me, Bill Pigeon—is a man of honor."

"Yeah," said Colvert, "so you told me. Look, Benge, ain't you got no deputies here you can send out after 'im? I can't stand around here all God-damn day. I got other things to do, too, y'know?"

"The case is out of my hands now, Mr. Colvert. You should know that. The man that Wili Woyi killed was not a Cherokee citizen, and, as you know, your law will not allow us jurisdiction over such cases. Otherwise, why should you be here? If Wili Woyi has not broken Cherokee law, how can Cherokee law take any action against him?"

"Damn it, Benge, I know all that, but you know as well as I do that that's just a Goddamn technicality. He's killed a man, and I got a legal warrant for his arrest right here in my coat pocket."

"And it's your job to serve that warrant. I have no intention of interfering with you in the line of your duty. Serve the warrant, Mr. Colvert, any time you please. I, however, will not break the laws by arresting a man outside of the jurisdiction of my court."

"Aw, son of a bitch!"

"Mr. Colvert, I suggest you go inside and relax. I believe it's going to rain any minute now. I'm sure that if you'll just be patient, Wili Woyi will show up, and then you can arrest him."

"You people think you're pretty Goddamn smart, don't you? You think you've made a fool out of a duly appointed officer of the law of the United States government. Well, it ain't gonna work. I can tell you that. Maybe I ain't got Bill Pigeon right now. Maybe I ain't gonna get him to-day, but I'll be comin' back, and I'll get the sonafabitch, and I'll have him at Fort Smith in the court."

Colvert stalked to his horse which was tied nearby. He jerked the reins loose from the hitching rail, mounted up hurriedly, and started to ride off immediately, but an afterthought made him turn back to shout over his shoulder to Benge and all the other Cherokees within hearing.

"And I'll see to it personal that you all get a invitation t' the hangin'."

When Wili Woyi and Turtle Brashears arrived at the cabin below the great rocks, they took the saddles from their horses' backs and turned the animals out to graze. Wili Woyi invited Turtle into his house.

"*Da na tlas da yun ni.* We will eat," he said.

He poured coffee grounds into a pot, picked up a heavy iron skillet and handed pot and skillet to Turtle. He found half a cake of cornbread left from earlier in another pot and, taking it up, he led the way back outside and around behind his cabin. There he soon built a small fire, filled the coffee pot with water from a bucket, and set it on to boil. He walked to the small smokehouse he had built up against the great rocks and returned with several medium sized perch, cleaned previously, and put them in the skillet to fry.

"Ha," said Turtle, "are these the largest you could catch in the Illinois?"

"I caught one very large," said Wili Woyi, "this long," and he held his hands apart so far that Turtle raised his brows.

"It was the first one," said Wili Woyi.

Turtle chuckled. He knew that Wili Woyi, according to tradition, always threw back into the water the first fish he caught no matter what the size, and upon throwing it back said to the fish, "It was the Fishinghawk." This was, of course, a ruse intended to misdirect any vengeful spirits who might seek restitution for violence done to the fish by sending into the body of the fisherman some dread disease.

Later, fish fried and eaten, coffee drunk, the two friends settled back. Now is the time for talk—after eating. Turtle stared up at the grey clouds.

"This thing is not over, Wili Woyi," he said.

"No," answered the other, "it will not be over. With Parker's men after me, it will not be over."

"What will you do?"

Wili Woyi had been rolling cigarettes. He finished, handed one to Turtle, picked a faggot with a glowing end from the fire and held it out while Turtle lit his smoke. Then he lit his own. He leaned back again on his elbows drawing deeply on the cigarette.

"I will live, Turtle," he said finally. "What should I do? As usual, I will live my life. These men from Parker, they must simply become a part of my life."

Wili Woyi felt the first few drops of rain fall against his cheek.

"*A ga sga,*" he said. "It's raining."

They gathered up the pots and went back inside the cabin.


Horse Jackson had a bad pain in his stomach. He had had it for three days. On the morning of the fourth day of his misery he awoke still in pain. As he moaned audibly, his wife, Quatie, said, "Your insides still hurt you?"

"Ahhh," Horse groaned, "yes, as much as ever."

"Some angry spirit has gotten inside you because of something you have done—or have neglected to do," said Quatie, who was a good Baptist, as was her husband, but saw no reason why the spirits should not attack Baptists as anyone else.

"*Ayo,*" said Horse, "it is three whole days now."

"Today will be four," answered his wife. "Four is a good day. Go to Wili Woyi. If anyone can find the cause of your pain and drive it away, Wili Woyi can."

"Perhaps you're right. There is no wiser *didahnuwisgi* in our Nation than Wili Woyi. He has more charms for healing than anyone else, but how can I pay him? We have no money."

"Take these tobacco seeds," said Quatie. "I was saving them for our own use, but what good will even this good Georgia tobacco do us when you are ill if we do not know the charms with which to use it? Wili Woyi has much use for good tobacco. Take the seeds."

Deputy Marshal Glenn Colvert squinted his eyes through the rain and through the stream which was running off the brim of his hat. There before him was what, according to directions he had been given, should be the house of Bill Pigeon. The sharp rise of the hills behind the cabin would make a quick escape to the rear, if not impossible, at the least, slow and difficult.

"That's good," thought Colvert, "first damn thing all day. That's good."

He climbed creaking down out of his saddle and slapped the reins of his mount twice quickly round the trunk of a nearby *bois d'arc* sapling, removed the rifle from the saddleboot and started slowly toward the cabin keeping well in under the trees. His boots squished with each step.

"God damn rain," he thought.

He was headed for a large boulder which was nestled just beside the trees in front of and slightly off to the left, Colvert's left, of the cabin of Billy Pigeon.

Inside, Wili Woyi and Turtle Brashears drank coffee and smoked the cigarettes which Wili Woyi had rolled.

"It is a good rain," Turtle was saying. "It will be good for my corn."

"And for everything else," added Wili Woyi. "It was much needed."

Outside, Colvert cranked a shell into the chamber of his rifle. He aimed above Wili Woyi's house and fired. Then he yelled at the top of his lungs, "Pigeon. Bill Pigeon."

Wili Woyi was up, rifle in hand, at his front window in an instant, and Turtle was not much slower. He, too, held a rifle.

"Pigeon."

"Who's that?" shouted Wili Woyi in English. "Who are you?"

"This here's Depitty Yewnited States Marshal Glenn Colvert, Pigeon, an' I've got a warrant f'r y'r arrest right-chyear in my coat pocket. Now, I don' want no trouble from you. I don' wanna kill nobody if I don' hafta. My orders is to take you in f'r trial."

Turtle asked Wili Woyi, "How many with him, do you think?"

"I do not know, Turtle. He is alone, I think. I am not sure."

"We two can kill him."

"No, Turtle. Then there would be warrants for two."

"We can go out the back way into the hills."

"And maybe then we would get shot in our backs, too."

Colvert called again. "Pigeon. Whattya say?"

Wili Woyi turned to Turtle.

"Turtle, the time is not right to fight or to run. Later will be the right time, maybe. Right now I will go with this deputy. Take my rifle and do not show your face. I do not think he knows that anyone is with me."

Turtle Brashears took the rifle. He did not say anything.

"Deputy," called Wili Woyi, "I am coming out. I will go with you."

"No Goddamn guns. No funny stuff," said Colvert.

"No guns, deputy."

Wili Woyi kicked open the front door of his cabin and walked out into the rain, hands held high.

Deputy Marshal Glenn Colvert made Wili Woyi saddle his own horse at gun point, then he put handcuffs on him and told him to mount up. He tied the Indian's feet together underneath the belly of the horse and led them to the *bois d'arc* to which he had tied his own mount, then they headed toward Muskogee and the nearest railroad depot. Wili Woyi had not spoken a word since coming outside. They rode most of the rest of the day—as long as there was much light, and because of the heavy rain the light did not last as long that day as was usual for a summer day. On the west bank of the Grand River Colvert ordered Wili Woyi to stop at the mouth of a small cave. There was enough overhanging rock above to give the horses some shelter. Colvert staked them out, untied Wili Woyi's feet in order to allow him to dismount, tied them again, and then prepared a camp for the night. He built a small fire, made some coffee, and heated a can of beans. Wili Woyi refused the beans but accepted a cup of the hot coffee. Still, he did not speak.

When Colvert had finished his beans and coffee, he unlocked the cuffs from one of Wili Woyi's wrists and locked them again with the Indian's hands behind his back. He checked the ropes binding his prisoner's feet together. Satisfied, he tossed a blanket over Wili Woyi and crawled into his own bedroll with a loud fart. Soon he was snoring peacefully. Wili Woyi was still awake, still sitting upright. It was not yet quite dark. It was no longer light. It was the next best time of the day for speaking to the spirits, the best time of all being the similar time between dark and light in the morning. Wili Woyi turned his eyes toward the clouds. He spoke out loud but in a very low voice. He spoke, in Cherokee, the following words.

> *Hey, you spirits on high,*
> *you anidawe,*
> *you who dwell*
> *in umwadahi,*
> *come down at once.*
> *go into the brain of that man—*
> *that man who thinks evil of me.*
> *Hey, instantly you have come down.*
> *you have gone into that man.*
> *he will not hear me.*
> *he will not see me.*
> *he will not even awaken*
> *until well past dawn.*

> *Hey, you* anidawe
> *who dwell on high,*
> *I will escape from that man.* Yu.

Wili Woyi spat four times toward the sleeping Colvert and repeated the charm four times, spitting again at the end of each recitation. By the time he had finished his ritual, total darkness had set in, and the hard rain had diminished to a light but steady drizzle.

While the heavy rain was still falling, before the light of day had fully disappeared, Turtle Brashears still sat in the house of Wili Woyi pondering what to do when he heard the sounds of an approaching wagon. The events of the day had made Turtle a bit jumpy, and he ran to the window with his rifle in hand. As he looked out into the rain, he recognized the wife of Horse Jackson sitting on the driver's seat. He put down the rifle and ran out into the rain.

"Quatie, *osiyo,*" said Turtle.

Then he saw that Horse Jackson was lying in the bed of the wagon wrapped up in blankets, the hard rain pouring over him. Horse did not speak. He did not even show any sign that he had seen or heard Turtle.

"We must get him inside, quickly," said Turtle.

And quickly, he and Quatie Jackson carried the ailing man inside where they undressed and dried him and wrapped him in dry blankets. They made him a pallet beside Wili Woyi's fireplace, and Turtle built the fire up. Then he went back out into the rain to care for the Jacksons' horses before returning to the fire to make coffee. He and Quatie drank coffee. Then Quatie spoke.

"My husband has been very ill these four days," she said. "We said that he should go to Wili Woyi and take tobacco. Then he became worse and could not even drive, so I had to bring him here."

"Ahh," replied Turtle, "Wili Woyi is not here. I do not know when he will return. You know, he killed that man awhile back, and there was to be a trial today at Illinois Courthouse with Judge Benge. Wili Woyi was not worried as that man needed killing and Benge is a fair judge. But then they discovered that the man was not of our Nation, and so the trial could not be held at Illinois Courthouse. A lawman came from Fort Smith, and arrested Wili Woyi today. I wanted to kill the lawman, but Wili Woyi would not let me. He said it was not the time."

Turtle paused.

"I do not know when he will be back."

Quatie stared at the floor.

"I do not know what I should do."

"Wait here," said Turtle. "Wait a little. Perhaps Wili Woyi will return, and Horse needs to rest and stay dry anyway. Wait here. Wili Woyi will come back maybe."

He poured more coffee.

The sun had been up and the rain had stopped for about thirty minutes before Glenn Colvert opened his eyes. He yawned and stretched. He propped himself up on one elbow, hacked and spat, then he looked over toward where he had left his prisoner. All he could see was his blanket lying there in a wad.

"God damn," he said as he threw his cover back from over him. He jumped to his feet and started for the blanket. His left foot became entangled in his bedroll, and he dragged it a couple of hopping steps with him before he managed to get it loose. Running in his sock feet, he reached the blanket and jerked it up from the ground. There were the handcuffs, still locked, and there, too, were the ropes with which he had tied Bill Pigeon's feet, his knots still in them. He picked up the ropes and the cuffs, looking hard at them as if they might tell him something. He looked around himself at the rocks and the trees. His horse still stood where he had hobbled it, but Bill Pigeon's mount was gone. There were no tracks to be seen, neither human nor animal. The rain had seen to that.

"God damn it," he thought, "he could be anywhere out there. He could be long gone or he could be layin' for me."

Another thought occurred to Colvert, and he hurriedly checked his weapons. Bill Pigeon had not touched them. Then he was still unarmed, and the chances were that he was as far away as time had allowed him to be. Colvert considered going after him, but could not decide where to look. Bill Pigeon would surely not return to his cabin so soon after having been arrested there, not with the same man who had arrested him likely to be on his trail. If he was not returning to his own home he might be going in any direction, and with the tracks having been washed away by the rain, Colvert could only guess at a direction in which to look. Pigeon likely had Cherokee friends and relatives all through the hills. He might be anywhere. Colvert thought a moment, and then forced himself to admit that he had simply lost his prisoner. He picked up the ropes and cuffs once more and looked at them.

"God damn it," he thought, "it just ain't possible. There just ain't no way."

The rain was still falling when Wili Woyi rode up to his cabin, and neither Turtle Brashears nor Quatie Jackson heard the sound of the approaching horse. When Wili Woyi walked through the front door the other two jumped quickly to their feet.

"Wili Woyi," said Turtle, "I am glad to see you back. That lawman . . ."

"I left him snoring, Turtle. But what is this? Quatie? Your man is ill?"

"For four days now, Wili Woyi. In his stomach it hurts, and now his head is hot. We have tobacco seeds from Georgia."

"*Wado,*" said Wili Woyi. "Thank you, the seeds will wait. We do not know if Horse will wait."

Wili Woyi removed his wet hat and coat and knelt beside the sleeping Horse Jackson. He looked long at his patient. He felt the head, the chest, the stomach. He looked at Quatie.

"Four days?"

"Yes."

"How long has he been this way?"

"He was awake when we left our home, but he was in much pain. Sometime on the way here he went to sleep."

Wili Woyi poured himself some coffee from the pot which Turtle had kept fresh and hot and took a long sip. Then he went back to Horse Jackson.

"Horse," he said, "Horse. This is Wili Woyi. Do you hear me?"

"Ahh," Horse struggled to comprehend.

"How do you feel, Horse?"

"*Ag wes da ne ha,*" said Horse, "I am in pain."

"We will fix it, Horse. It will go away."


When Glenn Colvert stepped off the train at Fort Smith, he headed directly for the office of his immediate superior, United States Marshal Moss Berman. Colver desperately wanted a glass of whiskey, but he knew Berman well enough to know that the drink had better wait until he had made his official report—a report which he, by the way, did not relish making. He had failed, and Moss Berman did not take failure lightly. He, himself, seldom failed to accomplish his purpose, and he expected the same from the men who rode for him—for the law. Colvert took a deep breath and knocked on the door.

"Come on in."

He did.

"Moss."

"I heard the train pull in, Glenn. You got your prisoner turned in already?"

"Well, no, Moss, . . ."

"Where is he? You hafta kill 'im?"

"No, but, damn it, I shoulda. Hell, Moss, I ain't got 'im."

Colvert stood shuffling his shoes on the floor like a teenager waiting for a scolding, but he was waiting rather for an explosion from Moss Berman—an explosion which never came. That was much harder on the deputy's nerves than if it had. Moss Berman took a long, black cigar from inside his coat pocket, bit off an end, spat it out, took his time wetting down the cigar, and finally struck a match on the front of his desk and lit it.

"What happened?" he asked in a quiet voice.

"Well, you know, Moss, that there Pigeon, he was lined up for a trial in the Cherokee courts. He was s'posed to show up at that Illinois Court-house, so that's where I went to fetch 'im. The injun judge an' a whole mess a injuns was standin' around there a waitin' f'r 'im, an' they kept swearin' to me that Pigeon 'uld be there most any time, but he never showed. So I went on out t' his house, an' he was there jus' bigger'n shit, and he never even give me no trouble. I hollered out for 'im t' come on out, that he's under arrest, an' he come. I tied 'im up, an' we tuck out. Well, come night-fall I bedded us down. Now, Moss, God damn it, I know how to hogtie a prisoner. You know I know. I tied that son-of-a-bitch up good. I tied his feet, an' I cuffed his hands. There wasn't no way nobody coulda got outta them ropes an' arns. Nobody."

"But Bill Pigeon did?"

"Yessir. God bless me, Moss, he did. When I woke up come mornin', his horse was gone, an' he was, too. Right there where I left the son-of-a-bitch, there on the ground, there was my blanket that I'd throwed over 'im, an' under the damn blanket—Moss, this here next is crazy, but I swear, Moss, them cuffs was layin' right there still locked, and them ropes was layin' right there with my knots still tied in 'em. Right here they is. I ain't done nothin' to 'em but jus' bring 'em along to show you."

Colvert pulled the ropes and the cuffs out of the pocket of his yellow slicker and held them out to Moss Berman. Berman took them, and Colvert continued to stare accusingly at them.

"Well," he went on, "I looked around, but I never seen no sign of no kind. If Pigeon left any, the rain wiped 'em on out."

Moss Berman tossed the ropes and cuffs back across his desk toward Glenn Colvert, and puffed on his cigar.

"Glenn, go on over an' get y'se'f a drink an' a good meal an' a bath. You need all of 'em. Then you get y'se'f a good night's sleep. In the mornin' round up Monk an' Estey. The three of y're takin' the first train outta here f'r Muskogee t'morra. That warrant you're carryin's for murder. I want it served, and I want it served now."

Wili Woyi had given him the specially prepared drink and had sung over him, and Horse Jackson was resting. Wili Woyi and Turtle Brashears were outside in back of the cabin smoking.

"Wili Woyi," said Turtle, "what will you do about this lawman? I think you should have killed him. Or you should have let me kill him for you when I wanted to. He did not follow you back here when you escaped from him probably because he did not expect you to be so fool-ish to return straightaway to your own home, but he will come back here looking for you one day. Will you kill him then? Perhaps there will be more of them with him that time. It will not be so easy as it would have been before."

"He will come here again, of course," answered Wili Woyi, "and most likely he will have others with him, but this time I will be prepared for him. There are ways, you know, to protect one's home from intruders."

"So I have heard, but I have never seen it done."

"Nor will you, Turtle. Some kinds of magic must be worked alone or the power will be lost. You know, for instance, that I cannot allow you to look upon my tobacco—that which I have prepared."

"Yes, I know."

"As soon as Horse Jackson is ready to move, I want you to go with them to help Quatie get him home safely. He will be ready soon. When I am alone again I will prepare my home. I will be ready from now on. The lawmen will not enter my house."

Horse Jackson slept the rest of that morning. At noon Quatie fed him some stew which Wili Woyi had prepared. About the middle of the after-noon the Jacksons, having given over the Georgia tobacco seeds to Wili Woyi, left for home accompanied by Turtle Brashears. Wili Woyi un-dressed and slept. He slept soundly until just before dawn the next morn-ing. Then he arose and went to a corner of his room where he kept a leathern pouch. He untied the thongs with which the pouch was bound and withdrew from inside a small handful of tobacco. He was still naked. He did not bother to put on any article of clothing. It was dawn.

Off to the left side of Wili Woyi's cabin, coming from the rocks be-hind, ran a small stream. The water in the stream was cold and clear. To the edge of this stream Wili Woyi walked taking with him tobacco. He faced the east and held the tobacco before him in his left hand. With the four fin-gers of his right hand he stirred the tobacco in his palm in a motion counter-clockwise as he repeated four times the following words.

> *Ha.*
> *From the four directions*
> *they are bringing their souls.*
> *Just now*
> *they are bringing their souls.*

After each repetition Wili Woyi blew his breath upon the tobacco, and when he had finished, he held the tobacco up toward the rising sun. He re-turned to his cabin, wrapped the tobacco in a piece of newspaper, and placed it under the pouch in the corner of the room. Then he dressed and made his morning coffee.

63

When he had finished a leisurely breakfast and had plenty of coffee, he rolled and smoked a cigarette. Then he went back to the spring where he was keeping a bucket of crawdads to be used for fishing. He took the crawdads and disappeared into the woods.

Wili Woyi returned home just in time for sundown. He set aside his catch of fish for cleaning later. Then he took up his pipe. It was only a handmade, corncob pipe, but it was serviceable, and it would do. He retrieved the tobacco which he had that morning prepared, and then, pipe in one hand, tobacco in the other, he went outside and to the east of his house. He filled the bowl of the pipe and lit it. Puffing slowly but steadily, Wili Woyi began to walk around his house. In a counter-clockwise direction he walked in a huge circle. He paused to blow smoke toward the south, and again toward the west, the north, and finally the east when he had arrived back at his starting point. This circling he repeated four times, making each circle larger than the last. Then he returned to the cabin to clean his fish, confident that he would not be disturbed in his home for at least six months.

Turtle Brashears was driving the wagon for the Jacksons. Horse was lying in the back, but he was awake and was feeling much better. Quatie Jackson rode on the seat beside Turtle.

"Wili Woyi is a marvelous doctor," Horse was saying. "I cannot begin to tell you how much better I feel already. He has much power."

"Indeed he has," answered his wife. "You could not have known, of course, but when we arrived at his house, Wili Woyi was not there. He was carried off by some lawman."

"What?"

"Yes," said Turtle, "I was worried about him, but I shouldn't have been. Wili Woyi escaped from that man, and he did not even have to kill him. His magic is very great."

"This lawman," said Horse, "what was he?"

"He was from Parker," said Turtle. "Recently, as you may know, Wili Woyi was forced to kill a man who was trying to rob him. He reported this killing as any good citizen would do, and there was to be a trial at Illinois Courthouse, but before the trial happened, they discovered at Fort Smith that his man, the thief, was not of our Nation. He was a *yoneg*. So a lawman came from Parker to arrest Wili Woyi, and he got him. I was there, and I wanted to kill the lawman. Wili Woyi said that I may not, and he went with him, but as you know he came back later. He escaped by magic. He did not need to fight with the fool."

"Turtle," said Horse Jackson, "if Wili Woyi has escaped from a white lawman, there will be more of them. They will not stop looking for him, and since he has made a fool of one of them, they will not be so careful next time just to arrest him. They will maybe kill him. Maybe we should go back there with our guns and help him. Wili Woyi is a great man, and it would not be right to let those dogs from Fort Smith get him."

"I agree with you, Horse," said Turtle, "but Wili Woyi sent me away with you just now. He is working some magic—I think against the lawmen. I think Wili Woyi will not be so easy for them to catch or to kill."

"I have heard that Wili Woyi is not only a great *didahnuwisgi*," said Quatie, "but that he is also a master of *didisgahlidhodhiyi*."

"Ah, yes," said Turtle, "indeed, he can make himself invisible, and not only that, but if he wishes to, he can put his soul into the body of something else. Sometimes he will go into an owl. I have seen these things."

"Well," said Horse, "perhaps you are right then. Perhaps Wili Woyi will be all right. Perhaps he does not need us."

"Perhaps," added Quatie, "he will be even better off without you."


Glenn Colvert was approaching the home of Wili Woyi for the second time in less than a week, but the second time he was not alone. With him rode Harper Monk and Birk Estey, both deputies from Fort Smith assigned by Moss Berman to ride with and assist Colvert in the arrest of Billy Pigeon. Berman considered a man who was wanted for murder and had already escaped once from an experienced deputy to be a serious enough threat to merit the additional manpower. It had been a source of embarrassment to Colvert, but as he had lost his prisoner there was not much he could say. Usually a loud, talkative man, Colvert had been amazingly quiet the whole of the trip from Fort Smith to Muskogee by rail and thence on horseback with Monk and Estey.

Just before the point in their journey at which Wili Woyi's cabin would become visible to them, Colvert reined in his mount and called a halt.

"Now, boys," he said, " 'course, we ain't got no way a knowing if Pigeon's at home 'r not, but let's not take no chances. He's sneaky as hell. B'lieve me. I know. Now, what I suggest we do is I think you two had oughta spread out 'n' go th'ough the woods so's one of you comes up on each side a the house. You c'n cover the back as well as the front thataway. I'll give you time t' git in position, then I'll move in on the front. I'll call out to 'im first. Give 'im a chance t' come on out peaceable. But if he takes out the back, you all cut down on 'im right quick. If he don't come out neither door, then I'll move on in."

It took only a few minutes for Monk and Estey to position themselves, and when Colvert was sure that they had had enough time, he stepped out in the open, facing the front of Wili Woyi's cabin, rifle in hand.

"Pigeon," he shouted. "Bill Pigeon."

Then aloud but only to himself he muttered, "Seems as how I've been here before, an' not too God damn long ago."

"Bill Pigeon. You in there?"

The only sounds to answer him were the gentle rustling of the breeze through the giant oaks and walnuts, the scamperings of busy squirrels, the flight of some crows, and off in the distance the rapid rat-tat-tat of a woodpecker hard at work. Colvert began moving toward the cabin. Slowly. Cautiously. About half way across the clearing which lay before the cabin he let his eyes dart rapidly from one side of the cabin to the other. There were no out-buildings in sight. The only place that looked as if it might be used to shelter animals was a depression in the rock behind the cabin and off to Colvert's left. It looked as if it might accommodate two or three horses, but that was about all. It was not too deep, and although it was heavily in shadow, Colvert could see that Wili Woyi's horse was not there.

"Shit. He ain't home," Colvert muttered.

He stopped when he reached the door, paused for an instant, then called out again.

"Pigeon, you in there?"

There was no answer.

Colvert, his heart pounding, tried the door. It opened easily. He pushed it just a few inches, peering inside. There was dim light inside the cabin.

"Anybody home?"

Still no answer. Colvert shoved the door all the way inside to the wall to be sure that no one could be lurking behind it. Then, with one foot across the threshold, he poked his nose inside and slowly looked around. He stepped back outside quickly with a strange and eerie sense of relief.

"Monk. Birk. Come on out, boys. Ain't nobody here. God damn it."


As the three riders from Fort Smith disappeared back down the road by which they had come, inside the cabin, Wili Woyi uncrossed his legs and rose to his feet. He walked straight across the room to the still open door, leaned with his left hand on the doorframe and stared after his departing visitors. With his right hand he raised to his lips the cup of steaming coffee which he held and took a long and satisfying sip.


Glenn Colvert, Monk and Estey had spent the entire day riding in circles in the woods around Wili Woyi's house—counter-clockwise. Colvert thought that Wili Woyi would not have gone far from home, and he was determined that if they searched long and hard enough in the area they would be certain to find some sign of the fugitive. When darkness fell and they could no longer search effectively, the three deputies began to look for a good camp site. As things worked out, they made their camp in the woods along the bank of the same stream which flowed by Wili Woyi's cabin. They built a small fire, made coffee and supper, and ate. When they had finished off all the coffee and cleaned their dishes in the stream, Glenn Colvert told the other two men to get some sleep.

"I'll stay up for a couple a hours an' keep watch," he said. "Pigeon might be onto us by now, an' there ain't no sense in bein' careless. In a couple a hours I'll wake you up" (he gestured toward Birk), "then you c'n watch for two hours, an' then wake up Monk. OK?"

The other two crawled into their bedrolls and were soon asleep. Colvert made more coffee. He built the fire up just a little for there was a slight chill in the night air. Then he sat down near the fire with a cup of coffee, his rifle across his knees. The two hours dragged slowly by with about the only break in the monotony the eerie hoot of a near-by night owl. When his time had passed, Colvert jostled Birk with his foot.

"Two hours is up, Birk," he said, "you're on."

As Birk yawned, stretched and moaned, crawled out of the sack, Glenn Colvert laid aside his weapons and pulled off his boots. Soon Colvert was snoring, and Birk was sitting beside the small fire with his rifle. Birk yawned and rubbed his eyes. His head fell forward, and he jerked it back upright.

"Shit," he muttered to himself, "cain't fall asleep on watch. Cain't do that."

He laid aside his rifle and poured himself a cup of coffee from the pot which Colvert had brewed. The owl hooted. Birk jumped.

"Just a hootowl," he said. "Goddamn hootowl."

Even having thus reassured himself, Birk found that each time the owl hooted, he jumped. He began to feel that the owl knew that it was startling him and was taking delight in the fact. He thought about trying to locate the villain to shoot it, but immediately realized that such a course of action would bring Monk and Colvert rapidly to their senses and almost certainly put them in a very bad humor. But the owl hooted again, and Birk jumped again, and he knew that he must do something. He put aside his rifle once more and began to look about on the ground for a stone just the right size. He found and hefted two or three before he settled on one. It was smooth, nearly round, and was not quite a fistfull. It should do nicely.

Birk stood up slowly with the rock in his right hand and faced in the direction from which the hoots had seemed to come. He strained his eyes into the darkness but could see nothing. Suddenly he heard it again, and he threw the rock with all his might in the direction of the sound. There was a rustling of leaves and the sound of the rock falling to the ground—then silence. Glenn Colvert snorted and rolled over in his sleep but did not wake up. Monk showed no sign of having been in the least disturbed. Birk went back to the fire and squatted. He took up his cup and sipped from it. As he reached to place the cup back on the ground, he stiffened. He heard what he would have sworn was the sound of footsteps, and it was very near. He reached for his rifle and was astonished when he saw that it was not there where he had left it. He drew his revolver, clumsily in his haste, and looked around the camp in all directions. There was no one to be seen. Nothing moved. Poised, ready to shoot, he continued to look. He thought about waking Colvert but did not know what he would tell him. Then he saw his rifle lying beside Colvert's where Colvert slept. He retrieved it.

"I know I left it over here," he muttered, "I know it. But there ain't no one here. I musta moved it over yonder when I'us gettin' after that damn hootowl. I musta moved it an' never knowed it. Too damn jumpy."

He picked up his coffee and lifted it to his lips to drink. It was empty.

"Glenn, Glenn," he yelled. "Get up. Monk?"

Glenn Colvert came out first. He had a pistol in each hand. Monk was reaching for his rifle and trying to get his legs out from under his blanket at the same time.

"What is it?" said Colvert.

"Glenn, they's somebody here."

"Where?"

"Here."

"Well, didja see 'im?"

"No, I never."

"Where'd the sound come from?"

"Right by God here. Right here."

Birk was stamping and pointing to the ground just back of the campfire from where he had been sitting.

"Come on, Birk," said Colvert lowering his guns. "You mean he 'us right here behind you, an' you never seen 'im? You been sleepin', Birk?"

"No, Glenn. Goddamnit, I swear it. I never went to sleep. I was settin' here with a cup of coffee in my hand, and I heard footsteps right here. I looked around, and they wasn't nobody there, so I got up to look around somemore. Then I seen my rifle was gone. I found it over yonder. Right beside yours. I swear, I never put it there. Well, I figgured I must be gettin' spooky, so I went back t' the fire, an' I found m' cup empty, an', Glenn, I hadn't tuck but a sip out of it. I don't know who 'r what it is, but Goddamnit, they's somebody here."

Again Birk stamped the ground around the fire.

"All right, all right," said Colvert, "you go on an' get some sleep. Monk, you awake? You take on over your watch now. It's a little early, but Birk's too . . ."

Colvert didn't finish what he was saying, for just then there was a loud splashing, followed by a hissing and a clank. All three deputies turned at once and raised their weapons. The fire was almost out, steam was coming up from the ashes, hissing still, and the coffee pot was on its side rocking a tiny bit in the dirt.

> Three miles southeast of Illinois Courthouse,
> near the Illinois River. Winter 1891.

"Looks like he's been here for sometime," one of the men in the group was saying. There were about a dozen of them gathered around to get a good look at the body so recently discovered.

"Yeah," said another. "Hogs 'r somethin's been after 'im. Bet his own mother couldn't recanize 'im now."

Glenn Colvert shoved his way through the crowd.

"Make some room here, fellas. This here's the law comin' through. Make some room."

A path to the body was more or less cleared, and Moss Berman followed Glenn Colvert through it.

"God damn," said Colvert, "that's a hell of a sight."

Moss Berman turned and walked away again. He paused a few feet distant under a large walnut tree to light a cigar.

"Reckon who it is?" said one of the men.

"Who it was, you mean," said Colvert.

Berman spoke out in a strong voice.

"It was Bill Pigeon," he said. "I recognize him, even like that."

There were murmurs of surprise and disbelief. Glenn Colvert hurried over to Berman. He spoke in a harsh whisper.

"How c'n you tell, Moss? I mean, the shape he's in? I had Pigeon under arrest that time, an' I can't tell. Fact a the matter is, I don't recall him bein' as big as this here feller looks to a been."

Berman sucked at his cigar. Slowly an expression of great puzzlement came over Colvert's face.

"Moss?" he said. "Whenever did you set eyes on Bill Pigeon?"

Berman reached out and took hold of Colvert's necktie. He gave it a gentle tug as if to straighten it. The crowd of spectators was still milling about the body as if they could not get their fill of the gruesome sight—all but one who seemed to be more interested in the two lawmen than in the body. Turtle Brashears, though being careful not to be too obvious about it, was watching Berman and Colvert with great interest.

"We been after this son-of-a-bitch for goin' on six years now, Glenn," said Moss Berman, his voice still low. "I got a damn good record, an' all I been gettin' from you is a bunch of hoodoo stories. Now, that there body over there looks a hell of a lot like Bill Pigeon t' me."

Just then one of the crowd spoke out.

"Hey, how the hell's he know who this is?"

Glenn Colvert turned to face the man.

"Fellas," he said, "this here's United States Marshal Moss Berman. You've all heard a him. I reckon he oughta know Bill Pigeon when he sees 'im. Even in that shape."

Berman turned to walk back to his horse, and Colvert followed him. As they mounted up they could hear the conversation continuing behind them.

"That there's Moss Berman?"

"Bill Pigeon, huh?"

"Well, I be God damned."

As Moss Berman and Glenn Colvert rode away from the scene, they heard a loud screech from the top of a tall cottonwood which was standing nearby. They paid it no mind, but back in the crowd Turtle Brashears turned his head toward the tree, and his keen eyes found, sitting on one of the topmost branches, a great horned owl, and he smiled.

# LUCI TAPAHONSO

## The Snakeman (1979)

*Boarding school is a common setting in Native literature, particularly in writing published before the 1970s, but still used in more recent works. Often, as in "The Snakeman," boarding school stories are modern treatments of abduction narratives from the Native tradition. In "The Snakeman," the boarding school at Fort Wingate, just outside the Navajo Nation's eastern border near Gallup, New Mexico, becomes the setting for dynamic interaction between the Navajo and American agendas. The children take both at face value, and out of the intersection create a mode of consciousness, of bonding, and of interpreting their experience that is at once Navajo traditional and American bureaucratic. Rather than advancing only through interplay between the local community and the supernaturals, "The Snakeman" is developed by way of an intricate interplay between three settings: the local community far away, the alien community of the boarding school, and the world of the supernaturals, spirits, and mystery.*

*Like the autobiographical narratives written by Luther Standing Bear and Don Talayesva (included in* Voice of the Turtle*), "The Snakeman" gently informs us that American social modes are mere costumes Native people don. The children know who and where they are, and how the world around them is defined: the Snakeman lives in the boarding school's attic; the mother loves her child as strongly in death as in life; and homesick, frightened children take care of one another, forging bonds to their traditional worldview that will inform their lives far beyond boarding school. American educators who believed that boarding schools and christianization would remake Native peoples in their own image didn't count on the power of loneliness to strengthen ties to indigenous traditions. "The Snakeman" lets us know that separating Native*

*children by way of Western education from their spiritual traditions is a
failed enterprise.*

*Diné writer Luci Tapahonso herself attended boarding school at Fort
Wingate. Her story borrows from her own attendance there as well as from
the ceremonial tradition of the Diné (the Navajo's name for themselves).*

*According to that tradition, it was during a conflict long ago that two
young women were abducted from their village by the enemy. They were
taken to a mountain fasthold, where they spent the night, each with one of
the abductors in different caves, separated from one another and their community. The men who abducted them were kind enough, given the vicissitudes of combat, and the women spent the night in relative safety. Imagine
their horror in the morning when each awoke to find the man she had slept
beside was a corpse!*

*From one corpse emerged a large snake, and from the other a bear.
Neither woman knew what had befallen her sister. The woman taken by
Snakeman was compelled to follow him to his land among the supernaturals, where she lived with his mother and performed, always badly,
whatever tasks the old woman assigned her. But although she was undisci-
plined and inattentive, she eventually gained the old woman's approval and
was given a Yei-bei-chi, a chantway, to take to her people so they could restore their bond to the sacred and regain peace. Tapahonso's story is an off-
shoot of the main ceremonial tradition of the Diné, known as the Yei bei
chi. It is connected to* Beautyway, *the mother of the Yei bei chi.*

T he child slid down silently and caught herself at the end of the fire escape. She eased herself down until she felt the cold, hard sidewalk
through her slippers—then she let go.

The night was clear and quiet. The only noise that could be heard was
the echo of the child's footsteps in the moonlit alley behind the old, brick
buildings.

The little girls, watching her from the top floor of the dorm, swung
the window screen in and out, catching it before it struck the window
frame. They always talked about what would happen if the top hinges suddenly gave way but they hadn't yet.

"Good thing—it's spring," one of them said.

"She would freeze her toes off for sure," another hissed.

"SHHH-H," the biggest one hissed.

They whispered in lispy voices and someone on the other side of the
room would only hear "s . . . sss," hissing and an occasional "shut-up!"
The room was large with windows on three sides. The fire escape the child
slid down was in the center of the north windows, which faced a big, dark
hill, its slope covered with huge, round rocks and dry tumbleweeds. Opposite the fire escape was the door to the hall.

Sometimes the dorm mother, who lived at the other end of the hall, heard them giggling or running around. She would walk down the dark, shiny hall so fast her housecoat would fly behind her in billows. The girls would scurry to their beds, tripping over their long nightgowns, finally faking snores as she turned on the harsh, bright lights in each room. After she went back to her room, the children jumped up and laughed silently with wide, open mouths and pounded their fists into their beds.

One of the girls whispered loudly, "She's coming back." They all ran noiselessly to the window and watched the small figure coming. The little girl walked briskly with her hands in her housecoat pockets. She wore the soft, wool slippers all the little girls made for their sister or mother at Christmastime. But she had neither, so she wore them herself.

"Seems like she floats," one girl commented.

"How could she? Can't you hear her walking?" the biggest retorted.

The girls went back to their beds and the ones that were closest to the fire escape window opened the window and held it up until she was in. Then they all gathered at one bed and sat in the moonlight telling ghost stories or about how the end of the world was REALLY going to be. Except for the girl who left, she always went to sleep and wasn't noisy like the rest.

Sometimes late in the night or towards morning when the sun hadn't come up completely and everything was quiet and the room filled with the soft, even breathing of the children—one of them might stand at the window facing east and think of home far away and tears would stream down her face. Late in the night someone always cried and if the others heard her—they would pretend not to notice. They understood how it was with all of them ... if only they could go to public school and eat at home everyday.

When they got up in the morning before they went downstairs to dress, two of them emptied their pockets of small, torn pieces of paper and scattered them under the beds. The beds had white ruffled bottoms that reached the floor and the bits of paper weren't visible unless one lifted the ruffles. This was the way they tested the girl that cleaned their room. When they returned to their bedroom in the evenings, they checked under their beds to see if the paper was gone. If it wasn't, they immediately reported it to the dorm mother, who never asked why they were so sure their room hadn't been cleaned.

The building was divided into three floors and an attic. The little girls who were in grade school occupied the bottom and top floors and the junior high girls had the middle floor. The top floor was used only for bedrooms and all daytime activity was on the bottom level. The building was old, like all the other buildings on campus, and the students were sure it was haunted. Besides, there was a graveyard a little ways away. How could it not be? they asked among themselves.

This was especially true for those little girls in the east end of the dorm, since they were so close to the attic door. There was a man in there, they always said in hushed voices, he always kept the attic door open just a little, enough to throw evil powder on anyone that walked by. For this reason, they all stayed out of the hallway at night. Once they had even heard him coming down the attic stairs to the door and the smaller girls started crying. They all slept two-to-a-bed, and the big girls made sure all the little girls had someone bigger with them. They stayed up later than usual, crying and praying, so that no one woke early enough to get everyone back into their right beds. The dorm mother spanked each of them but at least, they said, that night nothing happened to any of them.

Once when the little girl went on one of her walks at night, the other children were waiting for her as they usually did. Two of them were by the hall door trying to figure how to get to the bathroom two doors down the hall when they heard a scratching noise outside on the sidewalk.

"You guys! come here! he's over here!!" they whispered loudly.

They ran to the east window and saw a dark figure go around the corner and the biggest girl took control.

"You two get over by that window. You on that side. Someone get on the fire escape in case he tries to get up here."

They watched the man below and tried to get a description of him, in case someone asked them. They couldn't see him very well because he was on the shady side of the building. Some of the girls started crying, and some crawled quietly back into bed. Two of them, the bigger ones, waited to open the window for the other girl when she got back. When she came back, they all huddled around her and told her and started crying again. She said it was probably someone's father trying to see his daughter. Probably the mother won't let him see her, she said. So the girls calmed down and tried to figure out whose parents were divorced or fought a lot. They finally decided that he was the boyfriend of a junior high girl downstairs.

When a new girl came, she asked why the girl always walked at night, and the biggest one had said:

"Wouldn't you if you could see your mother every night, dummy?"

"Well, where's her mom? Can't she see her on weekends like us? That's not fair."

"Fair? FAIR??" they had all yelled in disbelief.

Then the girl who walked explained that her parents had died years before, when she was six, and they were buried at the school cemetery. So that's why she went to see them. Just her mother, mostly, though.

"How is she? Does she talk?"

"Can you REALLY see her?" the new girl asked.

"Yeah," she answered patiently. "She calls me and she waits at the edge of the cemetery by those small, fat trees. She's real pretty. When she died, they put a blue outfit on her. A Navajo skirt that's real long and a shiny, soft, light blue blouse. She waves at me like this: 'Come here, shi yashil, my little baby.' She always calls me that. She's soft and smells so good."

The little girls all nodded, each remembering their own mothers.

"When it's cold or snowing, she lets me stand inside the blanket with her. We talk about when I was a baby, and what I'll do when I get big. She always worries if I'm being good or not."

"Mine, too," someone murmured.

"Why do mothers always want their girls to be goody-good?"

"So you won't die at the end of the world, dummy."

"Dying isn't *that* bad. You can still visit people like her mother does."

"But at the end of the world, all the dinosaurs and monsters that are sleeping in the mountains will bust out and eat the bad people. No one can escape, either," said the biggest girl with confidence.

Then the little girl who talked to her mother every night said quietly:

"No one can be that bad." She went to her bed and lay there looking at the ceiling until she fell asleep.

The other girls gathered on two beds and sat in a little circle and talked in tight, little voices about the snakeman who stole jewelry from some of the girls.

"You can't really see him," one said, "cause he's sort of like a blur, moves real fast and all you can see is a black thing go by."

He has a silver bracelet that shines and if he shines it on you, you're a goner cause it paralyzes."

They talked about him until they began looking around to make sure he wasn't in the room.

The bigger girls slept with the littler ones, and they prayed that God wouldn't let that man in the attic or the snakeman come to them, and that the world wouldn't end until after their moms came to visit.

As the room got quiet and the breathing became even and soft, the little girl got up, put on her housecoat and slid soundlessly down the fire escape.

# DEAN ING

## Eagles (1980)

*At the same time Luci Tapahonso was writing a story crafted from her experience, her Diné tradition, and Western literary forms, writers from other segments of the Native community were preoccupied with matters equally cosmic in their import.*

*Dean Ing had been publishing for several years before the novel from which "Eagles" is excerpted came out. The novel,* Systemic Shock, *is, like most of Ing's work, devoid of overtly Native characters or style, but is nevertheless securely seated astride the Native and the Western narrative traditions. One of the more intriguing aspects of contemporary Native American fiction is its ability to overleap cultural boundaries: It needn't confine itself to subjects or characters that are stereotypically "indian," but can address itself to the international scene, speaking to global events, as has the oral tradition.*

*In "Eagles," the only reference to anything tribal is the location—the story is set on ancient Cherokee lands. Ing, himself Cherokee, seems to make some reference in his works to his ancestry; in another book, the heroine drives a Jeep Cherokee. However, its structure, which oscillates between nature-centered and highly technological perspectives, is one of the many signals that relate his work to First Nations' traditions.*

*Cherokees as a group have for centuries been among the most international of nations, involved and engaged with leaders and trends from the Western world, while remaining grounded in Cherokee tradition. Thus Ing, internationalist in one of the oldest of Cherokee traditions, weaves a tale of global genocide and human survival—a subject in which the Cherokee, of all nations, have long experience. "Eagles" provides us with a sample of how the historical experience of entire communities, along with the underlying values of their civilization, transcend set limits and cross the rigid lines more limited minds draw in time's ever-shifting sands.*

I

In early August of 1996 the Atlantic states baked like some vast piecrust under a paralyzing heat wave. It moved scoutmaster Purvis Little, in Raleigh, to plan the Smoky Mountain pack trip that would save a few lives. It also moved the President of the United States to his retreat in the Shenandoah hills.

The weather relented on the evening of Friday, the ninth. Young Ted Quantrill hardly noticed, racing home after his troop meeting in Raleigh, because he knew he'd have to politick for that pack trip. The President noticed it still less; despite the air conditioning in his hoverchopper, a tiara of sweat beaded his balding head. The bulletin that had drawn him back to Washington suggested complications in the sharp new rise of foreign oil prices; a rise that in itself further impeded his race for reelection against Utah's Senator Yale Collier. The President considered Yale Collier a charismatic fool. Ted Quantrill's parents thought the same of scoutmaster Little. In any case, a modest proportion of fools would survive the next week, while some of their critics would die.

2

Through twenty years and three administrations, pundits in American government had watched helplessly as the Socialist Party of China wooed lubricious favors from the Middle East. Every few years some think-tank would announce that global addiction to oil was on the wane, thanks to this or that alternative energy source. Just as regularly, the thinkers went into the tank. Fusion was still an elusive technique. New fission plants had been banned in the UN General Assembly after the pandemic of fear that peaked in 1994. Partial meltdown (Chernobyl, '86), outgassing (Wales, '93), and accidental scatter of confined radioactive waste (Honshu, '94; Connecticut, Shantung, '95), had taken only a few thousand lives—fewer than offshore oil rigs had taken.

But the fission boojum had scared the bejeezus out of voters from Reykjavik to Christchurch, and even autocrats reluctantly agreed to decommission some of their reactors. It was not that fission plants no longer existed, but they were fewer while power requirements grew.

The death tolls over Middle East oil seemed acceptable to governments, perhaps because their citizens remained hooked on the stuff. In some quarters a global perception began to grow that developed nations should find cleaner energy sources. Meanwhile, everyone continued to burn oil.

Direct solar conversion, wind-driven generators, and alternative chemical fuels plugged part of the energy gap, while the price of energy made conservationists of most Americans. Still, fossil fuel remained a favored energy source: storable, compact, simple. While developing one's own oil resources, one was wise to import as much as practicable. So said the Chinese; so said we all. As early as 1979 China's ruling party, the SPC, served notice of its intent to anyone who might be paying attention. The SPC's official news agency, Xinhua, said:

Nearly 160 Moslem mosques of Northwest China are being reopened ... after damage to varying degrees in the past few years. The mosques are under repair with government funds, including the famed Yin-chuan edifice and a Tonxin mosque known to be 800 years old.

And again:

The Koran, the scared book of Islam, is now being retranslated into Chinese ...

Though riddled with dissent on many topics, the Associated Islamic Republics was quick to thank China for her turnabout. The Chinese could pivot as effortlessly on oil as anybody, with better coordination than the reconstituted, ham-fisted Russian Union of Soviets.

After its economic collapse, the newer and smaller RUS retained the frozen mineral wealth of Siberia; had lost nothing directly to China. But lands lost to the RUS were in the temperate zone where grain—and Islam—could be grown, and even exported.

No war, or any other movement, could be considered truly worldwide if it did not directly involve the two billion residents of China and India. Between 1992 and 1996, China's heavy industry expanded with Chinese supertugs towing icebergs to (ex-Saudi) Arabian shores, bringing desalinization equipment to rival Israel's and aiding the transformation of desert wastes. If a few million Chinese suffered from lack of that equipment in 1995, the SPC could wax philosophical so long as those old Japanese-built oil tankers kept sliding into ports near Peking.

China did not lack oil, but what she had she proposed to keep while importing more from reluctant Mexicans and willing Arabs. India was not rich in oil; but she was well-positioned to obtain it easily from Islamic friends.

All this, Americans knew. What had alarmed the State Department a week previously was the first of a series of urgent communiques from

Mikhail Talbukhin, the RUS ambassador. The Supreme Council of the RUS had decided that Talbukhin should share a maddening discovery with us: recent price hikes on Arab oil were by no means uniform.

The Russians had voice-printed tapes to prove it. China and India were obtaining massive kickbacks, and had done so for years. Somehow, under the noses of US and RUS spy satellites, the SinoInd powers were obtaining *twice* as much Middle-East oil as we had thought.

At first the notion of smuggled oil seemed wildly unlikely, but State Department people agreed that the evidence was convincing. The President addressed the question, What Do We Do About It? He did not address it quickly enough for RUS leaders, who saw that something was done about it the following Tuesday.

On Tuesday, August 6, a tremendous explosion had been noted by a US satellite over India's coastal state of Gujarat. It was no coincidence that Gujarat lay directly across the Arabian Sea from the source of India's, and China's, oil. Within hours the United States had stood accused, on the evidence of Indian ordnance experts, of sabotaging a huge Indian water conduit. The RUS backed US denials; not merely because Russians had in fact done the job themselves, but for a much better reason. The RUS craved Western support against the communists next door.

By Thursday, August 8, alliances had crystallized in the UN. Every active unit of the National Guard went on standby alert.

### 3

Ted Quantrill had given up hope of shouldering a backpack until his father, an active reservist, took a hard look at his orders on a Thursday evening. The following day, Ted was en route to the high Appalachian Trail. On that day the boy assumed his own argument—the trek would be his fifteenth birthday present—had caused the change of heart. Only later did Ted Quantrill begin to suspect the truth.

### 4

From satellite and local report, it was obvious that the Gujarat disaster was more than the loss of a water conduit. Whole square kilometers were ablaze in an area known for its experimental cotton production by Indians with Chinese advisors. But cotton did not burn this way; and even if it did, China would not have risen to such fury over a trifling setback to India's agribiz. The blaze and the fury might be appropriate if both were rooted in oil. Not a few thousand gallons of it, but a few million.

Ranked fourth behind Arabia, the RUS, and Mexico in her known reserves of oil, China could have been providing India's supply, and the scenario was studied. But China exported the stuff only to Japan. With its expertise in shipbuilding and manufacture of precision equipment, Japan slowly forged her co-prosperity link with China, and shared the fuel supply. Some of China's imported oil came from Mexico and Venezuela and some, for the sake of appearance, came in tankers from the Middle East. American satellites yielded an estimate, based on a nosecount of tankers through the Strait of Hormuz, that China was buying a third of her oil from Arabs.

But no satellite had penetrated the bottom of the Arabian Sea. No research vessel had identified the progress of a stunning Chinese engineering project which, using an acid-hydraulic process, quietly tunneled a meters-broad pipeline under the continental shelf from Arabia to Gujarat on the western plain of India. It was known that China had invested in a scheme to run water conduits from the Himalayas to western India. What no one had suspected was that the conduit was double-barreled. Water ran toward the southwest. Oil ran toward the northeast, then on to China herself. No wonder, then, that China had exploded so many nuclear devices under the Tibetan plateau; the resulting cavities were being filled with oil pumped from the AIR. It was an immense undertaking, yet it required no technical breakthroughs. Its strength lay primarily in its secrecy.

With one well-placed demolition device just upline from a pumping station, the RUS severed water and oil conduits. Automatic cutoffs could not prevent the immediate loss of fifty thousand barrels of crude oil, which gravity-flowed from its conduit and spread atop the water as it burned. The RUS had well and truly blown the cover of the SinoInd conduit. Now, everybody's fat would sizzle in that fire.

## 5

The train clung to its monorail and hummed an electric song as it fled in a lateral arc from Raleigh past Winston-Salem. The scoutmaster, Little, was too busy controlling sixteen of his charges to worry about the seventeenth. The Quantrill boy lazed alone by a window, one hand cupped to his ear, watching an unusual volume of traffic stream near their track that overhung the highway median strip. As always, most highway traffic was cargo; some old diesels, mostly short-haul electrics. But today a surprising number of private cars shared the freeway.

Bustling down the aisle, Purvis Little promised himself to confiscate the Quantrill radio, which defied Little's orders on a pack trip.

Ray Kenney flopped into the seat next to Ted, jabbed an obscene finger in Little's direction. "Old fart," he muttered, "took my translator. Said we were only looking for the dirty words."

Quietly, without stirring: "Weren't you?"

"If I'm gonna learn the language, I gotta know 'em all," Ray said, innocence spread across the pinched features.

Ted smiled at the tacit admission. What Ray lacked in muscle and coordination, he made up by honing his tongue. If words were muscle, Ray Kenney could outrun the monorail.

Ray leaned toward his friend, pretended to stare at the traffic, and whispered, "Got a fiver? Wayne's gonna buy some joints in Asheville. If you want in, I can fix it."

Ted considered the idea. A few tokes by the underaged on a weed in a sleeping bag was nothing new, a token rebellion to relieve chafing under Little's authority. But Wayne Atkinson, their only Eagle scout, seldom did favors without three hidden reasons for them. Atkinson probably had the joints already. "I'll pass, Ray. Thanks anyway."

"Scared?" Ray caught the cool glance from Ted Quantrill's mint-green eyes. The scar over Ted's nose and the sturdy limbs furthered the impression that Ted did not yield easily to fear. He might, however, yield to a claim of it. "Wayne isn't scared. He's cool, he never gets caught."

"But you do; you're not Little's pride and joy."

"If I had merit badges coming out of my ass like Wayne does," Ray began, and then jerked around.

There was no way to tell how many seconds Little had been standing behind them. Ray braced his knees against the seat ahead, thrust his hands between his thighs, slumped and stared at nothing.

"I'll take that radio, Quantrill," said the scoutmaster after waiting long enough to make Ray Kenney sweat. He took the radio, slipped it into his shirt pocket, pursed his zealot lips. "Was it reggae jazz, or polluting your mind with a porn station?"

Not sullen, but weary: "Just a newscast, Mr. Little."

"Oh, no doubt," said Little, suddenly favoring Ray Kenney with a we-know-better smirk. "How will we ever explain your sudden interest in current events, Quantrill?"

Little turned away expecting no answer. He was halfway to his seat when Ted replied, "No mystery, Mr. Little. My father's in the Reserve, flies patrol from Key West to Norfolk. And there's a big tanker gone off the Florida coast."

Little frowned. "Sunk, you say?"

"Just gone; disappeared." Ted's shrug implied, *you tell me, you've got the radio.*

"Get your gear together boys," Little called. "Asheville is the next stop." Then he hurried to his seat, fumbled in his shirt pocket, and cupped one hand to his ear.

Ted Quantrill was wrong; a compelling mystery *was* unfolding in the Florida Strait sea lanes. The tanker *Cambio Justo*, under Panamanian registry, had last been reported off Long Key, lumbering north toward Hampton Roads with a quarter-million deadweight tons of Mexican crude oil in her guts. The *Cambio Justo* could hardly run aground in four-hundred-fathom straits. She could not just fly away, nor could she evade satellite surveillance while she thrummed over the surface of a calm sea. But she could always sink.

Two hours after the *Cambio Justo* vanished, a sinking was everybody's best guess, and as far as it went that guess was dead accurate. What no newsman had guessed yet was that she had not sunk very far.

## 6

The interurban coach disgorged Little's brood in Cherokee. From there to Newfound Gap they invested an old diesel bus with their high spirits. At the Tennessee border they reached the old Appalachian Trail, streamed off the bus, watched the vehicle drone up a switchback and out of sight. The bright orange paint and the acrid stink of diesel exhaust bespoke a familiar world that, for a few of them, vanished with the bus as completely as had the *Cambio Justo*—and for the same reasons.

"Wait up," Ray Kenney puffed as the youths ambled down the trail under a canopy of oak, hemlock and pine. He pulled a light windbreaker from his pack, zipped it over slender limbs as Ted Quantrill sniffed the sweet tang of conifers in the mountain air.

"Move it, Kenney," a voice commanded from behind. Wayne Atkinson, the oldest of the boys, enjoyed a number of advantages in Little's troop. Wayne wouldn't have said just what they were; not *couldn't*, but *wouldn't*. His rearguard position was one of responsibility, which Wayne accepted because it also carried great authority. Below average height for his age, he was strongly built, fresh-faced, button-bright and sixteen. Wayne Atkinson gave the impression that he was younger, which enhanced his image to adults. The biggest members of the troop, Joey Cameron and Tom Schell, accepted Wayne's leadership without qualm and, because they could look down on the top of his head, without fear. Among themselves, the smaller boys called him "Torquemada."

Ray was already shrugging his backpack into place when the last of the others eased past on the narrow trail and Atkinson got within jostling distance. Lazily, self-assured: "If your ass is on the trail at sundown, I get to kick it." He followed his promise with a push and Ray, stumbling, trotted forward.

Atkinson reached toward Ted Quantrill with a glance, let his arm drop again, motioned Ted ahead. Ted moved off, trotting after Ray, leaving Atkinson to ponder the moment. Quantrill's part-time job at the swimming pool had toned his body, added some muscle, subtracted some humility. Sooner or later that kind of insolence could infect others, even little twits like Ray Kenney, unless stern measures were taken. Wayne considered the possibilities, pleased with his position, able to see the others ahead who could not see him. It would be necessary to enlist Joey and Tom, just to be sure; and they could provoke the Quantrill kid by using his little pal Kenney as bait. All this required isolation from Purvis Little, who would sooner accept the word of his Eagle scout than that of God Almighty. Wayne's roles at award ceremonies reflected glory on his scoutmaster, and God had never seen fit to do much of that.

To give Little his due, he took his duties seriously and imagined that he was wise. He called rest stops whenever Thad Young faltered. The spindly Thad, long on courage but short on wind, made every march a metaphor of the public education system: everyone proceeded at the pace of the slowest.

The summer sun had disappeared below Thunderhead Mountain, far to their west, before Little reached their campsite near a sparkling creek. The National Park Service still kept some areas pristine; no plumbing, no cabins. The more experienced youths erected their igloo tents quickly to escape the cutting edge of an evening breeze, then emerged again, grumbling, in aid of the fumble-fingered.

Tom Schell slapped good-naturedly at Ted's hand. "Take it easy with that stiffener rod," he said, helping guide it through a tube in the tent fabric. "It's carbon filament. Bust it and it's hell to repair."

"Thanks. It's brand-new; an advance birthday present," Ted replied, imitating Schell's deft handiwork.

The Schell hands were still for a moment. "If you have a birthday up here, I don't wanta know about it."

Ted thought about that. "Aw, birthday hazing is kind of fun."

"Not if Wayne's got it in for you. Look: you've got your friends and I have mine, Teddy. If you're smart, you won't talk about birthdays until we're back in Raleigh."

"How do I get outa this chickenshit outfit," Ted grinned as they pulled the tent fabric taut. No answer beyond a smile. Tom Schell flipped his version of the scout salute from one buttock and wandered off to help elsewhere, leaving Ted to pound anchor stakes. Ray had forgotten the stakes, sidling toward the big campfire site where Little was talking with the strangers.

When he finished, Ted fluffed his mummybag into the sheltering hemisphere of fabric. He found Ray with the others, who by now had abandoned their weiner roast to listen to the tall stranger and to gawk wistfully at his two stalwart daughters. "We'll sleep on the trail if we have to," the man was saying. "We're taking the first ride back toward Huntsville, Mr. Little. I hope it's still there tomorrow."

"We've got a radio too." Purvis Little did not try to hide his irritation.

"I heard all about that tanker. I'm sure it has nothing to do with that mess in India and even if it did, you're only scaring the boys."

A murmur of denial swelled around him; no young male liked to let his visceral butterflies flutter before young females. The stranger said, "*I'm scared,*" in a shaky basso, "and I'd like to see all of us go back together. If there's to be a war, we should be with our families."

"Good luck on the trail," Little replied, his hands urging the man and his silent daughters toward the path. Then he added, with insight rare for him: "If there's another war, those families would be better off here than in Huntsville, or any other big city."

The older scouts were plainly disappointed to see the girls striding from sight in the afterlight. "What the heck was that all about," Ted asked.

"Beats me," said Thad Young. "What's an escalation syndrome?"

"It's when one government tries to hit back at another one," Ray said, "and hits too hard."

"Like Torquemada Atkinson," Thad guessed.

Ray, following Ted back to their tent: "Naw. That's annihilation." Pleased with his definitions, Ray Kenney did not realize that the first was genesis of the second.

## 8

Eight o'clock in the morning, or almost any other time, off Novaya Zemlya was broad daylight in August. Transmuted to a campsite near Clingmans Dome in the Smoky Mountains, that same instant was lit only by dying embers of a showy, wasteful Friday night campfire. While Wayne Atkinson outlined the sport he proposed the following day with the help of Joey and Tom, a "Bulgarian" radioman's assistant on the *P. Tuzhauliye* received a signal through his microwave unit.

Wayne did not bother to tell his confederates that hazing Ray Kenney might bring on violence with Ted Quantrill. The radioman's assistant had not told anyone his secrets, either. One, that he had been raised an Albanian, scornful of Russians; two, that he had emplaced explosives with remote detonators on every communication device he could find aboard ship, including sonar; and three, that he was one of Peking's many agents in place. The Albanian mole had been in place for over a year. Wayne Atkinson had been enjoying the sleep of the innocent for only a few minutes when, a continent and an ocean beyond, the Albanian paused at his breakfast in the ship's mess.

After a moment the man checked his watch, decided against filling his belly because of the icy water he expected to feel soon, sought his exposure gear, then paid attention to his receiver again. He encoded a signal on his watch while standing in the shadow of the broad fo'c'sle, estimating his chances of surviving the wake of 50,000 horsepower screws after a free leap of ten meters from deck to salt water.

From widely-spaced points down the length of the four-block-long tanker came sounds, hardly more than echoes, of muffled detonations. The Albanian eased himself over the rail, inhaled deeply, and leaped out as far as adrenaline could carry him.

The Albanian heard faint alarm hoots over the splash of his own struggle and the hissing passage of the *P. Tuzhauliye*, braced himself to enter the great vessel's wake, then felt a series of thudding impacts through the water. More alarms were going off aboard ship, which began to settle visibly as gigantic bubbles burst around her.

In itself, the ship's wake would not have been fatal. The Albanian resurfaced, pulled the "D" ring on his flotation device, then felt it ripped from his hands by an enormous eddy—the kind of eddy that might accompany the sudden sinking of four square city blocks. The inflating raft fled in the direction of the *P. Tuzhauliye*'s radar mast which was rapidly submerging and, as the Albanian gasped, he rolled and strangled on ice brine.

## 9

Purvis Little finished gnawing a breakfast chickenbone and began on a cuticle. Ted Quantrill's radio finished its newscast as the scoutmaster turned to his Eagle scout. "First time I've ever been sorry I didn't bring a transceiver. Maybe I'd best hike to the Ranger Station and call some of the parents."

"I'll hold the fort here," said Wayne Atkinson. *And make war on some of our little Indians,* he added to himself.

Thad Young took his skillet from the coals and wandered from Little's vicinity spooning Stroganoff. In common with most twelve-year-olds, Thad had bizarre notions about breakfast. He listened to Ted and Ray argue the demerits of ashes in their omelet, then remembered the morning newscast and pointed his spoon at Ray. "What's a measured reprisal?"

Blink. "Uhh—exactly two litres of shit in Atkinson's hat," Ray said. "I dunno, Thad; where'd you hear it?"

"Oh, the President's afraid the Russian's won't make a measured reprisal. What're you laughing about, Teddy, it's your radio they're listening to."

Ted jogged Ray's shoulder in rough endorsement of the joke, then turned serious. "I think it's about that missing tanker; a lot of politics in the air. My dad'll find the tanker; wait and see."

"In the Arctic? This is another one," Thad said, with a roll of his eyes. "Mr. Little is gonna hike out and see about it. Or somethin'," he added, consigning all adult motives to limbo.

The warble of Little's whistle convened the troop a few minutes later. Nothing to worry about, said Little, looking worried; but while he visited the ranger station, the troop would be in Wayne Atkinson's care. There were to be no excursions far from camp, and—a hesitation—their gear should be packed in case they had to move to another site.

"I'll bet," said Ray as they watched Little's head bob from sight. "A tenner says we're going home."

"Knock it off, Kenney," from the gangling Joey Cameron. Joey, no great mental specimen, hewed to one cardinal principle: he worshiped authority. Joey enforced his religion whenever possible.

Ray again: "Betcha I'm right. We won't even get to swim in the pond."

"I'll *throw* you in if you don't strike that tent and pack up." With that, Joey swept his brogan toward a tent stake. They all heard the *snap* as the stiffener rod broke near the stake.

Ted came to his feet with an anguished, "Cameron, you klutz! That's my—"

Joey Cameron caught Ted off-balance with a big hand on his breastbone, pushed the smaller youth who fell backward over a log. "That's your tough luck," he said. He had intended neither the injury nor the insult, had acted on impulse. But Joey patterned his behavior on Wayne's. Contrition was a weakness to be avoided.

"We can fix it," Ray said quickly, fearful that Ted might come up swinging. He extended his hand to his friend, watched Joey back away with long careful strides, managed to deflect Ted from anger as they studied instructions and ferrules in the mending kit.

In half an hour the rod was repaired, their gear repacked in backpacks. Robbie and Tim Calhoun, thirteen-year-old twins, aided in rigging a line between trees so that packs could be hung above the range of marauding ants. Robbie nodded, satisfied. "Now let's take a swim. Joey can be lifeguard."

"Who'll guard *his* life," Ted muttered, half in jest.

Ray patted the air. "Forget it, Teddy. You're like the damn' Russians, trying to make a war out of an accident."

"And you're like the damn' UN, trying to get me to do nothing and hiding it with big words." The Calhoun twins stood listening, mystified.

"You mean like 'measured reprisal'? Just remember to measure Joey Cameron first, Teddy. He's a mile high and a year older."

"So? Next Thursday I'll be a year older too."

"You'll be a few days older, just like everybody else. Come on, let's see how deep the pond is."

The pond had been dammed a century before; local flat stones fitted by long-dead hands of pioneers. Descendants of those folk still lived nearby in the valleys, with the help of legislation in Tennessee and North Carolina. Sites in Utah, Idaho and Oregon were also set aside for people who kept the old ways; living anachronisms who spun their own cloth, cured their own meat, distilled their own whiskey. There were still other repositories of ancient crafts and ethics in the north among the Amish, in the west among separatists from Mormonism, and in the southwest among latino Catholics, Amerinds, and just plain ornery Texans. City-bred in Raleigh, Ted Quantrill knew little about the back-country ways in his own region and next to nothing about those beyond it. Late Saturday morning, he only knew the sun felt good on his back as he spread himself to dry on moss-crusted stones after his swim.

Gabe Hooker was a boy who went along. He was roughly Ted's age and size, with a special talent for being agreeable. Across the pond, affable Gabe basked in the momentary favor of Wayne Atkinson. He heard Wayne suggest a cleanup project for the tenderfeet back at the campsite, and found himself selected as leader of the cleanup. Gabe rounded up the tenderfeet and went along.

Ted Quantrill's first intuition came with the silence, and the repeated soughing gasp that punctuated it. He opened one eye, surveyed an apparently empty pond, half-dozed again. He enjoyed the breeze tingly-cool on naked arms; lay cat-smug and mindless as a stone in celebration of idleness. During the early part of the summer Ted had worked half-days at a Raleigh pool, checking filters and diving for lost objects, scrubbing concrete and learning to catnap. And losing baby fat, and gaining inches in height. Unnoticed to himself, Ted was emerging from the cocoon of boyhood. Wayne Atkinson had noticed it—which explains why he was drowning Ray Kenney.

Again the quiet cough, a wheezing word through water. Ted opened the eye again, moved his head very slightly. Twenty meters away was Tom Schell, legs dangling from the lip of mossy stones into deep water at the dam. Tom frowned down at Joey Cameron, neck-deep in water, and at Atkinson whose muscular left arm encircled a log. Wayne's right arm, and both of Joey's, were busy.

"Let him up a minute," Tom urged quietly. "He's swallowed water twice."

"You afraid pissant Quantrill will hear?" Atkinson sneered at Tom Schell, hauled something to the surface, let it burble.

"You *want* him to?" Tom glanced quickly at Ted, saw no movement.

Wayne and Joey glanced too. "Who cares," Wayne said, caring a great deal. The Kenney kid had allowed himself to be drawn into the game, duck and be ducked, and had realized too late that Wayne had vicious ideas about its outcome. "You're the little shit that gave me that nickname, aren't you?"

No answer. Schell, reaching out: "Enough's enough, Wayne."

Joey saw his leader nod, wrestled a limply-moving mass to the lip of the dam. Ted Quantrill recognized the face of Ray Kenney as it drooled water.

Flashes of thought rapid-fired through Ted's mind. Purvis Little: no help there. Ray was coughing and gagging as Schell dragged him from the water. Schell, Cameron and Atkinson had deliberately set the stage with only one witness, or at least Atkinson had, and none of them doubted that they could overpower Ray and Ted together. Quantrill went to a crouch inhaling deeply, quietly, hyperventilating as he ran on silent feet. Joey saw him then, yelled an alarm in time for Wayne Atkinson to turn.

Quantrill was unsure of the murky bottom and chose to leap feet-first. He chose to plant one foot where Joey's solar plexus should be, and made his next choice in grabbing the handiest piece of Atkinson. It happened to be the sleek blond hair.

Ted's inertia carried him past them and instinct made him slide behind Atkinson as he gripped and shook the blond mop underwater. He hammered at the face with his free hand, knew from the sodden impacts that his fist caused little damage, released his grip, thrust away and surfaced.

Atkinson emerged facing Joey Cameron, dodged a roundhouse swing by his friend. "It's me, you fucker," he sputtered, and whirled to find Ted.

Their quarry made his eyes wide, began to swim backward into deeper water bearing all the signs of terror. Even Joey Cameron was not tall enough to stand on the bottom farther out.

A brave scenario occurred to Mr. Little's pride. "Stay put, this 'un's mine," said Atkinson, who was a fair swimmer.

Ted continued his inhale–exhale cycles; noted that Ray Kenney was trying to sit up as Joey climbed onto the dam. Dirty water hid his legs as Ted drew them up to his chest, still simulating a poor backstroke, mimicking mortal fear of the older youth. Atkinson swam in a fast crawl, grinned, paused to enjoy the moment as he reached for Ted Quantrill's hair. The doubled blow of Quantrill's heels onto his shoulder and breastbone knocked him nearly unconscious.

Wayne blanched, shook a mist of pain from his eyes. "For that," he began, then realized that Quantrill had used the double kick to start a backward somersault. Wayne kicked hard, encountered nothing, then felt himself again dragged backward by his hair. He managed to gargle Joey's name before being hauled under, inhaling more water than air as he gasped. His thighs were scissored by another's, his right hand cruelly twisted by another's, his world a light-and-shadow swirl of horror until his groping left hand found another's locked in his hair. Then Atkinson's head was free, but both arms were now pinioned by another's, and in his spinning choking confusion he tried to breathe. It was not a very smart move.

When Quantrill felt his struggling burden grow spastic, less patterned in its panic, he released it and treaded water calmly as Atkinson, sobbing, floundered toward shore. Joey Cameron thought about loyalty instead of terrain and stalked Quantrill across the pond. Here the silt was unroiled. Joey could see the stones on the bottom. He did not see the one Quantrill was holding until it crashed under his chin, and from that instant his vision improved remarkably. He saw that a fist with a rock in it beats a long advantage in reach, and he saw the futility of swinging on someone you cannot find when your eyes are swollen shut and your opponent waits to slash like a barracuda.

Throughout the fight, Quantrill coupled his terrible slashing fury with utter silence as he mastered the urge to weep in rage, and with an increasing clarity of purpose. The cries and sobs that drew younger boys back to the pond issued from older throats than his. By the time Ted Quantrill chased a galloping blood-streaming Joey Cameron to shore, he was dimly aware that he had done several things right; things that were new to him but that seemed very old and appropriate.

Item: let the other guy make all the noise. You know how he's taking it, and your silence rattles him.
Item: make the other guy fight your fight in a setting you choose.
Item: one enemy at a time, please.
Item: don't expect help from weak friends.
Item: don't expect thanks, either. Your friends may not see it the way you do.

Tom Schell qualified for a merit badge in first aid that day; would have qualified for another if they gave them for diplomacy. Tom listened to the wound-licking growls of Atkinson and Cameron, kept his own counsel, and found Ted nursing skinned knuckles at the pond. "You won't get a date with Eve Simpson for that dumb stunt," he said, invoking the name of a buxom teen-aged holovision star. "Wayne was just teaching Ray a lesson. When Little gets back he's gonna be plain pissed off."

"Let him take it out on Wayne. I did," Quantrill smiled.

*This kid is all wire and ice water,* thought Schell, staring at Quantrill as if seeing him for the first time. The chill down his back only aggravated Schell. "Su-u-ure. And why'd you tell the twins about your goddam birthday? They passed it along. A word to the wise, Teddy." Tom Schell shook his head as though superior to all that had happened, as though he had not lent tacit support to the worst of it.

Ted nodded, attended to his knuckles and the pursuit of new thoughts. He was in the process of realizing that each of them—Wayne, Joey, Tom, Ted—thought himself more sinned against than sinning. It never occurred to Ted to view the hapless Ray Kenney as a sinner; that for an individual or a nation, placing oneself in a helpless position against known danger might be an evil that generates its own punishment.

## 10

The scoutmaster felt reassured by his calls to Raleigh, and by the phrasing of media releases over the Quantrill radio. The emergency session of the UN, he was sure, would do the job. Purvis Little had never heard of I. F. Stone, whose journalistic accuracy grew from experience: "All governments are liars; nothing they say should be believed."

Little's first act on returning to camp was to call his own emergency session. He blew three short blasts on his whistle, saw the bandages on Joey Cameron's face, then glanced at his Eagle. "Good to see you practicing first aid with Joey," he began. "I need to talk with my patrol leaders."

"Practice hell," Atkinson said, regarding his splinted left middle finger. Then he remembered to smile. Regardless of the facts, Little always favored the one who was smiling.

"Language," Little tutted; "settle down, now." He draped an arm over Wayne's shoulder, raised his voice over the hubbub as other scouts surrounded him. "I've got good news, boys. Despite some rumors among our—" he sought the gazes of Ted and Ray, "—young worrywarts, we're not going home. I've talked with some parents, and they're confident that our country is not about to make war on China or Atlantis or Venus."

As every boy knew from holovision, the Venus probes had returned with wondrous samples from the shrouded planet. Mineral specimens suggested only a form of primitive quasilife there, and holo comics had extracted all available humor from the notion of intelligence on Venus. Dutiful laughter spread from the patrol leaders.

Little went on to warn his scouts against further worrisome talk about the outside world, and ended by announcing that he'd found a berry thicket not far from camp. Wayne Atkinson bided his time. When the patrols were out of sight searching for berries, he doubled back to find his scoutmaster. Somewhat later he brought Schell and Cameron back, and later still the rest of the troop straggled back with their booty. By then, Purvis Little understood the hostilities in his world roughly as well, and with roughly the same amount of bias, as India understood her problems after her secret session with her Chinese allies.

## 12

Quantrill was scouring his messkit after supper on Saturday when Tom Schell, without elaborating, told him he was wanted by the scoutmaster. Ted paused long enough to slip on his traditional kerchief, plodded through the dusk with a naive sense of mission in his soul. He felt sure that Little wanted to hear the truth until he entered Little's tent, saw the smugness in Wayne Atkinson's face.

"Sit down, Quantrill," said Little. It was either the best or the worst of signs; for minor discipline, you stood at attention. "What I have to say here is very painful for me."

Ted didn't understand for a moment. "I'm not happy about it either, Mr. Little. When I saw that Ray was unconscious, I just—"

"Don't make it worse by lies," Little cut him off wearily. "I've had the whole story from my patrol leaders, Quantrill. They were all witnesses, and they agree in every detail."

Tom Schell would not meet Quantrill's glance, though Atkinson and Cameron were more than happy to. Ted, angrily: "Do they all agree they'd nearly drowned Ray Kenney?"

"I'm sure Ray Kenney would say anything you told him to," sighed Little, and went on to describe a fictional scene as though he had seen it. Ray, running from a harmless splashing by a good-natured Eagle scout; Wayne, alone, brutally attacked from behind; Joey, trying to reason with the vicious Quantrill after Wayne's aloof departure; Ted Quantrill, hurling stones from shore at the innocent Joey. "It was the most unworthy conduct I have ever encountered in all my years of scouting," Little finished.

"You didn't encounter it at all, Mr. Little," Ted flashed. Anger made him speak too fast, the words running together. "It didn't even happen."

Little swayed his head as if dodging a bad smell. "Oh, Quantrill, look at the lads! I'm sure you'd like to think none of it happened. You may even need—psychological help—to face it," said Little, leaning forward to brush Ted's shoulder with a pitying hand. "But we can't have that sort of violence—mental imbalance—in a scout troop, Quantrill." Almost whispering, nodding earnestly: "It all happened, son. But we can't let it ever happen again. The best thing I can do is to let you resign from the troop on your own accord. Wouldn't that be easiest for you? For all of us?"

A sensation of prickly heat passed from the base of Ted Quantrill's skull down his limbs as he let Little's words sink in. Fairness, he saw, was something you gave but should never expect to receive. In the half-light of the single chem-lamp he noted the simple deluded self-justification on Joey Cameron's face, the effort to hide exultation on Wayne Atkinson's part. Tom Schell fidgeted silently, staring upward. Ted showed them his palms. "What else can I do, Mr. Little? You wouldn't believe me or Ray. Maybe I *should* resign. Then I won't have to watch Torquemada Atkinson hit on my friends."

"You're the hitter, Quantrill," Joey spat.

Quantrill's head turned with the slow steadiness of a gun turret. "And don't you ever forget it," he said carefully, staring past Joey's broken nose into the half-closed eyes.

Purvis Little jerked his head toward a movement at the tent flap. "Go away, Thad; this doesn't concern you, son."

"Durn right it does," sniffled Thad, pushing his small body into the opening. Behind him, Ted saw, other boys were gathered in the near-darkness. "We been listening, Mr. Little."

A wave-off with both hands from Little: "Shame on you boys! Go on, now—"

"Shame on *them*," Thad blubbered, pointing an unsteady finger at the patrol leaders. He ducked his head as if fearful of a blow but, now helplessly crying, he rushed on: "I seen part of it today an' Teddy's right, those bastids is liars, you don't know diddly *squat* about what happened—what those big guys been doing all along!"

A chorus of agreement as others streamed into the tent, some crying in release of long-pent frustrations.

Little had to shout for order, but he got it. Thad disabused him of some errors, and Ray's version was similar. The Calhoun twins, Gabe Hooker, even the shy Vardis Lane all clamored to list old injuries; reasons why the nickname "Torquemada" had stuck. The sum of it shed little glory and less credibility on Wayne Atkinson, who still hoped to brazen his way out.

Finally, Little turned openmouthed toward his patrol leaders, awed by his own suspicions. Joey saw Wayne's steady glare of denial and aped it until—"Wayne lied, Mr. Little," Tom Schell said quietly. He did not bother to add that he had endorsed every syllable. Maybe no one would notice.

"That's right," said Joey. If Tom was flexible, Joey could be flexible.

"I see," said Purvis Little; and the glance he turned on Ted Quantrill brimmed with hatred. Holding himself carefully in check: "I misjudged you, Quantrill—and some others, too. Forget what I said, but now I have to talk to my patrol leaders and," between gritted teeth, "the rest of you please, *please* get out."

## 13

The murmur of voices from Little's tent was distant, carrying only sad phatic overtones. Ted, quarreling internally with new unwelcome wisdom, thought Ray Kenney asleep until Ray said, "I'm glad we got you out of that."

"After you got me into it? The least you could do—but thanks." It had not escaped Ted that his friend had asked for gratitude without once giving it.

"We kept you from getting booted out," Ray insisted.

"Getting out anyway, soon as we get home."

"You can't; you're our leader."

Silence. Ted Quantrill knew that he could lead; knew also that he did not want followers.

Ray, through a yawn: "Things'll be different now that Little understands what happened."

"He doesn't. He never will," Ted replied, and discouraged further talk. Ted knew that with one hostile glance, Purvis Little had given him a valuable discovery: most people will hate you for killing their illusions.

The lesson was worth remembering; the whole day was memorable. Ted Quantrill wondered why he felt no elation, why he wished he were alone so that he could cry, why it was that he felt like crying. He had not yet learned that new wisdom is a loss of innocence, nor that weeping might be appropriate at childhood's end.

# PATRICIA CLARK SMITH

## Flute Song (1982)

*Volcano Cliffs is a region on the West Mesa of Albuquerque, New Mexico, where petroglyphs abound. At the time "Flute Song" was written, only a couple of housing developments interrupted the mesa's wild solitude. Recently, development interests have been winning their fight to build a highway through Volcano Cliffs, and soon enough the petroglyphs—which must be thought of as Native people's books and, in some cases, records of sacred ceremonies—will be painted over and bullet riddled, as so many such treasures across the continent have been.*

*Even so, perhaps the flute song of Kokopelli, Hump Back Flute Player, will occasionally sweeten the dusty wind along those ancient haunts. Perhaps another young woman will, from the kitchen of her life, hear his call and walk out into wilderness for a lovers' tryst.*

*Kokopelli has been among us since the People emerged from the third world, which they were fleeing because evil had overwhelmed their society there in the world below this one. They waited at the threshold to the fourth world as their goddess Iyatiku instructed them not to emerge until the sun rose in the east. When the time was ripe, she said, she would lead them to their new home in the fourth world. Alone, the sun rose in the south, then in the west, then in the north. On the fourth day, Iyatiku rode the rising sun up from the eastern horizon. She was heralded by Kokopelli, from whose flute emerged thousands of butterflies, ensuring prosperity, harmony, and beauty in the People's new lives.*

*Not so long ago, young Pueblo men would cluster about the door of the corn-grinding room to serenade the young women inside who were grinding corn and chattering among themselves. The swain and the young woman he courted hoped for a tryst with their chosen—which was why she was grinding and he was playing flute. If she joked about him to her companion at grinding, or glanced however shyly toward a certain boy, a girl could signal her regard. If the young man she so graced returned her interest, he would riff on his flute directly to her, and thus they would arrange a date to meet that night under the stars.*

*Among some Pueblos, on certain days the young women, hair arranged in elaborate figure-eight-shaped coils over their ears in a maidenhood style known as butterfly whorls, would flit among the newly planted crop, the young men chasing them, until they caught each other. Then what rollicking upon the warming spring earth!*

*"Flute Song" was written about ten years before the Kokopelli craze put his emasculated image on tea towels, pot holders, and greeting cards. Smith's story honors the spiritual history of this land, reminding us that the old gods still beckon; they have gifts for us—the ancient gifts of food and life-affirming sexuality. "Flute Song" reminds us that the true Kokopelli must possess humpback, flute, and penis rampant. So you see, it is not Kokopelli who adorns the pop market sundries to which his supposed icon is attached. The true Hump Back Flute Player weaves his enchanting songs out there on the mesas, calling a newcomer home.*

Before they moved to Albuquerque, Carol read the brochures Ed brought back with him from the development where he'd made the downpayment, and learned she would be living at the foot of volcanoes. There were dead cones there, five of them, lined up on the mesa west of the city a mile or so behind the development. She thought of the PBS documentary she'd seen about Pompeii and Herculaneum. Those towns had been suburbs too, in a way, and there had been bakeries there, and bars, and local elections, and women spending quiet days in their houses with their children. She remembered the lava molds of the dog curled around the stake where he'd been chained, and the old man who tried to escape toting his bags of gold, and she smiled to herself, imagining, *What if we had to run?* Ed would be at work when it happened, and she pictured herself, the stroller heaped high with canned goods, Jesse wailing, her holding her mother's crotcheted afghan over their heads with her free hand to protect them and bumping the silly tires over big ruts while the lava bombs whistled and thudded around them. He said most of the roads around there were still unpaved.

It was only the kind of thing she always imagined, and there was more pleasure than fear to it. Even here in Massachusetts, making toast, running errands, scraping applesauce off Jesse's chin into his mouth and hearing the spoon chink on his tooth, she pictured plane crashes, semis careening toward them across the median, she and Jesse taken hostage at gunpoint at the bank. She planned out carefully what she would do to be safe, but nothing ever happened.

And Ed said the house was beautiful. The Polaroids were good. It was high up on the West Mesa, and you could see the five volcanoes from the kitchen windows. Outside the sliding glass doors of the living room was their patio. Below, to the east, the city lay strung out along the Rio Grande Valley, and beyond that, the Sandias, big mountains the brochure said were part of the Rockies. The brochure went on about Indians and rodeos and Mexican restaurants and National Forests nearby, and a city that had everything, hospitals and museums, discos and a symphony.

The truth was that it didn't much matter, since it had to be Albuquerque. There were only so many places where Ed could work in nuclear medicine. Sometimes she thought she wouldn't have minded so much being a woman living by those Italian volcanoes. Those were near the sea, and there must have been water and birds and green gardens. On the United States map in their encyclopedia, New Mexico was colored tan, and she thought of it that way. In the Polaroids the river valley showed up blurrily as a dull green winding, but where the big black rocks of the lava flow stopped, high above the valley where their house would be, there would be brown dust, dry creaky plants, hot wind. Her mouth felt dry when she thought about it.

She knew how it would be. She was always slow to make friends. There would be first visits with casseroles and invitations to join things, from women who would grow quickly less interested when they found out she didn't play bridge after all, that she wasn't good at spending long afternoons in shopping malls and registering voters, that she mostly reacted with embarrassment to confidences given and invited. Once in a while Ed said she should get a job or take a class. But she had only been an English major, one who couldn't type, and as for classes, it seemed easier not to. There never was anything listed in community college catalogues she really cared to learn.

Here in Waltham she read and took long walks with Jesse and dreamed of Peterbilts crossing the median, of shattering forces closing in, and it would be that way there, too, wide days alone with books and the baby and a quiet house, and a view below them she couldn't imagine ever changing much. Summer and winter, it would be a city in a valley with mountains behind it, for what seasons could they have there?

It was better than she expected, in most ways. They moved in October, and the whole valley beneath them and patches on the rock faces of the mountains were yellow, not the fine varied fires, orange and burgundy, of New England, but yellow into old gold and brown, a definite turning. The river valley was a major flyway, and in those first days flocks of cranes and snow geese and other birds passed over her house. She was out in the yard raking stones when she first heard the cranes' trilling drift down to her, so otherworldly and filling the air it took her moments to figure out where it was coming from and look up, look up to see the sun flashing on their wings as they wheeled south. Ed was away most days, even weekends, setting up his new project. The mice he worked with started getting tumors in the right places, and the neighbors, as expected, settled into remote friendly presences. She read and dreamed, learned how to watch the mountains and the sky. Jesse grew. She wasn't unhappy.

Once, during that first month, when a neighbor was standing with her in the yard, she puzzled aloud over the penny-sized holes here and there in the ground, wondering what animal could bore so neatly in the hard-packed dirt. Cicadas, the neighbor told her, and walked over to a gray–green spray of chamisa growing wild by the cinder-block wall. She plucked something off the bush and handed it to Carol. It was the cast-off shell of an insect, about an inch long. It had a big segmented grub-body, all its legs intact, and a face with bulging eyes and complicated mouth-parts. "Just wait," the neighbor said. "You can't hardly sleep for them some nights in the summer, they make so much racket." She looked down at the husk in her hand, stroking its split back with one finger, loving its completeness. She wondered what color it would be if it were alive, what weight it would have in her hand.

At Ed's insistence, and with the cicada-neighbor's help, she got someone to clean once a week, a woman from Jemez Pueblo. She resented the idea of a stranger in the house, not really needing the help, but Delphine moved quietly around the kitchen and utility room in her solid body, cheerful and self-contained. Most of their conversation was about Jesse— babies and weather, easy talk. One day after Thanksgiving, Del said the three of them ought to drive up to Jemez on the second of December for Matachines. Carol was unsure of what she'd heard—machete? machines? and asked "What, Del?" feeling dumb.

"—Matachines. It's a big dance. You drive up in the morning and watch, and you come eat at my house. It's about Cortez comes here and he marries this girl, Montezuma's daughter, but Montezuma doesn't like her to marry him. It's a good dance."

Unexpectedly, Ed wanted to go.

"Local culture," he grinned. "I figured we'd start doing more stuff like that when the project settles down and it gets warmer, but we can't pass up an invitation."

That Saturday they drove north to the pueblo under a cold blue sky, on a two-lane lined with cottonwoods. Their bark showed strangely silver in the bright air.

The pueblo lay in a hollow just before the road started to climb into the Jemez mountains. One and two story adobes clustered against a big background of red cliffs and chalky tent rocks, like pillars of salt. They parked near the trading post and followed the sound of chanting down to a central plaza lined with people, Anglo and Indian. More Indians sat on the roofs, teen-age boys mostly. No one seemed especially reverent. Children raced around, and in front of her two old Indian women in flowered house dresses and bright patterned shawls sat in green and white plastic lawn chairs, talking in English about the bad luck of somebody named Willy. The air smelled sharply of wood smoke and frying dough.

The chanting stopped, and there was some bustle at the far end of the circle from her, where she couldn't see: the sound of bells receding. The crowd started to break up. They'd gotten a late start; it must be over already. Del appeared at their side: "Everybody's goin' to lunch now, you come and eat, and there's more later on."

They followed her off the plaza to her warm kitchen filled with people, relatives probably. Del insisted on serving the three of them and wouldn't let Carol help. The others smiled at them, and talked among themselves in their quick language; they grinned when Ed, after a spoonful of the chile stew, choked and grabbed his thin paper napkin off the oilcloth table, rubbing at his streaming eyes and nose. The children giggled, and Carol was ashamed for him, even knowing she would have done the same thing if she'd tasted it first. Del thumped his back and handed him the whole box of napkins, a glass of koolade: "It's real hot, you got to eat it with bread, wash it down." Taken in small sips, it was wonderful, with chunks of hot crusty bread to each mouthful, and koolade alongside. She fed Jesse jello salad and small bites of bread. He sat on her lap, kicking at the underside of the table and sucking on a spoon. The women kept taking things from the oven, big cookies brushed with cinnamon, and a crumbly cake-mix devil's food. She'd expected the chile, but not the jello and the Betty Crocker, and she smiled at herself. *Did you want her to be dressing out a deer with a bone knife?*

When they got back to the plaza, the dancing had already begun again, but the crowd was thinner, and this time they politely eased their way to the edge of the circle. One Mexican man, his dark face seamed and his hair combed wet, sat in a kitchen chair in front of a wooden booth hung with evergreen. He played a thin, scratchy fiddle, and another man who seemed unsure of the music strummed a guitar for rhythm. The whole while they stood there she tried to follow the tune. It kept pausing when she didn't expect it to, taking unforeseen turns, but part of it reminded her of a song they used to sing in kindergarten:

> *Put your little foot*
> *Put your little foot*
> *Put your little foot right there . . .*

There were dancers, maybe thirty of them, in two lines, wearing bright shirts and what seemed to be cheap iridescent patterned table-cloths pinned around their shoulders like capes. Straps hung with bells circled their ankles. They did not stomp the ground, but set their feet down gently, the emphatic motion to the beat coming instead when they raised their knees. An unsmiling little girl in a white communion dress and veil, long white stockings and maryjanes, danced with a big-bellied man in a mask. The two of them shuffled in and out among the lines of dancers, always circling back to another man, also masked, who sat at the far end of the circle from the musicians. They paused before him while he waved a light wooden frame laced with colored ribbons over them as though he blessed them. Carol couldn't help fitting her own words to the tune:

> *Did you see my*
> *Did you see my*
> *Did you see my new shoes?*
>
> *Papa bought them*
> *Papa bought them*
> *Papa bought them for me . . .*

The music changed pace. The little girl danced to one side of the ring. The seated man stood up, very tall in his horned mask, and suddenly the girl's partner bent down and grabbed his ankle. Slowly, he pulled the horned man by the leg through the whole line of dancers, the two of them moving toward the musicians in hesitant hops, while a skinny boy wearing a cowhide and loud cowbell ducked and feinted around the circle, charging at the dancers and the spectators. It was courtship and conquest, and the bride perhaps twelve. The man returned to his chair, the music paused, then started up, and they went through the whole thing all over again. She watched them, forgetting her earlier impression of cheap tablecloths pinned on like Batman capes, slowly being drawn in by their steady movement and bright color, losing herself in hot rose and white and beetleback green, moving, moving.

Again, it ended abruptly, before she was ready, and she stood there, a little dazed, as the two lines of dancers filed out, the sound of bells moving away. The man who had danced with the little girl turned around now, scanning the crowd, walking toward them. He walked toward her. She stared at him. She felt herself being taken by the hand and led gently, irresistibly, into the center of the ring. The bull-boy raced around them, clanking, his head lowered, pretending to charge her. Her head snapped around, looking for Ed. He had not noticed her yet. He was holding Jesse and talking to another Anglo couple.

The man pulled her close to his belly. She could smell beer on his breath, and the fresh paint of his mask. Waving his free hand gaily around in the air, he bumped his hip against hers, once, twice, three times, catching her off balance and making her clutch at his shoulder. The fiddle haltingly started up again, the same tune, and the crowd had noticed now and was laughing, watching them.

> *Papa bought them*
> *Papa bought them*
> *Papa bought them for me . . .*

She pushed loosely at his chest, no, please, still gripping her big shoulder-bag with the extra diapers and Jesse's bottle. *Naw*, he whispered in a husky voice from behind the mask, *come on, you dance with me, you do just like this*, and leading her strongly, his hand firm on the small of her back, he did the simple hopping step he'd done with the little girl. She was going to cry, please, I can't. *Naw, like this here*, and *there*, he said, and she did it, for one, two, three steps, faltering, dancing. The crowd cheered and whistled. He spun her around, and her shoulderbag flew out and hit her on the back, and then he released her and bowed to her deeply. She stood, arms at her sides, breathless. And then, as though her body knew better than she what to do, she curtsied to him, and turned and walked formally back to her husband, whose tight face and nervous grin she could see above the circle of the crowd who parted to let her pass. Before he could say anything to her—you ok? Why you?—Del appeared again beside them, grinning, giggling, "Ooo, you done good! You like that dance?"

All the way home Ed said little, commenting sometimes on the scenery—Indians lounging outside the bar at San Isidro, the salty crust on the banks of a little river, a jackrabbit crossing the road. She wondered what crack in the world had blinked open. Who in the world was looking at her.


One night in February, Jesse was teething. His cheeks flamed red, and he drooled and fretted, uhhh, uhhh. Ed slept, having taken his turn, and she rubbed Jesse's gums with wine, and rocked and walked, jiggling him up and down, afraid to break the rhythm, singing anything, all the songs from college, and slipping mindlessly from one into another:

> *Lord Jeffrey Amherst was a soldier of the king*
> *And he came from across the sea*
> *And he conquered all the Indians that came within his sight*
> *In the wilds of this wild countree . . .*

She reached further back, into the songs of her own childhood, not think-ing, moving and singing. Jesse's heavy head dropped to her shoulder.

*Put your little foot*
*Put your little foot*
*Put your little foot right there . . .*

she sang, dazed with sleep, and danced with him slowly, easily in her bare
feet around the darkened kitchen, moving in and out of the circle of soft
light from the lamp over the sink.

There was a little state park only a few miles up the road from their
house, but it was March before she went there, packing up Jesse and folding his stroller into the back of the car. The sun was hot, but an intermit-
tent breeze blew icy, as if it had just nosed off some glacier. She turned off
onto a blacktop drive at the sign, INDIAN PETROGLYPH STATE PARK.

It was a miniature valley, with the steepest side formed by the curve
of the lava flow, a hill set about with giant tumbled black blocks. Basalt,
said the folder the young ranger handed her at the entry station. From here,
where the ground dipped especially low at the base of the flow, she could
not see the development at all, and the lava curved around and cut off most
of the view east toward the city and the mountains. She was encircled.

For such a small-scale place, most of the trails were surprisingly
steep, winding in and around the great black chunks. The stroller was out
of the question, and she carried Jesse around the base of the flow and halfway up one of the trails, stopping often to rest and read the trail markers.
The petroglyphs showed pale against the black rocks, pecked out or incised
in varying degrees of clarity. They were oddly jumbled, running into one
another, some of them pecked out right on top of older pictures, at random
and disturbing angles to one another. None of the vanished artists had apparently cared how his picture stood in relation to the others. Or maybe
that was the point, she thought, abundance more important than order, like
the crowded meal Del had set out for them.

Some rocks were barren, while others teemed with pictures. There
were small human foot and hand prints, spirals and zigzags and tennis-
racquet shapes and other designs, bird and animal tracks, and the animals
themselves, some roughed-out, some delicately drawn. She counted lizard,
snake, rabbit, deer, mountain sheep maybe, something four-legged, wolf or
coyote, flying hawk, strutting grouse and quail. They delighted her,
pocked out so long ago and so precisely. She traced them with her finger.
The indentations were very shallow, almost imperceptible.

The human ones were disturbing, the carvings much more harsh and
stylized than the animals. Most of them had big swollen trapezoidal
bodies with stick arms and legs, and square or triangular heads with lines
or big dished out hollow O's for eyes and mouth. Some were beaked. Fantastic projections grew from their heads, like a child's spikey drawing of
hair—headdresses, maybe, on top of masks. The folder said little, just that
some of the pictures were casual doodles, while others showed "deities

and ceremonial aspects of life among the ancestors of the present-day Pueblo societies." They must be gods, she thought. How could you make a quail so neatly, right down to the little bouquet of feathers on his head, and then make one of these things and say it's human?

Jesse began to fuss. Her hands ached in the cold wind, coming up stronger now as the afternoon wore on. She started back down, but the trail was clearly marked only for people climbing upward. You were supposed to make a big circle and come down by a different path. She noticed a line of three small footprints leading off to the left that hadn't been visible on the upward hike. Curious and disoriented, she edged around the rock in the direction they pointed. She turned to check her bearings, and found she had stepped into what seemed like a small roofless room, a walled garden, ringed around by the footprint rock and by other rocks just as large. It was sheltered from the rising wind she could hear now making music through all the angles and crannies of the lava flow. She was suddenly conscious of the sun, warm on her back through her light windbreaker. The ground was level, a floor covered with fine white sand, six or seven feet square. Low plants grew here and there, different leaf shapes, dried out now. One of them still bore a few wrinkled yellow berries.

She noticed another petroglyph on the head-high rock opposite her. It was a plant, a thrusting central stalk with long narrow leaves arching off it, set about with elongated bumps with spidery threads at their ends. The Mazola commercial flashed into her mind, a lank and lovely Indian girl in cutoff jeans, her mouth in an insolent slant as she fondled a full kernelled ear and said to the camera, "YOU call it corn. WE call it maize." I call it corn, she thought, and then she turned and saw him on the uphill end of the rock room, the walled garden.

He was no smaller than the other humanoid petroglyphs. But she had unconsciously assumed that the trapezoid people, if they were alive, would be immense. She knew at once that this one depicted a presence close to her own size.

Unlike the other figures, he was alone on his rock. He reclined on his back, legs crossed, his heels kicked up in the air in a way that should have seemed an awkward position for a man, but somehow was not. Two plumes curled off his head, another from his stomach, and he crooked his elbows and raised a stick to his mouth, a bone or an instrument of some kind. His back had something protruding from it that looked a little like a cup handle. Maybe the whole thing was a picture of some kind of pottery. But no, she thought, it wouldn't be practical; the stick-thing and the plumes would break off too easily. Besides, this one was clearly a person, a man. He had one open eye on his flat-profiled face, and a thinly pocked line for a smile. But it was a real face, not all slash and beak and gaping O's, not like the trapezoid people, with their stiff legs and arms and mask faces. He seemed so gay and fluid and at ease, lolling there on his rock.

Jesse had stopped fretting. She stood there a long time in the warm sheltered place, looking at him, listening to the wind piping on the far side of the rock. When she turned to go, edging past the corn plant and the footprints, it seemed to her that the tracks were a sign, here, this way. What she was leaving was neither room nor garden, but a shrine.

She asked the ranger about him on the way out, framing her question cautiously, though she wasn't sure why: not what was that petroglyph back there, but had he ever seen one like that anyplace?

"Oh, sure, none like that here that I know of, but they're all over the southwest, even down into Mexico and South America. That's the flute player, Kokopelli. He's pretty nearly always got a hunch back."

"Do the feathers mean something," she asked, "that he's some kind of chief, or a priest?"

"Just feathers, just a headdress probably. But that one you talk about on his middle ain't a feather, it's probably his male part. They usually show him that way."

She thanked him and drove off, a little awkward about the clutch. Her face was burning. It was only partly the ranger, who of course might laugh about her later, she had a kid with her and everything, and she asks why there's this feather poking out of its belly. But he had been polite. He was a very young ranger, looking down, a little embarrassed himself as he did his duty and explained. It wasn't for his sake she was ashamed. Driving home, she felt as if a larger laughter, male, and tolerantly amused, surrounded her. She remembered her father and uncles at family dinners after a few beers, when she was little and would say things like about how her dog Silky must have gotten married because she was going to have puppies. She remembered their belly laughter, and her mother smiling a little while she told them hush, and her own shame and anger. She'd learned gradually to say nothing, to stay quiet in her corner and listen until she figured out all the possible things they might make fun of if she said them.

All the short drive home, the wind off the lava cliffs buffeted the car, playing rough. She carried Jesse into the house and closed the door against it. All afternoon, all night, it kept up, rattling the window frames. In the morning she saw how it had driven the dust in, silting under the jambs in fine curls and plumes on the kitchen floor.


The wind blew like that for days. She'd never lived in a place where dark clouds meant dry wind and no rain. Grit in their teeth, their eyelids grainy, and the house impossible to keep clean. Del said the rain would come later.

She stayed inside mostly and read, not novels now, but books about Indians, starting with the ones she'd picked up at museums in town, and then trying the branch library. She remembered the name the ranger told her, Kokopelli, the syllables like flute notes, and looked especially for news of him. She didn't find much. Most of the books just said what the ranger told her, that he was drawn on rocks from Guatemala up to the Canadian border. The authors annoyed her. Probably they said so little because they themselves didn't know much about him, but it seemed to her that they pretended they did, naming him casually as though the reader was supposed to say ah yes, him, as though everyone knew about him but her.

She had mostly been looking at modern sources, assuming they'd know more. But one day she came across an old book in the library stacks. It was a thin book in an olive cover, privately printed. She stood there skimming pages. The author had been a trader in the last century at the Hopi mesas over in Arizona; anthropology and languages were his hobby. Mostly he wrote to prove that the Hopi were remnants of one of the ten lost tribes. He said all the Pueblo languages had recognizable Hebrew roots, that elements in their legends suggested their Semitic past. But she could read between the lines that the people had liked him, had probably been amused by him, and polite to him:

> My friend Wikvaya is reluctant to accede to the truth about the origins of his people, being much attached to the story they have evolved in their exile and degeneration of their coming forth from four worlds beneath the earth, but he has always received me cordially, and assures me he believes in the brotherhood of all the nations. His rank in their religious societies is high, and I believe it would be impolitic for him to betray any further degree of agreement. He displays a great particular interest in the story of the giving of the tablets on Sinai, and owns it curious that his ancestors as well should have been given tablets to guide them in their wanderings, though he maintains stoutly that their sacred stones speak of different matters than the Commandments and are to this day in the keeping of certain people of the towns. These I have not yet seen, but I persevere in my efforts, and have great hope they shall forge yet another link in my proof. . . .

She checked the book out, not in hopes of finding any accurate information, just intrigued by this earnest scholar, this mild lunatic among the mesas, happily immersed like her in his private quest.

She read the book that night with pleasure. He rambled cheerfully all around, mixing his personal experiences and theories with tales the people told him, giving his estimate of "the character and condition of their race," describing daily life and ceremonies. He had illustrated the whole thing himself, with charts painstakingly drawn of Hebrew and Hopi words, the migration routes he imagined his lost Semites to have followed, drawings of baking ovens and kachina masks. And there was a small sketch of a man reclining on his humped back, playing a flute, and a story about him:

*This spirit whom they style Kokopilau, being a man of humped
back who plays upon a flute, is much depicted in their rock-
pictures, often more crudely than I have here rendered, for his
member is displayed in most of their carvings. He is called also
mahu, which is their name for locust, the connection in their
minds no doubt being that this insect, which is much in evidence
here in the summer months, as well makes music of a shrill sort,
and emerges from the earth where its larval stage is undergone.
Kokopilau they say came from out the lower worlds in company
with them and helped them in their early trials. His hump contains the seeds of all plants which he scatters before him, and his
music engenders warmth which speeds their growth. Wikvaya
says that as with certain of the other kat'sinas he is sometimes to
be met with in summer among the rocks, in particular places he
favors; further, that this happened to a woman of the village
when he was but ten or twelve years of age. She became with
child by him, but died later in childbed, the infant being of unusual size, and this is supposed a judgment on her for having
spoken to her relatives of the child's father and betrayed other
secrets concerning him. Yet for them he is in the main a jocund
spirit, immodest of his prowess, in which Wikvaya and the others
take great relish, saying the corn and beans and their other crops
advance the better for Kokopilau's sometime dalliance with the
daughters of men. We note that the locust as well among the He-
brews was a source of divine supply, as we find in the account of
the Baptist's wanderings in the wilderness: "AND HIS MEAT
WAS LOCUSTS."*

The wind slacked off and the weather warmed. The skinny saplings
in their yard fuzzed yellow–green. She went back to the park often now,
nodding briefly at the ranger and parking as far as she could from the
entrance. She explored all the trails, gradually. She found no other flute
players, no more hidden gardens. Few other people came there on week-
days. When there were people, she stayed clear of the trail that led past his
rock, watching carefully, from a distance, any other visitors who climbed
it. None of them ever took the wrong turning she had taken, not that she
could see.

She went to him when no one else was there, saving him for last, at
the end of the afternoon slipping through the passage by the footprint
rock. She sat quietly on the white sand, nursing Jesse on her lap, but looking at him, the man, her mind becoming grooved like the rock with the
flowing outlines of his body, the curve of his back, the jaunty angle of his
crossed legs, the thrust of flute and phallus, his whole joyous, carefree being. She would stay perhaps ten minutes, as long as Jesse was quiet, and

then rise and return to the car, her house, her life. She did not mention him to Ed, only saying she loved the park, that Jesse was beginning to recognize some of the animal pictures and point at them. She was afraid Ed would want to go there himself some Saturday. But he never did.

It was no lie that she loved the whole park. As the year moved into summer, she noticed more and more life on the floor of the valley. The sand was criscrossed with delicate tracks, mouse and beetle, snake and rabbit, and she began to see how many different kinds of plants grew there. One kind of spikey bush had purple flowers so small that the bushes, seen from a distance, seemed dusted with haze. As she stood beside one of them on a hot June afternoon, her knee brushed against it and she started at the sudden flurried movements all over it. Walking-sticks, ten or so of them, readjusted themselves irritably. When they were quiet again, their long segmented gray–green bodies were indistinguishable from the bush. She picked one up tentatively, saying "Look, Jesse." It high-stepped indignantly up her bare arm, tickling a little, and tumbled back into its bush.

After that, she knew that walking sticks were there on the purple-flowered bushes, but even though she tried for long periods of time, standing very still beside them, she could seldom spot one unless she shook the bush and forced one into movement. She wondered how many other things there were in the valley, living invisible, in her plain view.

It was in early June, too, that she first noticed the other regular visitor. On a late afternoon, coming down from a recess off the trail, she turned a corner of the marked path around a big boulder and almost fell over him. He was a young Indian man in his early twenties, wearing a denim shirt and levis, with a red bandana bound around his black hair. He sat so still she might almost have passed him by, squatting there right off the trail, leaning against a rock. Sorry, she mumbled, and he smiled and nodded up towards her, saying nothing. She wondered if he had seen her slip out from behind the footprint rock, and decided he couldn't have. If he had been sitting there the whole time, rocks would block his view. And he looked somehow as though he had been sitting there forever. She would know him again, she thought, and she did.

He was not there every time she came to the park, and he never seemed to be there when there were other people around besides herself. But he was there often. Mostly, after that first time, she saw him at a distance, high up and hard to spot against the sun, among the rocks at the top of the slope. Or she would glimpse him at the far end of the park as she was driving in, and by the time she was out of the car he would have disappeared. Maybe, against regulations, he climbed where there were no trails. I suppose it's more his place than the state's anyway, she thought. But she was more careful now, always looking around her before she cut off the trail into the little sanctuary, to where Kokopelli smiled and played his inaudible music.

But twice she came close to him, once at the base of the trail. Again he sat on the ground, but this time in full view as she approached, a little nervously. She was going to have to walk directly past him, and prepared her face to smile, her voice to say hi. Again, he did not speak, but looked up and smiled back, clearly recognizing her. She glanced down. Two blue-tail lizards, like the ones that lived in her yard and scuttled to the cinder-block wall at her faintest approach, rested on his denim knees, basking in the sun. Her shadow fell over his lap, and they spun about, dived into the crevice between his knees. One pale azure tail still protruded, draped along the curve of his thigh. He laughed. She gasped and hurried down the trail, sure of what she had seen. When she looked back, holding Jesse close, he was gone.

Another time she came upon him near her car, his back to her. She felt a little ashamed of the suspicions that arose in her, at her relief in remembering clearly having locked both doors. She felt an urge to turn back and linger for a while, to give him a chance to go away. But it was late, Ed would be home in an hour, she had to start dinner. She kept walking toward him, thinking *it's my car, I have to leave now.* She was within ten feet of him before she realized what he was doing. He turned toward her, shaking off, tucking himself in and buttoning the fly of his faded jeans. There was an irregular dark splotch on the ground. Again he smiled, perfectly unembarrassed, knowing her. She fumbled with the keys, unlocking the door. It took an interminable time to buckle Jesse in his car seat, to start the car. This time he did not disappear, but stood there, lean and at ease, hip cocked, thumbs in his pockets, watching her drive away. She stared at him in the rearview. He was still smiling.

She stopped at the ranger station. But when the ranger came out, she could not think what to say, what to complain of, that she had accidentally come upon a man pissing near her car, that he had turned and smiled at her. The ranger would put that together with their first encounter, what do the feathers mean? She gestured back toward the lava flow. "Does that young guy work here, that Indian man?"

He shook his head. His sunburn looked very red against his blond close-cropped hair. "No ma'am, no one else works here. I'm not sure who you mean. There's no one else driven in here, an old couple about eleven, but they left before you got here. Could be someone sneaked over the fence. Indian guy? I better check . . ."

She had a sudden revulsion at herself. She was someone betraying a secret.

"No, I didn't mean he was here now. Just somebody I've seen here a couple of times before."

That night she dreamed. She was in the park at night. It was full moon, and all the plants of the valley floor bulked strangely tall in the light. She climbed, dressed in shorts and a thin shirt, and the wind played through it across her breasts and ruffled her hair. It was light enough to see her way to the trail, to find the darker shadow of the narrow passage between the rocks that led to him, and she found her way not just by her eyes, but by the music.

He was waiting for her, reclining on the soft white sand, and she knew the pleasure he had had in waiting, in knowing she would come. He smiled at her around the mouthpiece of the jutting flute, welcoming her. His body was lean and compact and smoothly muscled. He lay there, crested erect in the soft night air, very plain in the moonlight. A knapsack lay beside him on the sand, army surplus maybe, but covered all over with embroidered designs in bright yarn, corn and lizard, locust and squash vine.

She stood there waiting until the song was done, because above all there was no hurrying this, and at last he was finished. He set aside the flute, laying it carefully on the knapsack to keep it free of the sand, and she knelt beside him, a few inches away from him. She could feel the warmth from his body. Lazily, he reached out and ran his hand between her legs, stroking her slowly there, back and forth, one finger firm. He paused sometimes to cup her with his whole hand, as if she were something precious, a fruit to be eaten, but good enough to wait for, a fruit good to heft and cradle in the palm. Still she did not touch him, but she knelt there, breathless, balancing on her wobbly knees, feeling him, until at last she too stretched out her hand, resting a finger lightly on his warm lips. He grinned and tongued it, and sucked at it, drawing her finger in the inside of his mouth, hot and wet, and his teeth nibbled at her lightly. She played her finger gently back and forth, in rhythm with his hand. It was an old game of symbols she instinctively knew, but had never played, waking or in dreams, with any man. His hand moved on her more surely, and she moaned, then, and woke herself. Moonlight slanted through Venetian blinds across a bed, and Ed slept beside her. His back was turned, one arm flung across his face. She shook him awake, in fear and desire, aching, *Love me, love me.*

She slept afterward, a thickened, dreamless sleep. But he lay awake for a long time, pleased and a little alarmed by her fierceness.

After that, she stayed away from the park. Something knew about her; someone had touched her. And maybe Ed guessed. He watched her face, the next morning, whenever he thought she was not looking. All that Saturday he kept reaching for her hand, asking if she'd like to get a sitter and go to dinner, to a movie, smiling at her in a half-embarrassed, questioning way. She shrunk from his looks, his hand, from all his kindness, this sudden burst of attention. She wanted to scream at him that she was all right, that he should go play with his mice, anything. Instead she smiled and hugged him, saying her head hurt, it was the heat, the summers here would take some getting used to.

She dreamed often now, almost every night, but not the same dream she'd had before. This dream broke in upon others, the more usual dreams, as though someone had flicked the channel on a TV set. She would find herself dressed in a light shift, or one of Ed's old T shirts, whatever she had worn to bed that night. She walked down the road to the park, the road where no one ever walked, but only drove. The ruts and the sharp stones, the dust between her toes, seemed very real. She was conscious of each step, not like the floating, diffuse passages from one place to another that happened in other dreams. When she turned in at the sign, the chain link gates to the park would be locked. She stood outside and laced her fingers through the wide mesh, pressing her face against the cold wire, straining to catch the voice she could almost hear calling her from inside. After a while, she would find herself back in the dream that had been taken from her, and she would be arguing with her father, or back in college, taking a final in a course she had never attended, the channel snapped back. But, waking in the mornings, it would be this dream she would remember above the other, vaguer dreams. At breakfast, she felt still the powdery dust of the road, the woven wire cold against her cheek.

July came in with bright unblinking heat. The yard baked, and outside her wide windows, the city wavered below in hot light. When she drove out to the main highway, small puddles of mirage on the pavement ahead receded forever before the car. She no longer had the patience to read. She couldn't endure the house, with only Jesse and herself for distraction. She did anything to get out, away, driving to shopping centers on made-up errands, taking Jesse into the city to grassy tree-shaded parks with swings and slides, so different from the petroglyph park, or to the community pool. She spread their blanket on the coarse scratchy grass and sat him on it, and lay down beside him, willing the strong sun to burn whatever it was out of her, listening to the chlorinated water flop in the safe concrete gutters, to the low normal voices of other women and their children.

The rains came almost every afternoon now. Dark clouds would begin to bunch up on the western horizon about three, behind the volcanoes. A breeze would swell, and the first faint thunder slowly drew closer. She could hear the storms approaching for hours, but when they came, the rain was hard and short, over in twenty minutes. By morning the yard would be baked hard again, waiting.

With the heat and the rains came the cicadas. Now she found their stranded shells everywhere, clinging to the siding of their house, on the chamisa ringing the patio, on the utility pole by the driveway. Their hollow feet clung tenaciously, even after the living creature had freed itself and dried off and flown away. Their keening filled the air, even if she were shut in the house with the swamp cooler turned on. One of them would begin it, to be joined immediately by another, a third, a fourth, the shrilling soon coming from everywhere, as though it were a sound made by the hot tremulous air itself. It was not so much unpleasant as strange, so much more insistent and overwhelming than any locusts she had ever heard.

She wanted to see one sing. She wanted to know that it was really an insect who made the noise, to understand that it really was wings or legs vibrating together. She would walk carefully up to one of the new saplings in their yard, scarcely twice as tall as herself, and stare up into leaves gone limp with the heat, trying to locate the source of the swelling sound, so close to her as she stood there beneath the little tree that it seemed almost a noise within her own mind. Unlike the crickets or frogs she had tried to sneak up on when she was little, the cicadas never stopped at her near approach. Their song would not be hurried no matter what threatened, as though it had to fill some preordained period of time. But there seemed no one length she could discern to the space between the first long sawing notes and the whirr scaling abruptly down into silence.

She never was able to see a cicada while it sang. But sometimes, after one had wound down and she had given up looking for him, she would see its big body fly clumsily out of one tree and over to another.

One morning as she sat on the patio before the sun grew too strong, one startled her by landing on her. It thudded off her shoulder and tumbled into her lap, then righted itself and took a few scrabbly steps. It was astoundingly big for an insect. Its thick body was splotched with black and yellow–green, the color of new corn shoots. Its great bulbous eyes stared straight ahead at her bare knees. She reached out tentatively to touch it, and it flew lumberingly off in widening circles, with a large buzz of wings.

She stood up to see where it had gone, turning the corner of the house as she marked its flight. She halted there, at the corner. The young Indian man from the park was walking past her house, down the dusty road where no one ever walked. He did not stop, but he slowed his pace. He looked at her across the low cinder-block wall and waved to her, smiling, gesturing with his head up the road, in the direction of the petroglyphs. She ran inside, fumbling with the sliding door's catch, breathing hard, and into the room where Jesse napped, snapping the lock of that door, too. She knelt on the thick carpet, peering out through a slat of the blind drawn against the light and heat. He had passed the house, and now he turned, looking directly at the window where she hunched shamefully, knowing she was there, knowing she was looking at him. Then he went on, striding easily up the road, satisfied. She could see now that he wore a knapsack on his back, and even at this distance, far enough away now for his image to begin to waver in the layers of hot air that lay between them, she could make out the bright yarn embroidery that covered the canvas. Kneeling there on Jesse's bedroom floor, still holding the gritty slat of the blind, she began to cry.

Jesse woke. She changed him, boiled two eggs, and sat beside him as he chased crumbs of yolk around his highchair tray and lunged for the cup he was learning to drink from. The routine calmed her. It was all right. She must have seen that knapsack before, one of the times she'd run into him, and it just hadn't registered on her waking mind. He was just a man, maybe a little strange, but friendly enough. If he meant harm, he'd had the chance.

Ed phoned later. He was going to have to work late at his lab that night. The whole thing was at a critical stage. There were tests to be monitored, he didn't trust his assistant to read off the results right. He stopped his explanation, aware of her silence. Was she all right? It wasn't that critical, he could come home.

She could not tell him. There was nothing wrong. After she hung up, she walked around the house checking locks and feeling foolish. They were secure. She was enclosed. She would be all right.

The rain held off that afternoon, and even with the cooler running, the heat was hard to bear. She fed Jesse supper and put him to bed. Some time after it was fully dark, she thought she heard a faint breeze, and opened the door against the chain. The breeze was there; it brushed against her face, smelling like rain. Lightning lashed weakly in the west, beyond the volcanoes, and almost a full minute went by before she heard the thunder, very faint. But it was coming.

She turned off the TV, wanting to hear the thunder coming on, and wanting to listen for Ed's car turning into the driveway, although it was much too early to look for him yet. She poured herself a drink, and picked one of her old texts from college off the bookshelf. She leafed through it, finding a comfort in the familiar feel of the dog-eared covers, the pages annotated in the hand of the person she'd been, the one who never got much more than low B's, but who had loved Roethke and Dylan Thomas and D. H. Lawrence. Her professor had been very big on Lawrence's animal poems. He musn't have been much older then she was now. She remembered him in his black turtleneck, earnestly explaining what Lawrence really meant by the incarnate moment. She smiled at her own solemn marginal notes: *N.B. snake = phallus; passage shows dark consc. of body.*

She got up to check on Jesse. He slept warm and tangled in the crib sheets, his thin hair flattened damply in licks across his skull. She stood beside the crib for a while, resting her hand lightly on his back, feeling the soft rise and fall of his breathing. The dark consciousness of the body. When she had first read Lawrence, she had had no man, no son.

When she returned to the living room and picked up the book, the poem leapt out at her. She had not thought of it in years, but she remembered it now, how she had puzzled over it at the time, a little frightened by it, and loving so much better the man in his pajamas watching the snake, the bat that looked like a black glove, the slow elephants mating. Now the words meant something:

> *Not I, not I, but the wind that blows through me!*
> *A fine wind is blowing the new direction of time.*
> *If only I let it bear me, carry me, if only it carry me!*
> *If only I am sensitive, subtle, oh, delicate, a winged gift . . .*

She read on, remembering before she came to it the ending that had so disturbed her seven years ago in a distant place, another body from this:

> *What is the knocking?*
> *What is the knocking at the door in the night?*
> *It is somebody wants to do us harm.*
>
> *No, no, it is the three strange angels.*
> *Admit them, admit them.*

Cicadas droned on outside, the storm still too distant to trouble them. The breeze was only a messenger, come to them far in advance. She read the poem over and over.


She saw it now. It was all right. She would go back to the park tomorrow, with Jesse, and Ed could come too, if he wanted. She had been selfish, blind, and who knew, maybe there was something there for him, too. And even if there wasn't, his presence could spoil nothing for her. Nor could the Indian man's, for surely it was all right, he was just a man, a coincidence, and separate from the other thing, from what talked to her out of those rocks. When something like that happened to you, it was personal, and other people could be all around, and still what drew her would come only to her. It was drawing her now, it was with her now. It was very large, but it was not something to be frightened of. It was something meant to open her up, something to learn from, and it was very private, but it would make her be better for all of them, for her husband, for Jesse. Look how different she was from the girl who had made notes in the book, how changed already, these last months. Once she had dreamed only of running from things, never, never of being drawn, borne, of yielding. And this, he, was not something to run from or hide from. She could not, even if she wanted to.

The book slipped from her lap. The wind was rising, or perhaps it was still the cicadas.

The song rose around her, stronger, less uncertain now that she was on the road, and the cicadas behind her. She was sure of it; reedy notes, running together in a trill, and then individual ones coming slowly, each one ringed by silence. A stone slipped into her sandal, rode with her for twenty paces, and then edged out again. She hardly noticed it.

The entrance signs showed dimly in the starlight, and she turned down the blacktop drive, her pace wholly uneven now, stumbling. The gate, she thought, it'll be locked again, I'll have to climb over it, never doubting that she could. But the gate was open, both flaps swinging in the wind that was part of the song, that smelled of rain. Both halves of the

chain-link were bellied out, twisted as though they had been wrenched vio-
lently apart. She leaned against the nearer one to catch her breath, because
she was going to enter calmly, not gasping raggedly, and she felt then the
heat of the metal. She looked about quickly to see if some car had rammed
drunkenly through. But there was no car, no accident, only the shut entry
station, and the small valley opening, and beyond, very far away, a small
visible slash of lights, the lights of the city. And even they were going away.
They were going out, not as though people in houses and public service
authorities were turning them off, but like chalk wiped from a blackboard,
visible in blurred outline for a few strokes, then a faint dusty smear, and
then gone, gone back to the fine original flat black. And the stars came clear
as single notes.

She moved further into the park, humming very lightly in good
counterpoint to the song that was always rising, and now she knew where
to put her voice always, which note would come next, and how to reply to
it and blend with it, and what the words were. They came to her effortlessly, one syllable at a time, as she needed them:

> *Kitana-po ki-ta-na-po ki-tana-PO*
> *Ai-na ki na wah ki na weh*
> *Chi li li cha chi li li cha*
> *Don-ka-va-ki*

She paused by a bush. She could see it plainly, each spike of it, and
saw clearly now, *all* over the bush, the walking sticks, perhaps twenty of
them, in pairs, one atop the other. She saw the intensity of the male's grasp,
the quiver in the abdomen of the female, the consummate fitness of bush to
ground, leaf to stem, creature to branch, male to female.

She breathed deeply, consciously, and listening to her own breath, became aware of a bigger breathing in the darkness. She tried to still her own
breath so she could be sure of it, but there was no need, for the other lungs
took in and gave out the air so largely, so calmly, compared to her own
small human breath. Ahead, a hundred yards, blocked out in the starshine,
there were shapes, like giant road signs, great trapezoidal forms. They were
moving, a little. She watched the two who bulked in front of her. They
raised their feet off the earth, set them down gently, making no noise, moving in time to the music that was not only in her head, but rising from the
rocks to her left. She thought, for one moment, of Jesse, of Ed, of her
kitchen, of the defective can opener that snagged and whined, of the boxes
of cereal lined up on the shelves, of the hard green pears she had bought the
day before, left on the windowsill to ripen. She turned back then toward
the wrenched gate, saying *Jesse, pears*. Another shape loomed there. Now
she could see more plainly the trapezoidal body, the elongated legs and
arms that no longer seemed stiff now that she saw them in motion, and the

double horn of the head, the beaked mouth. It turned toward her. The beak opened widely and clacked shut. It was a sound made in the direction of a child, in caution. No, not that way. Over there.

All right, she thought, walking toward the rocks, unbuttoning her blouse, wondering still, a little, in some far part of her mind what she was doing. She began to climb the trail. The sound of male laughter surrounded her. Someone was waiting for her, at ease, glad of her coming.

# ROXY GORDON

## Pilgrims (1983)

*Roxy Gordon, a Choctaw wild man from Texas, is one of the more innovative writers of the second wave of Native writers. He usually works in multimedia forms, but his story, "Pilgrims," is one of his more formally crafted works.*

*"Pilgrims" is a story guided by an underlying irony, as its title suggests. After all, the Pilgrims were the Anglo people who celebrated their first Thanksgiving, having survived the first several months (though many didn't make it) thanks to the efforts of local Algonquians. You remember Squanto, the Algonquian man who spoke English and helped the newcomers, acting as interpreter for them. His people showed them how to plant corn, a crop strange to English people, as well as pumpkin, squash, and beans. They also gave the Pilgrims sassafras tea, rich in vitamin C, which helped them survive the scurvy and other diseases caused by their chronic vitamin deficiency. So important to Anglo-European health was this plant that the English boat people were soon harvesting it in large amounts and exporting it to England and Holland, from whence it found its way to markets throughout Europe.*

*The long-range effect of the Algonquians' helpfulness was a modest population boom over there, which in turn resulted in more and more boat people sailing across the Atlantic and populating the Mid-Atlantic region, displacing the peoples of the loose Algonquian Confederacies that had held political sway. The flood of illegal aliens moved inexorably westward, taking their bacterial and viral diseases with them. The result, in time, was the loss of some 96 percent of Native American lives. While Americans are taught in grade school that democracy's beginnings are planted in the Pilgrim settlements, Gordon's treatment implies an alternative view. The tree of liberty's seed was not English but Algonquian, and it is to them that the democracies of the world owe their freedom.*

*All of which is a kind of gloss on Gordon's text, where the pilgrims are Indians, refugees, and the local natives are whites, among them a few surviving wartime enemies of the elder race. Another faint resonance, implied in the setting—Texas—and the interactive dynamics between old mountain men and Indians, is the voice of that quintessential American hero, John "the Duke" Wayne. We can almost hear his voice whispering just above the whistling of the wind in the tall prairie grasses, "Mount up, pilgrims."*

*According to old Lakota prophecies, the birth of a female white buffalo calf named Miracle, which occurred in the summer of 1994, signals the beginning of an age of reconciliation between the white and Native peoples. If so, Gordon's "Pilgrims," published in 1983, foreshadowed that great event. In it we discover that shared history makes deep, lasting bonds.*

When the Indians came to town, Charlie Tabor, the barber, called old Dock Middleton and asked him to come by the barber shop. Then Charlie Tabor needed an excuse to keep the Indians at the barber shop till Dock Middleton could get there, so he told the Indians they'd have to wait until Pink Isaacs came to town to give them permission to go out to Bead Mountain. Pink Isaacs did indeed own Bead Mountain but nobody needed permission to visit the place. Charlie Tabor called Pink and Pink said it was a curious story but he guessed it was true. Bead Mountain was called Bead Mountain, after all, because of all the clay Indian beads that used to lay scattered about. Pink said he wouldn't mind meeting the Indians and taking them but he was, that day, too damn busy pulling rusty pipe on his windmill, and he said to tell them to feel free to camp there if they felt like it.

Charlie Tabor had taken charge of the Indians that morning because he'd been the first to see them. He'd been walking to the barber shop about 7:30 and he'd seen them parked down by the Home Creek bridge where they'd spent the night. He didn't know they were Indians, but Charlie Tabor was always bound to check anything, so he'd walked to the bridge. At first he'd guessed they were Mexicans, but Mexicans weren't apt to be traveling about in touring cars and certainly not apt to be camping beside Home Creek. So as Tabor walked up on them, he'd decided they must be gypsies.

There were four of them, two men dressed in denim overalls, a woman, and an old man wearing a dirty, shapeless wool dress suit. When Tabor saw that the old man was wearing braids, he realized with surprise that these had to be Indians. Charlie Tabor had never before seen an Indian. He'd come to west Texas as a young man from Alabama thirty years after the last Indian had gone.

So Charlie Tabor had introduced himself and spoken of the fine morning, and the younger of the two men in overalls answered him carefully and none-too-happily.

"You people traveling, are you?" Charlie Tabor had asked the young man and the young man had said they were. Charlie Tabor asked where they'd come from and the young man said Oklahoma. Charlie Tabor asked where they were going and the young man seemed hesitant to answer. Charlie Tabor, who was bound to do his best to understand everything, had decided there was something about these Indians camped on Home Creek that he needed to know.

Charlie Tabor never was a man without words, so he had talked. He had talked nonsense, passing the time of day, commenting on the weather and how the creek was low, and he supposed he'd go up to the Blue Hole one of these evenings and catch some perch. The young man appeared confused; the old man paid no attention. The other man in overalls, he seemed to listen.

The two in overalls had stood by the car while the old man squatted by the dying breakfast fire as if to soak up heat though it was August and the old man was wearing a woolen suit. The woman cleared dishes.

The man who seemed to listen had finally spoken. He said, "My name is Amos Horn. This is my son; he's called Brian. And this is my father. That woman there, she's my old woman."

Charlie Tabor had introduced himself and asked again, "You folks just traveling?"

Amos Horn said, "We brought my father. This is the country where he was born and lived. He was a child over by that big mountain." Amos Horn had pointed east and Tabor guessed he meant Santa Ana Mountain. Twelve or fifteen miles east, Santa Ana Mountain was the only hill in that part of Texas which might deserve the name mountain.

"We camped there a few days," Amos Horn said, "and then my father wanted to come here to another place." Charlie Tabor had glanced at the old man who still paid no attention. "There is another mountain over that way," Amos Horn said as he pointed to the southwest. "He says it's the other side of these hills." Low wooded hills banked the south side of the creek. Tabor guessed he meant Bead Mountain. It wasn't a mountain like Santa Ana Mountain, but setting as it did on the prairie alone, it was a widely noted landmark and could be seen from miles in any direction. Bead Mountain was maybe four miles away, on the other side of the breaks of Home Creek. Being down in the creek bottom, they couldn't see it.

So Charlie Tabor had decided to situate them in his barber shop till he could check all this over more carefully, and he'd told them he'd call Pink Isaacs, the man who owned Bead Mountain.

Amos Horn and Brian sat on straight wooden benches in the barber shop and the old man and the woman waited in the car while Tabor did his calling.

Dock Middleton didn't need a haircut and he couldn't figure out why exactly Charlie Tabor was anxious to get him to the barber shop. Charlie Tabor was a man who liked to talk but there were enough loafers in Valera that Tabor never lacked for conversation. Dock Middleton, nevertheless, pulled on his boots and took out for the barber shop.

Dock Middleton was seventy-two years old. He'd lived in western Texas all his life. His childhood had been spent on the Llano in the hill country and he'd come to Coleman County to cowboy when the range was still open and run by the big cow outfits. He'd lived here ever since, first cowboying and later raising cows himself down on the Colorado— except for a time in the early seventies when he'd joined the Frontier Battalion of the Texas Rangers to chase Indians and horse thieves.

The Ranger service, that was the reason Charlie Tabor had wanted Dock Middleton in his barber shop—not the Ranger service itself but the mold of mind it seemed to have given Dock Middleton. And, particularly, it was a conversation Dock Middleton had carried on in the spring; that conversation, Tabor's memory of it, had led Tabor to call. Middleton and an old doctor named Zeller had been sitting on the wooden benches, killing time, when Dock Middleton had complained about a pain. He'd said he guessed it was his liver hurting him. The old doctor asked him where exactly was the pain and Dock Middleton had pointed out a patch of midriff which Doctor Zeller told him couldn't possibly be the liver because that wasn't where the liver was located and he was a doctor and he ought to know. But Dock Middleton had strongly disagreed. He'd said he didn't know much about doctoring but, by God, he'd damn well cut open enough dead Indians when he was a Ranger that he knew exactly where lay the liver.

Charlie Tabor had been amused and a bit shocked to hear the old man say such a thing. It was an image he couldn't grasp, this skinny cowboy-hatted old man, two generations earlier butchering the dead bodies of human beings. It was a curious thing to Charlie Tabor. And Charlie Tabor, the man who checked everything, naturally remembered that conversation when he saw the Indians that morning down by Home Creek.


Burned Black Horn had never been greatly sentimental, and it was not sentiment that had led him to wish a return to the localities of his childhood and young manhood. It was, instead, a mystery which sent him back. Burned Black Horn was not of a philosophical turn of mind either. He had little need to understand the universe or his place in it. Indeed, had his universe not turned itself upside down so unbelievably, he would have spent the balance of all his days with no mysteries at all, with everything fitting exactly in the place it should have fit. But nothing fit anymore; the universe which should have fit right-side-up was right-upside-down. Burned Black Horn had been much younger when things flip-flopped but, then, he had seen no particular mystery. It had been the whitemen who were out to turn it and if the whitemen could have been destroyed, then the universe would have stood upright. The People were, in the end, unable to stop the whitemen, so the universe had had no protectors. But, of course, as a young man Burned Black Horn had not really thought in such terms at all. What he really had thought was something like this: The Tejanos have killed my relatives at The Place Where Salt Seeps and, therefore, I must kill me some Tejanos. And this thing that he had thought had meant the exact same thing as if he had planned some defense of a right-standing universe.

It was after Burned Black Horn had passed middle age that he had begun to have flashes that something was more dreadfully wrong than he had suspected. True, many of his relatives and friends had died a long time ago at the hands of the Tejanos and the army and, true, he and his surviving relatives and friends had been in most ways confined and kept from the haunts and pursuits of earlier days. But still the Wichita Mountains where the Burned Black Horn family camped was a good place and the Burned Black Horn camp was full of his friends and relatives and many descendants. Burned Black Horn was never very hungry—those Wichita Mountains provided better than the white agent provided.

And in the part of his self that listened, Burned Black Horn heard the same murmuring of that-which-is-and-was-and-will-be that he had always heard. Burned Black Horn was neither particularly philosophical nor, in the mumbo jumbo terms of the whiteman's explanation of religion, was he particularly religious. It was just that part of his self that could hear always clearly heard the sweet murmur of that-which-is-and-was-and-will-be. This was what Burned Black Horn heard every moment of his life until one bad hot August when he was past middle age and then he didn't hear anything at all.

Burned Black Horn wouldn't have been able to say that he'd lost the murmur in the part of his self that heard. And he wouldn't have been able to say that at long last, these years later, the universe was truly turned upside down. But after a generation of silence in the part of his self that heard, he had said to his son, Amos, "I want to go back to the places I lived when I was a boy."

Dock Middleton was called Dock because his full first name was Dockery which had been his mother's maiden name. Most every new acquaintance assumed he was a doctor. Dock didn't much care. God knows he'd done his share of horse and cow doctoring and he'd cut bullets and a stray arrow or two out of men and set more than one old boy's broken leg. But Dock

Middleton didn't in any way consider himself a doctor. In most ways, it never occurred to Dock Middleton to consider himself anything. He was just old Dock Middleton, a cowman too old and stove-up to work cows—old Dock Middleton whose wife, Audrey, died in 1912, who had two sons, one in San Angelo trying to sell real estate and one in Eldorado raising sheep, an old man who played dominos and wasn't any too clean.

Dock Middleton was an old man in Valera, Texas during the Great Depression, right now hobbling on his bad left leg—that leg damaged these forty years since one of Clay Mann's bad horses fell on it—hobbling beside the deserted blacktopped highway into the center of town toward Charlie Tabor's barber shop. Dock Middleton had by now ceased to wonder why Charlie Tabor had phoned. Dock Middleton never had much truck with mysteries. He was not a religious man, but he'd been raised a good hard-shelled Southern Baptist and that is a religion largely without mystery.

He hobbled into Charlie Tabor's barber shop and sat down quickly to take the weight off his bad leg. There were two Mexicans sitting on one of Charlie's benches and a couple more in a car parked outside, the only stray automobile parked in downtown Valera. Charlie Tabor was cutting old man Lawlis' hair. He introduced Dock to the Mexicans. "This is the Horn family," the barber said. "They're Indians from up in Oklahoma." Dock looked them over and, by God, they weren't Mexicans. They were right enough Indians. Tabor pointed his scissors toward the strange automobile. "That old man out there, he was born and raised around here." Dock Middleton squinted his near-sighted eyes to see Burned Black Horn with his braids and dirty, black woolen suit. They were right enough Indians and it had been many a year since Dock Middleton had looked upon any Indian.

"The old man out there," Charlie Tabor said, "he used to live around Bead Mountain and he wants to go out there. Pink thought maybe you'd show them the way." Dock looked at Charlie Tabor and he thought: Pink didn't think any such thing. Charlie Tabor had to stick his nose into everybody's business and if there wasn't no business, Dock thought, then Charlie'd make some up.

Amos Horn shook hands with Dock Middleton and introduced his son. Dock Middleton looked at both their faces and he was reminded of things he had not in years remembered. He was reminded of no particular event; he was, instead, reminded of the way it had been, of the way it had felt then.

In the spring of 1873, Dock Middleton was camped not ten miles from Valera with Captain Maltby's company on Home Creek when word came from Camp Colorado that Ross Hubbard had lost sixteen horses and had trailed a band of a dozen Indians south along the Mukewater. So the company broke camp and headed for the Trickham country hoping to cut their trail. Seven or eight miles north of Trickham, they cut trail. A rock house was still smoldering. The house belonged to a man named Stoddard. Dock Middleton knew him by sight but Dock Middleton didn't recognize him. Stoddard was scalped and disemboweled. Hot coals from the house fire had been heaped into his belly cavity. Stoddard's boy, who was maybe fourteen, was dead and scalped, a mesquite limb thrust through his nose. A baby lay in a mass of gore. It would have been much better if the baby's mother had been dead but she wasn't—yet. She wouldn't die for another three or four hours.

Burned Black Horn sat in the backseat of the touring car with his daughter-in-law and stared straight ahead. Burned Black Horn was a study in blankness; Burned Black Horn was a master of blankness. He did not approve of his son's continual insistence on dealing with local whitemen. No whiteman needed to tell him how to find the landmarks of his past. He was quite sure he knew this land better than any whiteman could. Still now, Burned Black Horn knew every landmark, minor and major, between Chihuahua and the Kansas plains. The Comanche Crossing of the Pecos was as familiar to him still as was his son's horse pasture on Cache Creek. Whitemen, quite imponderably, professed the strange notion of owning this land but never seemed to know the land they professed to own. In the old raiding times, raiding parties had little trouble hiding within plain sight while white pursuers passed them obliviously by. The whitemen rarely seemed to even notice the land—that was the army whitemen and bands of outraged stockmen who would chase the raiders. The son-of-a-bitch Tejanos Diablos—the Rangers—they were something else. The son-of-a-bitch Tejanos Diablos, they were hard to hide from and they were bad to fight. Burned Black Horn remembered his relatives at The Place Where Salt Seeps; he remembered when he and the other raiders had come in from Mexico only hours too late. He remembered how the old men's bodies had been castrated, how the women's breasts had been cut off. He remembered how his uncle had had no skin at all. The son-of-a-bitch Tejanos Diablos would skin dead people and make bullwhips and quirts and sometimes moccasins from their hides.

Amos Horn had been born to his father's middle age and he knew little of the life the old man had lived in this country. Amos Horn was a Methodist preacher and a fairly successful cattleman. He got along with whitemen. Any affection he had for the old life was akin to racial memory and, as in most first generations after immigration, his racial memory was dim and usually not very important. He loved his father though—and respected him—so when the old man had asked to return to Texas, he'd felt compelled to undertake the trip. Amos Horn had enjoyed the trip. He enjoyed seeing sights he'd not before seen. He even enjoyed dealing with the whitemen. He enjoyed watching their initial surprise turn to a kind of amazed friendliness when they'd talked with him for a few minutes. These Texas whitemen seemed surprised that an Indian could talk to them—and certainly surprised that he could be a Methodist preacher. A white Methodist preacher in the town of Santa Ana at the foot of the mountain had taken them home for supper, and, so far as Amos Horn knew, it was the only time in his father's life that the old man had sat at a whiteman's table.

Amos took the old whiteman out to the car. They'd drive to the mountain, but they had to wait a few more minutes for the barber to finish cutting the other old man's hair. The barber wanted to go along. The barber, thought Amos Horn, was a man bound to involve himself in everything. Amos Horn noticed nothing out of the ordinary about the old whiteman who was to guide them. He looked like any other old white cowboy, like many an old man Amos Horn had bought cows from and sold cows to. The old man limped like many another stove-up old cowboy.

"This is my father," Amos Horn said to Dock Middleton, motioning toward Burned Black Horn. "And this is my old woman," he said, motioning toward his wife who was named Elsie and was an Osage Amos had met when she'd come to Cache as a young girl with her brother who was a great breaker of horses.

Dock Middleton did not glance at Elsie Horn; his eyes snagged on the face of Burned Black Horn.

Dock Middleton was not a philosophical man and he did not think in philosophical terms. And thus the thing that came to him now had no exact words to define it, but a new thing did come to Dock Middleton that morning in the street in Valera and if he could have defined it, he would have asked himself finally at the age of seventy-two, stove-up and no fancier of mystery: How did I come to be the human being that I am? What was the thing that made me who I am? What enigma has formed this old man without enigma? Dock Middleton, had he been another man than Dock Middleton, might have asked these questions but Dock Middleton was Dock Middleton and so his eyes hung on the face of Burned Black Horn.

And this was the thing that Dock Middleton really thought. He thought without anger or even resentment: What are these people doing here? We fought them and we beat them. We drove them north of the Red River. What reason brings these people back here? What right do these people have here?

Burned Black Horn looked at Dock Middleton and he thought, Well, this one is no Methodist preacher.

•　•　•

Brian Horn wished he'd never come on this trip. In his own way, he'd wanted to come as badly as had his grandfather. Like most of the second generation after immigration, Brian had a passionate regard for pre-immigration people and places. He'd wanted to see the places of his grandfather's young manhood. He'd wanted some way to grasp the reality of his grandfather as a raider and hunter and killer and man of place. He had been sorely disappointed. The countryside was scarred by countless hardscrabble dry-land farms and maintained by sad, almost pathetic whitemen who wore looks of defeat in their shapeless clothing and in their desperate eyes. In the mythology of Brian Horn's childhood, this land of the Penateka was a glorious place of great wars and warriors. Brian Horn could only see the southern edge of a worn out dustbowl, the pathetic end of a westering whiteman condemned forever to patched overalls and the ass-end of a flea-bit mule. Good God, it was worse than Oklahoma.

Elsie Horn was having a nice enough time on their trip. She saw her husband was enjoying himself and that made her happy. Elsie Horn was a woman without many needs, physical or emotional. She had never shared her husband's passion for the Methodist religion; she cared little for any religion. Elsie Horn had seen both her mother and father die of measles despite the best ministrations of an Osage medicine man. He had called powerfully for the intervention of the spirits. Had any spirits existed, Elsie Horn had reasoned, they likely would have responded. None had. Elsie had not been distraught to discover there were no spirits; she had not even been surprised. But Elsie Horn did truly love her husband and her son and whatever things they needed, she needed. So she was glad to have come; she was glad to see her husband enjoying himself. Elsie Horn had no idea if her father-in-law was enjoying himself. Burned Black Horn had lived in her household for seventeen years, yet she understood almost nothing of what he thought. Elsie had never spoken to her father-in-law, for he spoke only Comanche and she understood almost no Comanche. Her husband and virtually everyone she knew spoke English to her. She supposed she had no talent for picking up other languages, but she cared little.

Amos Horn could understand and speak English well. But, like most people meeting Dock Middleton the first time, he misunderstood Dock's given name. In translating it to Burned Black Horn, he told his father that Dock Middleton was a doctor. Amos Horn was a bit surprised that Dock Middleton should be a doctor. The old man was obviously a cowman, but

Amos Horn guessed that among these Texans who were widely known as cattlemen anyway, even a doctor might be a cowman.

Burned Black Horn was not so surprised. He was, in fact, somewhat pleased. He'd seen whitemen's doctors before and never had they impressed him as doctors. They were nervous men with shifty eyes or else they were fat, clumsy red-faced men. None of them seemed possessed of the power he expected in a man deemed doctor. But this one did seem to be doctor material.

Dock Middleton wasn't too sure of Charlie Tabor's motivation, but he was certain that Charlie Tabor had arranged this strange trip. His initial impulse had been to beg off, beg previous business, beg illness. Then he'd looked again out the barber shop window at Burned Black Horn outside in the touring car and that thing had come to him, that ill-defined mystery had seized itself upon him and he'd ceased to care about Charlie Tabor and Charlie Tabor's manipulations. Now he stood a bit uncomfortably beside the touring car while Amos Horn spoke to Burned Black Horn in Indian, explaining, Dock Middleton assumed, who he was and what was to happen now.

Charlie Tabor didn't know what would happen. That was the fun to Charlie Tabor. Charlie Tabor wasn't a bad man, nor did he mean badly with the games he played. He was a man who found the dynamics of human existence eternally intriguing. And he was a man who found no reason not to sweeten the intrigue. Cutting old man Lawlis' hair, Charlie Tabor examined what had happened up to now this morning and he was pleased.

Burned Black Horn paid no attention at all to Charlie Tabor. That whiteman was a man who chattered like a woman. He was a man who knew not the essential dignity of silence. He was like too many whitemen.

Though Burned Black Horn spoke no English, he had never known a time when whitemen were not about. Even in his earliest childhood there in the Penateka camp by Two-Flows Creek in the shadow of Santa Ana Mountain, even then there were whitemen and rumors of whitemen all about. The men of his band raided south to the whiteman's town of San Antonio and along the San Saba and sometimes even so far south as the coast of the ocean. They brought back whiteman's things—rolls of red cloth they loved, and umbrellas and tall silk hats. Already when Burned Black Horn was a young man, the existence of the whiteman had imposed a kind of definition, a kind of border onto the lives of the People. But always, the center held; no one guessed the whiteman might even approach the center—no one could possibly have guessed the whiteman might indeed someday destroy the center. Such change had Burned Black Horn seen in his life. But Burned Black Horn was not one to dwell upon the obvious.

Amos Horn drove the touring car and Charlie Tabor sat in the middle with Dock Middleton next to the door. In the backseat, Elsie Horn sat between her son and her father-in-law. Charlie Tabor no longer even pretended that Dock Middleton had any real function here. Charlie Tabor, himself, directed Amos Horn southwest, off the highway, down into the Home Creek breaks, across the bridge, not the same one they'd camped beside but another, newer iron bridge with timber flooring. Then they followed, roughly, Bead Mountain Creek up out of the breaks onto the prairie and suddenly the mountain loomed before them, the only real landmark on a horizon of miles and miles of rolling prairie.

Burned Black Horn was not a religious man, but even to a man of little religion, the sight of the mountain was suddenly affecting. Burned Black Horn remembered how it had been that afternoon those many years, those generations ago. He remembered how he'd come walking up out of the breaks, not here, but south several miles; he remembered how the mountain had looked then and it was much the same as now. He had walked resolutely, carrying a blanket. Comanches carried blankets when they went seeking; they had little use for penitence. He had walked to that place, that center, that place of spirits, that place where the dead were buried standing up facing east, facing east to face the sunrise over Santa Ana Mountain. He had gone to that place of spirits and of his people's dead. He had gone to beg for nothing because Comanches did not beg. He had not gone to prostrate himself; Comanches never prostrated themselves. He had gone to ask, respectfully and determinedly.

He had climbed the mountain and he'd spread his blanket on the east rim to face the sun to rise come morning. Four days and four nights, Burned Black Horn had sat there. And, of course, as he had never doubted, the center had held; a message had come. In twilight, a single buffalo, an old bull expelled from the herd, had approached the foot of the mountain. It had looked up, straight at Burned Black Horn, and there had appeared around its head an aura, a halo of fiery orange. Burned Black Horn had become then Burned Black Horn.

Burned Black Horn had lived in that country not much longer after that. The army had come, and the Rangers, to gather the Penateka to go live up on the Brazos reservation and though some Penateka went, many, including Burned Black Horn, scattered themselves among other bands far north out of reach of the army. Burned Black Horn went to the Naconis band of Peta Nacona which soon rejoined the Kwahadis, and thus Burned Black Horn was among the last to come into Fort Sill, coming in with Quanah, Peta Nacona's son. Quanah ultimately set up this camp on Cache Creek and, following his friend, so did Burned Black Horn.

The two of them, Quanah and Burned Black Horn, remained steadfast friends for all of Quanah's life. Quanah took well to the whiteman's way and became, among the whitemen, one of the best known Indians in America. He toured county fairs lecturing and went wolf hunting with Teddy Roosevelt while Burned Black Horn stayed in his own camp, never seeing whitemen for months at a time, never learning English.

•  •  •

Charlie Tabor directed Amos Horn off the road near the base of Bead Mountain and they drove across open prairie to park as closely to the mountain as possible. The car stopped and no one moved. "Well," Charlie Tabor said, "well, we're here." No one moved. "Well," Charlie Tabor said, "we'll have to hoof it now." For another moment still, no one moved. Then Amos Horn opened his door; then the others. Then they hoofed it. None of them doubted the old man wanted to climb the mountain; Bead Mountain was always meant to be climbed. There was never satisfaction in standing at the foot of Bead Mountain. So with hardly a pause, they climbed. Amos Horn and Brian helped Burned Black Horn; one took each arm, half lifting, sometimes pulling. They worked their way up the steep little mountain.

Neither Brian nor Amos had any real idea what this particular place might mean to Burned Black Horn. They had known since the beginning of the trip that this place was awfully important to him. Amos Horn never really wondered why. All the places on this trip were landmarks of his father's long ago; that was enough for him. Brian Horn had wondered a lot and still he continued to wonder. Brian Horn wondered at it all. Brian Horn was a young man beset by mystery.

Brian Horn was an educated young man. The Indian Department had sent him away east to school with the full cooperation and support of his father. Amos Horn knew that a man needed schooling. Brian Horn had spent the last summer before his schooling—eastern schooling at the age of fourteen—like all his available time, in the presence of Burned Black Horn. The old man had not been convinced there was any such need for white-man's schooling, but he had kept away from discussion of it. As he was about to leave, Brian had expected some kind of advice, some word from his grandfather. None had come. Burned Black Horn was not one to give advice. Brian Horn had always wished his grandfather could be a little less taciturn. Brian Horn was a young man in need of some center.

Dock Middleton had no one to help his climb and his bad leg gave him hell. He'd be damned if he'd hold up the others, so he gritted his teeth and shifted his weight with each step—and he hurt.

Charlie Tabor was impatient to reach the top. He realized that in his many years in this country, despite the fact that he'd grown used to Bead Mountain on the horizon, he'd never before climbed it. He was anxious for the top not only for whatever might happen among this bunch but just to see what was up there.

Amos Horn climbed because he climbed; Elsie Horn climbed because her family climbed.

Burned Black Horn climbed because, in old age, to a man who had no understanding of, nor need for mystery, there had come a mystery; there had come a mystery more important than any other that might come to a man. How could it be that that-which-is-and-was-and-will-be could have, all along, been a mistake? That old buffalo bull, he had stood there unmoving in failing light and he had looked directly up at Burned Black Horn. The old buffalo bull's head had been bathed in unearthly fire and Burned Black Horn had smelled burning hair. He had seen and smelled a thing no man had ever before seen or smelled in such a way. So, it had had meaning.

But, Burned Black Horn, truth to tell, being neither a religious nor a philosophical man, had taken his vision home and had lived with it all those years, all those generations, with no real idea upon this earth what it had meant. It had been a vision, a thing expected and needed to keep the universe upright, to re-affirm for him the center, and for all those years, that had been enough.

But then that thing had happened; the part of him that could hear had gone deaf. So he'd begun to wonder; a mystery had come to a man who was not meant for mystery. In another time, in an earlier time of his life, Burned Black Horn might have gone to some kind of medicine man; he might have gone to some old holy man to ask for guidance and for help. But that was another time. The medicine was gone; the medicine men were gone. How could a man go to a wise old man for help when that man needing help was by far the oldest man for many a mile around?

Burned Black Horn thought of the old white doctor and he glanced at him; he watched the old white doctor painfully climbing. This was a doctor of the people who lived here now, the people who saw the eastern sun rise here everyday now. Maybe this old doctor himself had spoken with the spirits of this place.

Burned Black Horn thought those things and he knew there was no way he could use his son, Amos, as a translator to ask the old white doctor. Perhaps, he thought, he could use his grandson. He thought, when we reach the top and both of us old men are no longer suffering this climb I will ask Brian to translate for me to the old white doctor. And, for the first time in his long life, Burned Black Horn wished he himself could speak the English language of the whitemen.

Dock Middleton could walk no longer. The pain was unbearable and he was exhausted. When they were a bit more than half-way up the mountain, he sat down. Charlie Tabor sat down beside him. The others paused, puffed a bit, looked around, and then they all sat down. They were all silent in their own exhaustions, too silent for Charlie Tabor. Charlie Tabor, who was never a man without words, spoke to Dock Middleton. He asked, "Does all this country here look about like it used to?" Dock Middleton, who was in pain and without breath, looked at Charlie Tabor and could hardly restrain himself.

"I guess it does," Dock Middleton said.

No one would say anything and Charlie Tabor was a man who

abhorred silence. He tried to think of a relevant thing to say. "Were there buffalo here?" he asked Dock Middleton.

Dock Middleton was close to calling the barber a damn fool, but Dock Middleton didn't say things like that so he answered him; he said, "Yeah, I remember when there was buffalo here."

Then, they climbed to the top of the mountain.

It was the east side of Bead Mountain they climbed so that when they reached the top, a flat table of several acres sprinkled with mesquite bushes and salt cedar trees, they paused, heaved breath, and turned, almost as one, to look east.

Blue Santa Ana Mountain trembled gently in the heat rising across the prairie. A few puffy white summer clouds floated in an immense faded blue bowl of sky.

There was absolute silence on top of Bead Mountain. The entire group of pilgrims stood themselves silently. And then slowly, they turned to survey the circle of prairie around.

North, they could see a low range of wooded hills, dark grey–green from a growth of liveoak that fringed them. To the west, only rolling prairie so far as they could see. To the south, almost beyond vision on such a shimmering summer day, the blue–green breaks of the Colorado. A mile away that direction, south, buzzards floated slowly, marking some place of death. No other animal nor human thing could they see, no other movement.

Dock Middleton was still irritated; he was disquieted he supposed by the barber's silly questions. Yet it was not the barber's questions. This disquiet had begun at the sight of Burned Black Horn. Dock Middleton was suffering from some old uneasiness. What had it been like? What was it like now? Dock Middleton was not a philosophical man, but with the oppressive heavy, silent weight of late summer upon him, he suffered silently great-growing uneasiness.

Amos Horn thought the view from the top of Bead Mountain was quite nice. It reminded him a bit of the prairie south of the Wichitas where ran Cache Creek. Elsie Horn was glad to be no longer climbing. It was a fine place to be to her though, and she was glad to be here. She sat down.

Brian Horn was not much affected by this place. It had been much the same on top of Santa Ana Mountain; it was much the same at home in Oklahoma. Still, he sought to see whatever it was that might be seen. Brian Horn was, like many another displaced and homeless refugee, a profoundly philosophical and religious man.

He surveyed the electric vacuum of hot August Texas prairie and he wished mightily that he might see as his grandfather saw. So he turned to look at Burned Black Horn.

And he saw there had come upon Burned Black Horn a strangeness; he was, somehow, not the same. Burned Black Horn was always a composed man, but now he might be more composed. He was a man who affected blankness, but now he might be much more blank. Brian ceased to study the countryside; he studied his grandfather. Then, as if by command or design, Burned Black Horn turned stiffly to face his grandson.

"I want you to do something for me," Burned Black Horn said to him. "I want you to ask the old white doctor something for me." At Burned Black Horn's sudden voice, all the others turned toward him. They all waited. But Burned Black Horn, try as he might, could think of no way to make the question he wanted his grandson to ask Dock Middleton. He shifted his eyes to look into Dock Middleton's face.

Dock Middleton guessed that Burned Black Horn had meant to direct some statement at him. He tried to drag up the bits and pieces of Comanche language he'd once known. He tried to understand what Burned Black Horn wanted of him.

Having no need for mystery, Elsie Horn, who could understand none of Burned Black Horn's words, first understood that the word hardly mattered.

Amos Horn was surprised at his father's request and he was anxious at the desperation he heard. When he looked at Burned Black Horn, like Brian he was startled at the strangeness he saw. As Burned Black Horn turned his gaze to Dock Middleton, Amos followed. And then Amos Horn too understood. A man of practical and universal humanity, a man who earnestly believed that any mystery could be reduced to parable, Amos Horn saw that Burned Black Horn and Dock Middleton were now as mirror images to one another.

Brian Horn waited for his grandfather to finish and he wondered what on God's green earth it could be that the old man should ask with such urgency. Brian Horn looked from one of the old men to the other, and then he, too, caught the wordless thing that passed between them. It was a moving and memorable moment for Brian Horn. For the first time in a long, long time, he lost his own sense of loss and expectation.

Caught up as he was in great mute union, Brian Horn understood, or at least, without clear definition, began first to suspect, that mystery itself was its own answer.


Only poor Charlie Tabor the barber didn't understand. His eyes careened from Dock Middleton to Burned Black Horn and back to Dock Middleton and back to Burned Black Horn. What in the world was happening? What in the world was happening? A man who tolerated no mystery, he was swept up in a swirling, desperate rush he could not hope to understand.

# MARY RANDLE TALLMOUNTAIN

## Tender Street (1982)

*Deftly and delicately, Mary Randle TallMountain depicts life on the Ten-*
*derloin, a district south of Market Street in downtown San Francisco where*
*many elderly pensioners, small-time hustlers, homeless people, and all man-*
*ner of society's rejects mingle with businesspeople, clerks, public service*
*providers, tourists, and one another. TallMountain lived on the Tenderloin*
*for a number of years, and resided in downtown San Francisco for decades.*
*During the time she lived in the senior residence facility she named The*
*Green Brick Box, she had many hours to observe life on the streets of San*
*Francisco. The places that figure in these three pieces of life on the Tender-*
*loin were favorite TallMountain haunts, and the men whose stories she*
*voices were people with whom she was familiar.*

*"Tender Street" reflects the compassionate eye of a careful observer, as*
*well as the predominant Native theme of transformation. In the first*
*account, the man at Sum Ling's appears and disappears—as do the Native*
*people, the homeless, the poor, those who are highly evolved spiritually, and*
*Old Man Coyote. In a particular kind of street way, the man at Sum Ling's*
*is a modern shaman, echoing on the hard streets the trickster powers Wili*
*Woyi displays in another region. You see, given the powers of trickster, one*
*can always survive.*

*In the second account, Jamb is in a liminal state. Close to death on the*
*cold 5 AM cement, he sees a guardian angel appear out of the fog. The long-*
*haired ragged angel wears jeans and offers kindness, a drink, and relief*
*from worry. He calls the "wagon" for the dying man, gives him hot coffee,*
*and takes Jamb's doggy companion Satin into his care. "Not to worry," the*
*apparition comforts Jamb, "hear?"*

*The third account in this urban transformation cycle locates the chroni-*

*cles in their context: It's transformation time, "Indin" Bilijohn's liminal event tells us. And magically, we understand: The tender streets help souls make significant crossings, guiding them into safety, into all that is unknown. The mystery of the streets becomes the Mystery of life and death, and human beings are shown as supernaturals, as spiritual entities, to our jaded and denial-veiled eyes. In liminal states, in transformation time, the filthy streets are transformed, and the streets' citizens are drawn into magic, mystery, miracle, sacred change.*

I

He was going slowly through the cafeteria when she noticed him this time, his light eyes flickering unobtrusively over the vacated tables. He was almost colorless except for his eyes, which had faded to ashgray. This colorlessness made him virtually invisible. She thought that you might see him standing on the other side of a crowded street, but before he had crossed it he might be able to disappear without a trace. This was a mysterious and fascinating idea. She believed that he, with utmost nicety, in some physical manner, shunned the casual observer's glance, although she had never seen how he did it. Think of such secrecy, such timing, such efficiency! She marveled. She imagined he spent the early evenings wandering from one shabby eating establishment to another. Often she had watched him here, and speculated about him. In her endless inner monologue she told herself he was a phenomenon of this society. She recognized him as one of the regulars, the street persons, of this city on the western seaboard of the wealthiest country in the world.

A fiery crown upon the city's fabled hills, entire banks of windows were aglitter with cerise and orange reflections of sunset. But no roseate echo infiltrated the cavernous recesses of Sum Ling's Cafeteria. The nocolor man plodded softly along the aisles, which at this hour of seven were shadowed under the dimmest of lightbulbs. The front booths were alive, filled with the noise and motion of the young Asians who made Sum Ling's their night's rendezvous.

More than usual, tonight she relished the cheerful sounds of the young people and the comforting homey clink of china. She was talking on the phone at the cafeteria's mini-booth, when suddenly she saw that the man had seated himself in her abandoned booth, only an arm's length away. She had never been this close to him before. Everything became clear and extraordinarily precise. A button was missing from his earth-colored Burberry. He carefully removed his blurred, bodiless hat with its stained sweatband. He gazed with warm interest at nothing at all, then shifted his look to another empty space. So that is how he avoids looking into our eyes, she thought. She trembled a little and made herself smaller. But he did not notice. He evidently hadn't seen her leave the booth, then, she realized; he didn't know she was the diner whose place he had appropriated. He has successfully erased all of us. How innocent! whispered her mind. How shameful to eavesdrop on him! But she could not stop.

Feeling abysmally surreptitious, she watched him slide toward himself her tray and its leftover heap of Ling's Special Oyster Beef with Rice which she had scraped together in the center of the plate. With a trace of long habitude, he did not look down, but let his right hand fall, grasp the fork between carved-stone fingers, and raise it laden to his lips. The merest hint of apology appeared in his vague eyes, his posture, even the quick return sliding motion of the fork. (I shall have done, and be gone from your sight. The echo in her mind seemed to come from him.)

His sharp profile tweezered; his Adam's apple bobbed with his chewing. The pile of brown-gravied rice vanished rapidly. I should have left him more meat, she thought with a flash of tenderness. Then she proposed to herself brightly: I could go back and sit down and talk with him. At once she was breathless with her bold idea. She started to intone the farewell ritual into her friend's ear. She felt eager, as if she must begin to run.

He pursed his straight mouth, wiped it with fastidious care on her crumpled paper napkin which he laid with a gentle gesture on the worn laminated tabletop. The pale eyes swept a benevolent glance over the adjacent booths. She swerved hers fast away, thinking, He almost caught me! When she looked back, he had risen and was moving at the edge of a crowd of bantering youths. As she bobbed and swayed, peering between them for a glimpse of him, she keened lightly to herself. She raised a hand and fluttered it toward his back in a pleading gesture. At the other end of the telephone wire, her friend began the ritual responses. She heard nothing. Her lips were busy with silent phrases.

Without a sound she cried, "Wait!"

She noticed, even from here, that the seat of his raincoat was very wrinkled; then among the dwindling crowd his shapeless figure became smaller and smaller until he was gone.

## 2

Jamb didn't know whether it was day or night, or how long he and Satin had been lying there. As soon as his eyes opened he knew he had hit the cement again. He moved his arm and felt the familiar street gritting against his skin. Satin's head came up off his shoulder and he saw her shining fur profiled against a strange building. Her ears turned like a weather-vane in several directions, and she looked questioningly at him.

"Easy, Satin," he croaked. Her ears dipped. He concentrated on her dark eyes, his own a wavering glaze. No movements of his body were possible. He had no idea how long he'd been unconscious. All he knew for sure was that Satin was here; she hadn't been taken away. But where was this? He couldn't move to get up, to find out.

Satin had come down on her elbows again and was scanning the street. He stared at the scintillating wet pores of her nose, black like the rest of her whole massive Labrador shape; about as black as he himself was.

Watching the legs of passers-by, he knew no one would stop. He had plenty of experience in that area. Then he heard the familiar police ambulance siren, coming to take him downtown. Satin would bark and growl to no avail. He'd have to leave her here on the street. Again. A pair of blue-jeaned legs halted in front of them. Jamb tried to lift his head, but it wasn't any use. A face emerged out of the fog that seemed to swarm in front of Jamb, and he saw a shock of uncombed hair over a ragged shirt collar.

"Hey, man, take a slug of this," came the young man's voice. Jamb saw a brown hand, a styrofoam cup, and a bent plastic straw. The hand came closer and Jamb opened his mouth. The coffee hit his stung dry lips sharply. He tried to drink though, and got a few sips as the coffee cooled down in the chilly 5 AM wind. Tried, too, to say something. The young man butted in, "Don't talk, man, rest your face." There was a pause. "The wagon's on its way. I have an idea. I'll take your dog to the SPCA, and see to it that they get your name. What is it?"

"Jamb Roland," he mouthed painfully, as one split tooth knifed an already cut lip. The siren whined closer, and the dipping wail stopped at the nearby curb. Through his ruined ears he heard very little besides the mumble of the van cops and some buzzing words about an ambulance.

The young man's voice was quiet, assertive, "Where will you take him?"

"Emergency, for now." The cops lifted Jamb to a makeshift gurney, and the young man took firm hold of Satin's leash. "Not to worry, Jamb. I'll see that she gets a square right away, and I'll tell them the whole bit at the SPCA. Not to worry, hear."

Jamb couldn't see Satin but he dimly heard her loud complaining barks as the van started up and howled along the street. The barks echoed through his mind over and over, interspersed with the words, "Thanks, thanks, thanks."

"And he didn't know me from nothin'. Oh, God," Jamb thought.

### 3

Meteorologist Pete Giddings sounded as husky as if he was out in this rain himself, Indian Bilijohn thought, twisting his shoulders deeper into his soaked Burberry. "Office workers on the fifty-first floor of Embarcadero

Four are watching snow fly past the windows. It's a weird November traditionally the tag end of Indian Summer in San Francisco."

Inside the St. Anthony Drop In Center Pete's voice rattled away in static and Bilijohn muttered, "Lucky dude, nothin' to do but yak in the warm." Those guys come in before midnight, he thought, and suppose to take turns, but sometimes they stay till daylight 'fore they get run off. He peered into the Center. The figures hulked inside, just lumps of gray. The bare bulb above the doorway came alight, dim orange against the early dark. In out of the slanting rain, four mummy bags lay fanned out like spokes around the center post. Bilijohn's ruined eyes blinked trying to find the guys' faces. Maybe he knew somebody, could scrounge a decent, whole butt for a change. But the faces were muffled. Huh, he said aloud. In Florida, they'd die right away with pneumonia, but here takes 'em least six months to run themselves down enough to get sick. Everybody thinks they got it good since they ripped off them sleepin' bags so they can stay dry this weather. Naw. Just takes 'em a little longer that's all. They ain't so lucky.

He flicked the flying rain from his nose with the back of his hand. Rivers ran down his heavy club of graying hair, soaked his faded blue headband, slithered into the collar of his raincoat, so shiny with age that it felt slick; too old to be warm anymore, like himself. Cold old Indian, he muttered. He stomped his feet. The boots squished. He realized he couldn't feel his feet today. Sure don't help the artheritis, this rain. Gee if I could, I'd go to Fresno. Mike McGarvin would get me a dry place to sleep. Somewhere near the Poverello. Warmer in Fresno, even when it rains. He approached a knot of people having a conference in the street. His lemur-dark eyes focused on them. He noticed they were soaked too. What's keepin' them out here in the streets?

Then he saw the yellow truck parked; two little old gents getting out of it handing out armloads of wax-wrapped packets from the truckbed. Suddenly the street was awash with drenched and tattered street people. The little old gents were just about lost in the surge. Bilijohn inched his way closer until he saw what they were passing out, though it didn't make any difference. Any give-away was better'n nuthin'. He took his three-pound packet of cheese with a mumbled thanks and moved on down the street.

In half a block he found himself in another line. He craned his head to see where it was leading. He saw a pair of women standing down the curb a ways. They were buying the cheese. Bilijohn's chest wheezed with a sudden sigh. He reasoned that the cheese ought not to go for any less 'n five bucks. And he sure could use a shot of 'Bird. A great wave of spit washed up in his gullet.

When he got to the front of the line, some woman he couldn't look into the eyes of, took his cheese, held out two dollars. His stomach spasmed in an acid drench, and he almost grabbed back the cheese, but he couldn't do it. He wanted to vomit. You thief, he wanted to yell, but he couldn't. The two paper dollars wadded in his fist, he headed down the street to Merrill's Drug. A jug of lousy Thunderbird. Hell, I'm an Indin, man, I can drink Thunderbird in public, he muttered. Us Indins got choices. Two. Thunderbird or Coors.

The cheese could have kept him off the St. Anthony bread line for at least a day if he'd resisted the woman. Lousy mooch, he thought. Naw forget it, he told himself, shrugged and kept putting his soggy feet down, shuffling along Market Street.

He bent to pick up a long butt that wasn't real wet, lying close in under a building's eave. He fished in the pockets of the Burberry. Not a match to my name he growled. When he came out of Merrill's, the bottle stuck into his pocket, he was still fumbling for a match. He aimed toward the next man passing in the street, then veered away, seeing NO chiseled in the hard lips and granite stare.

"All's I want is a light, man," Bilijohn mumbled at him wagging his hand. Now he felt the good electricity of his first gulp of wine radiate over the ache of his ulcers. The trembling in his legs was getting less. At the corner, standing for a red light, he laid his head back and tossed half the wine down his throat, feeling the stuff zig-zag sharply across the harsh desert of his long thirst. Dude thought I was a derelict, he mouthed, but the swords in his stomach pierced his thought and he winced in pain. Hah! Derelict.

He never seen me ride, did he? Bet he wouldn't know what to do with a quarter-horse. Naw, he's probably never even stepped in cow shit. Shoo, I wasn't gonna hit on him; all's I wanted was a flame, he reiterated angrily. Then seeing it as a ridiculous joke he let his lips turn up at the corners. His half blind eyes searched the clouds, as if he shared his laughter with the gods.

And the filthy street changed into the long grass of a strangely familiar valley, and Bilijohn was riding. Riding. He didn't hear the high keening screech of brakes, didn't see the lithe swerve of the shining town car. He heard only a distant call: Billy! Billy John! and his own answering holler. Yeah I'm coming as fast as I can! He didn't feel the massy jolt as the sharp hood scooped him sky ward, his eyes still measuring the weeping clouds. The half empty gray-green bottle arced into the gutter and tumbled down the torrent of flotsam, the Thunderbird belching out of it. Indian Bilijohn galloped on through the long amber grass, heels pummelling the bright flanks.

# RALPH SALISBURY

## Aniwaya, Anikawa, and the Killer Teen-Agers (1983)

*In a compelling tale, Salisbury gives an account of Indian wars past, present, and future, coiled cunningly into one. "Aniwaya, Anikawa, and the Killer Teen-Agers" echoes his fellow Cherokee Robert J. Conley's "Wili Woyi," in its surreal and shamanic dimensions and tribal understandings, though Salisbury locates his narrative in a futuristic space that, however desolate and corporate, is nevertheless tribal.*

*The image of the Native workers laboring under the overseers' lash and on starvation rations is one common to Native American storytelling since interface with whites became the norm; in some ways it is a variation on "Woman Singing," by Simon J. Ortiz, in* Voice of the Turtle. *It is the nature of tales in the Native tradition, whether categorized as "fiction" or "narrative" by literary experts, to contain multiple stories that intertwine, each illuminating several others. Rather than creating a separate body of criticism in which, ideally, the depths and resonances within a particular story are explored and made clear, the storytelling tradition decrees that one story be clarified and its meaning deepened by means of another and another and another.*

*"Aniwaya, Anikawa, and the Killer Teen-Agers" reminds us of the enduring power of the tradition, the strength of human bonds, and the transitory nature of present circumstance. Salisbury's, story is in content and structure trickster, possessed of liminal twists that occur when humor and extremity meet on the threshold of life and death, as in every good trickster tale.*

In their own logical way, High Command values time as much as I do; four wonderful, restful hours of beautiful dreams—after my last night of steak, beaujolais, dancing and the companionship of a beautiful patriot—I am rushed to an airstrip, flown over enemy mountains and parachuted into a meadow covered with small, fragrant blooms.

Before dawn, I have followed a river's glistening snake's subtle natal-cord curvings down to tracks which form a game of tic-tac-toe and have climbed onto a sawdust-piled gondola-car in a long, slow freight-train headed toward collision with the rising sun.

For awhile, then, I am on what my espionage instructors called "Native Time," watching the same range of mountains I grew up in across the border taper down to disappear under farms patterned as precisely as designs on a ceremonial-blanket, watching the sun's burning fist drive itself into the blue ice belly of the west—where a country that designates me "Native" not "Citizen" exists—watching the stars move beautifully along their invisible tracks.

The next dawn, I step down from the train slowing to a bone-jolting stop beside mountainous sawdust piles, one of which I climb, burrowing in to make myself a hiding place, a soft, resin-fragrant nest.

My orders are: to "infiltrate the Native work-crews immediately."

> Im
> med
> i
> ate
> ly
> is a wonderful long, slow word.

She is with me, my beautiful beaujolais-haired companion but rejecting me, contemptuous of the little Native in patched blue jeans and too-big sweat-shirt faded the color of a street. Where is her warrior resplendent in blue tunic, chest a rainbow signalling mysterious deeds, some so secret, so important, they will only be acknowledged by a crimson rectangle flecked with gold, until final victory.

Naked, we were young and equals in splendor.

The only splendor I awake to is the final suicide lunge of sun against factory-smoke.

It is noon. My companion of two nights ago will be awakening about now, in the big crimson bed where I last saw her, naked, tanned gold like the leaf on my medal.

There is no immediately visible work-crew to infiltrate, but there soon will be, I know because of pile after pile of sawdust and the big concrete building whose cannonshape smoke-stack has just obliterated the sun.

I look for a heavy stick to tie my blanket-bundle to, a heavy stick, a weapon that does not look like a weapon. No luck. Two nights ago I could have chosen among strong branches up in the mountains, but then I was hurrying to catch a train down to these mountains of sawdust—enough wood in them to make an army of clubs, but all that wood will only go to fuel the factory in making whatever war-weapons it supplies.

The first human I see is a tall, skinny Native, the second a cop.

"Come here, you." The cop sees two Natives.

For the rest of the day, I am dancing with a long-handled shovel, unloading the train which brought me.

Slowly, slowly the dozens of golden rectangles of sawdust shaped by gondola cars is translated into one more sawdust mountain, at first gleaming gold in daylight, then rising gray as ash in smoke-subdued moonlight, the only illumination in a city blacked-out to prevent bombing planes from locating it.

My side's bombing planes, I have to remind myself.

Here it is the same as when I left the reservation—caught, put to work, hard work—insults, cuffs on the head.

Caught for war, first draft—dog soldier. Volunteered for Commando, endured things worse so they'd get, finally, better. Enduring hard duty now in hope of another successful mission, reward, another great dinner, lovely companion, big bed crimson as the ribbon of a Distinguished Service Medal.

Here no steak and beaujolais, for sure, no dinner of any sort, only a cop-stick poked into my gut.

Then he demands, "What's your age?"

I say, "Fifty-two," which is my age, twenty-five, turned backwards. Remembering is a behind the lines agent's most important weapon, especially if he has not even a club.

"Get back to work."

It's dark, the cop can barely see that my hair is gray, its dye as dingy as the factory-smoke. The cop's memory of this afternoon tells him my body looks younger than the gray-dyed hair suggests and that I am a likely military recruit, but his memory is jostled aside by his need to keep watch over ten gondola cars and on two Natives unloading each car. He has to keep moving, keep us moving, get the job done, or his high command may decide he'd be of more use dancing with a shovel himself.

No dinner and no pay, but when the cars are all unloaded, about midnight, we are marched to the factory cafeteria to eat leftovers off plastic trays waiting to be washed. After eating, we are ordered to wash the trays, hundreds of them. Then we are marched out under the smoke-paled stars and told to report for more unloading tomorrow.

"Where do we sleep?" I ask the tall, skinny Native I'd worked with.

"On your back."

To keep him from being suspicious, I have had to tell him I'm newly arrived off the reservation most distant from his and am Anikawa, Deer Clan. He's Aniwaya, Wolf Clan; we will not be friends.

Another Native tells me to sweep my tracks behind me and climb a sawdust pile, where I can sleep dug in out of sight, because White gangs come hunting us on Saturdays after the guards have gone home to bed.

"It's too late tonight," the Wolf Clan man says. "They probably were here but left when they saw us still unloading, with a cop still on duty."

He might be saying this to get me killed. I sweep my tracks, climb high and dig deep into sawdust.

Thus it is that I wake from dreams of tree ghosts searching for their lost shapes in the sad smoke, and the screams are those of the tall, skinny Wolf Clan Native, not mine.

A gang of eight have him staked to the ground between sawdust piles, and, as flames flare up from his clothing, I see that his captors are big early-teenagers, not quite old enough yet for their army.

The Wolf Clan man is so skinny his arms look like burning sticks— and, from a head burned bare and blackened like the burl of a tree, the screams could be those of the tree ghosts I have dreamed, the Wolf Clan man's body slowly going up in smoke to be lost in the sawdust smoke.

Now his lips are burned off, but his glistening jaw muscles still move the white teeth, the glistening tongue, and I know what sounds are stirring the smoke from his burning flesh. Shock, that blessing the Creator gives us, numbing him to pain at last, he is chanting his death song, asking that his spirit be taken into the shadow land of the sunset, and, at the same time, invoking revenge. He is Wolf Clan, and throughout Creation spirit after spirit is joining him in the force of hatred and pride.

Deer Clan, I join my prayer to his.

His torturers are now uttering a graceless, drunken chant of their own, threatening all of the Natives hidden among the sawdust piles.

I immediately heed their threats, burying myself up to the nose in the flesh of a thousand trees.

For a long time I lie and breathe the sweet powerful scent of resin, my second skin, my armor. Lodgepole Pines, the trees where I parachuted down—Lodgepole because they are tall and straight and we'd used them for building our lodges, where all of the people came together. In the old days, the Wolf Clan people and my own had shared such a lodge.

With many pine-scented breaths, I pray while the stars move in their stately dance through the smoke of a factory functioning all night for war. I pray for revenge and for a life of dignity and beauty beyond victory day.

"We'll be back," the killer teen-agers are shouting.

They keep their word. The next night, Sunday, all eight of them come, drinking, threatening, their knives gleaming in the occasional victories of the moon.

I slip from shadow to shadow while they run from sawdust pile to sawdust pile, seeking a victim.

They find no one. Just as the cop had found no one to unload his sawdust in exchange for leftovers off plastic trays. All of the people swarmed onto the first empty train to leave after the death of the Wolf Clan man. The people have a little revenge; a factory crew has to take time off from their skilled work inside and labor, unloading the gondola cars, the enemy teen-agers unintentionally as effective as our own saboteurs. I witness this from a sawdust pile already too high for any more unloading but still safely far from the piles where bulldozers load trucks that will deliver sawdust to the plant-furnaces.

The Wolf Clan man has shown me our revenge. The crucifix shape of his burning flesh charred an outline four times his size with the spread of gasoline in earth more sawdust than clay. All day, I have seen this sign amid the labors of my enemies preparing for war. The shape so huge, so vividly black amid the golden sawdust, I can see it even after I have slipped up to the little hill where supply cars are sidetracked, waiting until they are needed—on a hill so they can roll down without an engine.

When the eight dark shapes appear in moonlight atop a sawdust mound, I release the brakes of the first huge, gasoline-filled tank-car, letting it roll down toward the small campfire I left amid the sawdust. I have opened all the hose valves. I have waited to do this just as an empty train has begun slowly moving out into the night.

"It's lucky we were scheduled to move out just before the whole damned place blew up," I hear the train crew telling each other, stopped, up in the mountains now, switching rails.

Their "luck" has already left the train, his dark-clothed shape become one with that of a small pine.


Their "luck" has been some time now with his tall, skinny brother's people.

No gold-leafed crimson medal-ribbons here, no gold-leaf-skinned ladies in huge crimson beds. But I have a wife.

No steak and beaujolais. Food is hard to get here. But, well warned, no more of our people go down to eat garbage—become overcooked meat.


The High Command will have aerial photos.

"The Native agent lost no time getting started. What will he accomplish next?" I hear them saying—as I harvest my crops, drag wood up close to my log hut for winter, dreaming of the flower that will still be blooming between my wife's graceful legs, even in snow-living on Native Time.

# LINDA HOGAN

## Amen (1983)

*From the mesas around Laguna to the hills of Georgia, from the West Mesa to the hills and towns of Oklahoma, there is a song on the wind, in the soil, in the sky. It is the song of "the earth power coming" as writer and scholar D'Arcy McNickle put it in his last novel,* Wind from an Enemy Sky. *It is the song of the Supernaturals, of the Earth herself, of the sky. It is the song of the moon, the water, and the fish. In "Amen" the people sing a Baptist song, repeating "Amen" in chorus, "just like they'd always been good Baptists." The irony in the statement underscores that which informs the entire narrative. Jack was a cowboy and an Indian, as so many were and are in Indian Territory, now named Oklahoma. He has the conjurer's skill, as the eye he keeps hidden signifies.*

*Like Jack's pearly moon eye, the people are hidden—in Georgia, in Alabama, in Tennessee, among cowboys, ranchers, university students, and Protestant congregations—and the Spirits are hidden—in the lava cliffs, the state police forces, the boughs of the great oak trees, the moonlit, jacklit rivers, the swamps, the sea. And though the magic eye is covered by an unsightly patch, though the spirit is skinny, old, and often too full for words, it survives. The Spirit people, like the traditions of First Nations people, survive—fat, huge, nourishing. That is the food for Indians upon which they and their ancient wisdom thrive.*

He was born with only one eye and maybe that's why he saw things different than most people. The good eye was dark. The sightless eye was all white and lightly veined.

"There's a god in the light of that eye," Sullie's mother said.

Sullie only saw the old man's eye once in her life. It was the night of the big fish and she thought it was more like a pearl or moon than like an eye. And it was all the more unusual because Jack was, after all, only an ordinary man. He had an old man's odor and wasn't always clean.

He carved wood and fished like all the men. With his small hands he carved tree limbs into gentle cats, sleeping dogs and chickens. And he carved chains to hold them all together.

"It's the only way I can keep a cat and dog in the same room," he joked.

Sullie kept most of his carvings. She watched the shavings pile up on the creaking porch until a breeze blew them into the tall grass or weeds. On a hot windless day they'd fall onto the gold back of the sleeping dog or on its twitching ear. She sat at old Jack's feet and watched and smelled the turpentine odor of wood. His unpatched eye was sharp and black. She could see herself in it, her long skinny legs folded under, her faded dress, dark scraggly hair, all in his one good eye. The other eye was covered, as usual, with a leather patch.

Even then he had been pretty old. His skin was loosening from the bones. He was watching with his clear and black eye how the sky grew to be made of shadows. And some days he didn't have room for one more word so they sat in silence.

The night of the big fish people had been talking about Jack. He wasn't at the picnic and that was a good invitation to gossip.

"Jesse James was part Chickasaw," said Enoch. "Pete has one of his pistols. Word has it that Pete and Jack are related to the James brothers."

Gladys waved her hand impatiently. She leaned her chair back a little and stuck her chest out. "Go on. That old man?"

"That old man was a pallbearer at Jesse James' funeral, yes sir."

"They wouldn't have had an Indian at the funeral, would they?" she asked.

"Look it up. Besides, in his younger days he wore a coal black shirt, even when it was hot. And he had one of them there Arabian horses no one else knew how to ride. And a concho belt made out of real silver. Had a silver saddle horn, too."

Will smiled at the other men. He removed his hat and rubbed back his thick black and gray hair. "That's right. Rumor has it his own brother stole that saddle and belt."

People still kept watch for it, for the stirrups dangling like half-moons and the hammered conchos down the sides. There had also been the horsehair bridle he brought back from Mexico. It was red, black and white horsehair with two heavy threads of purple running through it. The purple dye had come from seashells. Greek shellfish, someone had said and Jack liked to touch the threads and feel the ocean in them, the white Greek stucco buildings, the blue sky. He liked the purple thread more than all the silver. Almost.

"You wouldn't have crossed him in those days. He won that horse in a contest. The trader said if anyone could ride it, they could have it. Jack got on and rode it. He sure did. And then the trader said he couldn't give it to Jack. 'I'd be broke,' he said. So Jack said, give me fifty dollars. The man said he didn't have that kind of money. Jack pulled out his pistol and said, 'If I kill you, you won't have no worries about money or horses.' "

Everyone nodded. A couple of old folks said, "Amen," like good Baptists do. A cheater was a bad man. Jack's brother killed a man for cheating him out of thirty-eight cents. It didn't sound like much but there wasn't much food in those days and the thief had been an outsider. The old folks then also had said, "Amen." They had to feed their own. Not much grew out of the dry Oklahoma soil except pebbles. Word had it that this was just a thin layer of earth over big stone underground mountains. Close to the hot sun and the corn-eating grasshoppers.

And even Sullie had lived through two droughts, a dozen or more black and turquoise tornadoes rolling through the sky, and the year that ended in October. That year cotton grew up out of soft red soil and it grew tall. At first the old people praised the cotton and said "Amen" to the ground. But it kept growing until it was tall as the houses, even the houses with little attics. It stretched up to the wooden rooftops, above the silvered dried wood.

Jack went out in the mornings looking for signs of blossoms. Every morning he stood at the far end of the field and sang a song to the cotton. Sullie snuck out behind him and hid in the tall green plants. She heard parts of the song and silence and the cotton whisper and grow. No pale flowers ever bloomed. No hint of anything that would dry and burst open with white soft cotton inside. Jack went out daily. He stood and sang. He walked through the plants as if his steps would force the stems to let out frail blossoms.

Sullie's mother watched from the door. She dried her hands on the back of her skirt. "I don't think nothing's going to work." She whispered to Sullie and it was true because when October came the taller than houses plants froze, turned transparent and then dried a dull yellow. And the banks closed. And the new red mules died of bloat. And Sullie learned to keep silent at the long empty table.

"He even shot his own brother-in-law for beating up his sister. At a picnic just like this one."

"Amen," the women said, good Baptists. They nodded their round dark faces in agreement.

"After that he'd never sit by a window or go in a dark room. Why, he wouldn't even go in a barn unless it had two doors because he was sure the law or someone from the family would get him."

"He was mean, all right, a man to be feared. You'd forget he had such tiny little hands. And he only wore a size two shoe. Don't know how he ran so fast or handled them guns. And all the time turning his head like a cock rooster to make up for the missing eye."

It grew dark and several men went down to the lake to jack fish. They shined big lights into the water and it attracted fish the same way it paralyzed deer or other land animals. They wouldn't have done it if Jack had been there.

Sullie went down to the water. She was almost a teenager and she liked to watch the big men. She liked their tight jeans and shirts and hats. The women didn't like girls following the men but they forgot about her soon, they were so busy talking about new cotton dresses, their own little children sleeping now on blankets on the hillside. And later they'd talk about woman things, men, herbs, seeing Eliza George the old doctor woman who healed their headaches and helped them get pregnant. Sullie would be back in time to hear about Miss George and how to get pregnant.

But for now she watched the lights shine on the water. And some underneath showing up like sunset. A few miles away in the dark she saw the passing headlights of trucks. She sat in a clump of bushes and trees for a while, then went down to the dark edge of the lake. The men couldn't see her. They were blind to darkness because of the bright lights in their eyes.

She waded in the warm water. The hem of her dress stuck to her legs. She went a little deeper. She stubbed her toe and felt something move and give way. Whatever it was made a large current and she felt frightened. It was cool and slippery and swam like a large fish. Then it stopped. She reached her hand into the water, wetting even her hair, but it was gone. She felt nothing except the fast motion of water.

She smelled the water. She swam a little and looked at the light the women kept on the table, and the black trees.

She heard voices of the men out in the center of the lake. "Over there," someone said. And the lights swayed on water.

Jack walked down to the lake. Sullie started to call to him but then kept still. In the moonlight she saw that he wasn't wearing his eyepatch. And he walked stiff like maybe he was mad. So she kept silent and waded a little further into rocks and weeds and darkness near the shore.

He didn't have a boat or canoe and he stood a moment at the edge of the dark water. Then he dunked himself and stood again. Sullie saw his knobby shoulders beneath the wet shirt, the bones at the neck. Then he submerged himself in water and swam toward the other men. There were only a few splashes, an occasional glimpse of his head rising out of the water.

Before he reached the men with lights, Sullie heard them all become noisy at once. "Lordy," one of them said. The water near them grew furious and violent. One small canoe tipped and the lights shone off all directions.

Sullie waded out again to her chest to watch, forgetting about the women's talk. She heard the men's voices. "I could put my hands in that gill slit." Someone else said, "Watch his fins. They're like razor blades."

They were pulling something around, taking ropes out of the boats when Jack arrived. Sullie didn't hear the conversation between Jack and the other men but she saw him breathing hard in one of the boats and then he was gone, swimming again toward shore, her direction.

"Pry it out of those rocks," Enoch yelled. The men were jubilant, dredging up the old fish with only one eye. It was an old presence in the lake and Jack must have known about it all along. His absence had given the young men permission to fish with illegal light.

He came up from the water close to Sullie and walked through the rocks and sand out into the night air.

Sullie followed Jack a ways. In the darkness there was a tree standing in moonlight, the moon like a silver concho. Jack's hands were small and the light outlined the bones and knuckles. They were spotted like the sides of the ancient fish.

She held herself back from the old man. His shoulders were high and she remembered how he had made cornbread on the day of her birth and fed her honey so she'd never be thin. Sullie's mother had been surprised that Sullie knew this. "Who told you?" she asked.

"Nobody."

"You remember it on your own? Babies are supposed to be blind."

"I just remember, that's all."

And now he stood breathing in the dark. And there were yucca plants at his feet. After the first freeze they would scatter a circle of black seeds on the earth like magic. Like the flying wisteria seeds that had hit and scared Sullie one night. So much mystery in the world, in the way seeds take to air and mimosa leaves fold in delicate prayer at night.

"Who's there?" he said.

"It's me." Her voice was weak. She was afraid to go near him, afraid to run off. He turned and the sight of his eye made her pull her breath too fast into her lungs. It was bright as the moon and the lanterns on water. He watched her a moment and then turned. He looked toward where the cotton was growing this year, toward a few scattered houses with dark windows. Fireflies appeared while he stood. And the sounds of locusts and crickets Sullie hadn't noticed before.

"Let's go back to the rest of the folks," he said.

And they walked, the skinny wet girl, the skinny wet man. The women shut up when they saw them coming. The men didn't notice. They were dragging the rope-bound old fish up on the shore and all the children were awake and running and splashing the water.

Its fins slowed. The gills quit opening while they cut at it and cleaned it of red and yellow ropey intestines and innards. Dogs lapped at its juices.

In the moonlight the sharp scales were scraped off like hunks of mica in a shining glassy pile.

The smell of fish cooking. The dogs eating parts of the head. So large, that dull-colored thing. They'd all talk about it forever. Something that had survived the drought, the famine, the tornadoes and dead crops. It grew large. It was older than all of them. It had hooks in it and lived.

Sullie refused to eat. She pushed her dish away. Her mother hit the table with a pot. "Eat," she said.

Jack's one eye looked far inside Sullie. She was growing old. She could feel it. In his white gaze, she grew old. She grew silent inside. She pulled the plate toward her and looked at the piece of fish, the fried skin and pale bones of it.

"Eat it," Jack motioned with his fork, his own cheeks full of the pink meat. "Eat it. It's an Indian fish."

"Amen," said the women just like they'd always been good Baptists.

# LOUIS OWENS

## Soul-Catcher (1984)

*According to Louis Owens, Chocktaw-Cherokee writer and professor of English at the University of New Mexico,* nalusachito *is a Chocktaw word that translates roughly as soul-catcher, soul-eater, or soul-snatcher. A* nalusachito *is akin to the European ghoul or vampire, surviving by ingesting the life force of human beings indirectly, via their blood, or directly, by eating their souls.*

*Owens' story is based on an event in his childhood. His father had gone hunting, working his way along the Yazoo river in Mississippi. Somewhere on his way home a black panther—"painter" as he pronounced it—began stalking him. He reached the door of their cabin and shut it behind him before the big cat could pounce. The frustrated animal leapt to the roof, where the family could hear its footsteps on the roof and its screams.*

*"Soul-Catcher" is a cautionary tale, warning us that neither lack of understanding nor lack of agreement exempts one from certain consequences. Or, as the justice system has it: Ignorance of the law is no excuse.*

*"Soul-Catcher" centers on a cross-boundary child. Chocktaw on his father's side, the youngster is spending time with his isolated, very traditional great-uncle in the southern swamps. A California boy, he has gotten much of his sense of Native identity, as all too many have, from ethnographies and folktale collections. Uninstructed in the presence of wilderness and its denizens, the boy finds himself unable to cross the boundary that divides the secondhand nature of experience in suburban American life from the swamps of the Great Mysteriousness. The child has no way to understand a world where boundary crossing is taken as fact, and stories are told to help the uninitiated navigate the perilous crossing.*

*"That cat ain't got no surprises for me because I'm old, and I done*

*heard all the stories," the elder tells his nephew. The boy looks at the ethnography on Chocktaws he's been reading. Following his glance, the old man remarks, "It don't work that way. . . ." To the unstoried boy, trained to believe that the material contained in academic texts is factual while stories are untruths, the old man's pronouncement is confusing. His confusion has just the sort of consequences familiarity with the old tradition could prevent.*

The old man held the rifle in one hand and walked bent over under the weight of the gunnysack on his back, as if studying the tangle of roots that was the trail. Behind him three lanky brown-and-black-and-white hounds crowded close to his thin legs and threw nervous glances at the wet forest all around. The only sound was that of the old man's boots and the occasional whine of one of the dogs. The sliver of moon had set, and the trail was very dark. The light from the carbide lamp on his hat cast a phosphorescent glow around the group, so that the old man, with his long silver hair, might have been one of the Choctaw shadows on the bright path home.

Out of the dark to the old man's right came a scream that cut through the swamp like jagged tin and sent the hounds trembling against his legs.

"Hah! Get back you!" he scolded, turning to shake his head at the cringing dogs. "That cat ain't going to eat you, not yet."

The dogs whined and pushed closer so that the old man stumbled and caught himself and the light from the headlamp splashed upon the trail. He shook his head again and chuckled, making shadows dance around them. He knew what it was that stalked him. The black *koi* hadn't been seen in the swamps during the old man's lifetime, but as a child he'd heard the stories so often that he knew at once what the *koi* meant. It was an old and familiar story. He'd felt the black one out there in the swamps for a long time. The bird, *falachito*, had called from the trees to warn him, and he had listened and gone on because what else was there to do? All of his life he had been prepared to recognize the soul-catcher when it should come.

The old man also knew that the screamer was probably the panther that the fool white man, Reeves, had wounded near Satartia a couple of weeks before. He could feel the animal's anger there in the darkness, feel the hatred like grit between his teeth. And he felt great pity for the injured cat.

The boar coon in the sack was heavy, and the old man thought that he should have brought the boy along to help, but then the forest opened and he was at the edge of his cabin clearing, seeing the thread of his garden trail between the stubble of the past year's corn and the dried husks of melon and squash vines. Behind him, this time to his left, the panther screamed again. The cat had been circling like that for the past hour, never getting any closer or any farther away.

He paused at the edge of the clearing and spoke a few words in a low voice, trying to communicate his understanding and sympathy to the wounded animal and his knowledge of what was there to the soul-catcher. For a moment he leaned the rifle against his leg and reached up to touch a small pouch that hung inside his shirt. All of his life the old man had balanced two realities, two worlds, a feat that had never struck him as particularly noteworthy or difficult. But as the cat called out once more, he felt a shadow fall over him. The animal's cry rose from the dark waters of the swamp to the stars and then fell away like one of the deep, bottomless places in the river.

When the old man pulled the leather thong to open the door, the hounds shot past and went to cower beneath the plank beds. He lowered the bag to the puncheon floor and pushed the door closed. After a moment's thought he dropped the bolt into place before reaching with one hand to hang the twenty-two on nails beneath a much larger rifle. Finally, he looked at the teenage boy sitting on the edge of one of the beds with a book in his lap. The lantern beside the boy left half of his upturned face in shadow, as if two faces met in one, but the old man could see one green eye and the fair skin, and he wondered once more how much Choctaw there was in the boy.

The boy looked up fully and stared at the old uncle. The distinct epicanthic fold of each eye giving the boy's face an oddly Oriental quality.

"*Koi*," the old man said. "A painter. He followed me home."

After a moment's silence, the boy said, "You going to keep him?"

The old man grinned. The boy was getting better.

"Not this one," he replied. "He's no good. A fool shot him, and now he's mad." He studied the air to one side of the boy and seemed to make a decision. "Besides, this black one may be *nalusachito*, the soul-catcher. He's best left alone, I think."

The boy's grin died quickly, and the old man saw fear and curiosity mingle in the pale eyes.

"Why do you think it's *nalusachito*?" The word was awkward on the boy's tongue.

"Sometimes you just know these things. He's been out there a while. The bird warned me, and now that fool white man has hurt him."

"*Nalusachito* is just a myth," the boy said.

The old man looked at the book in the boy's lap. "You reading that book again?"

The boy nodded.

"A teacher give that book to your dad one time, so's he could learn all about his people, the teacher said. He used to read that book, too, and tell me about us Choctaws." The old man grinned once more. "After he left, I read some of that book."

The old man reached a hand toward the boy. "Here, let me read you the part I like best about us people." He lifted a pair of wire-rimmed glasses from a shelf above the rifles and slipped them on.

The boy held the book out and the old man took it. Bending so that the lantern-light fell across the pages, he thumbed expertly through the volume.

"This is a good book, all right. Tells us all about ourselves. This writer was a smart man. Listen to this." He began to read, pronouncing each word with care, as though it were a foreign language.

*The Choctaw warrior, as I knew him in his native Mississippi forest, was as fine a specimen of manly perfection as I have ever beheld.*

He looked up with a wink.

*He seemed to be as perfect as the human form could be. Tall, beautiful in symmetry of form and face, graceful, active, straight, fleet, with lofty and independent bearing, he seemed worthy in saying, as he of Juan Fernández fame: "I am monarch of all I survey." His black piercing eye seemed to penetrate and read the very thoughts of the heart, while his firm step proclaimed a feeling sense of manly independence. Nor did their women fall behind in all that pertains to female beauty.*

The old man looked at the boy. "Now there's a man that hit the nail on the head." He paused for a moment. "You ever heard of this Juan Fernández? Us Choctaws didn't get along too good with Spanish people in the old days. Remind me to tell you about Tuscaloosa sometime."

The boy shook his head. "Alabama?"

The old man nodded. "I read this next part to Old Lady Blue Wood that lives 'crost the river. She says this is the smartest white man she ever heard of." He adjusted the glasses and read again.

*They were of such unnatural beauty that they literally appeared to light up everything around them. Their shoulders were broad and their carriage true to Nature, which has never been excelled by the hand of art, their long, black tresses hung in flowing waves, extending nearly to the ground; but the beauty of the countenances of many of those Choctaw and Chickasaw girls was so extraordinary that if such faces were seen today in one of the parlors of the fashionable world, they would be considered as a type of beauty hitherto unknown.*

He handed the book back to the boy and removed the glasses, grinning all the while. "Now parts of that do sound like Old Lady Blue Wood.

That unnatural part, and that part about broad shoulders. But she ain't never had a carriage that I know of, and she's more likely to light into anybody that's close than to light 'em up."

The boy looked down at the moldy book and then grinned weakly back at the old uncle. Beneath the floppy hat, surrounded by the acrid smell of the carbide headlamp, the old man seemed like one of the swamp shadows come into the cabin. The boy thought about his father, the old man's nephew, who had been only half Choctaw but looked nearly as dark and indestructible as the uncle. Then he looked down at his own hand in the light from the kerosene lantern. The pale skin embarrassed him, gave him away. The old man, his great-uncle, was Indian, and his father had been Indian, but he wasn't.

There was a thud on the wood shingles of the cabin's roof. Dust fell from each of the four corners of the cabin and onto the pages of the damp book.

"*Nalusachito* done climbed up on the roof," the old man said, gazing at the ceiling with amusement. "He moves pretty good for a cat that's hurt, don't he?"

The boy knew the uncle was watching for his reaction. He steeled himself, and then the panther screamed and he flinched.

The old man nodded. "Only a fool or a crazy man ain't scared when soul-catcher's walking around on his house," he said.

"You're not afraid," the boy replied, watching as the old man set the headlamp on a shelf and hung the wide hat on a nail beside the rifles.

The old man pulled a piece of canvas from beneath the table and spread it on the floor. As he dumped the coon out onto the canvas, he looked up with a chuckle. "That book says Choctaw boys always respected their elders. I'm scared alright, but I know about that cat, you see, and that's the difference. That cat ain't got no surprises for me because I'm old, and I done heard all the stories."

The boy glanced at the book.

"It don't work that way," the old man said. "You can't read them. A white man comes and he pokes around and pays somebody, or maybe somebody feels sorry for him and tells him stuff and he writes it down. But he don't understand, so he can't put it down right, you see."

How do you understand? the boy wanted to ask as he watched the uncle pull a knife from its sheath on his hip and begin to skin the coon, making cuts down each leg and up the belly so delicately that the boy could see no blood at all. The panther shrieked overhead, and the old man seemed not to notice.

"Why don't you shoot it?" the boy asked, looking at the big deer rifle on the wall, the thirty-forty Krag from the Spanish-American War.

The old man looked up in surprise.

"You could sell the skin to Mr. Wheeler for a lot of money, couldn't you?" Mr. Wheeler was the black man who came from across the river to buy the coonskins.

The old man squinted and studied the boy's face. "You can't hunt that cat," he said patiently. "*Nalusachito*'s something you got to accept, something that's just there."

"You see," he continued, "what folks like that fool Reeves don't understand is that this painter has always been out there. We just ain't noticed him for a long time. He's always there, and that's what people forget. You can't kill him." He tapped his chest with the handle of the knife. "*Nalusachito* comes from in here."

The boy watched the old man in silence. He knew about the soul-catcher from the book in his lap. It was an old superstition, and the book didn't say anything about *nalusachito* being a panther. That was something the old man invented. This panther was very real and dangerous. He looked skeptically at the old man and then up at the rifle.

"No," the old man said. "We'll just let this painter be."

He pulled the skin off over the head of the raccoon like a sweater, leaving the naked body shining like a baby in the yellow light. Under the beds the dogs sniffed and whined, and overhead the whispers moved across the roof.

The old man held the skin up and admired it, then laid it fur-side down on the bench beside him. "I sure ain't going outside to nail this up right now," he said, the corners of his mouth suggesting a grin. He lifted the bolt and pushed the door open and swung the body of the coon out into the dark. When he closed the door there was a snarl and an impact on the ground. The dogs began to growl and whimper, and the old man said, "You, Yvonne! Hoyo!" and the dogs shivered in silence.

The boy watched the old man wash his hands in the bucket and sit on the edge of the other bed to pull off his boots. Each night and morning since he'd come it had been the same. The old uncle would go out at night and come back before daylight with something in the bag. Usually the boy would waken to find the old man in the other plank bed, sleeping like a small child, so lightly that the boy could not see or hear him breathe. But this night the boy had awakened in the very early morning, torn from sleep by a sound he wasn't conscious of hearing, and he had sat up with the lantern and book to await the old man's return. He read the book because there was nothing else to read. The myths reminded him of fairy tales he'd read as a child, and he tried to imagine his father reading them.

The old man was a real Choctaw—*Chahta okla*—a full-blood. Was the ability to believe the myths diluted with the blood, the boy wondered, so that his father could, when he had been alive, believe only half as strongly as the old man and he, his father's son, half as much yet? He thought of the soul-catcher, and he shivered, but he knew that he was just scaring himself the way kids always did. His mother had told him how they said that when his father was born the uncle had shown up at the sharecropper's cabin and announced that the boy would be his responsibility. That was the Choctaw way, he said, the right way. A man must accept responsibility for and teach his sister's children. Nobody had thought of that custom for a long time, and nobody had seen the uncle for years, and nobody knew how he'd even learned of the boy's birth, but there he was come out of the swamps across the river with his straight black hair hanging to his shoulders under the floppy hat and his face dark as night so that the mother, his sister, screamed when she saw him. And from that day onward the uncle had come often from the swamps to take the boy's father with him, to teach him.

The old man rolled into the bed, pulled the wool blanket to his chin, turned to the wall, and was asleep. The boy watched him and then turned down the lamp until only a dim glow outlined the objects in the room. He thought of Los Angeles, the bone-dry hills and yellow air, the home where he'd lived with his parents before the accident that killed both. It was difficult to be Choctaw, to be Indian there, and he'd seen his father working hard at it, growing his black hair long, going to urban powwows where the fancy dancers spun like beautiful birds. His father had taught him to hunt in the desert hills and to say a few phrases, like *Chahta isht ia* and *Chahta yakni*, in the old language. The words had remained only sounds, the powwow dancers only another Southern California spectacle for a green-eyed, fair-skinned boy. But the hunting had been real, a testing of desire and reflex he had felt all the way through.

Indians were hunters. Indians lived close to the land. His father had said those things often. He thought about the panther. The old man would not hunt the black cat, and had probably made up the story about *nalusa-chito* as an excuse. The panther was dangerous. For a month the boy had been at the cabin and had not ventured beyond the edges of the garden except to go out in the small rowboat onto the muddy Yazoo River that flanked one side of the clearing. The swampy forest around the cabin was like the river, a place in which nothing was ever clear: shadows, swirls, dark forms rising and disappearing again, nothing ever clearly seen. And each night he'd lain in the bed and listened to the booming and cracking of the swamp like something monstrously evil and thought of the old man killing things in the dark, picturing the old man as a solitary light cutting the darkness.

The panther might remain, its soft feet whispering maddeningly on the cabin roof each night while the old man hunted in the swamp. Or it might attack the old man who would not shoot it. For the first time the boy realized the advantage in not being really Choctaw. The old uncle could not hunt the panther, but he could, because he knew the cat for what it really was. It would not be any more difficult to kill than the wild pigs he'd hunted with his father in the coastal range of California, and it was no different than the cougars that haunted those same mountains. The black one was only a freak of nature.

Moving softly, he lifted the heavy rifle from its nails. In a crate on the floor he found the cartridges and, slipping on his red-plaid mackinaw, he dropped the bullets into his pocket. Then he walked carefully to the door, lifted the bolt, stepped through, and silently pulled the door closed. Outside, it was getting close to dawn and the air had the clean, raw smell of that hour, tainted by the sharp odor of the river and swamp. The trees were unsure outlines protruding from the wall of black that surrounded the cabin on three sides. Over the river the fog hovered in a gray somewhat lighter than the air, and a kingfisher called in a shrill *kree* out across the water.

He pushed shells into the rifle's magazine and then stepped along the garden trail toward the trees, listening carefully for the sounds of the woods. Where even he knew there should have been the shouting of crickets, frogs, and a hundred other night creatures, there was only silence beating like the heartbeat drum at one of the powwows. At the edge of the clearing he paused.

In the cabin the old man sat up and looked toward the door. The boy had an hour before full daylight, and he would meet *nalusachito* in that transitional time. The old man fingered the medicine pouch on the cord around his neck and wondered about such a convergence. There was a meaning beyond his understanding, something that could not be avoided.

The boy brushed aside a muskedine vine and stepped into the woods, feeling his boots sink into the wet floor. It had all been a singular journey toward this, out of the light of California, across the burning earth of the Southwest, and into the darkness of this place. Beyond the garden, in the uncertain light, the trunks of trees, the brush and vines were like a curtain closing behind him. Then the panther cried in the damp woods somewhere in front of him, the sound insinuating itself into the night like one of the tendrils of fog that clung to the ground. The boy began to walk on the faint trail toward the sound, the air so thick he felt as though he were suspended in fluid, his movements like those of a man walking on the floor of the sea. His breathing became torturous and liquid, and his eyes adjusted to the darkness and strained to isolate the watery forms surrounding him.

When he had gone a hundred yards the panther called again, a strange, dreamlike, muted cry different from the earlier screams, and he hesitated a moment and then left the trail to follow the cry. A form slid from the trail beside his boot, and he moved carefully away, deeper into the woods beyond the trail. Now the light was graying, and the leaves and bark of the trees became delicately etched as the day broke.

The close scream of the panther jerked him into full consciousness, and he saw the cat. Twenty feet away, it crouched in a clutter of vines and brush, its yellow eyes burning at him. In front of the panther was the half-eaten carcass of the coon.

He raised the rifle slowly, bringing it to his shoulder and slipping the safety off in the same movement. With his action, the panther pushed itself upright until it sat on its haunches, facing him. It was then the boy saw that one of the front feet hung limp, a festering wound in the shoulder on that side. He lined the notched sight of the rifle against the cat's head, and he saw the burning go out of the eyes. The panther watched him calmly, waiting as he pulled the trigger. The animal toppled backward, kicked for an instant and was still.

He walked to the cat and nudged it with a boot. *Nalusachito* was dead. He leaned the rifle against a tree and lifted the cat by its four feet and swung it onto his back, surprised at how light it was and feeling the sharp edges of the ribs through the fur. He felt sorrow and pity for the hurt animal he could imagine hunting awkwardly in the swamps, and he knew that what he had done was right. He picked up the rifle and turned back toward the cabin.

When he opened the cabin door, with the cat on his shoulder, the old man was sitting in the chair facing him. The boy leaned the rifle against the bench and swung the panther carefully to the floor and looked up at the old man, but the old man's eyes were fixed on the open doorway. Beyond the doorway *nalusachito* crouched, ready to spring.

# BETH BRANT

## Coyote Learns a New Trick (1985)

*No cycle of transformation stories can be complete without the Trickster, the sly Old Man or Old Woman who in salaciousness, shrewdness, cunning, selfishness, and devious duplicity uncreates and re-creates self and the Earth. In many Coyote stories, Old Trickster is a painful but amusing exemplar of the kind of activities we must not engage in. If we hoodwink others into giving up their lives when they think they are participating in a ceremony, or when we talk them into trading their good eyes for pretty but useless rose petals, or when we run around having indiscriminate sex with whatever strikes our fancy for reasons not directly connected to sex or bonding, we will suffer the consequences of humiliation and ignominy: Everyone will know our shame and laugh at us.*

*Some kinds of trickery are far more serious than the shenanigans Brant's Coyotesse is up to. Her Trickster is a modern scalawag, a rakish bit of a rogue who is engaged in nothing more threatening than hilarious seduction. Punning on "trick"—which can mean sleight of hand, four cards taken at bridge, or someone who pays money for sex—Brant instructs us on a modern Coyote activity in which some may well choose to engage.*

*Old Trickster knows all there is to know about transformation, being change-artist par excellence. In "Coyote Learns a New Trick," Coyote indulges in one of his/her favorite changes, that of gender. In some old stories Coyote trades his penis for a vagina in pursuit of a joke; in this one, she cross-dresses, and finds that the joke is on her.*

*In the old stories, whether the trick works or backfires, Coyote's tricky maneuvers are instructive. After all, teaching about transformation is a major function of the old narrative tradition. And coping with change is some-*

*thing Old Coyote excels at, especially in this time. We do well to learn from Wile E. Coyote's example.*

Coyote thought of a good joke.

She laughed so hard, she almost wanted to keep it to herself. But what good is a joke if you can't trick creatures into believing one thing is true when Coyote knows truth is only what she makes it.

She laughed and snorted and got out her sewing machine and made herself a wonderful outfit. Brown tweed pants with a zipper in the front and very pegged bottoms. A white shirt with pointed collar and french cuffs. A tie from a scrap of brown and black striped silk she had found in her night rummagings. She had some brown cowboy boots in her closet and spit on them, polishing them with her tail. She found some pretty stones that she fashioned into cufflinks for her dress shirt.

She bound her breasts with an old diaper left over from her last litter, and placed over this a sleeveless undershirt that someone had thrown in the garbage dump. It had a few holes and smelled strong, but that went with the trick. She buttoned the white shirt over the holes and smell, and wound the tie around her neck, where she knotted it with flair.

She stuffed more diapers into her underpants so it looked like she had a swell inside. A big swell.

She was almost ready, but needed something to hide her brown hair. Then she remembered a fedora that had been abandoned by an old friend, and set it at an angle over one brown eye.

She looked in the mirror and almost died laughing. She looked like a very dapper male of style.

Out of her bag of tricks, she pulled a long silver chain and looped it from her belt to her pocket, where it swayed so fine.

Stepping outside her lair, she told her pups she'd be back after she had performed this latest bit of magic. They waved her away with, "Oh Mom, what is it this time?"

Subduing her laughter, she walked slowly, wanting each creature to see her movements and behold the wondrous Coyote strutting along.

A hawk spied her, stopped in mid-circle, then flew down to get a good look. "My god, I've never seen anything like it!" And Hawk screamed and carried on, her wing beating her leg as she slapped it with each whoop of laughter. Then she flew back into the sky in hot pursuit of a juicy rat she had seen earlier.

Coyote was undaunted. She knew she looked good, and besides, hawks have been known to have no sense of humor.

Dancing along, Coyote saw Turtle, as usual, caught between the road and the marsh. Stepping more quickly, Coyote approached Turtle and asked, in a sarcastic manner, if Turtle needed directions. Turtle fixed her with an astonished eye and hurriedly moved towards the weeds, grumbling about creatures who were too weird to *even* bother with.

Coyote's plan was not going so well.

Then she thought of Fox. That la-di-da female who was forever grooming her pelt and telling stories about how clever and sly she was. "She's the one!" said Coyote.

So she sauntered up to Fox's place, whistling and perfecting her new deep voice and showful walk. Knocking on Fox's door, she brushed lint and hairs from her shirt, and crushed the hat more securely on her head. Fox opened the door, and her eyes got very large with surprise and admiration.

"Can I help you?" she said with a brush of her eyelashes.

Coyote said, "I seem to be lost. Can you tell a man like me where to find a diner to refresh myself after my long walk?"

Fox said, "Come on in. I was just this minute fixing a little supper and getting ready to have something cool to drink. Won't you join me? It wouldn't do for a stranger to pass through my place and not feel welcomed."

Coyote was impressed. This was going better than she had planned. She stifled a laugh.

"Did you say something?" Fox seemed eager to know.

"I was just admiring your red fur. Mighty pretty."

"Oh, it's nothing. Inherited you know. But I really stand in admiration of your hat and silver chain. Where did you ever find such things?"

"Well, I'm a traveling man myself. Pick up things here and there. Travel mostly at night. You can find a lot of things at night. It sure smells good in here. You must be a fine cook."

Fox laughed, "I've been known to cook up a few things. Food is one of the more sensual pleasures in life, don't you think?" she said, pouring Coyote a glass of red wine. "But I can think of several things that are equally as pleasurable, can't you?" And she winked her red eye. Coyote almost choked on her wine. She realized that she had to get this joke back into her own paws.

"Say, you're a pretty female. Got a man around the house?" Fox laughed and laughed and laughed, her red fur shaking.

"No, there are no men around here. Just me and sometimes a few girlfriends that stay over." And Fox laughed and laughed and laughed, her long nose sniffing and snorting.

Coyote couldn't figure out why Fox laughed so much. Maybe she was nervous with such a fine-looking Coyote in her house. Why, I bet she's never seen the likes of me! But it's time to get on with the trick.

Now, Coyote's trick was to make a fool out of Fox. To get her all worked up, thinking Coyote was a male, then reveal her true female

Coyote self. It would make a good story. How Fox thought she was so sly and smart, but a Coyote got the best of her. Why, Coyote could tell this story for years to come!

One thing led to another, as they often do. They ate dinner, drank a little more red wine. Fox batted her eyelashes so much, Coyote thought they'd fall off! But Coyote was having a good time too. Now was the time.

"Hey Fox, you seem like a friendly type. How about a roll in the hay?"

"I thought you'd never ask," said Fox, laughing and laughing.

Lying on Fox's pallet, having her body next to hers, Coyote thought maybe she'd wait a bit before playing the trick. Besides, it was fun to be rolling around with a red-haired female. And man oh man, she really could kiss. That tongue of hers sure knows a trick or two. And boy oh boy, that sure feels good, her paw on my back rubbing and petting. And wow, I never knew foxes could do such things, moving her legs like that, pulling me down on top of her like that. And she makes such pretty noises, moaning like that. And her paw feels real good, unzipping my pants. And oh oh, she's going to find out the trick, and then what'll I do?

"Coyote! Why don't you take that ridiculous stuffing out of your pants. And take off that undershirt, it smells to high heaven. And let me untie that binder so we can get down to *serious* business."

Coyote had not fooled Fox. But somehow, playing the trick didn't seem so important anyway.

So Coyote took off her clothes, laid on top of Fox, her leg moving between Fox's open limbs. She panted and moved and panted some more and told herself that foxes were clever after all. In fact, they were downright smart with all the stuff they knew.

Mmmmm yeah, this Fox is pretty clever with all the stuff she knows. This is the best trick I ever heard of. Why didn't I think of it?

# PAULA GUNN ALLEN

## Charlie (1987)

*Charlie is a construct of liminality. He is a shadowy being, a man who has taken up residence at the crossroads between states of consciousness, one who is poised at the intersection of the Four Corners of the soul. Allen's fiction generally contains such a figure. In her novel,* The Woman Who Owned the Shadows, *liminality personified is named Stephen—a cousin, perhaps a lover, an oppressor, an abuser. Allen's treatment of the abuser/oppressor as a state of chronic liminality suggests that what Jungians refer to as "the shadow" is a state of consciousness that is trapped between worlds, a consciousness that is unwilling or unable to transform.*

*Charlie is a Vietnam vet as well as a Native, a casualty of war upon war. His mother, Maggie, is a counselor at an Indian Alcoholic Treatment Center, and Charlie and his wife, Polly, have recently moved to Albuquerque from Los Angeles. They are staying with Maggie for a time, until they "get on their feet." Until Charlie finds a job, or Polly does. Until they find an apartment, a car, a life. Or until they move away. Charlie is trapped by more pain and rage than he can handle, wandering the territory of shadows that is located on the border between life and death.*

*A number of characters in Native fiction, both from the oral tradition and from the contemporary narrative applications of that tradition, are caught in a state of permanent liminality. It enables them, like Trickster, to keep on keepin' on, to maintain their existence—however fraught for them and dangerous to others. But it is a state of arrested consciousness, of a soul that, unable to engage in change, cannot accept the inevitability of death, and cannot grow, as we learn over and over from trickster stories told continent-wide.*

onely. He was so lonely. As though he was an arroyo, waiting for water that would never come. As though clouds forever moved over him, never blessing him with rain. He was parched and aimless. Dry and forever unfilled.

Not that he didn't try. He reached out over and over. Loved. Cared. He thought about the kitten he had taken in, the poor starving creature. How he had nursed her, crooned over her, held her close. How sweetly she had looked at him, small eyes blinking, claws softly kneading his chest, softly purring, content. How he had fed her cream even when he had nothing for himself to eat. If only he still had that small warm fuzzy animal now. She had loved him, and he had loved her.

He hadn't meant to hurt her. He was only so upset when she kept mewing at him. For food, he guessed. She was hungry and he didn't have anything to feed her. And it was the middle of the night. And she wouldn't let him sleep. He remembered the feel of her small body when he gripped her. How her bones and fur felt in his hand in that second he held her, raising his arm high behind him; how she felt just as he let go.

She had landed against the far wall. He hadn't meant to use so much force. He had lost control. Then he stood over her, watching the blood coming up from her, dribbling out of her mouth onto the floor.

After he was sure she was dead, he took her outside. He couldn't bury her; there was no unpaved ground where he lived. He put her body in the trash can in the alley and went back upstairs to bed.

Polly was like that kitten. Soft and helpless. When he'd found her she was hungry. She wore torn jeans and a scanty top. She had an old lightweight windbreaker that was her only protection from the cold. Pretty, though. She sure was pretty. So small and soft. She'd look up at him with her trusting eyes, smiling so softly. Just like the kitten.

He hadn't thought about that before. How she reminded him of his kitten. He wished he could remember the animal's name. If she had one. She had trusted him too. Too bad. He ached with unshed tears, for the kitten, for Polly, for himself. He reflected on how important it was for him to have a small creature relying on him. Looking at him with trust. Looking up to him.

He had taken Polly in. Fed her. Given her grass, beer, even good-quality whiskey, from his precious store of Black Jack. They'd been warmed by each other. Young faces gleaming in the half-light. He'd kept the light dim in his rented room in that crappy hotel he was living in then. In L.A. But it was good enough, he thought. It was okay.

After he'd been released from the hospital he'd drifted for a while, then found that room and moved in. He'd gotten odd jobs, hawking and bouncing for strip joints, running bingo games, parking cars. He'd made out all right. At least he'd had enough to take care of himself, and some party money. He'd planned to be a leather worker. Set up a booth, maybe. Go around and sell his work. He was good at it. People were always wanting him to make them something. He thought he could make a good living at it after a while. He'd been hopeful then. It seemed like the world was opening up. He would make it, he was sure.

Then something happened. He didn't know what. He had been drinking, of course, but he'd always drunk. Nothing new about that. But there he was, going into bars, walking up to strangers, punching them, belligerent. "Hey, man, you're screwy," he'd say. And more. He didn't remember it all. He was drunk. But he knew he kept getting beat up. He kept losing jobs. Getting fired. Getting eased out. Everything would be going along just fine, then, wham. Out on the street, buddy, out on the street. He'd call in to ask about the work schedule and they'd say, "You ain't scheduled, Charlie." Just like that. "Why don't you come on in and pick up your check."

The worst time was the day he'd been so drunk he'd fallen down on the street. Head cradled on his arm, he'd decided just to stay there. He was comfortable, he'd thought. No need to move. Suddenly out of nowhere this spade dude was kicking his head, telling him to get up. Taunting him, calling him names. Saying he was a bum, he was ruining his life. Saying, "Get up man, get the fuck up, motherfucker, get off you ass, man, GET UP," the whole time kicking him, hard.

Charlie had gotten up then, reeling. Trying to stand. Putting his hand out against the wall to steady himself. "Drunk on you ass, man," the black man had mocked, spitting. "Look at you, a damn drunk injun, just like in the flicks. Whassa matter with you, man?" he'd said, looking hard at Charlie. "White man get you?"

Charlie had been too shocked to be mad. His head hurt where the dude'd kicked it. He could barely focus his eyes. The man would go in and out of focus, blurring, looking like a bird flying up close somehow. His purple coat and light tan pants seemed to glow, like his eyes, his mahogany skin.

He grinned when Charlie finally focused on his face. A triumphant grin that broke into a huge, knowing smile. "Man, thought that'd get you. Now go on out of here. Get yourself cleaned up, get some food. Go on, now, split, man."

Charlie looked at the man for a minute, trying to understand what he was saying. Then he lurched down the street, back to his room. That was the bottom. Almost.

He'd sat there, puking and crying. His rage washing over him like sheets of rain. Rocking back and forth on the edge of the bed, he'd sat, getting madder and madder. Raging at himself, at what he'd become, what he'd done. The black man was right. He was a drunk Indian. He was a no-good bum. Just like they wanted him to be. But he was obedient. He obeyed them, after all, didn't he? Enraged, he had gotten up and begun tearing his clothes up, slashing the furniture, smashing the lamps. He gouged and slashed his leatherwork with his knife. He broke his records. He smashed his cassette player. He tore the tapes out of every plastic cartridge. When he had ripped everything in sight and smashed what he couldn't rip, he stood in the middle of the room, staring around. "It's no good, man," he said. "It's no fucking good." And he sat on the floor, wet from the whiskey he'd poured on it and his vomit. And he was filled with sorrow and revulsion. For his life. For what he lived. For what he was. He held out his wrist, raised the leather band to expose the veins beneath and took his knife to them, sawing hard, watching through narrowed tear-blinded eyes as the blood came. Satisfied with the job, he switched hands, cut deep into the veins in the other wrist. Then he put the knife down and waited for death. I should sing something, he thought. Heap big chief, noble Ind'in warrior. Should sing for my death.

Then he must have passed out because he didn't remember much after that. He remembered Polly's face, white with fear, her hazel eyes now dark and huge. She was talking to him, telling him it would be all right, he'd be all right. They were in an ambulance, medics working on him or sitting near him, something. It was vague in his mind, obscured by exhaustion, booze, loss of blood.

Later she told him that she'd come in as he was trying to cut his wrist band in half. She'd taken it from him, wrestling him for it. She'd gotten it and the knife away from him and then called the ambulance. The social workers had come too, talked to him about being suicidal, and did he want treatment. They'd stitched up the worst of his cuts, and released him the next day, giving him a small card with the number he could call for emergency counseling or to make an appointment for psychiatric care. "I'm not nuts," he'd said. "I'm just fucking pissed off." He'd glowered at them, the two serious-faced white boys, longhairs, bearded and too thin, who were talking with him. He and Polly had left, gone back to his room. When his injuries were healed they had left the coast, come to this dry southwest town to stay with his mother.

Walking along the busy boulevard now, shivering in the cold wind that blew off the mesa, he thought about that time, his anguish, his despair when they'd gone up the three flights to his room and switched on the overhead light. He'd torn it apart, completely. He'd left nothing. He felt again the despairing ache in his gut, tangled threads pulling tighter, snarling hopelessly. And the rage that grew out of the threads, a bright glow, warming him.

The kitten, the room, now Polly. He looked bleakly out at the traffic moving past him. Polly. Swearing, he clenched his hands into tight fists. Punched at the air, at the traffic, at the memory of the past few hours.

Polly, bleeding, screaming at him. Clawing him with her pretty nails. Hating him. Running out the door, screaming "You'll pay, you bastard, you'll pay for this, I swear it, you no-good rotten bastard. You wait. I'll get you, you just wait."

Then she was gone. He'd grabbed his leather vest and gone out behind her, slamming the door. Christ, he thought. I didn't lock it. Mom'll be mad as hell when she comes home and finds the whole place open. Shit. What the fuck am I gonna do now? How will I explain why Polly's gone? She thought I was getting a job. Doing fine. We talked about it last night. I told her all about how it's been with me. Oh God, Maggie, I'm sorry. Jesus H. Christ, I'm sorry. Your precious boy's nothing but a no-good bum, just like the man said.

He turned. Maybe I better go back. Straighten the place up a little. We must'a torn the hell out of it. Yeah, he thought. I'll go on back. Polly will come back, she has to. She can't go anyplace with no money. She doesn't know anyone here except sis and Mom. I'll go on back there and get cleaned up and maybe fix something to eat. There was a bottle of something under the sink in the kitchen. I saw it behind the soap. Bitch. Thought she was hiding it from me. Well, she'll never miss it. Not for a while. I'll have a few and get things straightened up. When Polly comes home we can talk. It'll be all right.

He hurried now, back the way he'd come. His feet were icy from the cold. He thought about being inside, in his mother's apartment, warm and safe, making things work out, making everything come out all right.

# N. SCOTT MOMADAY

## Tsoai (1989)

*Unlike Charlie in the preceding story, Momaday's protagonist Set Lockman makes it across the boundary of consciousness from the limited to the vast, from the mundane to wilderness. The novel from which these vignettes are taken,* The Ancient Child, *chronicles the passage of an alienated Kiowa from Bay Area artist to shaman. In this work, Momaday continues his exploration of states of liminality, which he began in his first novel,* House Made of Dawn, *and has pursued throughout his work as poet, essayist, painter of shields, and novelist.*

*Momaday draws from Kiowa myth, using it as the primary structural device of the story of an estranged man's movement from alienation and mundanity to belonging and self-realization. But Set Lockman's journey to himself does not take him to a state of Emersonian self-reliance or the kind of rugged individuality so deeply embedded in the American mind. Rather, it takes him from a state of parentless isolation, a chronic state of meaningless-ness and anomie where self-estrangement coupled with self-preoccupation is normal, to one of permanent, ineradicable connection to All-that-is. In the Kiowa way, he gets his name; he understands, recognizes, and accepts his nature, simultaneously receiving the gift of true selfdom from his grandmother, Kope'mah, from the young medicine woman of mixed Kiowa and Navajo blood, and from the ritual tradition of the Kiowa people.*

*Set Lockman is a transformation in the process of happening, as we see in his descent from rational urban affluence to madness, coupled with his name change from his earlier nickname Loki to his mature Set.*

*In the meandering and deliberately fractured course of the novel we are compelled to cross boundaries we didn't know existed, as is the protagonist. Loki, dangerous trickster, becomes Set, which means Bear—thought by the Kiowa and others to be itself a fundamentally liminal being who can change into human or into which humans can transform. Bear is also seen widely as possessing the power to heal. It is this transformation from spiritually ill boy-child to supernatural being, from earthbound to wilderness consciousness, that Momaday chronicles.*

*Set is a name that was held by a number of Lockman's Kiowa predecessors. There were before Lockman several Sets, each with a different modifying quality their whole name revealed: Set Angya, the historical Kiowa leader Sitting Bear; Set-tainte; and, in the distant place where human consciousness and myth intersect, Set-talee, Boy Bear, also known as Tsoaitalee, Rock Tree Boy. Set is also the name of the god in the Egyptian oral tradition who was brother and murderer of Osiris, the great Corn god of the Nile.*

*Liminality is a state that is by its very nature obscure: It is beyond narrative logic as it is beyond left-brain reasoning. Indeed, the text suggests that the process of transformation epitomized in Set's journey is as far beyond art as it is beyond myth and literature—or, as Momaday himself frames it at the opening of his novel in a quote from Argentine writer Jorge Luis Borges, "For myth is at the beginning of literature, and also at its end." The primary myth upon which* The Ancient Child *is founded is Kiowa, but on a deeper level, Momaday's work is an elegant exploration of that place where all the sacred traditions of the world meet. It is holographic, or "wholographic." It instructs us that entering vastness means to get out of line.*

### It shines like a vague, powdered mask, like a skull

Locke Setman—Set—studied the telegram that had been slipped under the door of the studio. It read:

GRANDMOTHER KOPEMAH NEAR DEATH.

PLEASE COME AT ONCE.

NOTIFY CATE.

He was completely at a loss. He knew of no Grandmother Kopemah. Obviously this was word from his father's people, but he did not know them. They had nothing to do with him. They were related to him, he supposed, but that was only an accident; they were his relatives, but they were not his family. His father had died when he was seven, and his mother, even more remote in his mind, had died giving him birth. All that he had of his forebears was a sediment in his memory, the memory of words his father had spoken long ago—the stories his father had told him. The longer he looked at the telegram, the more deeply it disturbed him. It was in Set's nature to wonder, until the wonder became pain, who he was. He had an incomplete idea of himself.

The ten words were compelling, after all. Cate was Catlin, Catlin Setmaunt on the tribal rolls, who as a young man began to sign himself Cate Setman.

The telegram was sent by Milo Mottledmare of Saddle Mountain, Oklahoma. Set studied it for a long time, moving his eyes from the address to the text and back again: LOCKE SETMAUNT, 1690 BEACH STREET, SAN FRANCISCO: KOPEMAH . . . DEATH . . . COME . . . CATE. The longer he looked at it the more extraordinary it became, a document which contained his name and his father's name, a thing of impenetrable meaning, an enigma, perhaps an omen. *It bore his father's name,* therefore his spirit. Here was an exigent message from one Milo Mottledmare, perhaps his father's friend or kinsman, who on the face of it seemed not to know that Cate Setman had died more than thirty years ago. But for his father's name, Set would have supposed there had been a mistake, that the telegram was meant for someone else.

The rest of the day he brooded, pacing about the studio, working sporadically at the easel. He tried to reach Milo Mottledmare on the telephone, but there was no listing. The brooding became a restlessness. In the evening he went out walking. It was clear, and there was a good breeze off the Bay. He stopped by the Edwardian for a sandwich and a beer, and he spoke briefly to a man he knew only as Gaetano, another painter and resident of the Marina. Set had never seen his work. Gaetano introduced his companion, a large, red-haired girl with a pretty face and a British accent. Her name was Briony. When they parted, she shook Set's hand and said, "Super. Look after yourself."

He had meant to go on up the hill to Scott Street and spend an hour with Bent, but he changed his mind and returned to the studio. He phoned first Bent, then Lola, and told them he was going out of town for a day or two.

Coming down out of the clouds toward Oklahoma City, Set thought of puzzles. He gazed upon the immensity of red and green and yellow geometry—rectangles, triangles, squares, jigsawn shapes. The geometry rolled out forever to the skyline. Oh, but there, he thought, look; there is exception and redemption, a redeeming disorder, the opposing aesthetic of the wilderness—the green belts slashing through the boxes like limbs of lightning, like sawteeth and scythes. It was a country of rivers and creeks, prairies and plains. In school Set was taught that art was resistance. In one way or another all his teachers said so, even Cole Blessing, whose drawings were alive. But Cate Setman knew better. Cate must have spoken the truth to Set, and Set must have known too, even when he was not looking, listening intently, and he would somehow keep the knowledge. Look, he said to himself, the wild, crooked courses, reaching in every direction. Water follows the line of least resistance, and it is itself irresistible. It has shaped some of the most impressive forms on the face of the earth.

Cate had long ago told him something about his name. What? What was it? It lay on the farthest edge of his memory. He had not yet begun to believe in names.

At Will Rogers Airport, with some trepidation, he rented a car. Lola Bourne made him keep current a driver's license, but although he traveled widely in connection with his exhibits, he almost never drove, and he had never owned an automobile. He said he wanted air conditioning. The freckled-faced girl behind the Hertz counter giggled and touched his hand. When he stepped outside the terminal the heat stunned him, and when he got into the car he had to open the windows in order to breathe. The girl had given him a map. He opened it and laid it out on the seat beside him, but he didn't think he would need it right away. He drove west. There was country music on the radio. The highway had been cut straight through the waves of grassland, and all along there were slashes of bright embankment on both sides—quick, bold strokes, as Jason Fine would say. Jason was Set's agent, and he was knowledgeable and shrewd, but he spoke of painting in clichés. This landscape of Indian red, Mars yellow, and burnt umber would be in Jason's terms brooding, vast, uncompromising, preeminently honest, and commensurate with man's capacity for wonder.

At a crossroads near Saddle Mountain he drank root beer from a can. It did not slake his thirst, but it tasted better than the water he had drawn from a great blue inverted bottle into a tiny paper cone; the water was warm, and there was a tincture of oil in it.

"Oh, yeah," said the small arthritic man at the cash register. "Miz Kopemah lives out yonder with the Mollymares—Reverent Mollymare an' his missus, you know—out a ways on Cradle Crick, I b'leeve it's called. Yuh cain't hardly miss it. Jist take the first left an' folley the road, oh, seben, eight mile, I reckon's all. Fine folk, them Mollymares, the Reverent an' his missus, fine Christian folk." Then a cloud seemed to pass over his face. There was a moment in which his concentration seemed prodigious. "But, say, I declare I b'leeve ol' Miz Kopemah passed on. Yessir, jist day before yestiddy. They was a burial out to the cemetery, I declare."

There was a house in a grove of trees, a creek beyond. It was an old house, in bad repair. He was glad to be done with the dirt road. All the way from the blacktop he had veered in and out of ruts and plunged into deep, soft dirt, granular like sand, barely keeping ahead of his own dust. He brought the car to a stop and turned off the ignition. The engine died hard, coughing and sputtering for a time.

At close range the house seemed even older and more dilapidated than it had from the moving car. He had never seen such a house; it seemed as old as the land. The ground was grown up with weeds and wild grass, and there were patches of bare red earth here and there, dusted with ash and stained with dishwater and cooking broths and other kinds of waste. There was an anthill at his feet. A rangy, tawny cur, her teats large, dark, and distended, ambled wearily in the shadow of the house, followed by three round, dusty pups; they paid him no attention. He wanted a drink of cold water. No one was at home, he thought; the house gave no sign of life. It was past five o'clock. There was a peculiar stillness on the earth; it seemed strangely appropriate to that place. Beyond the house and the grove, a long, rolling plain lay before the creek, extending east and west. It seemed almost white, like the moon.

Then, as he wiped the perspiration from his forehead, he saw the boy. The boy stood—seemed suspended—in the black interior of a lean-to, a brush arbor, perhaps thirty or forty yards away. He peered out of the depth as out of a cave, across the bright foreground, without expression. Set thought at first that the boy must be deranged, so strange and unsettling was his sudden and wild appearance. But his gaze was a good deal more incisive than an idiot's. It was indeed so insistent and penetrating that it made Set squirm.

"Hallo!" Set called loudly, surprised to hear the consternation in his voice. "Say, I'm looking for someone, an old woman. I'm afraid I—"

"Oh, you're too late, Mr. Setmaunt. Gran'ma . . . Kope'mah . . . well, Gran'ma died already."

Set was so intent upon the boy's face, as much of it as he could see, that the voice, nearer by, startled him, and he turned sharply around. It was a woman on the porch of the house who had spoken, a handsome, matronly woman, perhaps fifty years old, of medium height, rather stout, with thick black hair in which there were streaks of gray. He looked at her for a moment, trying to swallow, but his mouth was too dry. He felt suddenly very tired and depressed. He had come all the way to this remote and godforsaken place for reasons he could not fathom and, now it seemed, to no purpose whatsoever. The grandmother, Kope'mah, was dead. He was weary and off balance; he felt that he was about to collapse. For the first time in his life, it seemed, he could not bring the world into perspective. Why had he come here? What in God's name had compelled him, and what was he doing? He did not know. He wondered if he were losing his mind. He shot a glance toward the boy, but the boy was not there.

"I'm sorry," Set managed at last. "When? When did she . . . die?"

"Friday. Early Friday morning. She was buried on Saturday."

"Friday," he repeated and said again, "I'm sorry."

"You know, Mr. Setmaunt, we tried to call you, several times, from the church—we don't have no phone here—but there was no answer."

It was now Monday. He had received the telegram on Saturday. It had to have been sent on Saturday. It made no sense. Nor could he imagine how anyone here could have telephoned him. His number was unpublished, and it was known to very few people, none of whom knew anything about his father's family, not even Bent. A kind of nausea was coming upon him. He felt an ant crawling on his leg.

"Yes, I'm Set, Locke Setman. Please, may I have a glass of water?"

169

He turned his head again toward the arbor. There was only the black, empty space within.

Inside the house Set could barely see at first. The windows in the front room were small, and they admitted too little light. The screens were old and rusted, and there was no longer any tension in them, so they billowed in and out. An L-shaped tear in one had been crudely mended with a coarser, darker wire. It looked like a great black centipede, broken nearly in two. Flies were thick at the windows. Set blinked away the face of the boy, which had remained in his mind's eye. He had never been in such a room as this. The walls were wooden, of a teal color. The furniture consisted of a small drab sofa, three chairs of assorted shapes and sizes, a table, and a Franklin stove. There was a kerosene lamp on the table and several photographs on the walls, and there was one painting. The photographs were old and tinted by hand, of men and women who belonged to another age, with one exception—that of a young round-faced man in military uniform. The men and women, peering passively from oval frames, bore a certain family resemblance. They were in native Kiowa dress. From the time he had entered the room, Set was conscious of an odor, neither pleasant nor unpleasant, which he could not identify. It was both subtle and pervasive. He had known it before. It put him in mind of damp, rotted wood or of deep earth. And yet there was also something human about it. Had he been asked to name it, he might have said it was the smell of age.

"Anyway, we're sure glad you could come," said Jessie Mottledmare. "We sure been wantin' to meet you—you know, to meet Catlin's son. You must stay here tonight. You're probably tired and hungry. Milo, he's my husband, will be here soon; he'll bring some meat for supper. And in the morning you must visit the cemetery. The graves, our graves, are not very far apart."

"Our graves?" Set said lowly. It sounded not like a question. A suspicion, as cold and fragile as a snowflake, touched upon his brain.

Jessie burst into laughter. "Gran'ma's and Cate's, I mean," she said.

Set closed his eyes and held his breath. In the confusion and anxiety of being a child and an orphan, he had never come to know where his father was buried, only the abstraction: *out there, where he came from.* Catlin Setmaunt, as the name must appear on the headstone, was buried *here.* After a long moment Set simply accepted that he had been drawn unaccountably into some design of fate in which he belonged. He could not yet even begin to see the design, but perhaps he would see it clearly in time. The last words of the telegram returned to him: NOTIFY CATE. He felt that he was the butt of a bad, even insensitive joke, and he had been manipulated. He had played the part of a fool. In his naïveté he had indeed tried to summon the ghost of his father, but the ghost had summoned him instead, as it were. His life had begun to turn on ironies. In this close, quaint, ancient-smelling room, Cate was close, closer than Set knew.

After a while he wanted to stretch his legs, and he excused himself and went outside. He followed a path in the grass. It was sundown and the heat had fallen off. There was a breeze, very light, and warm rather than cool, but it felt good on his skin and it smelled of trees and grass. Again he looked for the boy, but he no longer expected to see him. The final light had withdrawn to the west, and there was a copper tint upon everything, even the shadows. The bare ground of the path was saturated with softest sanguine light. He could not remember having seen earth of that color; it was red: earlier a flat brick red, now deeper, like that particular conté crayon that is red and brown, like old blood, at the same time—or catlinite, the color of his father's name. He walked from the path along the creek. The growth there was dense, and the water was red like the earth, and the current was slow, so slow as to be nearly imperceptible. The orange bitch had followed him. He spoke to her now and then, but she paid him no mind; she ambled along in her own unhurried maternal perception of the universe, he supposed. He had the sense that she did not accompany, she merely happened to be traveling the same road.

He had a strange feeling there, as if some ancestral intelligence had been awakened in him for the first time. There in the wild growth and the soft glowing of the earth, in the muddy water at his feet, was something profoundly original. He could not put his finger on it, but it was there. It was itself genesis, he thought, not genesis in the public domain, not an Old Testament tale, but *his* genesis. He wanted to see his father there in the shadows of the still creek, the child he once was, himself in the child and in the man. But he could not. There was only something like a photograph, old and faded, a shadow within a shadow.

Then something moved. The motion was sudden and without sound. He had caught only a glimpse of it out of the corner of his eye. And then he was looking hard across the creek, into a small brake. Dusk had settled there; the dim light was like smoke, the foliage thick and black beyond. A time passed in which he held his breath, listening, searching. And he released his breath. "Well, whatever it was, it's gone now," he said to the bitch. She had set her head and was staring intently into the same recess. The hair on her nape was raised.

When he returned to the house, lamplight glowed from within, and Milo—the Reverend Milo Mottledmare—was there. Milo was extremely ill at ease. He offered Set a limp hand and undertook to make him welcome, as best he could; the dirt road was very rough, wasn't it? The light was very dim, wasn't it? But the old lady, the grandmother, you know, wanted to live in the old way. She didn't believe in plumbing and electricity. She had never talked on a telephone. Milo was sorry that Set had not been at the funeral ("Beautiful, just beautiful! A bronze casket, satin-lined; Gran'ma in a blue dress with white lace and ribbons, pretty new shoes; and she was smiling so sweetly); he was glad that Set had come in any case; he had spent the whole day at Lawton on church business—his regrets, but the Lord's work had to be done; gracious, the land needed rain, the crops were burning up. Set tried to respond reasonably, but he could not think what to say. Yes, he was sorry that he was not there; beautiful, yes, it must have been a beautiful ceremony; surely the old woman would have been pleased. The more the two men talked the less was said, and the air grew stale between them. They were both greatly relieved when Jessie called them to dinner.

Set was hungry, and Jessie had prepared a generous meal. There was boiled beef, and there were fried potatoes and onions and roasted corn. Simple as it was, it seemed to him exotic, for it was not familiar to him now. And yet it was a kind of cooking that he once knew, that lay somewhere in his memory. His father had liked to boil beef in salted water. The broth was to Cate a delicacy, as it was now to Set, and he savored it. He poured heaping teaspoons of sugar into his iced tea, after the example of his hosts. Cate had done so too. Lola Bourne should see him now, among the dark walls and the photographs of Indians, at table with the Mottledmares, lamplight flickering on the oilcloth, he thought. She would have been intrigued, and she would not have approved of the sugar and salt. Not only would she have disapproved—he smiled to himself—she would have nagged and held a grudge. He missed her.

The food revived him somewhat, and he felt decidedly better than he had when he arrived. Set liked Jessie from the first. She was warm and genuine, easygoing and full of good humor. There was nothing pretentious about her, and she was not in the least self-conscious. In this respect she and her man Milo could not have been less alike. He was painfully, comically shy. He appeared to mean well, but he was awkward and obsequious and inarticulate, and he could not look Set in the eye. Set could not be alone with such a man and be comfortable, he thought. But Jessie, in her candor and goodwill, enabled him to relax, and he conversed easily with her. Homeless again, he began almost to feel at home. In a certain way Jessie reminded him of Señora Archuleta.

After a time he brought himself to ask about the boy, whose face had become a caricature, a curious mask in his mind. Was the boy perhaps a member of the family? he asked. Both Jessie and Milo looked at him for a moment, then at each other, without comprehension. Then Jessie broke into laughter, and she said, "Oh, you mean—why, you mean Grey! Oh, she's a tomboy, all right. She's around here all the time, sure enough; but she lives with Worcester, my Uncle Worcester, across the creek. They have a little place across the creek."

"Bote," Milo said without expression. "Bote, Oklahoma."

Set was taken aback and embarrassed and was also entirely incredulous. He wanted to say, No, we're not talking about the same person. I saw a boy in the lean-to, a thin, wild-eyed boy who stared at me rudely and intensely, whose eyes expressed nothing—no, something, something like—

well, foreboding, something ominous and . . . unimaginable. Don't you see? There could be no mistaking it, that it was . . . *ominous*. No! The boy looked at me, looked inside me, through me, even. It was a look I cannot forget. But he said instead, "Do you mean . . . she . . . she is your cousin? She is your cousin, then. And you said her name . . . Grey?"

Why was he being so inquisitive? he wondered. He felt himself stumbling, intruding, on the verge of revealing his own secrets, but his curiosity had got the better of him. He felt a strange excitement growing within him, and he did not know why.

"We think they're married, Indi'n way," Milo said with a lascivious wink and a strange laugh like a grunt; then, seriously, "She's the Mayor of Bote, Oklahoma."

Jessie looked at him directly, and he returned to his plate.

"No," said Jessie, "she's my niece. My brother Walker was her father; he died a few years ago. But her mother is Navajo, and Grey grew up in Arizona. My brother lived there before he died."

"Shoot, we don't know too much about her," Milo offered.

There was a pause.

"How long has she been with you . . . with your uncle?" Set asked. He could not guess where his questions were leading. He had finished his food, and he wanted a drink of whiskey. He was not likely to find one here, he thought, but there was an unopened bottle of Scotch in the car.

"Oh, maybe two years now," Milo said.

"Yes, two years," Jessie said. "She just turned up one day—I still remember it, you know? We were sitting down to supper in the arbor, Milo and Gran'ma and me, and Grey, she just appeared, came from nowhere, it seemed. She sat down with us and helped herself to everything, like she had lived here all her life. Oh, we didn't know what to think at first. She didn't tell us who she was. But she was so nice and friendly, you know? We couldn't help but like her. And a funny thing, Gran'ma liked her most of all, and she didn't seem at all surprised to see her. It's funny, you know?— like she was expecting her."

"Yeah," Milo agreed. "It was like Gran'ma was expecting her all along, an' all." He wagged his head in wonder. "Her and Gran'ma, they sure did get along good together; gracious, they got along good. And that there Grey, shoot, she talks Kiowa better'n we do. You just don't find them young'uns talkin' Kiowa like that no more."

"Nobody's going to miss Gran'ma more than Grey, I guess, unless it's Worcester," Jessie said. "He's getting old too."

"Grey and your uncle . . . she's a young woman, isn't she? I thought I saw a young . . . person."

"Oh, I bet she's eighteen or nineteen," said Jessie, "though sometimes she seems a lot older. She's been around, to hear her talk. She doesn't really *confide* in us. But she knows what's going on, you know?"

"She don't really *confide* in us," Milo put in. "She's kind of wild." Set glanced at him; for the first time they were in agreement.

"And, uh, she's a mayor . . . ?"

"She's the Mayor of Bote, Oklahoma," said Milo Mottledmare as a matter of fact.

"Oh, that's what she says," Jessie laughed. "It's a joke, I guess. She and Worcester live across the creek. There are a couple of old sod houses over there. People, white people, used to live in them back in the Depression, maybe before that. They're just crumbling away. Nobody lives in them now, not for years and years. Anyway, Grey calls the place Bote, Oklahoma, and she's declared herself the mayor."

"She's the Mayor of Bote, Oklahoma," Milo said again.

"They get along all right, Grey and Worcester, despite the difference in their ages, do they?"

"Oh, my, yes," Jessie answered. "You see, Grey likes the old ones, and they know it, and they like her too. Sometimes when you listen to her talk, you'd think she's old herself. She can talk like an old, old woman. Worcester, he's seventy, probably. We tease him about Grey, you know. Well, they live together."

"And Grey is the daughter of your brother?—you said his name was Walker?"

"Yes, Walker. Walker the Younger, we say in the Kiowa way. Our father's name was Walker too."

"We think she went to boarding school," Milo said.

Set remained curious about Grey—Grey had taken hold of his imagination—but the conversation took a turn, and he had to put his thoughts of her aside for the time being. Jessie and Milo Mottledmare wanted him to talk about himself, and so he did. He told them briefly and rather self-consciously of having lived in an orphanage, of having been adopted, of having gone to art school and become a painter. He answered their questions as best he could and did not mind that Jessie's were now and then personal. He had not married; he was a successful artist; he lived alone. She tried to seem satisfied, but he could see that she wanted to know more. She amused him, and he did not resent her curiosity; she did not resent his, after all. And he too found out something. His grandmother, Cate's mother, and Kope'mah had been very close throughout their lives, until Agabai died in 1932. Although Kope'mah was older than Agabai and outlived her by forty years, they were like sisters, or like mother and daughter. And Cate had been to Kope'mah like her own child. When he died she placed a buffalo robe over his coffin. It was a magnificent heirloom, and the gesture was worthy of a great man. Set was deeply moved to hear this; not for many years had his father's memory borne so closely upon him. Cate Setman had married Catherine Locke at Santa Barbara in the year Agabai died. Catherine died in childbirth in 1934, and Cate died in a car crash in

Wyoming in 1941, when Set was seven years old. A maternal uncle inter-
vened, and Set was not told of his father's death until an orphanage had
been secured. Of course Jessie and Milo knew of Cate's death soon after
the fact, and long before Set knew. They attended the funeral, and Milo's
mentor, the Reverend Leland Smoke, spoke over Catlin Setman's grave.
NOTIFY CATE had been the instruction of the old woman, Kope'mah. She
had spoken of Set in her last days, Jessie said. And again Set was incredulous. The old woman could have known next to nothing about him, he
thought, and in spite of her devotion she could not have known much
about Catlin. She had to have known Cate as a child, inasmuch as he went
out into the world when he was still a boy, and he died away from home as
a young man. But the grandmother, in her final days, had spoken urgently
of him and *to* him, Jessie said. Set wished now with all his heart that he
might have been in time to hear Cate's name on the grandmother's lips.
Cate was very dear to her, and in her ultimate awareness of the past he
must have been intensely alive to her. NOTIFY CATE. The telegram was
Grey's doing; or rather it was the grandmother's, through Grey. So nar-
rowly had Set missed an opportunity to know something about himself,
something of who he was.

They sat for a long time at the table, and at last Set became very tired;
he and Milo began to yawn in concert. There was a large summer moon,
and he asked if he might sleep in the arbor. The next day there was to be a
meeting of one of the Kiowa dance societies near Anadarko. It was decided
that Milo would leave early in the morning and set up the camp. Later Set
would drive Jessie, and perhaps Worcester and Grey, there on his way to
the airport. And they would allow enough time to visit the cemetery and
watch a part of the dance.

The moon was high when he went out of the house. He was used to
city lights, and for him this moon was brighter than any he had ever seen.
In all the night it was the principal thing; every object on earth seemed to
stand out in a blue and silver wash, and he could see with great clarity
even the shadows of trees in the middle distance. The arbor was black inside, except the moonbeams splintered on the roof of boughs. The wide
bench, on which he was to sleep, was stitched with pale blue gunmetal
light. The night in its Plains vastness overwhelmed him, and just then a
cool, fresh wind lifted from the Washita, and he wanted to give himself
up to the deepest sleep. He wanted there to be nothing; he wanted to
enter wholly into the deep element of the Plains night in which he imagined nothing was.

The hours passed, and he dreamed. He heard himself say something,
and he awoke. He opened his eyes and was startled to see the girl standing
over him. She made no sound, but looked down at him with great compo-
sure. He could not see her face, only her form. The moon shone behind
her, set a wonderful radiance upon her. She was so perfectly still. His im-

pulse was to shout at her, to berate her. It was such a stupid and careless and dangerous thing for her to do, to steal up on him while he slept. He might have struck out at her, or he might have been frightened to death! This went through his mind in an instant—and then all at once his shock and anger were gone. Something in her attitude, in the very way she stood in the darkness seeming not even to breathe, expressed an irresistible calm, one that infected him.

"Grey?" he managed, after a moment.

She might have nodded. She seemed tentative, ephemeral, as if she might vanish in a moment. Her hair was edged with light like mercury, a thin, concentrated brilliance.

"What? What is it? What do you want?" He was stammering.

"It is what the grandmother wants," she said. She spoke deliberately, distinctly. Her voice was soft and measured.

There was a silence. He nearly laughed in his perplexity. He was confounded. Nothing he could say or do seemed appropriate. "The old woman is dead," he said in a whisper, simply, to no one. It did not matter, he supposed. It did not matter that the grandmother was dead, or that he said so, or that the girl standing before him spoke in riddles in the night, in a darkness in the light of the moon, in a darkness that comprehended the galaxies.

"The grandmother, Kope'mah, wants me to give you back your medicine. It belongs to you. You must not go without it."

When at last she moved, it was a decisive act. She turned and walked away rapidly. She appeared and reappeared among the shadows in the undulant plain, moving with long, silent strides toward the pitch-black band of trees on the creek. He looked after her until she was out of sight, and then he heard the hoofbeats of a horse muffled, dying away.

# DIANE GLANCY

## The Orchard (1990)

*A man comes to a place on his life's road where mortality closes in on him. Anglo-American society calls it midlife crisis. But "The Orchard" refers to it in other ways: male "menopause"; assimilated Indian or "apple"; paternity in the old world sense of planting the living seed in the inert earth to bring to life a plant, a child, more seeds; and the end of a man's migrations.*

*Many Native nations have an ancestral myth and allied ceremonial cycle that revolve around the migration theme. The spiral that often appears in petroglyphs and pictographs is thought by many to signify that the panel in which it appears is concerned with a given community's migration through that area. Glancy is Cherokee, and though I don't know that the Cherokee have a migration cycle in the many volumes of their mythic/ceremonial tradition, the neighboring Chickasaws and Chocktaws do, and all of them were forcibly removed to Indian Territory in what is now eastern Oklahoma early in the nineteenth century by the United States Government under President Andrew Jackson. That removal was not the last large migration though it was the most recent forced resettlement of entire nations of Native American Indians within the present borders of the United States. The Cherokee in particular have been migrating to America and overseas from the Cherokee Nation for generations. Even earlier, the ethnologist George Mooney recorded that Cherokee youth in the 17th century were migrating or longing to migrate north to join their cousins the Haudenoshonee ("Iroquois"), whose warfaring life held for them a great attraction.*

*The Cherokee stories of migration may indeed hark back to their earliest ritual tradition. In any case, "The Orchard," which holds a father's childhood memories and his seeds that make a star, is a bittersweet tale of transition, of a ceremony that in its time will find completion.*

• • •

Bill Navat woke that Saturday with the dream of apples.

Through the trees, the morning sun speckled the wall. He turned a moment and looked at his wife. She was still asleep; probably dreaming also before she woke.

A thin image of his dream spread itself inside his forehead again, feeling moist as the white inside of apples. He dozed momentarily. It was an orchard, probably one he'd seen long ago. Small patches of sunlight flickered from the window.

He came to consciousness again, firmly now, and got up. Maybe it was the cold autumn. He shut the window, quietly not to disturb her, and went downstairs.

Apples, he thought. Had he once eaten too many? Had he dreamed he was a boy climbing an apple tree in his backyard at the farm? Had he been in an orchard somewhere recently? Something must have reminded him of apples. There was a hard, round image pushing into his head again, a definite surge of his will. His mouth watered with the thought of tartness. Maybe he was only hungry. Small brown holes in the apples, freckles. A dried leaf on the stem.

He ran water into the coffeepot, thought he would like an apple fritter, one he remembered from childhood, but his wife didn't bake. She worked and was busy with the children—their music lessons and art lessons. He let her sleep on Saturday. She might rather stay in the kitchen and cook fritters, but she had to work. His salary as director of Indian exhibits at a museum didn't stretch far enough, and he remembered the fritters. A cold blue wedge of morning sliced the corner of the table. Shiny apples, red as sumac. He walked the edge of consciousness where images dance.

A man's hard voice called from the barn. He heard it in his head. The memory of it embedded his daydreaming. The harsh cold mornings he tried to shrink back into sleep startled him. Close the large and creaking door. Some neighboring farmer always disgruntled. Bill vowed then he would not let his life close in on him so that he felt cornered, and could only lash out with an ugly voice at his wife and children.

He remembered the chickens in a tree on the shed roof. The one time the creek flooded and his father sold the farm in eastern Oklahoma and they moved to Carthage, Missouri. Bill's father didn't let things close in on him. He got out in the yard and danced in a circle. He acted out what he had to do in the ceremonies passed down from the ancestors. Bill could follow them too. Yes. That's the way life was.

Bill wondered what had happened to the disgruntled farmer. He probably still yelled from the barn.

In Carthage, there was an orchard down one street and up another.

One of those old houses with some land between new tracts of houses in the surburbs. An owner who wouldn't sell to developers, but stayed until new houses surrounded him, retreating behind overgrown firs and bushes.

The morning light streaked the wall of the kitchen. Neighboring children would soon appear at the door to ask if his children could play. He thought of the path into the old orchard, already his sides ached. He poured a cup of coffee and made toast. He sat at the table and thought about the job he had been offered at a museum in New Mexico and he wanted to bolt. But he was settled where he was, though the walls of the small, private gallery closed in about him and his hands were tied by curators who wanted to keep it as it was and had always been.

His wife liked her job. His children were satisfied in school. He was a holy man in the Indian Church, a leader in the sweat lodge ceremony. His job at the museum was secure. He liked to walk along the display cases and show the feathered coup sticks, the baskets and blankets and spears he had arranged—the buffalo hunting-mask he had purchased for the museum—the tortoise-shell leg rattles and ceremonial gourds. Yes, he had done well. Why should he want to leave familiar surroundings for some distant museum in the desert?

He made a circle dance on the table with his fingers, walking them around and around. He would stay in one place. The migrations had ceased. He remembered the times he had gotten on a bus and ended up someplace far away. Calling back home for money to return. Where had it gotten him? He had to part with those ways.

He was from a small woodland tribe. His father had been able to farm. What would he gain by leaving? What did he know about southwestern Indians? The tribes were so different. He poured another cup of coffee and returned to the table. He read a letter left open from a relative—Uncle Redwing—one his wife intended to answer. His seeds in the core of her, their children asleep, or maybe awake, watching cartoons in their room. They had watched television late last night and had gone to sleep. He had wakened in the night, he remembered, and gone in to find them sleeping; the programs off for a while, the static filling the room, the milky face of the television like a sore moon through the dark.

The apple pushed itself into his consciousness again as an unwelcome guest, a reminder of what he didn't want to be reminded of: he had a will to run, to disobey, that whacked at him sometimes with an ax. How many workers had been fired at the museum? They showed up for a while, then wouldn't come on time. He had to get over that urge to drift. He would stay in one place! Unless there was reason to leave. That's what the world required. He had invested too much of his life where he was.

He heard other children playing outside though it was still early. He didn't want his children to come downstairs yet. He wanted to sit at the table by himself and think. He wanted to walk his fingers around the table in one place again. He was restless at the museum, but a man didn't leave his job. The curators praised him; he ran the museum with precision.

The moon was an apple without a core. Where was his core? Directing Indian exhibits in a museum? Discussing the collection at ladies' luncheons? Why wasn't he satisfied? Sometimes the world closed in on a man. But he would stay. He would pull himself away from that urge to bolt. He made his fingers circle in one place.

Besides, wouldn't he find the same old discontent in a new place?

He heard his children upstairs, their brown eyes flecked with seeds. What if his wife knew he kept the company of apples? he thought as he took one from the bowl. He turned the apple in his hand. It had the roundness of the earth. The core made a star when cut crosswise through its girth. He remembered the red coil of peel when his mother pared apples like the vision of a spirit horse with braided mane. He used his fingers as though they were legs. He got on the horse. Let's go, he said. He'd ride in place. Yes. That's the journey he'd make.

# EMMA LEE WARRIOR

## Compatriots (1991)

*There are boundaries more difficult to cross than the one that separates the mundane world from the world of the Great Mysteriousness, the profane from the sacred. "Compatriots" is a powerfully constructed depiction of one of the more troubling and ubiquitous of those boundaries: culture.*

*Culture crossing is a transformational boundary crossing that is as fraught with mystery as any other, and pulsing with powers of a sort that mortals cannot master. There are a number of these sacred—and thus dangerous—kinds of boundary crossing in modern life, though they are recognized as such only indirectly by modern people. Gender crossing, religious conversion, psychosis, psychicism, and movement across social classes are among them.*

*Warrior's story involves at least two such transitions, neither of which is successfully completed: One is from assimilated Indian to Native traditionalist, the other from Western consciousness to Native consciousness. Two homes are visited. Lucy's, very Native while seeming Anglo in many respects, is one in which the woman is clearly head of household. The other, a seemingly very traditional tipi camp, is clearly headed by an arrogant white man. In this household the woman wife is cowed, subservient, and victimized by the same verbal abuse Helmut directs at the visitors, especially his compatriot, Hilda.*

*The boundaries that are uncrossable in Warrior's story are essentially cultural, and the lines Warrior delineates are reflected with exactness in the relative positions of power held by men and by women, and in the economic status of each family. One of the most telling boundary markers is the so-called traditional Indian splendor over which Helmut presides, a splendor that is as much Hollywood as it is stolen.*

*You can steal horses, you can steal land, you can steal automobiles and other goods, Warrior's story implies, but you can't steal that which is before and beyond objects or words.*

Lucy heard the car's motor wind down before it turned off the gravel road a quarter of a mile west of the house. Maybe it was Bunky. She hurried and left the outhouse. She couldn't run if she wanted to. It would be such a relief to have this pregnancy over with. She couldn't see the colour of the vehicle, for the slab fence was between the house and the road. That was just as well. She'd been caught in the outhouse a few times, and it still embarrassed her to have a car approach while she was in there.

She got inside the house just as the car came into view. It was her aunt, Flora. Lucy looked at the clock. It was seven-thirty. She wondered what was going on so early in the morning. Flora and a young white woman approached the house. Bob barked furiously at them. Lucy opened the door and yelled at him. "I don't know what's wrong with Bob; he never barks at me," said Flora.

"He's probably barking at her," explained Lucy. "Not many whites come here."

"Oh, this is Hilda Afflerbach. She's from Germany," began Flora. "Remember? I told you I met her at the Calgary Stampede? Well, she got off the seven o'clock bus, and I don't have time to drive her all the way down to my house. I took her over to my mother's, but she's getting ready to go to Lethbridge. Can she stay with you till I get off work?"

Lucy smiled. She knew she was boxed in. "Yeah, but I've got no running water in the house. You have to go outside to use the toilet," she said, looking at Hilda.

"Oh, that's okay," her aunt answered. "She's studying about Indians, anyway. Might as well get the true picture, right? Oh, Hilda, this is my niece, Lucy." Flora lowered her voice and asked, "Where's Bunky?"

"He never came home last night. I was hoping it was him coming home. He's not supposed to miss anymore work. I've got his lunch fixed in case he shows up." Lucy poured some water from a blue plastic water jug into a white enamel basin and washed her hands and face. "I haven't even had time to make coffee. I couldn't sleep waiting for him to come home." She poured water into a coffeemaker and measured out the coffee into the paper filter.

"I'd have some coffee if it was ready, but I think I'd better get to work. We have to punch in now; it's a new rule. Can't travel on Indian time anymore," said Flora. She opened the door and stepped out, then turned to say, "I think the lost has returned," and continued down the steps.

The squeak of the dusty truck's brakes signalled Bunky's arrival. He strode toward the door, barely acknowledging Flora's presence. He came in and took the lunch pail Lucy had. "I stayed at Herbie's," was all he said before he turned and went out. He started the truck and beeped the horn.

"I'll go see what he wants." She motioned to Flora to wait.

When Bunky left, she went to Flora: "Maybe it's a good thing you came here. Bunky didn't want to go to work 'cause he had a hangover. When he found out Hilda was going to be here all day, he decided he'd rather go to work."

"If I don't have to leave the office this afternoon, I'll bring the car over and you can drive Hilda around to look at the reserve, okay?"

"Sure, that'll be good. I can go and do my laundry in Spitzee." She surveyed the distant horizon. The Rockies were spectacular, blue and distinct. It would be a nice day for a drive. She hoped it would be a repeat of yesterday, not too hot, but, as she stood there, she noticed tiny heat waves over the wheat fields. Well, maybe it won't be a repeat, she thought. Her baby kicked inside of her, and she said, "Okay, I'd better go tend to the guest." She didn't relish having a white visitor, but Flora had done her a lot of favours and Hilda seemed nice.

And she was. Hilda made friends with the kids, Jason and Melissa, answering their many questions about Germany as Lucy cooked. She ate heartily, complimenting Lucy on her cooking even though it was only the usual scrambled eggs and fried potatoes with toast and coffee. After payday, there'd be sausages or ham, but payday was Friday and today was only Tuesday.

"Have you heard of Helmut Walking Eagle?" Hilda wanted to know.

"Yeah, well, I really don't know him to talk to him, but I know what he looks like. He's from Germany, too. I always see him at Indian dances. He dresses up like an Indian." She had an urge to tell her that most of the Indians wished Helmut would disappear.

"I want to see him," Hilda said. "I heard about him and I read a book he wrote. He seems to know a lot about the Indians, and he's been accepted into their religious society. I hope he can tell me things I can take home. People in Germany are really interested in Indians. They even have clubs."

Lucy's baby kicked, and she held her hand over the spot. "My baby kicks if I sit too long. I guess he wants to do the dishes."

Hilda got up quickly and said, "Let me do the dishes. You can take care of the laundry."

"No, you're the visitor. I can do them," Lucy countered. But Hilda was persistent, and Lucy gave in.

Flora showed up just after twelve with the information that there was a sun-dance going on on the north side of the reserve. "They're already camping. Let's go there after work. Pick me up around four."

"I can't wait to go to the sun-dance! Do you go to them often?" Hilda asked Lucy.

"No, I never have. I don't know much about them," Lucy said.

"But why? Don't you believe in it? It's your culture!" Hilda's face showed concern.

"Well, they never had sun-dances here—in my whole life there's never been a sun-dance here."

"Really, is that true? But I thought you have them every year here."

"Not here. Over on the Blood Reserve they do and some places in the States. But not here."

"But don't you want to go to a sun-dance? I think it's so exciting!" Hilda moved forward in her seat and looked hopefully at Lucy.

Lucy smiled at her eagerness. "No, I don't care to go. It's mostly those mixed-up people who are in it. You see, Indian religion just came back here on the reserve a little while ago, and there are different groups who all quarrel over which way to practise it. Some use Sioux ways, and others use Cree. It's just a big mess," she said, shaking her head.

Hilda looked at Lucy, and Lucy got the feeling she was telling her things she didn't want to hear.

Lucy had chosen this time of day to do her wash. The Happy Suds Laundromat would be empty. As a rule, the Indians didn't show up till after lunch with their endless garbage bags of laundry.

After they had deposited their laundry in the machines, Lucy, Hilda, and the kids sauntered down the main street to a cafe for lunch. An unkempt Indian man dogged them, talking in Blackfoot.

"Do you know what he's saying?" asked Hilda.

"He wants money. He's related to my husband. Don't pay any attention to him. He always does this," said Lucy. "I used to give him money, but he just drinks it up."

The cafe was a cool respite from the heat outside, and the cushioned seats in the booth felt good. They sat by the window and ordered hamburgers, fries, and lemonade. The waitress brought tall, frosted glasses, and beads of water dripped from them.

"Hello, Lucy," a man's shaky voice said, just when they were really enjoying their lunch. They turned to look at the Indian standing behind Hilda. He was definitely ill. His eyes held pain, and he looked as though he might collapse from whatever ailed him. His hands shook, perspiration covered his face, and his eyes roamed the room constantly.

Lucy moved over to make room for him, but he kept standing and asked her, "Could you give me a ride down to Badger? The cops said I have to leave town. I don't want to stay 'cause they might beat me up."

"Yeah, we're doing laundry. I've got Flora's car. This is her friend, Hilda. She's from Germany."

The sick man barely nodded at her, then, turning back to Lucy, he asked her, "Do you have enough to get me some soup. I'm really hungry."

Lucy nodded and the man said, "I'll just sit in the next booth."

"He's my uncle," Lucy explained to Hilda as she motioned to the waitress. "His name is Sonny."

"Order some clear soup or you'll get sick," Lucy suggested to her uncle.

He nodded, as he pulled some paper napkins out of a chrome container on the table and wiped his face.

The women and children left Sonny with his broth and returned to the laundromat. As they were folding the clothes, he came in. "Here, I'll take these," he said, taking the bags from Lucy. His hands shook, and the effort of lifting the bags was clearly too much for him. "That's okay," protested Lucy, attempting to take them from him, "they're not that heavy. Clothes are always lighter after they've been washed."

"Hey, Lucy, I can manage. You're not supposed to be carrying big things around in your condition." Lucy let him take the plastic bags, which he dropped several times before he got to the car. The cops had probably tired of putting him in jail and sending him out each morning. She believed the cops did beat up Indians, although none was ever brought to court over it. She'd take Sonny home, and he'd straighten out for a few weeks till he got thirsty again, and he'd disappear as soon as he got money. It was no use to hope he'd stop drinking. Sonny wouldn't quit drinking till he quit living.

As they were pulling out of town, Lucy remembered she had to get some Kool-Aid and turned the car into the Stop-n-Go Mart. Hilda got out with her and noticed the man who had followed them through the street sitting in the shade of a stack of old tires.

"Hey, tamohpomaat sikaohki," he told Lucy on her way into the store.

"What did he say? Sikaohki?" queried Hilda.

The Kool-Aid was next to the cash register and she picked up a few packages, and laid them on the counter with the money. When the cashier turned to the register, Lucy poked Hilda with her elbow and nodded her head toward the sign behind the counter. Scrawled unevenly in big, black letters, it said, "Ask for Lysol, vanilla, and shaving lotion at the counter."

They ignored the man on the way to the car. "That's what he wants; he's not allowed to go into the stores 'cause he steals it. He wanted vanilla. The Indians call it 'sikaohki'; it means 'black water.' "

Although the car didn't have air-conditioning, Lucy hurried toward it to escape the blistering heat. When she got on the highway, she asked her uncle, "Did you hear anything about a sun-dance?"

At first he grunted a negative "Huh-uh," then, "Oh, yeah, it's across the river, but I don't know where. George Many Robes is camping there. Saw him this morning. Are you going there?"

"Flora and Hilda are. Hilda wants to meet that German guy, Helmut Walking Eagle. You know, that guy who turned Indian?"

"Oh yeah, is he here?" he said indifferently, closing his eyes.

"Probably. He's always in the middle of Indian doings," said Lucy.

"Shit, that guy's just a phony. How could anybody turn into something else? Huh? I don't think I could turn into a white man if I tried all my life. They wouldn't let me, so how does that German think he can be an Indian. White people think they can do anything—turn into Chinese or Indian—they're crazy!"

Sonny laid his head back on the seat and didn't say another word. Lucy felt embarrassed, but she had to agree with him; it seemed that Indians had come into focus lately. She'd read in the papers how some white woman in Hollywood became a medicine woman. She was selling her book on her life as a medicine woman. Maybe some white person or other person who wasn't Indian would get fooled by that book, but not an Indian. She herself didn't practise Indian religion, but she knew enough about it to know that one didn't just join an Indian religious group if one were not raised with it. That was a lot of the conflict going on among those people who were involved in it. They used sacred practices from other tribes, Navajo and Sioux, or whatever pleased them.

The heat of the day had reached its peak, and trails of dust hung suspended in the air wherever cars or trucks travelled the gravel roads on the reserve. Sonny fashioned a shade behind the house underneath the clothesline in the deep grass, spread a blanket, and filled a gallon jar from the pump. He covered the water with some old coats, lay down, and began to sweat the booze out.

The heat waves from this morning's forecast were accurate. It was just too hot. "Lordy, it's hot," exclaimed Lucy to Hilda as they brought the laundry in. "It must be close to ninety-five or one hundred. Let's go up to Badger to my other aunt's house. She's got a tap by her house and the kids can cool off in her sprinkler. Come on, you kids. Do you want to go run in the sprinkler?"

The women covered the windows on the west side where the sun would shine. "I'm going to leave all the windows open to let the air in," said Lucy, as she walked around the house pushing them up.

Lucy's aunt's house sat amongst a clutter of junk. "Excuse the mess," she smiled at Hilda, waving her arm over her yard. "Don't wanna throw it away, it might come in handy." There were thick grass and weeds crisscrossed with paths to and from the clothesline, the outhouse, the woodstove. Lucy's aunt led them to an arbour shaded with huge spruce branches.

"This is nice," cooed Hilda, admiring the branches. Lucy's aunt beamed, "Yes, I told my old man, 'Henry, you get me some branches that's not gonna dry up and blow away,' and he did. He knows what's good for him. You sit down right here, and I'll get us some drinks." She disappeared and soon returned with a large thermos and some plastic tumblers.

They spent the afternoon hearing about Henry, as they watched the kids run through the sprinkler that sprayed the water back and forth. Once in a while, a suggestion of a breeze would touch the women, but it was more as if they imagined it.

Before four, they left to pick Flora up and headed back to Lucy's. "It's so hot after being in that cool cement building all day!" exclaimed Flora, as she settled herself into the car's stifling interior. "One thing for sure, I'm not going home to cook anything. Lucy, do you think Bunky would mind if you came with us? I'll get us some Kentucky Fried Chicken and stuff in town so you don't have to cook. It's too hot to cook, anyway." She rolled up a newspaper and fanned her face, which was already beginning to flush.

"No, he won't care. He'll probably want to sleep. We picked Sonny up in town. Both of them can lie around and get better. The kids would bother them if we were there."

It was a long ride across the Napi River toward the Porcupine Hills. A few miles from the Hills, they veered off until they were almost by the river. "Let's get off," said Flora.

Hilda gasped at what she saw before her. There was a circle of tepees and tents with a large open area in the middle. Exactly in the centre of the opening was a circular structure covered with branches around the sides. Next to this was a solitary unpainted tepee. Some of the tepees were painted with lines around the bottom; others had orbs bordering them, and yet others had animal figures painted on them. Smoke rose from stoves outside the tepees as people prepared their evening meals. Groups of horses stood languidly in the waning heat of the day, their heads resting on one another's backs and their tails occasionally flicking insects away. The sound of bantering children and yapping dogs carried to where they stood.

"Let's eat here," the kids said, poking their heads to look in the bags of food. Flora and Lucy spread a blanket on the ground, while Hilda continued to stand where she was, surveying the encampment. Flora pointed out the central leafy structure as the sacred area of prayer and dance.

"The tepee next to it is the sacred tepee. That's where the holy woman who is putting up the sun-dance stays the entire time. That's where they have the ceremonies."

"How many sun-dances have you been to?" asked Hilda.

"This is my first time, but I know all about this from books," said Flora. "Helmut Walking Eagle wrote a book about it, too. I could try to get you one. He sells them cheaper to Indians."

Hilda didn't eat much and kept looking down at the camp. "It's really beautiful," she said, as if to herself.

"Well, you better eat something before you get left out," advised Lucy. "These kids don't know when to stop eating chicken."

"Yeah," agreed Flora. "Then we can go down and see who's all there." Hilda had something to eat, and then they got back into the car and headed down toward the encampment. They drove around the edge of the camp and stopped by Flora's cousin's tent. "Hi, Delphine," said Flora, "I didn't know you were camping here."

Lucy knew Flora and Delphine were not especially close. Their fathers were half-brothers, which made them half-cousins. Delphine had grown up Mormon and had recently turned to Indian religion, just as Flora had grown up Catholic and was now exploring traditional beliefs. The same could be said about many of the people here. To top things off, there was some bad feeling between the cousins about a man, some guy they both had been involved with in the past.

"Can anybody camp here? I've got a tepee. How about if I camp next to you."

Delphine bridled. "You're supposed to camp with your own clan."

Flora looked around the camp, "I wonder who's my clan. Say, there's George Many Robes, he's my relation on my dad's side. Maybe I'll ask him if I can camp next to him."

Delphine didn't say anything but busied herself with splitting kindling from a box of sawn wood she kept hidden underneath a piece of tarp. Jason spied a thermos under the tarp and asked for a drink of water.

"I have to haul water, and nobody pays for my gas," grumbled Delphine, as she filled a cup halfway with water.

"Oh, say," inquired Flora, "do you know if Helmut Walking Eagle is coming here? This girl is from Germany, and she wants to see him."

"Over there, that big tepee with a Winnebago beside it. That's his camp," Delphine answered, without looking at them.

"Is she mad at you?" Jason asked Flora.

"Yeah, it must be the heat," Flora told him with a little laugh.

Elsie Walking Eagle was cooking the evening meal on a camp stove outside the tepee. She had some folding chairs that Lucy would've liked to sit down in, but Elsie didn't ask any of them to sit down though she was friendly enough.

"Is your husband here?" asked Flora.

"No, he's over in the sacred tepee," answered Elsie.

"How long is he going to take?"

"Oh, he should be home pretty soon," Elsie said, tending her cooking.

"Do you mind if we just wait? I brought this girl to see him. She's from Germany, too," Flora said.

Lucy had never seen Helmut in anything other than Indian regalia. He was a smallish man with blond hair, a broad face, and a large thin nose. He wore his hair in braids and always wore round, pink shell earrings. Whenever Lucy saw him, she was reminded of the Plains Indian Museum across the line.

Helmut didn't even glance at the company but went directly inside the tepee. Flora asked Elsie, "Would you tell him we'd like to see him?"

"Just wait here. I'll go talk to him," Elsie said, and followed her husband inside. Finally, she came out and invited them in. "He doesn't have much time to talk with you, so . . ." Her voice trailed off.

The inside of the tepee was stunning. It was roomy, and the floor was covered with buffalo hides. Backrests, wall hangings, parfleche bags, and numerous artifacts were magnificently displayed. Helmut Walking Eagle sat resplendent amidst his wealth. The women were dazzled. Lucy felt herself gaping and had to shush her children from asking any questions.

Helmut looked at them intently and rested his gaze on Hilda. Hilda walked toward him, her hand extended in greeting, but Helmut ignored it. Helmut turned to his wife and asked in Blackfoot, "Who is this?"

"She says she's from Germany," was all Elsie said, before making a quick move toward the door.

"Wait!" he barked in Blackfoot, and Elsie stopped where she was.

"I only wanted to know if you're familiar with my home town Weisbaden?" said Hilda.

"Do you know what she's talking about?" Helmut asked Elsie in Blackfoot. Elsie shook her head in a shamed manner.

"Why don't you ask *her* questions about Germany?" He hurled the words at Hilda, then, looking meanly at his wife, he added, "She's been there." Elsie flinched, and, forcing a smile, waved weakly at the intruders and asked them in a kind voice to come outside. As Lucy waited to leave, she looked at Helmut whose jaw twitched with resentment. His anger seemed to be tangibly reaching out to them.

"Wow!" whispered Hilda in Lucy's ear.

Outside, Flora touched a book on the fold-out table. Its title read *Indian Medicine* and in smaller letters, *A Revival of Ancient Cures and Ceremonies*. There was a picture of Helmut and Elsie on the cover. Flora asked, "Is this for sale?"

"No, that one's for someone here at camp, but you can get them in the bookstores."

"How much are they?" Flora asked, turning the book over.

"They're twenty-seven dollars. A lot of work went into it," Elsie replied.

Helmut, in Blackfoot, called out his wife's name, and Elsie said to her unwelcome callers, "I don't have time to visit. We have a lot of things to do." She left them and went in to her husband.

"Do you think she wrote that book?" Lucy asked Flora.

"He's the brains; she's the source," Flora said. "Let's go. My kids are probably wondering what happened to me."

"I'm sorry I upset her husband. I didn't mean to," said Hilda. "I thought he would be willing to teach me something, because we're both German."

"Maybe you could buy his book," suggested Lucy.

"Look," said Flora, "if you're going to be around for a while, I'm going to a sun-dance this next weekend. I'm taking a few days off work. I have a friend up north who can teach you about Indian religion. She's a medicine woman. She's been to Germany. Maybe she even went to your home town.

"Oh, really!" gushed Hilda. "Of course, I'll be around. I'd love to go with you and meet your friends."

"You can come into the sweat with us. First, you'll need to buy four square yards of cotton . . ." began Flora.

But Hilda wasn't really listening to her. She looked as if she were already miles and miles away in the north country. Now, a sweat, she thought, would be real Indian.

# THOMAS KING

## A Seat in the Garden (1991)

*The boundary between the supernatural and the ordinary is permeable, as the tradition has long held. In "A Seat in the Garden," King approaches that theme with whimsy and perception. The "big Indian," who is seen only by the two Anglo men, Joe Hovaugh and his buddy Red Mathews, keeps shouting, "If you build it they will come," just like a similar character in a recent movie. He resembles a movie Indian as well, at least to Red's mind, and he is eerily familiar. Perhaps he's the late Will Sampson, the Big Indian who is most known for his performance in* One Flew Over the Cuckoo's Nest. *He reminds one character, Red, of Jeff Chandler, an actor who excelled at portraying the Hollywoodian "noble savage."*

*Whoever the big Indian in the garden is—or isn't—he is there and not there. The Native men, one Cree and two Nootka, are busily cleaning up the land. The white men approach them for help with the Indian, who the Native men pretend to see. But they're joking around, a usual Native response to the oddities of white behavior with respect to Native people and events.*

*"A Seat in the Garden" is a low-key satire, more humorous than Warrior's biting satire in the previous story. Like Warrior, King is concerned with boundary issues in his story, and the trickster-effect common to Native stories of a satirical nature lies in the twists on popular expectations about Native thought, perception, and consciousness. King and Warrior are both drawing from a similar narrative structure, stance, and plotting mode.*

*Some experts claim that humor is one way of expressing hostility, and has its basis in anger, and perhaps that is true of much humor that comes out of Western cultures. But Native humor is based on anomaly—on the distance between idealized reality and that which is actual. Whether the subject of the joke is tradition, intercultural relations (among Indians as much as between various Native and immigrant groups), history, gender relations, the weather, or common features of contemporary Native life, the point of the joke—as in "A Seat in the Garden"—is the disparity between what is expected and what occurs.*

Joe Hovaugh settled into the garden on his knees and began pulling at the wet, slippery weeds that had sprung up between the neat rows of beets. He trowled his way around the zucchini and up and down the lines of carrots, and he did not notice the big Indian at all until he stopped at the tomatoes, sat back, and tried to remember where he had set the ball of twine and the wooden stakes.

The big Indian was naked to the waist. His hair was braided and wrapped with white ermine and strips of red cloth. He wore a single feather held in place by a leather band stretched around his head, and, even though his arms were folded tightly across his chest, Joe could see the glitter and flash of silver and turquoise on each finger.

"If you build it, they will come," said the big Indian.

Joe rolled forward and shielded his eyes from the morning sun.

"If you build it, they will come," said the big Indian again.

"Christ sakes," Joe shouted. "Get the hell out of the corn, will ya!"

"If you build it . . ."

"Yeah, yeah. Hey! This is private property. You people ever hear of private property?"

". . . they will come."

Joe struggled to his feet and got his shovel from the shed. But when he got back to the garden, the big Indian was gone.

"All right!" Joe shouted, and drove the nose of the shovel into the ground. "Come out of that corn!"

The cornstalks were only about a foot tall. Nevertheless, Joe walked each row, the shovel held at the ready, just in case the big Indian tried to take him by surprise.

When Red Mathews came by in the afternoon, Joe poured him a cup of coffee and told him about the big Indian and what he had said. Red told Joe that he had seen the movie.

"Wasn't a movie, Red, damn it. It was a real Indian. He was just standing there in the corn."

"You probably scared him away."

"You can't let them go standing in your garden whenever they feel like it."

"That's the truth."

• • •

The next day, when Joe came out to the garden to finish staking the tomatoes, the big Indian was waiting for him. The man looked as though he were asleep, but as soon as he saw Joe, he straightened up and crossed his arms on his chest.

"You again!"

"If you build it . . ."

"I'm going to call the police. You hear me. The police are going to come and haul you away."

". . . they will come."

Joe turned around and marched back into the house and phoned the RCMP, who said they would send someone over that very afternoon.

"Afternoon? What am I supposed to do with him until then? Feed him lunch?"

The RCMP officer told Joe that it might be best if he stayed in his house. There was the chance, the officer said, that the big Indian might be drunk or on drugs, and if that were the case, it was better if Joe didn't antagonize him.

"He's walking on my corn. Does that mean anything to you?"

The RCMP officer assured Joe that it meant a great deal to him, that his wife was a gardener, and he knew how she would feel if someone walked on her corn.

"Still," said the officer, "it's best if you don't do anything."

What Joe did do was to call Red, and when Red arrived, the big Indian was still in the garden, waiting.

"Wow, he's a big sucker, all right," said Red. "You know, he looks a little like Jeff Chandler."

"I called the police, and they said not to antagonize him."

"Hey, there are two of us, right?"

"That's right," said Joe.

"You bet it's right."

Joe got the shovel and a hoe from the shed, and he and Red wandered out into the garden, as if nothing were wrong.

"He's watching us," said Red.

"Don't step on the tomatoes," said Joe.

Joe walked around the zucchini, casually dragging the shovel behind him. Red ambled through the beets, the hoe slung over his shoulder.

"If you build it, they will come," the Indian said.

"Get him!" shouted Joe. And before Red could do anything, Joe was charging through the carrots, the shovel held out in front like a lance.

"Wait a minute, Joe," yelled Red, the hoe still on his shoulder. But Joe was already into the tomatoes. He was closing on the big Indian, who hadn't moved, when he stepped on the bundle of wooden stakes and went down in a heap.

"Hey," said Red. "You okay?"

Red helped Joe to his feet, and when the two men looked around, the big Indian was gone.

"Where'd he go?" said Joe.

"Beats me," said Red. "What'd you do to get him so angry?"

Red helped Joe to the house, wrapped an ice pack on his ankle, and told him to put his leg on the chair.

"I saw a movie a couple of years back about a housing development that was built on top of an ancient Indian burial mound," Red said.

"I would have got him, if I hadn't tripped."

"They finally had to get an authentic medicine man to come in and appease the spirits."

"Did you see the look on his face when he saw me coming?"

"And you should have seen some of those spirits."


When the RCMP arrived, Joe showed the officer where the Indian had stood, how he had run at him with the shovel, and how he had stumbled over the bundle of stakes.

After Joe got up and brushed himself off, the RCMP officer asked him if he recognized the big Indian.

"Not likely," said Joe. "There aren't any Indians around here."

"Yes, there are," said Red. "Remember those three guys who come around on weekends every so often."

"The old winos?" said Joe.

"They have that grocery cart, and they pick up cans."

"They don't count."

"They sit down there by the hydrangea and crush the cans and eat their lunch. Sometimes they get to singing."

"You mean drink their lunch."

"Well, they could have anything in that bottle."

"Most likely Lysol."

The RCMP officer walked through the garden with Joe and Red and made a great many notes. He shook hands with both men and told Joe to call him if there was any more trouble.

"Did you ever wonder," said Red, after the officer left, "just what he wants you to build or who 'they' are?"

"I suppose you saw a movie."

"Maybe we should ask the Indians."

"The drunks?"

"Maybe they could translate for us."

"The guy speaks English."

"That's right, Joe. God, this gets stranger all the time. Ed Ames, that's who he reminds me of."

• • •

On Saturday morning, when Joe and Red walked out on the porch, the big Indian was waiting patiently for them in the corn. They were too far away to hear him, but they could see his mouth moving.

"Okay," said Red. "All we got to do is wait for the Indians to show up."

They showed up around noon. One Indian had a green knapsack. The other two pushed a grocery cart in front of them. It was full of cans and bottles. They were old, Joe noticed, and even from the porch, he imagined he could smell them. They walked to a corner of the garden behind the hydrangea where the sprinklers didn't reach. It was a dry, scraggly wedge that Joe had never bothered to cultivate. As soon as the men stopped the cart and sat down on the ground, Red got to his feet and stretched.

"Come on. Can't hurt to talk with them. Grab a couple of beers, so they know we're friendly."

"A good whack with the shovel would be easier."

"Hey, this is kind of exciting. Don't you think this is kind of exciting?"

"I wouldn't trip this time."

When Joe and Red got to the corner, the three men were busy crushing the cans. One man would put a can on a flat stone and the second man would step on it. The third man picked up the crushed can and put it in a brown grocery bag. They were older than Joe had thought, and they didn't smell as bad as he had expected.

"Hi," said Red. "That's a nice collection of cans."

"Good morning," said the first Indian.

"Getting pretty hot," said the second Indian.

"You fellows like a drink," said the third Indian, and he took a large glass bottle out of the knapsack.

"No thanks," said Red. "You fellows like a beer?"

"Lemon water," said the third Indian. "My wife makes it without any sugar so it's not as sweet as most people like."

"How can you guys drink that stuff?" said Joe.

"You get used to it," said the second Indian. "And it's better for you than pop."

As the first Indian twisted the lid off the bottle and took a long drink, Joe looked around to make sure none of his neighbors were watching him.

"I'll bet you guys know just about everything there is to know about Indians," said Red.

"Well," said the first Indian, "Jimmy and Frank are Nootka and I'm Cree. You guys reporters or something?"

"Reporters? No."

"You never know," said the second Indian. "Last month, a couple of reporters did a story on us. Took pictures and everything."

"It's good that these kinds of problems are brought to the public's attention," said Red.

"You bet," said the third Indian. "Everyone's got to help. Otherwise there's going to be more garbage than people."

Joe was already bored with the conversation. He looked back to see if the big Indian was still there.

"This is all nice and friendly," said Joe. "But we've got a problem that we were hoping you might be able to help us with."

"Sure," said the first Indian. "What's the problem?"

Joe snapped the tab on one of the beers, took a long swig, and jerked his thumb in the direction of the garden. "I've got this big Indian who likes to stand in my garden."

"Where?" asked the second Indian.

"Right there," said Joe.

"Right where?" asked the third Indian.

"If you build it, they will come," shouted the big Indian.

"There, there," said Joe. "Did you hear that?"

"Hear what?" said the first Indian.

"They're embarrassed," said Red under his breath. "Let me handle this."

"This is beginning to piss me off," said Joe, and he took another pull on the beer.

"We were just wondering," Red began. "If you woke up one day and found a big Indian standing in your cornfield and all he would say was, 'if you build it, they will come,' what would you do?"

"I'd stop drinking," said the second Indian, and the other two Indians covered their faces with their hands.

"No, no," said Red. "That's not what I mean. Well . . . you see that big Indian over there in the cornfield, don't you?"

The Indians looked at each other, and then they looked at Joe and Red.

"Okay," said the first Indian. "Sure, I see him."

"Oh yeah," said the second Indian. "He's right there, all right. In the . . . beets?"

"Corn," said Joe.

"Right," said the third Indian. "In the corn. I can see him, too. Clear as day."

"That's our problem," said Red. "We think maybe he's a spirit or something."

"No, we don't," said Joe.

"Yes, we do," said Red, who was just getting going. "We figure he wants us to build something to appease him so he'll go away."

"Sort of like . . . a spirit?" said the first Indian.

"Hey," said the second Indian, "remember that movie we saw about that community that was built . . ."

"That's the one," said Red. "What we have to figure out is what he wants us to build. You guys got any ideas?"

The three Indians looked at each other. The first Indian looked at the cornfield. Then he looked at Joe and Red.

"Tell you what," he said. "We'll go over there and talk to him and see what he wants. He looks . . . Cree. You guys stay here, okay?"

Joe and Red watched as the three Indians walked into the garden. They stood together, facing the beets.

"Hey," shouted Joe. "You guys blind? He's behind you."

The first Indian waved his hand and smiled, and the three men turned around. Red could see them talking, and he tried to watch their lips, but he couldn't figure out what they were saying. After a while, the Indians waved at the rows of carrots and came back over to where Joe and Red were waiting.

"Well," said Red. "Did you talk to him?"

"Yes," said the first Indian. "You were right. He is a spirit."

"I knew it!" shouted Red. "What does he want?"

The first Indian looked back to the cornfield. "He's tired of standing, he says. He wants a place to sit down. But he doesn't want to mess up the garden. He says he would like it if you would build him a . . . a . . . bench right about . . . here."

"A bench?" said Joe.

"That's what he said."

"So he can sit down?"

"He gets tired standing."

"The hell you say."

"Do you still see him?" asked the second Indian.

"You blind? Of course I still see him."

"Then I'd get started on the bench right away," said the third Indian.

"Come on, Red," said Joe, and he threw the empty beer can into the hydrangea and opened the other one. "We got to talk."

Joe put the pad of paper on the kitchen table and drew a square. "This is the garden," he said. "These are the carrots. These are the beets. These are the beans. And this is the corn. The big Indian is right about here."

"That's right," said Red. "But what does it mean?"

"Here's where those winos crush their cans and drink their Lysol," Joe continued, marking a spot on the pad and drawing a line to it.

"Lemon water."

"You listening?"

"Sure."

"If you draw lines from the house to where the big Indian stands and from there to where the winos crush their cans and back to the house . . . Now do you see it?"

"Hey, that's pretty good, Joe."

"What does it remind you of?"

"A bench?"

"No," said Joe. "A triangle."

"Okay, I can see that."

"And if you look at it like this, you can see clearly that the winos and the big Indian are there, and the house where you and I are is here."

"What if you looked at it this way, Joe," said Red, and he turned the paper a half turn to the right. "Now the house is there and the old guys and the big Indian are here."

"That's not the way you look at it. That's not the way it works."

"Does that mean we're not going to build the bench?"

"It's our battle plan."

"A bench might be simpler," said Red.

"I'll attack him from the house along this line. You take him from the street along that line. We'll catch him between us."

"I don't know that this is going to work."

"Just don't step on the tomatoes."

The next morning, Red waited behind the hydrangea. He was carrying the hoe and a camera. Joe crouched by the corner of the house with the shovel.

"Charge!" yelled Joe, and he broke from his hiding place and lumbered across the lawn and into the garden. Red leapt through the hydrangea and struggled up the slight incline to the cornfield.

"If you build it, they will come," shouted the Indian.

"Build it yourself," shouted Joe, and he swung the shovel at the big Indian's legs. Red, who was slower, stopped at the edge of the cornfield to watch Joe whack the Indian with his shovel and to take a picture, so he saw Joe and his shovel run right through the Indian and crash into the compost mound.

"Joe, Joe, . . . you all right? God, you should have seen it. You ran right through that guy. Just like he wasn't there. I got a great picture. Wait till you see the picture. Just around the eyes, he looks a little like Sal Mineo."

Red helped Joe back to the house and cleaned the cuts on Joe's face. He wrapped another ice pack on Joe's ankle and then drove down to the one-hour photo store and turned the film in. By the time he got back to the house, Joe was standing on the porch, leaning on the railing.

"You won't believe it, Joe," said Red. "Look at this."

Red fished a photograph out of the pack. It showed Joe and the shovel in mid-swing plunging through the corn. The colors were brilliant.

Joe looked at the photograph for a minute and then he looked at the cornfield. "Where's the big Indian?"

"That's just it. He's not there."

"Christ!"

"Does that mean we're going to build the bench?"


The bench was a handsome affair with a concrete base and a wooden seat. The Indians came by the very next Saturday with their knapsack and grocery cart, and Red could tell that they were impressed.

"Boy," said the first Indian, "that's a good-looking bench."

"You think this will take care of the problem?" asked Red.

"That Indian still in the cornfield?" said the second Indian.

"Of course he's still there," said Joe. "Can't you hear him?"

"I don't know," said the third Indian, and he twisted the lid off the bottle and took a drink. "I don't think he's one of ours."

"What should we do?"

"Don't throw your cans in the hydrangea," said the first Indian. "It's hard to get them out. We're not as young as we used to be."


Joe and Red spent the rest of the day sitting on the porch, drinking beer, and watching the big Indian in the garden. He looked a little like Victor Mature, Red thought, now that he had time to think about it, or maybe Anthony Quinn, only he was taller. And there was an air about the man that made Red believe—believe with all his heart—that he had met this Indian before.

# ANNA LEE WALTERS

## Bicenti (1991)

*Sometimes the transformational imperative gets out of hand, spills over the boundaries necessary for the ordered working of relationships among dimensions, among worlds. This is the theme of Anna Lee Walters' "Bicenti." What happens when the existence of one world threatens to break through, and shatter, the existence of another? We know what happens—or part of it, anyway— when diametrically opposed civilizations collide. We know what happens when certain incompatible chemicals are combined. And we know what happens when contradictory beliefs are held simultaneously within one person's mind. But we—that is, the general populace—do not know what happens when a universe whose basic physical properties and laws do not harmonize with another's threatens the boundaries between them. That is the subject of "Bicenti."*

*When reading Walters' story, consider the uncertainty principle, post-quantum physics, and other new science paradigms that attempt to describe the kind of events "Bicenti" chronicles. The uncertainty principle holds that between the moment that the "electron" is a wave/trace and an electron attached to a particular pattern, its identity is in flux, that is, its identity is uncertain. What it will become is also uncertain until it does become something identifiable, such as part of a DNA molecule, or an $H_2O$ or some other molecule. Similarly, Native thought holds that identity during a liminal or threshold state is in flux, and what it will become is uncertain until it becomes whatever it will after it crosses the threshold into a stable state.*

*Anna Lee Walters, an Otoe Pawnee writer, has lived for a number of years in the Navajo Nation, where she has served as an editor for the Navajo Community College Press. "Bicenti" is a deepening of the themes her work has been concerned with through the past two decades, acting as a gloss or critical text to earlier stories she published.*

• • •

Things weren't right.

Maya sat on the mattress and sank into its springs and lumps. She contemplated the squareness of the small room, sharpened by the afternoon shadows strewn across the floor. The angular walls, the floor and ceiling tiles cut impotently into infinite space and time, but the fragile structure confined her there indefinitely. She stared out the rectangular window to an identical house across the street, and closed her eyes tightly.

"I have this feeling that something is wrong," Maya said sheepishly to Wilma, when Wilma entered the room. Wilma was round and her circular shadow broke up the box space in the sparsely furnished room as Wilma gestured and moved around.

"Oh? What's the matter?" Wilma asked with concern. Her eyebrows lifted in a question.

Maya's oval brown face cracked slowly into a crooked smile. She asked, "Did you ever look at this room, Wilma? The squareness of our little worlds? The insignificant walls? Have you ever wondered if there were a futility and senselessness in these structures? Why are we so infatuated with squares? Are there squares in the real world?" Maya giggled at herself and pointed out the window with her last question.

As Wilma sipped her coffee noisily, she studied Maya's face. It wore a nervous frown that was there one minute and gone the next. "You didn't come here to ask me about this room," Wilma said matter-of-factly. "You didn't drive all the way from Albuquerque to Santa Fe, to question me about this room. Huh-uh."

Maya put down her own mug of coffee and looked into the eyes of her old friend intently for a few seconds, making a decision to tell Wilma everything. She dropped her voice to barely a whisper. Wilma had to lean toward Maya to catch the words Maya let go. The words visibly hung in the air between the two women for seconds.

Maya said, "Things have been happening to me lately. I've lost some things. Well . . . actually they were taken, you know, uh . . . stolen." Maya watched Wilma's response. Wilma's face was blank. Maya continued, "Then, there have been accidents on the highway, traffic accidents, all occurring within seconds from me. Too close!"

Wilma was sipping coffee. Her shadow slipped under her and stayed a step ahead of her as she glided to a chair, one of three pieces of furniture in the room. Maya bent and leaned even closer to Wilma. The wooden chair holding Maya's weight made a little sound. Planes of light and shadow played over Maya's face as she asked Wilma, "Do you know what I am talking about?" The frown was laying over Maya's face again.

Wilma nodded her head decisively. "Yes . . . , oh sure. I was just thinking about things you can do about it. First, tell me about the items you've lost. Did you get anything back? Returned to you?"

Maya leaned forward and held her oval face in her long fingers. Her pointed elbows were on her knees. "Well, first two blankets disappeared. That pretty purple one with the tan and black stripes. Then I missed a red one with green fringes, both taken from the place I am now staying, in Albuquerque."

"Go on," Wilma encouraged. Maya looked thoughtful and far away. Maya's round figure stood before the rectangular window. Clouds floated on her shoulders and through her black hair.

"A purse was taken next. Everything in it," Maya said. She waved her purse away with a soft bare arm. A streak of sunlight radiated under her arm.

"And the accidents?" Wilma prodded.

"Always to other people, just ahead, or just behind me, a split second from me. As far as you are to me. It's happened three times now, people died each time." Maya poured the remaining coffee into her mouth and sat back on the chair.

The room became quiet. The sunlight on the floor crawled from Wilma's feet to Maya's, halfway across the room. Maya's face went through a variety of expressions in this silence, while Wilma's face stayed blank, noncommittal.

Then Wilma soothed Maya's prolonged frown. "Stay here tonight, you can—can't you? We'll talk and think this thing through. Okay?"

Maya nodded her head, though she did not speak. She went again to the window, staring beyond the house across the street, into infinite space and time.

"If we can't come up with any answers or solutions, then you go to Bicenti. You ought to anyway, to find out about your missing things. He will locate them for you. Okay?" Wilma asked while Maya nodded her head again. Their shadows had stretched longer by then, and the planes of the room were elongated, distorted by the hour at hand.


The Sangre de Cristo Mountains loomed in the east, soft and rolling cones, under a melting orange and purple sky. This evening was cool, a gentle wind from the south played on the two women.

Maya and Wilma sat on the porch. Wilma hummed a tribal song as the two watched the mountains, and the sky and clouds dissolve into darkness.

Maya said, "Wilma, you've been listening to my problems all day. I didn't even ask you about the vandalism you have been experiencing out here. What's happening?"

Wilma answered, "Well, we are about ten miles from town. I guess distance may have something to do with it. But things have been quiet lately. If you don't count the weird incident that happened next door." She raised a finger and indicated her nearest neighbor's house. Then she continued, "It happened about a month ago. And Maya, you can't really call it vandalism. All that can be said about it is that it was *very strange.* Bizarre might be the word to describe it. That reminds me, Maya, you ought to park your car up here by the house."

"Well anyway," she went back to her story, "this lady and her husband next door, they're Spanish people . . . One evening they came home and parked their car out in the parking lot in front of their house. See? The next morning, *the car was upside down.* It was pretty strange. No one heard a sound during the night. But sure enough, the next morning there was this car sitting in the exact spot where it had been parked the evening before, but it was upside down!"

Maya laughed, "I guess so! I hope things like that don't happen too often. Are you afraid living out here by yourself?"

"Not at all," Wilma chuckled. "I usually enjoy it. I can't stand the thought of living cooped up in town. The houses are so close together. We're close here too—but it's different. Besides Raoul is here more often than not. You haven't met him but you'll like him, Maya, when you do meet him. He's mostly Spanish, but he's part Indian too."

"Is everyone here Spanish?" Maya wanted to know.

"Mixed, but mostly Spanish. There's a Taos family on the other side, an old Comanche woman down this street, and then there are *Dine*—Navajos." She laughed. "The rest are *Bilagaana* or *Nakai.*" As an afterthought, Wilma said, "Indians are everywhere, no matter where you go."

Maya smiled. "It's a nice, peaceful community," she said. "Too bad about the vandalism. As often as I've been here, I would never have known the problem exists out here—if you hadn't told me."

The two women sat there for a while longer until Wilma asked Maya if she were tired. Maya admitted that she was, stress had taken its toll. Before they retired, Wilma said, "Maya, why don't you move your car up here, beside the porch?"

Maya said, "Nothing's ever happened before. I'm sure that it will be okay. I'll just leave it where it is."

Maya stretched out on top of a sleeping bag in the middle of Wilma's square floor. Her eyelids soon twitched in a deep sleep.

Wilma stood over her friend for a long time that night, thinking of the words Maya had dropped in the next room. A frown creased Wilma's forehead now that Maya couldn't see. Wilma went to the only window in this room to close the drapes. She raised the window several inches to allow a breeze to circulate. She saw Maya's car sitting under a streetlamp that emitted a yellow circle of light around the car.

About midnight, Maya woke. Her eyes stared into the blackness of the square room. She was fully conscious. Her thoughts went immediately to her car. "They're doing something to it," she whispered. She rose, went to the window and looked out. The car sat safely under the high beam of the streetlamp. Maya breathed a sigh of relief. She sat in the rocking chair beside the window and kept a vigil over her car for a few minutes. Then, satisfied that for the moment it was safe, she lay back inside the sleeping bag. The breeze was stronger, billowing the drapes.

At 5:30 the next morning, the alarm clock buzzed.

The Sangre de Cristo Mountains were a faint shape outside Wilma's house. A white line curved around the horizon of the mountains, sun streaks spread fan-like at one end of the range.

Wilma got out of bed and stopped the buzzing alarm. The house was all dark. She walked from her room to the one where Maya slept. She pulled the cord at the window. The drapes, like stage curtains, parted on the glowing horizon. A cold wave slid into the room. The window was still open. Outside in the parking lot, the streetlamps were dark. Wilma could see the faint blue mountains in the east, the silhouette of night in the west engulfed nearby houses.

Wilma went to the kitchen to put coffee in the percolator. She turned on the radio. Its dials were fluorescent when Wilma flipped off the light switch.

Then she went into the bedroom, stripped off her clothes, and went naked into the bathroom. In a few minutes, the shower could be heard.

Maya woke to a country and western singer moaning on the radio and the shower beating into the bathtub. She lay there a moment with her eyes closed listening to the music drift into the room. The odor of perking coffee followed the music.

When Wilma entered the room in a long white terry-cloth robe, Maya asked, "What time is it? I have to be in Albuquerque by eight. I have one of those awful early classes today."

"It's about five forty-five," Wilma answered drying her long hair with a red towel. "I set the alarm a half hour early, so we can visit a little longer. I have to go to work too. I hope you don't mind my getting you up so early."

"Oh no, I'm glad you did," Maya said. She sat on the sleeping bag and added, "Wilma, thanks for everything. I feel much better, refreshed and in a clean frame of mind. I'll go to Bicenti this weekend."

"Good, I'm glad that's settled," Wilma answered, shaking out her long wet hair that had fallen to her waist. She said, "Maya, I think the coffee's ready. You want some?"

But Maya held up a hand and said, "I'll jump in the shower first." She gathered her clothes and carried a small suitcase into the bathroom. The light in there escaped from under the closed door. The rest of the house was dark.

Wilma went to lower the open window in the room. Her wet hair had chilled her. While she was pulling the window down, she looked toward Maya's car. It was assuming a vague shape in the dawn. Wilma paused momentarily straining her eyes at the car. "Hmm," she said and went into the kitchen.

She poured a cup of coffee and looked at the radio when the female announcer came on and said in a seductive voice, "Good morning, sleepyhead. It's six AM"

Not too long after, Maya padded into the room. Her hair was wrapped in a towel turban-style. She wore blue jeans and a turquoise blouse. Her toes stuck out of her house shoes. She poured herself a cup of coffee and took a taste. That's when Wilma said, "Maya, it looks like there is something on your car."

"Oh?" was Maya's response. Her feet padded to the open window. The sun had not risen yet, but the mountains were purple and the sky above them was a delicate pink. Daylight was spreading tentatively toward Wilma's community. The community buildings, however, were still square silhouettes against the fingers of dawn. "It's a beautiful morning," was Maya's first observation. Then her eyes went to the car.

There *was* something on it, but she was nearsighted and without her glasses. She said, "Yes, Wilma, there does seem to be something on it. But I can't make it out that well." Her words made her remember the vigil at midnight.

Wilma stood at Maya's side. She said, "Let's go see. Maybe they punctured the tires, or something like that."

The two women walked out of the house. Maya carried her mug of coffee. They stood on the porch. Wilma pointed to her flower bed. The flowers were uncurling. They walked past the marigolds and down to the parking lot. None of the other houses were lit, not even the apartment complex at the end of the block. The local streets were empty of early morning traffic. "That's strange," Maya said. "There doesn't seem to be anyone stirring but us."

Wilma looked up and down the streets, her damp hair clung to her shoulders. "Yes, that's right, isn't it?" she agreed with Maya. The domed sky was turning a pale blue. Clouds skirted the mountaintops.

Maya's car pointed north. As she walked toward it, she noted that the windows were unbroken, the tires inflated. The car appeared to be unharmed, at least on one side. But what was that on top of it? A black shadow lay on the roof of the car. It stretched the entire length of the roof. Maya and Wilma stopped about ten feet from the car. Their eyes locked briefly. Then both women had the same thought, they gazed at the houses around them. The houses were mute and lifeless forms. Wilma pulled her wet hair over her right shoulder and looked southwest. The Sandia Mountains were now distinguishable in the dawn. A crescent moon glittered on Sandia Peak. A few cars on Interstate 40 still had their lights on. These lights zipped east and west without a sound.

"Strange," commented Wilma. Maya took a shaky step closer to the shadow on her car. Wilma followed. And when Maya stopped just at the left headlight, Wilma did too.

"What in the world?" Wilma asked in a breathy and perplexed voice.

Maya was frozen for a second, desperately sorting images that flashed before her eyes. She saw herself standing in front of the car, moving like an actress in a bizarre play, detached from herself but nevertheless affected. The only thing she could say was, "What?" and again, "What . . . ?"

The thing on the car grew into a foreboding shape in morning light. A large dog was draped over the roof of the car. The outline of its head was clearly discernible.

"What?" Maya repeated. "How . . . ?" She didn't finish the question.

The animal did not move. Maya half expected it to pounce on her or off the car. Again Maya's eyes zeroed in on the houses. Not a curtain in any window fluttered. She noted that Wilma too was studying the houses. When the dog did not move, Maya put her coffee mug on the hood of the car and took another step.

It was then that she saw the spray of blood covering the front window, on the passenger side. It had dripped down the side windows on the other side of the car. Dried pools of red stained the cement.

The jaws of the dog hung open and it looked as if this was from where the blood had gushed until the animal was thoroughly drained.

Maya tried to make sense of the scene. She went through a flood of emotion; anger, compassion for the dead animal, and resolution not to submit to fear.

"Let's go inside," she told Wilma. Wilma nodded, grabbed the mug she had placed on the hood, and involuntarily shivered.

Inside the house, Maya grabbed Wilma by the shoulders and asked, "What's happening?"

Wilma's eyes were round and her mouth was round too as she said, "Oh, Maya, I don't know. It's like that incident with the car. Weird as hell. What shall we do?"

"I don't know," Maya said. "Let me think." She kicked off her house shoes and slipped on leather sandals. While she did this, Wilma threw on the clothes she wore the day before.

"We have to get rid of it," Maya said. "Someone gave that thing to me. I don't want it and I refuse it. I'm taking it back to wherever it came from . . ."

"We'll have to clean the car," Wilma said. She ran to get a plastic jar of dish detergent, and she filled a Tupperware bowl with warm water.

"I don't get it," Maya said, looking out the window once more. "Where is everyone? There used to be early morning traffic here, I remember that!"

"Don't try to figure it out now, Maya. Let's act, move, do something!" Wilma said. "This absence of the neighbors—maybe we can use it to our advantage."

"Yeah, okay." Maya nodded her head. She took a roll of paper towels Wilma handed to her.

Again, they ventured out. The sky was opaque, the sun had not yet climbed the lowest mountains. Not one car passed on this street, or down the side streets.

Maya and Wilma acted quickly and in coordination. The two women lifted the dead animal off the roof of the car. Its body was stiff and heavy. It must have weighed a good seventy pounds. They laid the rigid body just off the walkway in front of Maya's car. Again anger filled Maya as she poured soapy water on the dried blood. Wilma scrubbed the front of the car while Maya did the side, wiping the car clean and dry with paper towels. It took a few minutes. Wilma went back inside the house. Maya stayed to empty the remaining water on the pools of blood on the cement. The soapy water colored a pink tint and ran in rivulets down the street.

Then Maya noticed something she hadn't seen before. A trail of blood led to her car from across the street. She followed it and came upon another pool of blood just in front of the house opposite Wilma's house. From there the trail went down the block. Maya stood in front of that house for a moment. Then she quickly walked to the place where she and Wilma had carefully laid the animal, a few feet from the car.

She picked up the stiffened body by its front and back legs, and she carried it across the street, struggling with her burden and panting when she was done. She left the dog in the pool of dried blood there, stood defiantly and challengingly in front of that house. There were no signs of life in the neighborhood yet. She scooped up a handful of dirt from that yard and carried it to her car where she scattered it over the drying pools of water and blood. She rubbed the dirt over the cement viciously with her sandals. The blood darkened to brown spots.

"Now," Maya whispered, "we'll see what happens."

At that moment a light came on in a house on a corner. She heard a door slam somewhere. A quick look inside her car reassured her that nothing more had been done to it. The tires were in good shape. She retraced her steps to Wilma's house. Wilma met her at the door. Wilma's wet hair was tied with a rubber band and she wore a sweater.

"What now?" Wilma wanted to know.

"We wait and see what happens," Maya said. "No matter what does happen though, we don't know anything about that dog, okay?"

"It's the best way," Wilma said.

Maya unwrapped the towel around her head. "What time is it?" she asked.

"It's about six-forty," Wilma said. "You should leave before seven if you want to make that class."

Maya asked, "Will you be all right?"

Wilma went into the kitchen, searching for the coffee cup she'd put down someplace earlier. As she poured a hot cupful of coffee, she answered, "I'll go to work. No, maybe I won't. I have time I need to use for my leave anyway. But, I'll be all right."

Footsteps were coming down the sidewalk outside. Wilma came out of the kitchen and looked questioningly at Maya. The steps ended on her front porch. Someone pounded on the door.

Wilma opened it. Maya sat in the living room and listened. "What did you do with the dog?" a female voice asked in a huff.

Maya heard Wilma ask innocently, "What dog?"

The woman repeated the question. Wilma asked again, "What dog? What are you talking about?"

To this, the woman shrieked, "You're going to pay! Killers!"

Wilma then said, "Look, lady, calm down. If I can help you in some way . . ."

But the woman interrupted the offer of help, threatening Wilma with curses and vile names. Maya heard Wilma close the door.

Wilma returned to Maya. She looked calm, but Maya saw her hands shaking. "Did she frighten you? Who was she?" Maya asked.

"I don't know," Wilma said, "but it wasn't the woman who scared me. It was the man."

"The man?" Maya asked in surprise.

"Yes," Wilma said. "There was a man with her, standing behind her the whole time. He stood there in silence and made obscene gestures at me. His gyrations were so unnatural, not humanly possible. It scared the hell out of me!"

"You didn't show it, did you?" Maya asked in alarm. "Fear won't help us, Wilma."

"No, I don't think it showed. I was just so startled. But it was the damndest thing!" Wilma gulped her coffee. Maya put an arm around her friend. "Are you okay?" Maya asked. Wilma shuddered, but managed a smile.

"Listen, I'm going to have to leave. I hate to just walk away like this, I don't understand any of this," Maya said.

"It may be that walking away is the only way to respond," Wilma said, pursing her lips. "But I am convinced that you need to see Bicenti, now more than ever."

Maya nodded in complete agreement.

Footsteps were at the door again. Wilma looked at Maya and went to the door. "Killers!" the woman was screaming. "The state police are coming after you." Maya saw her lift a pudgy finger and stick it in Wilma's face. The woman was clownish in appearance, her face painted in brilliant hues. Maya stood behind Wilma.

There *was* a man with the woman. He was dark, possibly Hispanic or Indian. He bobbed up and down, as if there were springs in his legs and feet. He waved his arms imitating a grounded bird, and he contorted his face into grotesque masks that changed and flitted away as quickly as they settled over his features. Then his hands went to the crotch of his pants and he mimed an unearthly performance, contorting his body beyond the bounds of human ability. The woman with him blocking the doorway was unconcerned with his antics, she continued to shout obscenities at Wilma. They poured out in a torrent of stinging words.

Then Maya said to the woman, slowly and very clearly, "I don't know what's happening, or who you are—but you are not welcome here, and neither is anything that you bring with you." The words hung in the doorway for seconds.

The woman's eyes blinked surprise at Maya's words. For a moment, the woman's own stream of words stopped. She balanced her bulky weight on one foot. Her painted face became a frozen mask. The dark man behind the woman ceased his gyrations for a split second fracturing time and space after Maya spoke. He poised himself in the interlude, unnaturally immobile. The feat was startling. Maya was elated, felt a jab of tiny victory that her words had somehow paused his weird pantomime.

"Close the door," Maya said in Wilma's ear. Wilma pushed the door shut on the two figures. Outside, the woman again started her harangue, and then the din subsided. There were no sounds of departing footsteps. Only abrupt silence.

Wilma went to the window to observe the walkways and parking lot. "Nothing," she said in a low voice to Maya. "Nothing."

They gathered up Maya's things and prepared to go to Maya's car. Maya took out her keys from her pants pocket. They were ready to face whatever waited outside.

Before Maya opened the door, she said to Wilma, "Wait until I see if the car is going to start. Don't leave me until I know for sure. Then I'll wait until you're back inside before I drive away."

The streets were silent. None of the occupants of the dozen houses around them were visible. Wilma and Maya were completely alone. The orange rim of the sun was spreading up behind the mountains then.

"I'm sorry to have to leave like this," Wilma said. "But don't worry about me. I'll let Raoul take me to someone like Bicenti and learn something about this mess. I'll be all right. Now you just promise me that you'll see Bicenti as soon as possible. Promise."

Maya nodded and looked back toward Wilma's house. That dark

man who had been on Wilma's porch a few minutes earlier now stood on the walk. Maya's head went up sharply and she sucked in a deep breath. Wilma turned to see what had affected Maya this way. The man seemed suspended there on a background of cumulus clouds. He was detached from the earth and everything that Wilma and Maya knew. He began to bob, spring up and down, a jumping-jack. Again, his hands went to his pants crotch and Maya turned away. So did Wilma.

"Is it possible that I am cracking up?" Maya asked Wilma. Wilma smiled a caring and trusting smile. "If you are, I am too," she told Maya. "Look, Maya—don't mention this, *what's happened here*, to anyone. You know what I mean, other than the likes of Bicenti. Few people understand, have seen beyond . . ."

Maya looked again to where the dark man had been. He'd disappeared into Santa Fe's thin air. "Yeah," Maya said, "I know. I agree. Our people understand . . . this kind of fracture of space and time . . . But like you say, there's only a few who do. Don't worry, I won't say anything. Now you go inside as soon as the car starts." She unlocked the car, took her glasses from the glove compartment, and put the key in the ignition. The car started smoothly.

"Okay," Maya said to Wilma, "go on. I'll wait until you get inside." Wilma reached inside the car and hugged Maya, then she turned and retreated to the house.

Maya backed out of the parking lot slowly, noting that the curtains in a few houses were moving. She turned on the radio and set the dial on the Santa Fe station. The woman's voice had not abandoned the seductive tone. And it was now 7:05.

Wilma waited alone in her house all day, expecting something to happen but nothing did. About mid-morning, the neighbors showed some signs of life and activity. Cars cruised the streets.

Maya drove directly to Albuquerque, negotiating the tricky freeway traffic in time to make her 8:15 class at the university. But her mind played a reel of events that had happened to her recently; broken images of the dawning hours returned to her. By then, she was doubting her senses, asking herself if any of it had happened. In a university parking lot, she climbed out of her car, ambivalent about what she should do. She gathered her books from the car trunk and slammed it down hard. Then she went to put a quarter into the meter. Splotches of dried red blood on the car caught her eye. Suddenly her doubts vanished, her mind cleared. She set her jaw in determination, and she climbed back into the car. Bicenti was in Arizona, six hours away.

It was nearly four when Maya arrived home. Her family met her at the front door. "What's wrong, Mom?" one of her children asked. "You're not supposed to be home yet. Are you cutting class?" The boy laughed and then he noticed Maya's strained face. He asked, "Are you all right?"

"No," Maya answered. "Let's talk."


In Santa Fe, Raoul knocked on Wilma's door. Wilma let him in. He hugged her, his white even teeth showing in a wide smile. "How's my girl today?" he asked.

Wilma answered him, "Raoul, how would you like to take me for a long ride today?"

"How long?" Raoul questioned.

"To Cañoncito, thirty miles from Albuquerque," Wilma told him. "I'll make it worth your while," she said with a wink.

"Okay by me, but why are we going to Cañoncito?" Raoul inquired.

"I have to see a man there," Wilma said.

Raoul smiled and teased, "Won't I do?"

Wilma laughed, "Afraid not, lover boy. The man we're going to see finds things, tells you what's wrong. Know what I mean?"

Raoul nodded. He understood.


At dusk, Maya and her man were riding down a treacherous road that wound through sagebrush and piñon trees. The Chuska Mountains were dark green behind them and Black Mesa was ahead of them some forty miles distant. A cribbed log *hoghan* and a house were in sight at the end of the road. Sheep were penned in a nearby corral, and their bleating sailed through the evening's space and time.

Maya's man went into the house and not long after came to get Maya, waiting in the pickup truck. "Bicenti is in the hogan," he said. He opened the truck door. Maya followed him inside the dark hogan.

Maya's man greeted Bicenti who sat on a sheepskin that covered the earthen ground. They touched each other's hands, then Maya touched Bicenti's hand, and took a place on the sheepskin beside him. Through the smoke hole, Maya watched the pink sky fade. In time Maya told him everything. *Things weren't right,* she said intermittently while he sat and listened, not surprised at anything she said.

They left Bicenti's hogan over an hour later. The eastern sky was sprinkled with early stars and the world appeared as it should be. Bicenti would come to Maya's house the next night. He would quietly tell all. Then he would bind the tiniest fracture in infinite space and time. Then, he would go silently away, until the next time.

# DEBRA EARLING

## Jules Bart, Giving Too Much—August 1946 (1991)

*Sometimes transformative events come disguised as personal trauma, in cir-*
*cumstances where one must face one's truth. Unmasking the false person-*
*ality to reveal one's essential identity is one of the themes of Earling's story,*
*which is a form of trickster narrative. "Jules Bart, Giving Too Much—*
*August 1946" takes as its familiar theme the exploration of boundaries:*
*where they are located and how they pertain to issues of truth, falsehood,*
*honor, courage, and self-definition.*

*The borderlands of sexual identity directly address the largest issues of*
*our time; those hardy citizens of the crossroads, bisexuals and "closet"*
*homosexuals and lesbians, are in a state of perpetual liminality—much as*
*the Changer Coyote is portrayed as being. For it is on the threshold that the*
*most profoundly shaking, sacred events are likely to occur. Like the transi-*
*tional states of childbirth, near-death, puberty, and dying itself, sexual limi-*
*nality is heavy with danger and promise precisely because it is a border*
*state, the only state in which complete transformations can occur. "Jules*
*Bart, Giving Too Much—August 1946" asks us all to consider what we*
*would do when required to announce the truth of our hearts.*

I almost couldn't lift her from the water. She was so heavy and I thought to
myself I had to, that somehow it was all part of finishing the job, lifting
her up from the water, carrying her back to her mother. My legs were
shaking like my bones were bending and I said to myself a hundred times
while I was carrying her that she was only a young skinny girl. Hell, I've
lifted calves from drowning out of sucking mud and I never felt like they
were heavy enough to break me, to pull the muscles in my back tight as a

hoist tilting an engine. But she was heavy and unmoving. She was dead. And not in the way my mother was dead, like there was a measure of good peace. This girl was hard dead. She was a nightmare waiting to be dreamt. She was someone that just might be standing here by the river in the early morning dark of a good fishing day. And I thought to myself, even a lot of hard work, even a good many late hours in the barn dust couldn't chase the memory of her from me.

And I think it's funny when I'm in a room full of porch ranchers who are impressed by the fact that I'm a damn good cowboy, a cowboy who could rope a cow fart if I wanted, and I joke and laugh with them and they never know I get spooked by things. None of them know. I laugh with them at myself because of the crazy son of a bitch I really am when the cowboy hat comes off. Truth is, I once took a woman home with me and not because I wanted to rattle my balls. I had had a shit-the-bed nightmare three nights in a row and I was scared. And I'd never tell them, deny it on a long day until the dark comes and I'm walking home alone with a few beers in my belly like courage, my shoulders huddled up around my ears, my teeth chattering.

I've seen my face in the window, a reflection from a bare bulb, and I've jumped. I think that's why I get along well with horses. It never bothers me to hop a bronc that can butt my balls so far up my throat you'd think they were my Adam's apple. I can grab on. I can hold the fear to me like a good drink. But bad dreams make my muscles twitch. I know the meaning of spooked. I know how hard it is to let go of the day when you're living alone. I've seen a mean night come out of nowhere, a bad dream that stinks in your nostrils like a snort of cow shit. I've heard my dead mother calling from the other room on a calm night. And I have to breathe slow. Calm down. Light a smoke. I see things out of the corner of my eye and it scares the shit right out of me.

It's not always that way. Sometimes I go along for months not noticing the house settling or the sounds the barn animals make on a winter night. But just like some ornery horses are always looking around for a good scare, I guess I'm looking for a thrill. My mother used to say it was the sign of a restless heart always to be a little scared of things. "You're not telling the world what your heart's desire is," she would say. And deep down I know she was a little right and it embarrasses me. Still, I'm content to work hard and to sit out on my porch in the evening. Sometimes I pull my bed out there, out under the stars. A few nights back I counted seven falling stars. I wished on every one of them for a quick kiss and a good piece of ass. I had me a few smokes, wished that I played the guitar like Gene Autry.


I got drunk, shit-faced, ploughed, nozzled, stoned, tight, staggering, three-legged drunk not too long ago when I got a little jumpy. Some gal was telling me, Norma Lipscomb it was, that I was so drunk I unzipped my pants and pissed off the barstool. She said I was so drunk I tried to pick her up and that I showed her my dick. She said I promised to give her the meat from my best calf and that I said I would come chop all her wood and lay her right through the winter of next year. But I don't remember any of that. Don't remember saying a damn thing like that, think she was lying. Anyways I think when a man gets a little drunk he speaks the partial truth. And the truth is I'd never screw Norma Lipscomb not even if you paid me. The woman has tits she belts at the waist. She's got two mud moles with long whiskers on her chin. And besides that, you can see up her nostrils. I wouldn't dip water from her trough if I was dying a thirst. I wouldn't do a lot of things I thought. But when Antoine Pretty Chief asked me for a light under the neon red of the bar sign outside, something funny happened.

I stepped outside for some air and the summer night felt cool on my temples. I lit a cigarette and smelled small rain on the dry ground. A wind was coming up from the river and I leaned into it, feeling the cold alcohol in my blood swirling. Antoine Pretty Chief stepped from the shadows and I already knew he was close to me but I couldn't focus until he was standing in the light. I turned around and that son of a bitch was so pretty he took my breath. His hair was so black it looked glassy and his eyes were large and wet and he looked like he'd been crying.

"How the hell are you?" I asked.

I spun around a little too fast on my heels and fell on my ass. I sat there for a minute and it felt good to be sitting, to let the world stop spinning, when he reached over and easy pulled me up. I was so close to him I could smell his sweat and he was sweet as dry wood and I sniffed him. I couldn't stand on my own so he propped me up. He had shoulders like a good cowboy and I wanted to laugh because he's an Indian and I knew it wasn't funny. Funny to me drunk, I guess. I laughed anyway. He pulled me up close to him. He had a silver ring on his smallest finger, a ring that caught the light. His nails were white. I was trying to tell him something. Trying to tell him about being scared but I don't think I said a word to him, not a word he could recognize.

Hell, I was so drunk my heart was pounding through my shirt. And I feel sick now to remember I liked the son of a bitch. I liked his power like a horse. I had a hard-on the size of my gearshift but I wasn't sure why. He pulled me up by the waist and I could feel his cock behind me.

"You sick asshole," I said. "Get your hands off me. Get your goddamn hands off me." But he pulled me to the truck and hoisted me in. He didn't say anything. He didn't say a word. He fished in my pants for my keys and I made like I was trying to stop him. He just put me in my truck and drove me home. When we got to the house, he stopped the truck and set the brake. I could smell him. I wanted to get away. I wanted to go in the house. I looked up, feeling the alcohol again. My temples were ice and I looked out the window to the long path round back to the house. I tried to focus my thoughts on opening the door and standing on my own. A wind gust rocked the truck and I turned to him. I saw his neck. I could see his heartbeat in his throat. His heartbeat in his neck. His neck thick as a stallion's. There was a pale blue light. Blue light through his hair from the moon. Shit. I fumbled for the door. I was going to get my ass out of there. I could feel my balls swell. His teeth were so white they were blue as the moon in the darkness. I better get out of here, I kept thinking, but wanted to stay. And before I knew it he had his mouth at my fly and I wanted to kiss him. I wanted to kiss the son of a bitch. I wanted to strip buck-naked and feel his heavy muscles, his cock against my belly. And I never felt that way before, I swear to God. And I puked till there was nothing left in me, then I puked some more. But sometimes I find myself thinking about Antoine Pretty Chief. And I whisper to myself so I can deny it. I love him.

Now Louise comes along and I swear she's the most beautiful woman I've ever seen. I wanted her so many times but she's never noticed me. And the night her sister dies she comes home with me. A bad night for both of us. A hell of a night for me. I take her home and we sleep together. I hold her in my arms and squeeze her. She's so damn beautiful. She's got a mean wound on her left breast but she's tough. She's had a harder ride than most cowboys. I bury my whiskered face in her sweet tits. I've never had it so good. But then she wakes up crying in the middle of the night. And I think about her sister dead and gone. I think about myself alone. The night is strange and I cry too, but I don't let Louise know. In the night she can't see my face. I haven't cried since my own mother died and not so much even then. In the dark we smoke cigarettes. We talk about a lot of things, little things, nothing really, and I don't know what gets into me but I find myself flapping my gums to her about Pretty Chief. I tell her about me and Pretty Chief, what we've done. And it feels good to be talking in the dark, pulling on a smoke, good not to be alone. But in the morning comes gray and the rain stings and I've given myself away.

# ESTHER BELIN

## indigenous irony (1991)

*"indigenous irony" could also be called "so many borders to cross." In this ironic chronicle the all-too-contemporary dilemma of many young Native people is revealed. The narrator's awareness, torn by the conflicting strains of modern American Indian life, finds voice in biting commentary on the passing scene. In another time, or in this time but in another place, service in the United States has been seen as an honorable occupation for Native men. Perhaps they saw defense of the nation as a continuation of their ancient love for their land. A fine point perhaps, and one that escapes the awareness of this young urban Indian woman who, marginalized from her Navajo community, turns to radical thought for grounding.*

*Yet military service is a major current in the flow of Native life, as it has been since time immemorial. Military service and its consequences have informed much of Native fiction in the twentieth century. Belin's story is part of that tradition, adding a dimension to the war chronicles that has been muted or largely absent. Native writers who publish "war protest" work are generally women. Perhaps Indian antiwar writers thus signal their membership in the nationwide community of progressives, or perhaps their negative reaction to war echoes the protests of their grandmothers and granddaughters from time immemorial.*

*Whatever the case, Belin offers a perceptive and moving commentary on the recent American drama in the Persian Gulf. There the commanding officer, giving the troops the signal that Desert Storm had officially begun, thundered: "Heads Up! We're going into Indian Country!" Belin's story stands as a commentary on the irony of 13,500 Native men and women attached to the U.S. command on the borders of Kuwait who heard that announcement and obeyed.*

• • •

Didy Bahe never had to think about war as a reality. War was an experience shicheii almost went through and something shimasani's brother, Steven, had nightmares about. In 1988, Didy Bahe met an Apache man who was still living the Vietnam War in his sleep.

She always heard Indian men were overrepresented in the armed services and that they often enlisted. She also heard rez soldiers endured the rugged life of the military and were better than Anglo soldiers. Irony #1 (of many more to come). Didy Bahe (on her own) soon realized her survival was a similar irony. She speaks mostly of Navajo soldiers and what she's seen/read/heard—never experienced.

When the "Liberation of Kuwait" began, Didy Bahe was an unemployed/healthinsuranceblocked/nonregisteredstudentof UCBerkeley. The news reached her around four in the afternoon, but she still drove her friend to a haircutting appointment at 4:30. Perhaps out of anger. "I can stand it. Just see how I can stand it! Just see how I can stand taking Wilma BushyHead to get her hair cut during the war!" Or simply because she had previously scheduled-in assisting her friend with her appointment and she had definitely not scheduled-in a war. War. War. The word itself had no meaning to Didy Bahe. It was as if someone said "United States" or "Red, White and Blue" and expected a reaction from her.

When Didy Bahe was forced to think about war, only comical scenes from M*A*S*H flashed through her mind. The spicy juices of her mother's meatloaf set the scene for the Korean War that took place every weekday at six in the evening. She still enjoyed the show and still desired to secretly be Hawkeye, the surgeon who makes the war seem like a five-year-old's birthday party. Didy Bahe enjoyed her childhood and since M*A*S*H was part of it, she weirdly enjoyed war.

While maneuvering her black/hipNissan/dentedbyaman truck over the every-other-second-potholed Berkeley streets on the way to S.ka.p(long a)de Salon. Didy Bahe thought about her decision to drive Wilma to her appointment. The scheduling was definitely the reason. She did not need an (un)scheduled war to screw up her second-to-last semester in this institutionaljunglegym—especially when she'd just learned how to play by the *Big Man's* rules.

Yes, the scheduling was definitely it. Yes, she wanted everyone to see how she could stand driving her truck (fueled on Chevron gas) right after the war started. She wanted masses to guilt her into setting her truck on fire in effigy while shouting "No Blood for Oil!" (for the zillionth time). Yes, that was it. She knew the Anglo dude (aka Boogie Man) who sits in the ivory tower would be looking down at her smiling. His proudest moment. Didy Bahe was not only driving her bloodforoilfueled truck, but she was submitting herself to the ghostly/plasterfaced/depechemodefollower hairstylists for an hour as one clone stylist vogued Wilma out. Yes, the Anglo dude—just like the little man in the fridge who no one ever sees yet everyone knows exists—was proud. He won the war of institutional-genocide/assimilation/acculturation/annihilationofthesavagerace at least for now. Why should she jump up and burn cars in effigy if the white people around her at the time were carrying on business as usual?

Besides, Didy Bahe's generation of Indians was not concerned with a whiteman/pseudo"Americans"/equalityfornon-Indians,etal war. She was already fighting for her nation's sovereignty—she was shouting "Support Big Mountain! Give Back Mac $$! Justice for Navajo Nation!" She had no time for other brown people across the ocean . . . across the ocean. "Even though I'm across the ocean in another part of the world, I feel like I'm back home in the Navajo desert, except there are no mesas, sheep or frybread. . . ." Didy Bahe's cousin Eugene went on to describe the hot, sandy desert similar to where he grew up on the rez/ournation/land/BIA/DepartmentofInterior-givenhome.

She didn't know many things, but she definitely knew he shouldn't be there. Didy Bahe could see him surrounded by beige/perhapspink-colored/greenandbrowncamouflaged/dirty/scared men—men who would easily laugh at his rez accent and bowlegs. And Eugene—he'd smile long and slow like George Strait showing all of his shiny, white teeth—then chuckle fawn-like, as most rez Indians did. Eugene enlisted because Haskell Indian Junior College sucked. The faculty/materials/curriculum/mentality reflected its funders: the Bureau of Indian Affairs. When they said *educate*, they meant *assimilate*. When they had recruiters visit the campus, they meant *Army*, *Navy*, *Marines*, not *Princeton*, *Harvard*, *Yale*.

Eugene and all other Indians in the Persian Gulf were defending a country that they needed to be defended against. Didy Bahe heard some soldiers enlisted because they *believed* they were honoring the treaty obligations their tribal nation had made with the United States. Irony #10 to the fifth power. Didy Bahe wanted to scream, "Dope rez Indian! Can't you see what the Big Man is doing to Us? How can you be soooo stu-upid! The military is just another form of genocide. White people think we all died off in the 1800s—didn't you watch *Dances with Wolves*? Why contribute to that notion?" But Didy Bahe endures and prays. She hasn't walked their path. She hasn't had to pawn family jewelry for a sack of flour, potatoes, sugar, and a can of coffee. She doesn't cough up blood from breathing in yellow dust left from abandoned uranium mines used during WWII. No, she is one of *those* urban Indians who didn't have to go through reservation hardships. Didy Bahe's hardships are the same, but different. Irony—take a number.

In the salon, her hardship is listening to Chanel-painted clones argue equally about which Depeche Mode concert was the best and whether today was the best day to start a war. Didy Bahe doesn't say anything because she's brown and used to being silent. So she gets comfortable in the black leather chair and tries to modern-rock out to Depeche Mode while telling a blatant lie. "I thought 'Music for the Masses' was the best tour." Her life is an irony and irony is survival and survival is the most ironic resistance of them all.

# MICHELLE T. CLINTON

## Humiliation of the Boy (1991)

*"Humiliation of the Boy" is an autobiographical work of fiction, related to a major form of Native narrative—not only in its origin but in the bleakness and horror inflicted upon a child that it tells. In its basic theme, it resembles a number of Native stories published in this century. The story in this volume it most closely resembles is "Tony's Story," where hatred and violence breed their mirror image, one of the possible transformations that can occur when a person is forced to cross a threshold not meant to be crossed.*

*With unflinching attention to detail Clinton builds a narrative so full of pain it becomes almost unbearable. In her story she reflects the truth of human anguish, filling in the personal spaces that history leaves blank. "Humiliation of the Boy" requires us to face fully the consequences of neglect, abuse, racism, elitism, and the social devastation that ensues from neglect of the sacred, consequences suggested in "Indians and Ecstasy" and addressed in "indigenous irony."*

*Not all fiction written by Native writers has Native characters, just as not all Native people have bronze skin. Few wear buckskin and feathers; few ever did. Quite a few stories written by Native authors are concerned with people who live outside of Indian Country—as are Martin Cruz Smith's detective trilogy set in Russia, D'Arcy McNickle's stories about generic Americans in New York and London, and John Rollin Ridge's novel about a Mexican "Robin Hood," Joaquin Murietta. After all, it is the authorship, rather than the subject, that defines a work as Japanese, German, French, English, or Nigerian. Similarly, what defines a work as Native American Indian is the community of reference, blood, and upbringing from which the writer comes.*

•   •   •

It started with his teeth: huge, buck, dinosaur teeth that kept his lips chapped and his mouth wet because he couldn't close it. Strange for a skinny boy like that to have such big bones coming out of his face. They broke the skin at the right time for any child; in the days after the tooth fairy's coin changed into chocolate or snow cones, the tips of his front teeth broke the gums at the wrong angle, he was sure. Even in the beginning, they cut out at his front lips, as if his own bones hated him and always intended to make him hurt.

"Is this right, Mommy?" he asked. "This can't be right. Is my mouth going to be okay?"

"Honey, it's fine," she told him, "or your father will take you to the dentist and buy you braces. Really, don't worry about it, you'll be fine."

But the father evaporated in a silence that swept his mother into numbness, his sister into tears. One day a daddy, who ate more meat than anyone, always brooding and magnificent, with his fuzzy ties and mustache, and the next day no one. The next day empty shot glasses on the coffee table in front of his mother, the next day his younger sister hiding her crying in a locked bathroom. So he kept quiet and tried to close his mouth. (If he ignored the sharp pain and occasional dabs of blood, he could stretch his lip over the uneven edge of his teeth, and sometimes press his lips together.) No one mentioned the dentist ever again. The mixed promise of novocaine shots and pliers, the magic braces that would bend him into a proper shape, gone disappeared, leaving behind a cruelty that ate his mouth with laughter and hate.

Beaver. Buck tooth beaver. The boy's blue eyes never made up for it. He always hoped they would; he prayed the girls would see his blue eyes first and be blinded by racial preference, the flushed european color that gleamed like metal and marked him as mixed. It started in his body, cruel, fermenting, planted by the father inside the meat of his mother, the slimy birth of a light-skinned negro, speckled by unexplained color, a twist in the genes accented with animal teeth and slobber he couldn't control. Snot mouth snaggle tooth buck face beaver with no detectable signs of africa and blue eyes that forced him to pass for white.

He grew but he couldn't gain weight: his arms long and muscle-less, his toes fingerlike and monkeyish, the ridge at the top of his hip visible. Everything monstrous, everything ugly lived and commanded his life from all over his body, from inside himself.

You might think all this scorn would gather in the boy, like the dead white cells of an infected pimple, all the meanness thrown at him would collect in inner clumps and poison his shyness. Like some dogs, if you beat them long enough. Dobermans turn their teeth on you, abused german shepherds eventually get foulmouthed and bite. Ordinary logic assumes the boy might take to twirling the twitching bodies of flies over a yellow match, or watching salt sizzle the nervous system of unlucky snails. I could tell you the boy took to catching cats, pulling their legs off and staring at the meaty mess of their insides, and all this would make sense.

But no. Instead he collected and memorized facts. He learned the life cycles of insects, the origin of political theories, the behavioral practices of primates. He taught himself chess. (Black queen pawn opening was his favorite move.) He knew the webbing patterns of matriarchal arachnids, the territorial conflicts of the navaho, the hunting techniques of wolves. The cool and empty public library of Compton, brilliant and white-hot those unyielding summers, or soggy in september after school and on saturdays, her indifferent texts, her self-conscious librarians, her giant crowded bookcases, became the perfect place for this boy to hide.

Plus, he could always talk to his sister. She didn't know he was a nerd, she was so small. She was kept in a far part of the playground with the little kids, she never heard the new, animal descriptions of his chapped mouth, his bony body. She never saw the punches absorbed by his stomach, his back to the asphalt; she didn't see the spit thrown at his math book, his shoes, his hands.

He told her things. Too fidgety to learn chess really, but she liked him, she liked the special words, scientific nomenclature, about hairy mammals, the only ones with titties, the dolphins and whales who swam.

"I have to tell you something about communism," he told her. "Do you know what that is?"

"No," she said, twisting the ends of her braids, "but I know it's bad. Bad men made it up, I know that."

He frowned and sucked the sides of his mouth to let her know she didn't have a clue. "The word 'communism' comes from the word 'common,' like to have things in common, like you and me, we have Daddy and Mommy in common, we share that."

She squinted, which she did when she was lost, when he got too complicated. He went on, "Pretend there's a bunch of people. Say like you have a baker, someone who bakes bread and someone who makes shoes, and a chair maker. Say the baker makes some bread and the shoemaker makes three special pairs of shoes and the chair maker makes three chairs. Then everybody shares. The baker gets chairs and shoes and everybody has bread to eat. That's communism."

"Oh," she said, her eyes relaxing, "that sounds okay."

"Of course, that's not the whole story," he told her. "Everybody has different ideas about everything."

"What else," she said.

"The capitalists, that's us, the guys with the capital and capital means money. The capitalists say the communists want to take all the stuff from the rich, stuff they earned in a free marketplace, and give it to people who don't work."

"But sharing is better," she said.

"I know," he told her, "I know, it confuses me too." And he relaxed because someone else was finally lost with him. "That's part of being intelligent. Listening to all sides and worrying about the truth."

But in school, after the bell rang and he sat at his desk, his shoulders hunched up to meet his ears, his back and neck slumped down, and his love of learning was muted. And when forced to speak, he slurped his words and stammered. Pretty funny, his classmates figured whenever he talked, he was a cartoon stuttering, buck tooth mixed breed, his lips juicy and cracked, the class dweeb, the black nerd, not only ugly but stupid too. Busy, lazy teachers learned to avoid the fuss and overlook him. Another nobody, if you left him to himself, he made no trouble, another unimportant, mediocre child, shuffled forward every year to the next grade.

Every year the visiting school dentist would mark the green card with a red felt tip marker: THIS BOY HAS CAVITIES, THIS BOY NEEDS FILLINGS, BRACES, A RETAINER, THIS BOY NEEDS HELP. Holding the card made him dizzy, his stomach rock-hard with a pain the size of a balled-up fist, his head empty of emotion. He never cried. He was a man. The man of the house, like his mother told him, and he knew already the man of the house swallowed things he could do nothing about. Besides, if he showed his mother the dentist's card, she would be the one crying, she would drink and curse and remind him of his father's sin. All the ways he was just like the bastard, all the ways he was no good and had betrayed her.

So by junior high, he knew what to do with the green dentist card. He understood to get an ink pen, practice her writing, and fill in the line marked guardian's signature with a gentle, practical lie.

High school blurred into him, with faster and harsher crowds, the girls in lipstick and popping breasts, the senior boys with thin moustaches and thick chests made a messy force that spun around him. More subjects, more teachers to avoid, more waiting. He stood in line.

He began to forget things. Which room number, the combination to his locker, which book for which class, a pencil for algebra, an ink pen for english, he was late all the time.

"Three tardies and you're out of here," second semester chemistry teacher said straight out. "I don't put up with lazy students," he said as he paced the room and glared through his students. "I don't waste my time with losers," he said slow and loud while pacing, while searching through the faces in the last row, and zeroed in on the boy.

"This is an advanced science course. This involves serious work. I don't care about your problems. I am happy to fail all of you." The chem teacher's white skin gleamed with authority, his thin hair lay parted, greased, and flat. His eyebrows arched in indifference, his upper lip was straight and emotionless as a minus sign. There was plenty of gossip about him: give him a moustache, a green suit, and he'd be a perfect match for hitler.

He liked to weed out the weak ones, the nobodies, students with thin imaginations and watery memories. He declared death by anonymity for average students. He liked to clear space for winners, the ones who had the right kind of guts, the ones who would dominate and succeed. He stopped talking and stood silent, his elbows straight, his hands against his desk.

"Below is your chem locker. On your desk is the key to your locker. This key is as important to you as your name. Because inside the locker is very expensive laboratory equipment. You are lucky to have this equipment. Most inner city schools don't even offer chemistry lab. If you lose this key or break any of this equipment, your parents will be responsible for the cost. And if your parents can't pay, if you lose this key and somebody takes it and steals your equipment," he pushed his face toward the class and stressed every word, "I will have you expelled from this school." The chemistry teacher let a sharp, silent fear possess his students.

Between the fingers of the boy, the key felt cold and dead. He blinked at it and swallowed the saliva in the sides of his cheeks. He'd never had a key before, not even to his mother's apartment. Where would he keep it? In his pocket, his shoe, his mouth?

"Take your key now and try it in the lock of your locker," the teacher said, and passed out a paper with a name and number for each of the beakers and clamps and thin rubber hoses in the locker. The boy had to inspect each thing, list each one on a piece of paper that he then had to sign, a paper that said he intended to respect the equipment as the valuable property of the L.A. Unified School District. That he (or his guardian) would be financially responsible for loss, theft, or damage due to improper use or carelessness. The boy signed the paper in stiff, dark lines of ink, with hard black strokes that seemed to come out of his stomach. Then he lined up all the glass and metal from inside his locker, logged them and stared at all the letters and numbers enameled on the faces of the beakers.

Clear and vulnerable, all lined up from smallest to biggest, the beakers stood breathless and straight. His own. They held water and measured things. They had no expression, no opinion, no faces to make, no stingers to use. He promised to never lose the key. He promised to memorize and execute proper cleaning procedure, to always restore them to their steady beauty, he promised to polish each piece twice.

One piece at a time, he packed them back into his locker, so that no glass edge touched another (this would make scratches). He stacked the metal clamps and put away the Rosebud matchbox into the small drawer inside his locker. He looked out the window and waited for the bell to ring.

After the classroom cleared out, and the teacher's back was turned, the boy put the key in the ankle of his left shoe (he was left-handed), double-checked the subject, room number, and floor of his next class, panicked and rushed out the room.

The chem teacher rose from his seat and walked immediately over to the boy's locker and checked it. The door stood slightly ajar and fully open to whatever, unlocked, uncared for. He knew it, as soon as he'd spotted the boy slumping in the back row. Predictable. He knew a weakling when he saw one. They always proved themselves losers by the end of the term anyway. Good now as later, he thought, as he packed all the equipment from inside the boy's locker into a cardboard box and carried the box of equipment and set it behind his own desk.

The television was on, that night at home, his sister wasn't around, his mother had just started drinking. The hot dog dinner swam in glossy water, the baked beans crusted over. He ate, left his plate on the kitchen table, went into the living room, and started to take off his shoes.

"What's that?" his mother sneered, pointing to the other side of the room. Five pillowcases stuffed with dirty clothes were stacked and ready. The boy said nothing. "I want you to go out and find your god damn sister and wash these damn clothes."

"I don't know where she is," he said, adding a high tone to his words to distract her.

"She's probably in the streets. Playing," she said, "probably doing something nasty with those common boys. You find her. You're her brother. Why aren't you taking care of her?"

His sister was in the back room, her usual after-school spot, reading (hiding, the boy knew, hiding and waiting for him to come home). Together they loaded the hand shopping cart up with laundry and walked through the blue night air, past the wino corners, past the boarded-up shops and churches, toward the closest washhouse, a short eight blocks away. He counted them, secretly, and just kept talking. He told her about the metric system, the liters and centimeters. He told her about the chemistry key, the chemistry locker, his new responsibilities.

"Always divisible by ten. So you can get as big or small as you like. Very practical," he explained. "Inches and pounds don't work like that, so people are likely to mess up."

"Oh," she answered, her eyes following the cracks in the sidewalk. She wouldn't look up. She wouldn't smile at him, so he knew she was the most scared.

Inside the laundry room, two winos took quiet swigs out a paper bag, three large women cursed and laughed, while messes of small children ran circles around the washers. Most of the washers worked, but half the dryers were broken, so there were people waiting, mostly women with tight jaws and plain-faced adolescent girls, their stacks of wet clothes piled in laundry carts, on washers, cold and damp.

The brother and sister sat on separate washers, waiting like the rest, the girl mindlessly thumping her legs against the machine. The boy stared at the floor of the washhouse and tried to leave his body, but a smell, fermenting urine and vomit, began its slow assault on his nose. His eyes traced the shapes of stains, dark globs patched over the concrete, some of it was probably just old gum, some of it sticky pop somebody spilled, or oil tracked in from the street. He found the stinking mess, half-digested bits of something slimy, not quite dry, over by the winos, around their shoes. The paper bag was wet too, like the hands of the drinkers; he watched the two men lift the bag high and then toast or curse everything.

"Fuck this miserable ass place," the smaller one said.

"Yeah," said the other, "fuck this god damn misery." And then they'd drink and pass the bag and drink again.

Everything to think about was in front of him, stinking and waiting. His sister slouched and chewed her nails. He wished he was smaller, small enough to chase his sister around the loud washers, or big enough to not be there at all. He fingered the coins inside his pocket and wondered if the quarters and dimes would stretch far enough, maybe the dryers wouldn't work like last time and they would have to take the sheets home wet.

When one washer opened up, the boy and his sister started with the dark clothes, and then two more, the sheets and towels. When five were spinning, his sister laid her open palm on the front of one of the dryers to check if it was working. Dryer okay, so they carried armloads of clothes, careful not to drop them on the stained floor, to the opposite side of the washhouse, and stuffed the hot dryer full.

By the time the heavy dark clothes were dry, the washhouse had emptied of smaller children, the gruff heavy women had finished their work and left. The two wine drinkers slouched over, quiet, probably asleep. The brightness cast by the fluorescent lights blurred into shadows with no shapes, no edges. All the washers had stopped and the dryers rocked and hummed inside the washhouse. Alone with his sister, the boy felt the muscles in his neck soften. Sitting on the washer, he gently bumped his heels against the white metal, like younger children do.

With the commotion slowed down, he felt something pressing on his back. His feet stopped bumping. He felt his neck go rigid again, his breath tight.

"What you doing in here white boy," somebody said, words from behind him, from the back door of the washhouse, the heat spilling into the hum of the dryers. The boy could not get his head to turn. His body, hard like concrete, wanted to blend into the warm surface of the washer.

"Punk," a different voice said. "White faggot ass. What you doing."

"White mother fucker must not be able to talk," another said, and then they were around him, two coming from each side, four boys, almost men, bulky in the shoulders and thighs, their jeans the color of grease, with hard creased cuffs.

"We talking to you, buck tooth honkey."

And the boy finally looked into them, their shadowless faces, any humanness blasted out by the stark light, the harshness lining their mouths, all their eyes poised and aimed like weapons at his mouth.

"I'm black." He almost said "man," but he knew he was not a man, never could be a man. He was a sissy, a punk. He made himself smaller, pulled his front lip over his teeth and swallowed. "I'm just a ordinary nigguh, just like you," he stammered.

"White boy called me a nigguh, man," the smallest one said and snatched the boy's shoulder, pulling him off the dryer. The boy stumbled, broke his fall with his elbow.

"Get up faggot," he heard through his back, but he stayed there. He could crawl, he could disintegrate into pieces and leave his blue eyes, leave his slimy buck teeth broken on the floor.

He watched their shoes as they surrounded him.

"We should stomp the shit out your ass."

"Get up mother fucker," and one grabbed his arm and jerked him, dragging him over to the dryers. Then hands were on his ankles, his feet left the floor, his head, empty of will, went through the open door of the dryer. The four boys tried to push his feet into the dryer but he kept his legs rigid so the door wouldn't close.

"This is for what you done to our people," the smallest said. "Who got a dime?"

"I ain't wasting no money drying out a white boy," the biggest one said. "Let's get the fuck out of here." And they were gone, the warmth of the dryer soaking into his mind.

He could not find his body. He could not find thought or a reason to move. Then some life force that he could not wish away pulled him out of the dryer, forced him to face the numb eyes of his sister, the piles of soggy clothes, and the walk, the pounding of his feet against the city sidewalk, the slow walk back to the home of his mother.

Late. He knew he was separating from himself when he could not say, inside the quiet of his own mind, why was he always late. Chemistry was going to be his new god, his secret of purified knowledge, and here he was, second day, fumbling, stumbling, shoelaces dragging, last into class and late.

He expected to get dressed down, from the chem teacher's opening just the day before, but instead, he slipped in the back door, slid into his chair, stacked his books and joined class like nothing happened. Just the teacher passing out textbooks and everybody fidgeting. These perfect moments of aloneness, when no one had the presence of mind to notice him, were what he loved about school. Then he remembered the locker, the precious glass and metal magic things that would teach him, extend a new intelligence into him, and the key. His first key. He pulled it out the top of his sock and held it closed inside his fist, tight enough to almost cut him. The key to chemistry, the key to knowledge, the key to secrets he could keep from everybody, his own.

The tip of the key fit into the lock and tumbled the lock mechanism with no trouble at all. But inside the locker was nothing. His breath cut short. It was true: nothing. A panic, blood-rich and angry as knives broke open his chest, shot up into his throat and fell into his palms. He checked the number on the key against the number on the locker. He checked the seat. He heard himself think "please god" and open the locker again.

"Is there a problem?" The chem teacher stood over him and the class was doubled over, choking with laughter.

All red flushed into his face, no words, no ideas as defense.

"See this student," the teacher said. "He is an example of what will never survive in this world." He looked down at the boy.

"I can't kick you out today, but I want you to know I'm on to you. I know you are lazy, I know you have no respect for this school system. I can tell, just from your face, that you will flunk out of this class, just like you will fail at living."

The boy's head held tight, poised and balanced on an emptied body. The black line around everything blurred. Sound became speckled bits of color; color twisted like hot noise. He felt his head falling backward, slamming onto desks, floors, dryers, but he knew that, really, in this reality, his head was stuck. He couldn't go anywhere. Not with his mouth like this. Not with the spittle about to drip down. Not with the white punk inside him, making him late, exposing his core to the scorn and laughter of other people that would not stop.

"I want you to know and remember I'm on to you and I'm going to watch you. I'm going to watch you fail." And the chem teacher went back to the front of the class and went on with his introduction to the chemistry textbook.

Time was controlled by the jerking black tipped hands of the clock. Time was really his only problem, he knew that, all he had to do was make it through, through class, through the halls, through p.e., through all time and matter because this body and everything were fakes. Master design fakes as fake as the promise of braces and the father in his memory. Time was the only challenge except to not be drawn in and slaughtered by reality.

He willed himself out of the slight tremor in his hands and found the place behind the eyes where the waiting was easiest. Faces flattened. All color a smudge with no depth. Only the black tips of the clock hands held the power to affect him.

Then the bell cracked into the classroom and released him. He sat and waited for a clear room, locked and relocked his locker fourteen times (just in case), stacked his books, and rushed out.

Through the crowded hall, into history class and health science, everything seemed different. Behind his eyes he watched smeared faces overlook him. He forgot his pen, he forgot which seat he had been assigned, he brought the wrong book to class, but no one noticed. He experimented with stillness and the smallest breath he could live on, addicted to the jerking of the clock.

The final bell, a double bell for the end of the school day, opened reality out into the hallway again, with the threat of the remembering and forgetting. He counted his books ten times, double knotted his shoelaces eight times, drank from every water fountain between his last class and his main locker, thought maybe he should count his footsteps between places, so he could not possibly get lost.

How many steps home, how many stairs down from the second floor to the first, how many even steps, each with the exact stride and placement as the first, from crosswalk to streetlight. Six streetlights, eleven blocks, he could keep track the way he predicted the aggression of a knight in his chess games, always one step down at the corners, one step up back onto the sidewalk.

When he opened the living room door, the only door, the right door into his mother's house, a thick and sour sheet of air pushed into his face. Dirty dishes stink and a mother sleeping on the couch. He crept past her, aiming for the back room he shared with his sister. Sitting cross-legged on his bed, her back to him, his sister had taken out the chess pieces. She had them in mix match colored stacks, laid out like wounded army soldiers, out of order, out of rank.

"This one's the queen, isn't it?," she turned to him, her voice light and shrill. "I could learn to play if I could be the queen and have knights of my own."

Tension in his knuckles crunched his hands down into claws, then fists. "Who said you could touch my things," his voice whined out in a thin hostile line that was aimed right at her. Hatred in his hands curled into fists. She was so small, so stupid, always everywhere, following him, bugging him. He could see the scratches on his pawns, she'd ruin everything if he let her. "I hate you," he said, "I hate you for messing up everything," his voice shrinking into one last quiet curse. "Fucking bitch," he said and turned away from her, turned to face the dense smell in the living room.

He dropped into the living room chair and watched his mother breathe. The small opening in her mouth, the beat in her neck, the moisture at the corners of her eyes. He could not see her teeth, he could not count them. He knew then what he had to do: count his teeth, count the cavities, count the ones that grew in straight and remember the number of those that grew in crooked.

He could feel something. He could remember. He could remember a feeling that meant more than time, more than counting, something he would never tell his mother or sister, a heat that always forced him to keep living. His stomach exploded with a desire to throw up. He swallowed down, he pushed down onto the new thing that he knew he would have to keep silent and numbered forever, the hate that started in his mouth, moved deliberately onto his skin, and spread out onto all faces. He knew his mouth would never open to let the thing out.

# LOUISE ERDRICH

## Lipsha's Luck (1992)

*One of the interesting phenomena in contemporary Indian country is the rise of the bingo parlor. Bingo, poker, roulette, electronic slot machines and other Western forms of gambling are recent features of Native life and culture, but gambling itself is as old as the nations and their languages. The oral tradition of most First Nations is replete with stories about the Gambler, a mysterious figure who often deals in corpses, or who casts bones, sticks, or riddles with some hero for the liberation of locals he holds captive.*

*Gambler stories share certain elements with stories from other narrative cycles. These narrative relatives include the trickster stories, specifically stories about a male deity, often the Sun or Moon, who denies his children until they trick him into acknowledging his paternity, and abduction narratives. In gambler stories what is at stake is often the freedom of captives Gambler has taken.*

*"Lipsha's Luck," an excerpt from Erdrich's novel* The Bingo Palace, *draws on the northern variants of the Gambler cycle. In twists on the tradition, Lipsha is taken captive, while the old man, who in many respects—his dwelling, obscurity, size—resembles the Gambler, becomes the hero who frees him. The sense of danger and conflict between worlds, the idea of great mobility, the sexual undercurrent of the story, and above all the sense of magic and mystery that permeates it are elements of traditional gambler narratives. These traditional elements are intertwined with features of contemporary Chippewa life in the northern Midwest, elegantly merged by way of the bingo parlor, the van, Lipsha Morrissey, and the determining presence and voice of the elder women.*

*Traditionally, at least as far as second wave Native fiction is concerned, the figure of the grandmother has signified the old tradition and cultural transmission. Grandmother was generally used to mean "that which means traditional native ways." In many respects Erdrich conforms to second wave conventions, but puts her inimitable, third wave twist upon it: Grandma Lulu, an often-married women and mother of many sons like the sacred ancestress of the Chippewa. Lulu teaches her luckless grandson how to win at gambling. She is a good mentor and model because she wins big.*

*Another significant female persona is the determining, rather than merely influencing, presence of the Auntie, a central character in many First Nations oral traditions. Auntie or aunties appear in some of the fiction by Native women (but they are not as prominent as lineal ancestresses, in accordance with patriarchal norms for women with authority over men). Yet traditionally, for many, First Nations aunties are of greater significance than mothers or grandmothers, as Aunt Zelda proves to be in "Lipsha's Luck." There is a further twist on the tradition implicit here: The Gambler is usually a male figure, but here the Gambler is female, sly, cunning, vital, and tricky; a coyote-gambler character who appears in female guise as Lulu Lamartine, and as Lipsha's long-dead mother, June, both women who approach Luck in a purely businesslike manner.*

When I think of all of the uncertainties to follow, the collisions with truth and disaster, I want to dive, to touch and lift that broad feather. I want to go back in time and spin the Firebird around, screeching with a movie flourish, to zoom back into the story, separate the pipe, swallow that one lone seed. And yet, as there is no retreating from the moment, the only art left to me is understanding how I can accept the consequence. For the backwardness, the wrongness, the brush of heaven to the ground in dust, is a part of our human nature. Especially mine, it appears.

As I sit with Shawnee Ray in that blinding room, waiting for the police to drive up wailing their sirens, I talk fast. I am trying to edge out the one idea I do not want Shawnee Ray to pursue.

"Just picture the lab analysis when it comes back," I try to joke. "Raisins, dried buffalo meat, *pukkons*, suet, prunes, tire rubber . . ."

She doesn't answer. Her head stays bowed.

"You're thinking," I venture.

She just sighs, gets up, and walks over to the phone.

It only takes Lyman Lamartine a half hour to respond to the call that ricochets from Shawnee to Zelda and probably on all through the tribal partyline wire. He drives into the border station yard with a powerful crackle of his studded snow tires. I can't help but hope he might slide through to Canada, but Lyman never slips off course. Each tiny silver nail bites ice. Standing at the window, both Shawnee Ray and I watch as he confers with the guard, using soothing hand gestures, shaking his head, smiling briefly, and then examining with zealous eyes the pipe offered to him, holding forth then, explaining tradition with a simple courtesy I wish that I could imitate. He wears a tie and silver-bowed eyeglasses. His hair is long, but cut in a careful shag that brushes the collar of his overcoat. After a while, the conversation seems to take on a friendlier overtone, for the guard nods his head once, and then straightens with an air of discovery.

"Zelda must have called him," says Shawnee Ray. Her face, in its frame of harsh feathers, is flushed and anxious. I am going to ask her just how I should conduct myself in this unusual situation, what to say, whether she can give me any clues, when Lyman and the guard come inside.

Shawnee doesn't turn to greet Lyman, her stare just widens as she continues to gaze out the window, seemingly struck by the view of parking lot asphalt and dark-night snowy earth. I am at such a loss that I act completely normal, and walk over to Lyman to talk to him, far enough away so she will not hear our conversation. There aren't enough words on the reservation for our line of kin anymore. It's less confusing to decide on one thing to call them and leave out the tangles.

"Hello, my uncle," I say, once the guard has busied himself with a phone call and paperwork. "It's decent of you to show up and get this straightened out, so I just want to say thanks, and to assure you that Shawnee Ray had nothing to do with the mess."

"I never dreamed she did."

"And, see, you were right."

Lyman still holds the pipe carefully in his two hands. Weighing it, he slowly disconnects the bowl and stem. I reach to take them, but he keeps turning the pieces around and around in his hands as though they were magnetized. The stem is long as my arm, double barreled, one of a kind. It is quilled the old way, and the bowl is carved by some expert long forgot, the red stone traded from South Dakota.

"I'll give you three hundred," he says.

I don't register his meaning at first. I stand still, waiting for him to finish his inspection. Passed to Nector from his old man, Resounding Sky, that pipe is that very same one smoked when the treaty was drawn with the U.S. government. So there are some who say that it was badly used and has to be reblessed, and it is, I don't argue, a pipe that capped off the making of a big fat mistake. This is the same pipe refused by Pillagers who would not give away our land, the same one that solemnized the naming ceremony of a visiting United States president's wife, but it is also the pipe that started the ten-summer sundance. It is a kind of public relations pipe, yet with historical weight. Personal too. This pipe is my inheritance from Nector. I feel his love dishonored by the rude treatment it received from the guard, on my account. Standing there regarding it, guilty, I wait for the sky to drop. I wait for the earth to split, for something to go terribly wrong, but the only thing that happens is I take a job.

"I suppose," says Lyman, putting the pipe reluctantly back into my hands, "you don't have a place to keep this museum piece."

"I'm kind of between places," I acknowledge. "I had the pipe stowed in a little suitcase in my car trunk."

Lyman drops his chin low and looks up at me from under his brows. "You working?"

"I'm between jobs, too."

"Maybe," says Lyman, his teeth showing a little, "you could work for me again. Close by. Where I could keep an eye on you."

So I am hired to rise early and clean out the bingo hall. Once in a while, I substitute bartend too. My place of employment is an all-purpose warehouse containing an area for gambling that Lyman hopes to enlarge, a bingo floor that converts to a dance area, and a bar, and there are even a few older makes of video games blinking dimly against one wall. At five each morning I roll from bed in a room behind the bar, fill a bucket with hot water, add a splash of pink soap, wring out my mop, and set to work. After I swab the linoleum, I sling my rag across the seats and counters. I wash down the walls where people stagger, reach their hands out to break their fall, hands they've used to fix cars, calm horses, tie steel in the new interstate highway, hands that have slipped low with the oil of popcorn. Hands that are blood-related to my own hands, knuckle and bone.


From outside, my place of work is a factorylike Quonset hut—aqua and black—one big half-cylinder of false hope that sits off the highway between here and Hoopdance. By day, the place looks shabby and raw—a rutted dirt parking lot bounds the rippled tin walls. Bare and glittering with broken glass, the wide expanse is pocked by deep holes. The Pabst sign hangs crooked and the flat wooden door sags as if it was shoved shut in too many faces, against hard fists. But you can't see dents in the walls or rips or litter once darkness falls. Then, because the palace is decked with bands of Christmas tree lights and traveling neon disks that wink and flicker, it comes at you across the flat dim land like a Disney setup, like a circus show, a spaceship, a constellation that's collapsed.

Inside it's always sour twilight. The atmosphere is dense and low, as if a storm is on the wind. You don't walk through the door, it's more like you're swallowed, like God's servant who the fish gulped down. Steel ribs arch overhead and the floor is damp. I can't get it dry even with a fan. The booths are covered in a thick plastic torn and carved in old patterns, glued back together in raised scars where I've fixed them with Vinyl-repair. But nobody notices how it looks after nine o'clock.

On one side, the bar is fixed so all the bottles are backed by mirrors and the bartender can see the customers even when his hands are busy with the pumps. The popcorn machine is at the end of the counter, and it's the best lighted spot in the house. The bulbs in the hood flood golden radiance down on four or five barstools where women gravitate. They know how the light makes their eyes soft and dark, how the salt and butter clings to them, gets into their clothes, and mixes with sweat, cologne, and Salem smoke to produce a smell that is almost a substance, a kind of magic food that leaves a man emptier and hungrier after one whiff.

The bingo palace drives itself through wet nights according to these hungers. Except for the bright glow of the glass case of yellow popcorn, and the stage, bathed in purple, the great low room is a murk that hazes over and warms. Lovers in the booths or the unmatched dinette sets wrap their arms and legs together and send charged looks through rings of smoke. Smoke hangs low like a heavy cloud, collects at one level, shifts and bobs above the heads of the players and dancers. Smoke deepens, poised calm as a lake, over the tables.

People come and go underneath the cloud. Some to the bar, some to the bingo. There are the road workers, in construction, slab muscled and riding temporary money, new pickups with expensive options and air-brushed curlicues on the doors. Local businessmen with French names and Cree blood, guys with green eyes and black hair, talk in the quieter corners, making deals with flat hand gestures. Farmers visit—a Scandinavian family group or two—always quiet and half asleep and worked raw. When the men take off their Grain Belt or John Deere hats, the upper halves of their pale foreheads float and bob in the dark as they nod and talk.

Indian men, old ones with slicked-back gray hair, black-framed Indian Health Service glasses, and spotless white shirts of western cut and pearl snaps, sit straight up at the tables. Although they speak in low, soft voices, you can hear everything they say through the din. Within their company, there's sometimes a woman in a flowered pantsuit, hair swept into a bead rosette. She sips her beer, nods, adds a word at the right moment, and through the force of her quiet, runs the entire show.

Near the radiant circle at the popcorn machine, against the Lally poles, around the back entrance, lounge the younger Indian guys. Without seeming to notice the eyes that turn on them, or don't—and I know because I'm usually attempting to be one of them—these guys strut like prairie grouse. Some wear straw Stetsons with side or front medallions of pheasant feathers, and some wear mesh CAT hats, black and gold, with beaded brims. A few have long ponytails that flood to their waist, or thick loose hair they toss back over their shoulders. Some leave on their dark glasses, even inside. Some wear rude-colored western shirts, or fancy ones with roses and briars and embroideries of rising suns. Heavy-metal leather, surfer shirts, glow-in-the-dark rings around a few necks. Anything to make a girl look. There are tall men already with hard, belligerent paunches and slender boys with mysterious, clear faces and sly ways with their hands. But all of us, every one, wear boots and jeans within which our hips move, proud, with lazy joy, smooth as if oiled with warm crankcase or the same butter that the women at the bar lick off their fingers and smear on the men's hands when they dance—or go elsewhere. For the large unlit parking lot behind the palace is full of empty-looking cars that shudder, rock on their springs, or moan and sigh as the night wears on.

Now, you say, what about that truth and disaster I mentioned? It starts here at the bingo palace, with one of those ladies I just told you about who runs things by sitting quiet in the middle of the room. Aunt Zelda, of course.

Every time Aunt Zelda got annoyed with life in general she came to sit in Lyman's bar—not to drink, but to disapprove of her surroundings. On the night I get my luck fixed, I feel my aunt's presence the moment she steps through the doors. Her eyes flick and probe the dark booths as she sails forward, and her mouth twitches in righteous shock. I don't even have to turn around or look in the mirror to know it is her. She clicks across the floor loud as a calculator, then scrubs the end stool clean with a hankie fished from her sleeve.

"A tonic water, please," she requests in a controlled voice. I reach over and splash the stuff into a glass with ice. Then I squeeze a rag carefully to wipe the counter, and I set her glass on a little white square napkin from a special pile, unsoiled by liquor slogans or printed bathroom jokes. Cautiously, I put forth the question. "Lime?" She gives a short nod, a little yank of her cuffs. Her shoulders shrug slightly down. I spear not one, but two lime chunks on a little plastic sword and dunk them into her glass.

Only then does she take possession of her stool.

"On the house." I wave away the open metal jaws of her tiny purse. She snaps it shut, thanks me, cranks up her posture one more notch.

"You give this place just what it needs," I tell her, "an air of class."

When she doesn't respond, I repeat the compliment again, with more conviction, and she smiles, curving the corners of the pointed lips she has carefully painted upon her mouth.

"Salute," she toasts with light sophistication. Her sip prints the glass with her sharp lip-print, blurring her determined mouth further yet.

It will take glass after glass of formal prepared tonic waters very gradually laced with gin to bring the human shape back to her face. My motive is good—to make Shawnee Ray's life a little easier, for once the slight amounts of alcohol start having their effect, Zelda's basic niceness is free to shine forth. Right and left, she always forgives the multitude. Her smile relaxes—gleaming, melted pearls. From her corner she sheds a more benign opinion like a balm. No matter how bad things get, on those nights when Zelda stays long enough, there is eventually the flooding appeasement of her smile. It is like having a household saint.

But you have to light a candle, make a sacrifice.

Zelda is aware that her chemistry experiment has had unexpected results—here I am mixing drinks for my boss, the intended husband of the girl she fostered, while that girl herself, Shawnee Ray, is not out with Lyman Lamartine but at home intensively mothering her little boy. Zelda shouldn't play so hard and loose with the unexpected, that is my opinion. People's hearts are constructed of unknowable elements and even now, I feel sure, there is some unexplainable interest in me on the part of Shawnee Ray. I have to admit that our first date wasn't much. Still, she has consented to talk to me on the phone once or twice since that night.

I don't push my luck, but just go along for a while tending to my job, allowing the others to run interference with Zelda. As usual, she has a lot of people to maneuver, and so she hasn't had the time to concentrate full force on me. I am satisfied, want to stay that way. I like my aunt, even though I find it difficult to keep from getting run over by her unseen intentions.

Eighteen-wheeler trucks. Semis, fully loaded, with a belly dump. You never know what is coming at you when Zelda takes the road. Maybe it is the wariness, maybe I just want to head her off. Maybe I am stepping out in front of her with a red flag, or maybe I forget to put on my orange Day-Glo vest. Whatever happens, the fact is I get careless with Zelda's drinks. The trade is slow. I suppose I am tired and forget to measure. I add just that little bit too much to Zelda's tonics that sends her barreling at me full throttle. Too bad I am standing on the center line.

Starting out, she explains to me how my great grandmother, that dangerous Fleur Pillager, tried to kill herself by loading her pockets with stones and marching into Matchimanito Lake. Only, here's what stones she picked: the very ones that rested by her bedside, the very ones that she had always talked to. The perfect ones. The round ones. They knew her and so they helped her. They wouldn't let her sink. Spirit stones, they floated her up.

She says things that she should keep to herself, keep quiet about, never speak. She goes and tells me why I owe her everything.

"You're sweet," Zelda sways forward, her hair semifrowzled.

"I got it from the time I worked the sugar beet plant," I explain.

"You got it from yourself." Her black eyes wander. "Not from your mother."

"My mother?"

I can't help it, my ears flare for more. So I ball up my rag, lean on the counter, and ask the thing I shouldn't ask.

"What about her?"

And then Zelda tells me the raw specifics of how my mother left me with Grandma. She tells me facts that make me miserable. She does the worst thing of all: she tells me the truth.

"I don't know how she could have done it." Zelda shakes her head, her mouth rolled tight.

"What?"

"I hate to talk about it in front of you." She hedges to draw out the intensity. "But then, you already heard about the gunnysack."

My aunt is enjoying herself. She pretends not to, but actually loves giving out the facts and the painful details. I could stop her, but the mention of my mother makes me helpless. No matter what June Morrissey has done to me, no matter that she's gone, I still love her. I can't hear enough, or so I believe.

"That gunnysack was a joke." I speak confident. "Grandma kidded me once that my real mom was about to throw me in the slough. But no mother—"

Zelda interrupts me, nods agreement. "No mother, she was sure no true mother. June Morrissey, Kashpaw, whatever she was, she threw you in."

"N'missae," I say now, real slow, calling her my oldest sister. "You had a little extra to drink tonight. I spiked your tonic. Don't get mad at me. It's on the house."

But she is shaking her head at my version of the subject that has risen in her memory.

"She chucked you," Aunt Zelda continues. "I should know. It was me who dragged you out."

"You never said that before." I check the gin bottle. I cannot tell exactly how much I've poured.

"I was always a watcher, the one who saw. I was sitting on the back steps when I looked down the hill. There was June, slinging a little bundle into the slough."

"That's gin talking," I say. I tell her right out like that, and even throw down my rag on the counter. But I cannot turn away or stop listening as she continues in a voice that grows more hoarse, fascinated and too believable.

"I'll never forget that moment, Lipsha. Cloudy summer's day. I was all sly and I waited until June left. Then I went to see for myself what she had tossed into the water." Zelda stops here, bites her lower lip, and twists the glass in her hands. "I don't know how long I waited. If I'd known it was you, I would have ran down right away."

"Wasn't me." I make my voice firm, loud. "Wasn't Lipsha. No mother . . ."

No use. Zelda hardly notices me. She's talking about the moment she lived through at the edge of that pothole of water brown as coffee and sprouting cattails and lilies and harboring at its edges ducks and mudhens and flashy mallards.

"I waded in." Her voice grows strong, definite and sure. "I went in mud up to my knees and then into water over my head, so I had to swim around and try to remember where June had aimed the gunnysack. I started diving and must have made three, four tries before I touched the bag's edge. It took me two more dives to haul it up because"— now Zelda pauses for emphasis, glaring through me like I'm not there—"June had added *rocks*. I lugged that heavy sack to dry land, pulled it out. Then I packed it with the rocks banging, through the woods and into the field." Zelda bites her straw as she remembers me once more. "I would have opened it as soon as I got it out, Lipsha, if I'd known it was you."

I am getting this feeling now, this sick wrench that comes upon a person when they don't want to witness what is happening right in front of them.

"It wasn't me!" My voice is loud and one or two bleary loungers look over, curious. My mind is buzzing. My arms are weakening, deadening with the feeling that they want something big to hold on to, a tree, a rooted sapling, a hunkered crowd of earth, another person. But Zelda isn't someone to tolerate surprises. I can't grab her, and anyway she is the source of my confusion, so I stand my ground, even though I feel a tremble starting down low in my feet. I don't move as her voice continues.

"I opened that sack once I was out of the woods. I cried when I saw it was a baby! When you saw me you blinked your eyes wide and then you smiled. You were in that sack for twenty minutes, though, maybe half an hour."

"I was not."

"Maybe longer." She takes no argument. "Something else has always bothered me though." She scratches at the counter with a swizzle. "Lipsha, you were in that slough a long time."

"No, I wasn't."

She stops completely and stares at me, and then she whispers.

*"So why weren't you drowned?"*

And because I am mad at her for making up that stupid fucking story and all, I stare right back.

*"Watch out,"* I snap my eyes at her. *"You'll take my place!"*

I hiss these words into Zelda's face, using the same dangerous threat that my great grandmother, Fleur Pillager, is supposed to have said to her long-ago rescuer, who died soon and took her place on death's road. I employ the family warning, and Zelda does draw back. A tiny light of fear strikes itself in and out of her eyes as quick as a motel match. But she isn't one to accept into herself a curse. She is too strong a boss woman, and veers off my Pillager words with a quick sign of the cross.

I would like to do the same with hers, but odd thing is, I can't. I tell myself that in her cups she became inventive, that she embroidered my case history in her memory, beadworked it with a colorful stitch. She's wrong, I keep promising myself. Wrong as wrong.

*Wrong*, I repeat, turning in that night. *Wrong*, I keep insisting in my mind as I turn out the lights. *Wrong, wrong, wrong*, I fall into my dreams. I tell myself that Zelda scared the story up, she made it happen. She never found me in a gunnysack. I remind myself that I believe what Grandma Kashpaw told me—that I was given to her in a sad but understandable way by a mother who was beautiful but too wild to have raised a boy on her own. I had come to terms with that story, forgave how June was so far out on the edge of life that she couldn't properly care for me.

I want to keep that firm ground, that knowledge, but my dreams are frightening water.

That night, deeper places draw me down. I sink into black softness, my heart beating fast, straining in the trap of my chest. I wake with a thump, as though I've hit the bottom of my waterbed. I jump onto the floor and pull on my jeans, switch on the lights, decide to make a round, a kind of house check, and maybe, although I rarely do indulge, drink down a free drink.

I walk quietly into the shadowy echoes of emptiness. I pass the bar, then steer around to the other side. I am just in the process of selecting a bottle, when I look into the mirror.

And see June.

Her face is a paler blur than the dark, her eyes are lake quartz, and she gazes with sad assurance at me out of the empty silence. She wears a pink top that glows faintly, as does the Bailey's Irish Cream filling her small glass. Her hair is black, sweeps down along her chin in two smooth feathers. There is no age to her—ancient, brand-new, slim as a girl. Take your pick. She is anyone, everyone. She is my mother.

She looks the way she did when I was little, those times I glimpsed her walking back from her trips to town. She looks the way she should have if she stayed and kept the good ways and became old and graceful. She watches me across the long, low room. There is no smoke to part, to make way for her gaze. There is no noise to hear over. I can't claim that she is obscured. I can't claim her voice is covered.

June carefully opens her purse and taps out a cigarette. Darkness moves in front of her and by the time I turn around and shuffle to the other side of the room, her chair is empty. She has moved. My hair freezes on my neck to see her on the other side of the bar. I get a prickle down my back and I go fainting and weak all over. Stumbling, I almost turn tail.

"You have to face her," I tell myself, trying to calm my heart. "She's visiting for a reason."

In places, the concrete base of the bar has humped beneath the flooring and buckled. On cold nights, from my little den, I hear it shift. I catch that low sound now, a thump and crack. Then there is a still moment when nothing moves. Outside, there is no wind, not a faraway motor. No voice raised. No sound in the open fields. No dog barks, nothing.

Suddenly the furnace breaths out and complains. Ice tumbles in the freezer slot of the refrigerator.

I shake.

Now I always told myself before that there was a good side to ghosts. My reasoning goes along on the base of the following uncertainties: Beyond this world, is there another? Dimensions, how many? Which afterlife? Whose God will I face if there is one, whose court? A ghost could answer the basic question, at least, as to whether there is anything besides the world I know, the things I touch. If I see a ghost, possibilities will open. I have told myself all this, and yet, finally in the presence of one, I shake.

I keep telling myself that my mother means me no harm and besides, it can't have been easy for her to appear. She has surely walked through fire, crossed water, passed through the great homely divide of fenced pasture and fields scoured flat by the snow. She has walked the three-day road back, the road of the dead. She has put herself out royally to get here, is what I'm saying. I tell myself I should at least have the guts to find out why.

I take a deep breath and enter the vast, still plain of the bingo palace. I flick on the lights, but they are low-watt anyway, so dim they hardly make a difference. Each step I take, I stop and listen for the echo, the trail. Each time I stop, I hear the silence, loud as a rush of heat. My heart pushes the blood to my head in pulses that glow behind my eyelids, and my fingers burn at the tips as if they were dipped in ice. I reach the stool, the one where I've seen her sitting, and then I touch it with my palm and it seems to me the back is warm.

"Where's my car?" she asks right beside me, then, as if we are continuing a conversation in time. "I came back because I was just wondering where you put it. Where the hell is my car?"

"It's outside," I answer, but my voice sounds like I'm talking from a hollow well.

"What did you do with it?" Her tone is pointed. "Crack it up?"

"No."

"Well, what?"

"It's kind of stalled," I tell her.

" 'Kind of'? What do you mean 'kind of'?"

"All it needs is a little jump-start."

"I'll give you jump-start. Shit!"

She throws herself down at a table, angry, and nods at the chair. I am now in a weakened state, my legs wobble, soft rags. If I'd known that accepting the blue Firebird paid for with the insurance money from her death would piss her off this bad—even from beyond the grave—well, forget it. Even after what Zelda said, I guess I still imagined my mother as gentle toward me, hopefully guilt-struck, but either that was wishful thinking or she is in a mood that night. Her voice is hard and she has no time for small talk. I figure that there is maybe some trouble, something disagreeable going on wherever she has come from, a situation from which she needs relief, or at least transportation.

After sitting there and stewing in our own silence for what seems a long time to me, I get the nerve to speak.

"June . . . Mom," I gently begin, surprised to hear how the last word sounds in my voice, "what do you want from me?"

Lukewarm puffs of smoke quiver in the air between us, and she frowns.

"I'm in a rush. I gotta go, but listen here. Do you play bingo?"

"I never did yet," I inform her. "Well, hardly ever."

"Now you do."

She dangles the lighted cigarette from her lips and again opens her purse, searches with both hands, carefully draws out a flimsy booklet, and pushes it across the table between us. I see that the papers are bingo tickets, marked with little squares containing letters and numbers. I begin to flip through the book politely, the way you look at photos of someone's vacation to Sturgis, wondering what her intention could be, but there is nothing in the tickets that looks out of the ordinary. When I lift my head to thank her, no one is there. She has evaporated into the spent daze of smoke that wreathes her chair.

I run outside, coatless in the freezing black air, and I call my mother's name but there is no answer. Above me, in the heaven where she came from, cold stars ring down and stabs of ancient light glitter, delicate and lonely. Grand forms twist out of unearthly dust. As I watch, then, sure enough, one star breaks from its rank and plunges.

It is happening. I know it. My luck is finally shifting. I go back inside and crawl into my sleeping bag bed, and eventually I begin to lose the sense of fear and excitement, to float down through the connections. I wake slightly, once, imagining that from beyond the thickly insulated walls of the bar, I hear the muffled rev of an engine. I worry vaguely about my car, but sleep is a deep wave's trough. I turn over, roll down the watery slope.


When I walk into bingo that night in late winter I am a player like any regular person, drenched in casual wishes, in hopes. Upon first entering, I look for any friends I might have from the past or the present, or any relations, and right off, I see Grandma Lulu. She has five tickets spread in front of her. Her neighbors each have only one. When the numbers roll, she picks up a bingo dauber in each hand. It is the Early Birds' game, one-hundred-dollar prize, and nobody has got too wound up yet or serious.

"Lipsha, go get me a Coke," commands Lulu when someone else bingos. "Yourself too."

I hit the concession, snag our soft drinks and come back, set them down, pull up to the table, and lay out my ticket. Like I say, my grandmother, she plays five, which is how you get the big money. In the long run, much more than even, she is one of those rare Chippewas who actually profit by bingo. But then again, these days it is her preferred way of gambling. No pull-tabs. No blackjack. No slot machines for her. She never goes into the back room, never drinks. She banks all of her cash. I think I can learn from Lulu Lamartine, so I watch her close.

Concentration. Before the numbers even start, she sits down in her lucky place, a chair that nobody else dares take, fourth row and fourth to the right by the eastern wall. She composes her face to calm, snaps her purse shut. She shakes her daubers upside down so that the foam-rubber tips are thoroughly inked. She looks at the time on her watch. The Coke, she takes a drink of that, but no more than a sip. She is a narrow-eyed woman with a round jaw, curled hair. Her eyeglasses, blue plastic, hang from her neck by two chains. She raises the ovals to her eyes as the caller takes the stand. She holds her daubers poised while he plucks the ball from the chute. He reads it out. B-7. Then she is absorbed, scanning, dabbing, into the game. She doesn't mutter. She has no lucky piece to touch in front of her. And afterward, even if she loses a blackout by one square she never sighs or complains.

All business, that's Lulu. And all business pays.

I believe I could be all business too, like her, if not for the van that sits behind the curtain. I don't know it right away, but that is the prize that will change the order of my life. Because of the van, I'll have to get stupid first, then wise. I'll have to keep floundering, trying to catch my bearings in the world. It all sits ahead of me, spread out in the sun like a naming giveaway. More than anything, I want to be the man who can impress Shawnee Ray.

"Lipsha Morrissey, you got to go for a vocation," says Grandma Lulu, during break.

"Maybe I'll win at bingo," I say to her, in hope.

Her smile is still and curved as a cat's, her cheeks round and soft, her fingernails perfect claws of blazing tropic pink.

"Win at bingo," she repeats my words thoughtfully. "Everybody wins once. It's the next time and the next time you got to worry about."

But she doesn't know that I am playing bingo on the advice of a ghost, and I haven't mentioned my position as night watchman at the bar. I suppose I want her to think of me as more successful than I really am, so I keep my mouth shut although, after all, I shouldn't be so shy. The job earns me a place to sleep, twenty dollars per week, and as much beef jerky, beer nuts, and spicy sausage sticks as I can eat.

I am now composed of these three false substances. No food in a bar has a shelf life of less than forty months. If you are what you eat, I will live forever, I decide.

And then they pull aside the curtain, and I forget my prediction. I see that I wouldn't want to live as long as I have coming, unless I own *the van.* It has every option you can believe—blue plush on the steering wheel, diamond side windows, and complete carpeting interior. The seats are easy chairs, with little built-in headphones, and it is wired all through the walls. You can walk up close during intermission and touch the sides. The paint is cream, except for the design picked out in blue, which is a Sioux Drum border. In the back there is a small refrigerator and a padded platform for sleeping. It is a starter home, a portable den with front-wheel drive, a place where I can shack with Shawnee Ray and her little boy, if she will consent. If she won't live there, though, at least she will be impressed.

Now, I know that what I feel is a symptom of the national decline. You'll scoff at me, scorn me, say what right does that waste Lipsha Morrissey, who makes his living guarding beer, have to comment outside of his own tribal boundary? But I am able to investigate the larger picture, thanks to my mother's direction and thanks to Lulu, from whom I soon learn to be one-minded in my pursuit of a material object.

After that first sighting, I go play the bingo whenever I can get off from bar duty or cleanup. Lyman never stops me, for I think it seems economical for his workers to return their profits to the palace by spending off-hours at the long tables or drinking beers. Every bit of time that I spend listening for bingo numbers, I grow more certain I am close. There is only one game per night at which the van is offered, a blackout game, in which you have to fill every slot. The more cards you buy, the more your chance increases. I try to play five numbers like Grandma Lulu, but they cost five bucks each.

To get my van, I have to shake hands with greed.

I get unprincipled. As I might have already said, my one talent in this life is a healing power I get passed down through the Pillager branch of my background. It's in my hands. I snap my fingers together so hard they almost spark. Then I blank out my mind, and I put on the touch. I have a reputation up to now for curing sore joints and veins. I can relieve ailments caused in an old person by one half century of grinding stoopover work. I have a power in myself that flows out, resistless. I have a richness in my dreams and waking thoughts. But I do not realize I will have to give up my healing source once I start charging for my service.

You know how it is about charging. People suddenly think you are worth something. Used to be, I'd go anyplace I was called, take any price offered or take nothing. Once I let it go around that I expect a twenty for my basic work, however, the phone at the bar rings off the hook.

"Where's that medicine boy?" they want to know. "Where's Lipsha?"

I take their money. And it's not like beneath the pressure of a twenty I don't try, for I do try even harder than before. I skip my palms together, snap my fingers, position them where the touch inhabiting them should flow. But when it comes to blanking out my mind, I consistently fail. For each time, in the center of the cloud that comes down into my brain, in perfect focus, the van is now parked.

One afternoon, Grandma Lulu leaves word that I should come over to her apartment to work on a patient, and though she doesn't name money, I know from her voice it is an important customer. Maybe he's her latest boyfriend. For sure, he has a job or some SSI. So I go over there. Entering her place, as usual, I exchange salutes with my own father from his picture on her shelf of little china mementos.

"I'd like you to meet Russell Kashpaw," Grandma says, and with that, I shake the hand of our state's most decorated war hero, who is recovering from multiple strokes and antique shrapnel wounds. Russell sits in a wheelchair. His job, at which he does the most business after the bars close, is tattooing people with pictures of roses, skulls, Harleys, and kung fu dragons. He lives down a curved road, off in the bush, and you can see his work displayed on almost any night.

Russell looks like a statue, not the type you see in history books, I don't mean those, but the kind you see for sale as you drive along the highway. He is a native Paul Bunyan, carved with a chain saw. He is rough-looking, finished in big strokes. I shake Russell Kashpaw's hand, hoping to feel some pulse surge, some information. I shake it longer, waiting for electrical input, but there is nothing.

"Sometimes there's a lot of static in these old war wounds," I say out loud. "Where do you feel the knot?"

In a low and commanding voice, heavy on the details, he begins to describe his aches, his pains, his spasms, his creaks and cricks. My two grandmas and their neighbor, that gossiper Mrs. Josette Bizhieu, are in the room with me. The three of them nod and tut at every one of Russell Kashpaw's symptoms and in glowing words assure him that he's come to the right place for a cure. So I rub my hands together hard and fast, inspired, then I press my burning palms to the sides of his shoulders, for it is the back of his neck and spine that are giving him the worst aggravations today. But though I knead him like I see Grandma making her buns and rolls, and though I heat my hands up again like a lightning strike, and though I twist my fingers into wire pretzels, I cannot set the touch upon him proper.

He was so shot up there's metal in him, shorting out my energy. He is so full of scars and holes and I can't smooth him straight. I don't give up, though. I try and I try until I even seem to hurt him worse, gripping desperate, with all my might.

"Holy buckets," he yells.

"Damn, Mr. Kashpaw. I'm sorry!"

I'm all balled up like some kind of tangled yarn of impulse. I'm a mess of conflicting feedback, a miserable lump of burnt string. And worst of all, the eyes of my Grandma are on me with increasing letdown and disappointment, as I fail, and fail my patient once again. Russell pays me but he isn't happy, and neither am I, for I know, as soon as right now, the talk will gather and flash from lip to lip starting at the Senior Citizens and fanning through the houses, down the roads. My touch has deserted me. My hands are shocked out, useless. I am again no more than the simple nothing that I always was before.

I suppose after that I begin to place my desperations in the bingo. I long for the van like I've started to wish for Shawnee. And then, there comes an incident that sets me back in my quest.

Instead of going for the van with everything, saving up to buy as many cards as I can play when they get to the special game, I go short-term for variety with U-Pick-em cards, the kind where you have to choose the numbers for yourself.

First off, I write down my shoe and pants size. So much for me. I take my birth date and a double of it after that. Still no go. I write down the numbers of my Grandma's address and her anniversary dates. Nothing. Then I realize if my U-Pick-em is going to win, it will be more like revealed, rather than a forced kind of thing. So I shut my eyes right there in the middle of the long bingo table and I let my mind white out, fizzing like the screen of a television, until something forms. The van, as always. But on its tail this time a license plate is officially fixed and bolted. I use that number, write it down in the boxes.

And then I bingo.

I get two hundred dollars from that imaginary license. It is in my pocket when I leave that night. The next morning, I have fifty cents. But it's not like you think it is with Shawnee Ray, and I'll explain that. She doesn't want something from me, she never cares if I have money and never asks for it. Her idea is to go into business. To pay for college, she wants to sell her original clothing designs, of which she has six books.

I have gotten to know Shawnee a little better with each phone call, but the time has come that I can't think up another excuse to dial her number. She is so decided in her future that she intimidates me—it is her A+ attitude, her gallons of talents and hobbies. Though I want to ask her out again, the embarrassing memory of our first date keeps intruding on my mind. Finally I tell myself, "Lipsha, you're a nice-looking guy. You're a winner. You know the washer's always broken at Zelda's house. Pretend to run into Shawnee at the laundry."

So I scout the place for days until she finally shows, then I go right up to her at the Coin-Op and I make a face of surprise, which against my better judgment gets taken over by immediate joy. Just seeing her makes my head spin and my hands clench my chest. For the hundredth time, I apologize for how I've gotten her in trouble. Then I say, "Care to dance?" which is a joke. There isn't anyplace to dance at a laundromat. Yet, I can tell she likes me at least as much as the week before. We eat a sandwich and a cookie from the machine and then while her clean clothing dries Shawnee says she wants to take a drive, so we tag along with some others in the back of their car. They go straight south, toward Hoopdance, where action is taking place.

"Shawnee Ray," I whisper as we drive along, "I can't stop thinking of you."

"Lipsha." She smiles. "I can't stop thinking of you too."

I don't say anything about Lyman Lamartine and neither does she, but I have this sudden sense of him right then as perched behind us in the back window, head bobbing side to side like a toy car dog. Even so, Shawnee Ray and I move close together on the car seat. My hand is on my knee, and I think of a couple different ways I could gesture, casually pretend to let it fall on hers, how maybe if I talk fast she won't notice, in the heat of the moment, her hand in mine, us holding hands, our lips drawn to one another. But then I decide to give it all up, to boldly take courage, to cradle her hand as at the same time I look into her eyes. I do this. In the front, the others talk between themselves. We just sit there. Her mouth turns raw and hot underneath the weight of my eyes and I bend forward. She leans backward. "You want to kiss me?" she asks. But I answer, not planning how the words will come out, "Not here. Our first kiss has to be a magic moment only we can share."

Her eyes flare softer than I'd ever imagined, then widen like a deer's, and her big smile blooms. Her skin is dark, her long hair a burnt brown-black color. She wears no jewelry, no rings, that night, just the clothing she has sewed from her own designs—a suit jacket and a pair of pants the tan of eggshells, with symbols picked out in blue thread on the borders, the cuffs, and the hem. I take her in, admiring, for some time on that drive before I realize that the reason Shawnee Ray's cute outfit nags me so is on account of she is dressed up to match my bingo van. I can hardly tell her this surprising coincidence, but it does convince me that the time is perfect, the time is right.

They let us off at a certain place and we get out, hardly breaking our gaze from each other. You want to know what this place is. I'll tell you. Okay. So it is a motel, a long low double row of rooms painted white on the outside with brown wooden doors. There is a beautiful sign set up featuring a lake with some fish jumping out of it. We stand beside the painted water.

"I haven't done this since Redford," she says in a nervous voice. "I have to call Zelda and tell her I'll be late."

There is a phone outside the office, inside a plastic shell. She walks over there. I know without even listening that when Shawnee Ray asks whether it is okay with Zelda to stay out later than usual no names will be mentioned but Lyman's will probably be implied.

"He's sleeping," she says when she returns.

I go into the office, stand before the metal counter. There is a number floating in my mind.

"Is room twenty-two available?" I ask for no reason.

I suppose, looking at me, I look too much like an Indian. The owner, a big woman in a shiny black blouse, notices that. You get so you see it cross their face the way wind blows a disturbance on water. There is a period of contemplation, a struggle in this woman's thinking. Behind her the television whispers. Her mouth opens but I take the words from it.

"This here is Andrew Jackson," I say, offering the bill. "Known for booting our southern relatives onto the trail of tears. And to keep him company, we got two Mr. Hamiltons."

The woman turns shrewd, and takes the bills.

"No parties." She holds out a key attached to a square of orange plastic.

"Just sex." I cannot help but reassure her. But that is talk, big talk from a person with hardly any experience and nothing that resembles a birth control device. I am not one of those so-called studs who can't open up their wallets without dropping out a foil-wrapped square. No, Lipsha Morrissey is deep at heart a romantic, a wild-minded kind of guy, I tell myself, a fool with no letup. I go out to Shawnee Ray, and take her hand in mine. I am shaking inside but my voice is steady and my hands are cool.

"Let's go in." I show the key. "Let's not think about tomorrow."

"That's how I got Redford," says Shawnee Ray.

So we stand there.

"I'll go in," she says at last. "Down two blocks, there's an all-night gas station. They sell 'em."

Okay. Life in this day and age might be less romantic in some ways. It seems so in the hard twenty-four-hour light, trying to choose what I needed from the rack by the counter. It is quite a display, there are dazzling choices—texture, shapes, even colors. I notice I am being watched, and I suddenly grab what is near my hand, two boxes, economy size.

"Heavy date?" my watcher asks.

I suppose the guy on the late shift is bored, can't resist. His T-shirt says Big Sky Country. He is grinning in an ugly way. So I answer.

"Not really. Fixing up a bunch of my white buddies from Montana. Trying to keep down the sheep population."

His grin stays fixed. Maybe he has heard a lot of jokes about Montana blondes, or maybe he is from somewhere else. I look at the boxes in my hand, put one back.

"Let me help you out," the guy says. "What you need is a bag of these."

He takes down a plastic sack of little oblong party balloons, Day-Glo pinks and oranges and blues.

"Too bright," I say. "My girlfriend's a designer. She hates clashing colors." I am breathing hard suddenly, and so is he. Our eyes meet and take fire.

"What does she design?" he asks. "Bedsheets?"

"What does yours design?" I reply. "Wool sweaters?"

I put money between us. "For your information," I say, "my girlfriend's not only beautiful, but she and I are the same species."

He pauses, asks me which species.

"Take the money," I order him. "Hand over my change and I'll be out of here. Don't make me do something I'd regret."

"I'd be real threatened." The guy turns from me, ringing up my sale. "I'd be shaking, except I know you Indian guys are chickenshit."

As I turn away with my purchase, I hear him mutter something and I stop. I thought I heard it, but I wasn't sure I heard it. Prairie nigger.

"What?" I turn. "What'd you say?"

"Nothing."

The guy just looks at me, lifts his shoulders once, and stares me in the eyes. His are light, cold, empty. And mine, as I turn away, mine burn.

I take my package, take my change.

"Baah. . . ," I cry, and beat it out of there.

It's strange how a bashful kind of person like me gets talkative in some of our less pleasant border-town situations. I take a roundabout way back to room twenty-two and tap on the door. There is a little window right beside it. Shawnee Ray pulls the curtains aside, frowns, and lets me in.

"Well," I say in that awkward interval. "Guess we're set."

She takes the bag from my hand and doesn't say a word, just puts it on the little table next to the bed. There are two chairs. Each of us takes one. Then we sit down and turn inward to our own thoughts. The romance isn't in us now for some reason, but there is something invisible that makes me hopeful about the room.

It is a little place just over the reservation line, a modest kind of place, a clean place. You can smell the faint chemical of bug spray the moment you step inside it. You can look at the television hung on the wall, or examine the picture of golden trees and waterfall. You can take a shower for a long time in the cement shower stall, standing on your personal shower mat for safety. There is a little tin desk. You can sit down there and write a letter on a sheet of plain paper. You can read in the Good Book someone has placed in the drawer. I take it out, New Testament, Psalms, Proverbs. It is a small green book, no bigger than my hand, with a little circle stamped in the corner, a gold ring containing a jug, a flame.

As we sit there in the strumming quiet, I open the book to the last page and read, like I always do, just to see how it ends. I have barely absorbed the last two pages when Shawnee Ray gets curious, touches my hand, asks what I am doing. Her voice is usually bold but at that moment I think of doves on wires. Whatever happens, I think, looking at her, I want to remember. I want a souvenir. I might never be hopeful for the rest of my life the way I am hopeful right now. I suppose it says something about me that the first thing I think of is what I can steal. But there it is, the way I am, always will be, ever was. I think of taking the lampshade, made of reed, pressed and laced tight together. That is possible, but not so romantic. The spread on the double mattress is reddish, a rusty cotton material. Too big, too easy to trace. There is an air conditioner. That might not be noticed until winter finishes. There are ashtrays and matches, a sad, watery mirror, and a couple postcards of the motel itself with its sign of the fish. But what I finally close my hands on, what I put in my pocket, is the little Bible, the bright plastic Gideon's.

"I don't know why we're here," I say at last. "I'm sorry."

Shawnee Ray removes a small brush from her purse.

"Comb my hair?"

I take the brush and sit on the bed just behind her. I start at the ends, very careful, but there are hardly any tangles to begin with. Her hair is a quiet dark without variation. "Your lamp doesn't go out by night," I whisper, in a dream. She never hears me. My hand follows the brush, smoothing after each stroke, until the fall of her hair is a hypnotizing silk. I lift my hand away from her head and the strands follow, electric to my touch, in soft silk that hangs suspended until I return to the brushing. She never moves, except to switch off the light, and then the television. She sits down again in the total dark and asks me to please keep on and so I do. The air goes thick. Her hair gets lighter, full of blue static, charged so that I am held in place by the attraction. A golden spark jumps on the carpet. Shawnee Ray turns toward me. Her hair floats down around her at that moment like a tent of energy.


I sit on ground where Pillagers once walked. The trees around me are the dense birch and oak of old woods. Matchimanito Lake drifts in, gray waves, white foam in a bobbing lace. Thin gulls line themselves on a sandbar. The sky turns dark. I close my eyes and that is when, into my mind, the little black star shoots. It comes out of the darkness, though it is darkness itself. I see it pass and diminish and remember my mother's visit.

Here's luck. June's moment, a sign to steer me where I go next.

"This is the last night I'm going to try for the van," I tell myself. After my mother's visit, the book of bingo tickets that she gave me disappeared for a while and then, one early morning, cleaning out the bar, I found them stuffed into the seam of a plastic booth. To me, they are full of her magic—ghostly, charged. I never dared use them before. I'll use them now, I decide. This or never is the time. I'll use these last-ditch tickets, and once they're gone I'll make a real decision. I'll quit working for Lyman, go full out for Shawnee Ray, open the Yellow Pages at random and where my finger points, I will take that kind of job.

Of course, I never count on actually winning the van.

I am playing for blackout on the shaded side of those otherworldly tickets. As usual, I sit with Lulu. Her vigilance helps me. She lets me use her extra dauber and she sits and smokes a filter cigarette, observing the quiet frenzy that is taking place around her. Even though that van has sat on the stage five months, even though nobody has yet won it and everyone says it is one of Lyman's scams, when it comes to playing for it most people buy a couple cards. That night, I've just got one, but it is June's.

A girl reads out the numbers from the hopper. Her voice is clear and bright on the microphone. Lulu points out one place I have missed on the winning ticket. Then I have just two squares left to make a bingo and I suddenly sweat, I break into a chill, I go cold and hot at once. After all my pursuit, after all of my plans, I am N-36 and G-52. I narrow myself, shrink into the spaces on the ticket. Each time she reads a number out and it isn't 36 or 52 I sicken, recover, forget to breathe.

I almost faint with every number she reads out before N-36. Then right after that G-52 rolls off her lips.

I scream. I am ashamed to say how loud I yell. That girl comes over, gets Lyman Lamartine from his office in the hallway behind the big room. His face goes raw with irritation when he sees it's me, and then he cross-checks my numbers slow and careful while everyone hushes. He researches the ticket over twice. Then he purses his lips together and wishes he didn't have to say it.

"It's a bingo," he finally tells the crowd.

Noise buzzes to the ceiling, talk of how close some others came, green talk. Every eye is turned and cast on me, which is uncomfortable. I never was the center of looks before, not Lipsha, who everybody takes for granted around here. Not all those looks are for the good either—some are plain envious and ready to believe the first bad thing a sour tongue can pin on me. It makes sense in a way. Of all those who stalked that bingo van over the long months, I am now the only one who has not lost money on the hope.

• • •

Okay, so what kind of man does it make Lipsha Morrissey that the keys do not burn his hands one slight degree, and he beats it out that very night, quick as possible, completing only the basic paperwork? I mean to go tell Shawnee Ray, but in my disbelief I just drive around without her, getting used to my new self. In that van, I ride high, and maybe that's the thing. Looking down on others, even if it's only from the seat of a van that a person never really earned, does something to the human mentality. It's hard to say. I change. Just one late evening of riding the reservation roads, passing cars and pickups with a swish of my tires, I start smiling at the homemade hot rods, at the clunkers below, at the old-lady sedans nosing carefully up and down the gravel hills.

Once, in the distance, flying through my headlights at a crossroads like a spell, I think I see the blue Firebird, mine formerly and, I presume, now rightfully my mother's. After all, she told me she was coming for it on the night she gave me the bingo tickets. After all, the next morning it was gone. I reported it stolen and filed a complaint with the tribal police, but that was duty, for the car insurance. I know who has it now. Riding along in my van, I wish her well. I am happy with what I have, alive with satisfaction.

I start saying to myself that I shouldn't visit Shawnee because by then it's late, but I finally do go over to Zelda's anyway. I pull into the driveway with a flourish I cannot help. When the van slips into a pothole, I roar the engine. For a moment, I sit in the dark, letting my headlamps blaze alongside the door until it opens.

The man who glares out at me is Lyman Lamartine.

"Cut the goddamn lights!" he yells. "Redford's sick."

I roll down my window, ask if I can help. I wait in the dark. A dim light switches on behind Lyman and I see some shadows—Zelda, a little form in those pajamas with the feet tacked on, a larger person pacing back and forth. I see Shawnee arguing, then picking up her little boy.

"Come in if you're coming," Lyman calls.

But here's the gist of it. I just say to tell Shawnee hello for me, that I hope Redford is all right, and then I back out of there, down the drive, and leave her to fend for herself. I could have stayed. I could have drawn my touch back from wherever it had left. I could have offered my van to take Redford to the IHS. I could have sat there in silence as a dog guards its mate, its own blood, even though I was jealous. I could have done something other than what I do, which is to hit the road for Hoopdance, looking for a better time.

I cruise until I see where the party house is located that night. I drive the van over the low curb, into the yard, and I park there. I watch until I recognize a couple cars and the outlines of Indians and mixed-bloods, so I know that walking in will not involve me in what the newspapers term an episode. The door is white, stained and raked by a dog, with a tiny fan-shaped window. I go through and stand inside. There is movement, a kind of low-key swirl of bright hair and dark hair tossing alongside each other. There are about as many Indians as there aren't. This party is what we call, around here, a hairy buffalo and most people are grouped with paper cups around a big, brown plastic garbage can that serves as the punch bowl for the all-purpose stuff, which is anything that anyone brings, dumped in along with pink Hawaiian Punch. I grew up around a lot of the people, know their nicknames, and I recognize others I don't know so well but am acquainted with by sight. Among those last, there is a young red-headed guy.

It bothers me. I recognize him, but I don't know him. I haven't been to school with him or played against him in any sport. I can't think where I've seen him, until later, when the heat goes up and he takes off his bomber jacket. Then Big Sky Country shows, plain letters on a blue background.

I edge around the corner of the room into the hall and stand there to argue with myself. Will he recognize me or am I just another face, a forgotten customer? He probably isn't really from Montana, so he might not have been insulted by our little conversation or even remember it anymore. I reason that he probably picked up the shirt while vacationing. I tell myself that I should calm my nerves, go back into the room, have fun. What keeps me from doing that is the sudden thought of Shawnee, our night together, and what I bought and used.

When I remember, I am lost to the present moment. One part of me catches up with the other.

I have a hard time getting drunk. It's just the way I am. I start thinking and forget to fill the cup, or recall something I have got to do, and end up walking from a party. I have put down a full can of beer before and wandered out to weed my Grandma's rhubarb patch or to work on a cousin's car. But that night, thinking of Lyman's face, I start drinking and keep on going and never remember to quit. I drink so hard because I want to lose my feelings.

*I can't stop thinking of you too.*

I hear Shawnee Ray's voice say this out loud, just behind me where there is nothing but wall. I push along until I come to a door and then I go through, into a tiny bedroom full of coats, and so far with nobody either making out or unconscious on the floor. I sit on a pile of parkas and jean jackets in this alcove within the rising hum of the party outside. I see a phone and I dial Shawnee Ray's number. Of course, Zelda answers.

"Get off the phone," she says. "We're waiting for the doctor."

"What's wrong with Redford?" I ask. My head is full of ringing coins.

There is a silence, then Shawnee's voice is on the line. "Could you hang up?"

"I'm coming over there," I say.

"No, you're not."

The phone clicks dead. I hold the droning receiver in my hand, and try to refresh my mind. The only thing I see in it clear enough to focus on is the van. I decide this is a sign for me to pile in behind the wheel, drive straight to Zelda's house. So I put my drink on the windowsill, then slip out the door and fall down the steps, only to find them waiting.

I guess he recognized me and I guess he really was from Montana, after all. He has friends, too. They stand around the van and their heads are level with the roof, for they are tall.

"Let's go for a ride," says the T-shirt guy from the all-night gas pump.

He knocks on the window of my van with his knuckles. When I tell him no thanks, he leaps on the hood. He wears black cowboy boots, pointy-toed and walked-down on the heels, and they leave small depressions every time he jumps and lands.

"Thanks anyhow," I repeat. "But the party's not over." I try to get back into the house, but like in a bad dream, the door is stuck or locked. I holler, pound, kick at the very marks that a desperate dog has left, but the music rises and nobody hears. So I end up behind the wheel of the van. They act very gracious. They urge me to drive. They are so polite, I try to tell myself, they aren't all that bad. And sure enough, after we have proceeded along for a while, these Montana guys tell me they have chipped together to buy me a present.

"What is it?" I ask.

"Shut up," says the pump jockey. He is in the front seat next to me, riding shotgun.

"I don't really go for surprises," I say. "What's your name, anyhow?"

"Marty."

"I got a cousin named Marty."

"Fuck him."

The guys in the back exchange a grumbling kind of laughter, a knowing set of groans. Marty grins, turns toward me.

"If you really want to know what we're going to give you, I'll tell. It's a map. A map of Montana."

Their laughter turns hyena-crazed and goes on for too long.

"I always liked the state," I allow in a serious voice.

"No shit," says Marty. "Then I hope you like sitting on it." He signals where I should turn and all of a sudden I realize that Russell Kashpaw's place is somewhere ahead. He runs his tattoo den from the basement of his house, keeps his equipment set up and ready for the weekend, and of course, I remember how in his extremity of pain I failed him.

"Whoa." I brake the van. "You can't tattoo a person against his will. It's illegal."

"Get your lawyer on it tomorrow." Marty leans in close for me to see his unwinking eyes. I put the van back in gear, but just chug along, desperately, thinking. Russell does a lot of rehabilitation in the old-time sweat lodge, and for income or art has taken up this occupation that he learned overseas and can do sitting down. I don't expect him to have much pity on me, and I graphically imagine needles whirring, dyes; getting stitched and poked, and decide that I'll ask Marty, in a polite kind of way, to beat me up instead. If that fails, I will tell him that there are many states I would not mind so much, like Minnesota with its womanly hourglass for instance, or Rhode Island which is small, or even Hawaii, a soft bunch of circles. I think of Idaho. The panhandle. That has character.

"Are any of you guys from any other state?" I ask, anxious to trade.

"Kansas."

"South Dakota."

It isn't that I really have a thing against those places, understand, it's just that the straight-edged shape is not a Chippewa preference. You look around, and everything you see is round, everything in nature. There are no perfect boundaries, no natural borders except winding rivers. Only human-made things tend toward cubes and squares—the van, for instance. That is an example. Suddenly I realize that I am driving a four-wheeled version of the state of North Dakota.

"Just beat me up, you guys. Let's get this over with."

But they laugh even harder, and then we are at Russell's.


The sign on his basement door reads Come In. I am shoved from behind and strapped together with five pairs of heavy football-toughened hands, so I am the first to see Russell, the first to notice he is not a piece of all the trash and accumulated junk that washes through the concrete-floored cellar, but a person sitting still as any statue, in a corner, on his wheelchair that creaks and sings when he pushes himself toward us with long, powerful old man's arms.

"Please!" I plead with a desperate note in my voice. "I don't want—"

Marty squeezes me around the throat and tousles up my hair.

"Cold feet. Now remember, Mr. Kashpaw, just like we talked about on the phone. Map of Montana. You know where. And put in a lot of detail."

I try to scream.

"Like I was thinking," Marty goes on, "of those maps we did in grade school showing products from each region. Cows' heads, oil wells, missile bases, those little sheaves of wheat and so on. . . ."

Russell Kashpaw looks from Marty to me and back and forth again, skeptical, patient, and then he strokes his rocklike cliff of a chin and considers the situation.

"Tie him up," says Kashpaw at last. His voice is thick, with a military crispness. "Then leave this place."

They do. They take my pants and the keys to the van. I hear the engine roar and die away, and I roll side to side in my strict bindings. I feel Russell's hand on my shoulder and suddenly, from out of nowhere, caught in a wrinkle in my brain, words jump like bread into my mouth.

I start babbling. "Please, Russell. I'm here against my will, kidnapped by Montana boys. Take pity!"

"Be still." Russell Kashpaw's voice has changed, now that the others are gone, to a low sound that matches with his appearance and does not seem at all unkind. I fix my pleading gaze upon him. A broke-down God is who he looks like from my worm's-eye view. His eyes are frozen black, his hair crew-cut, half dark, half gray, his scarred cheeks shine underneath the blazing tubes of light in the ceiling. You never know where you're going to find your twin in the world, your double. I don't mean in terms of looks, I'm talking about mind-set. You never know where you're going to find the same thoughts in another brain, but when it happens you know it right off, just like you were connected by a small electrical wire that suddenly glows red hot and sparks. That's what happens when I stare at Russell Kashpaw, and he suddenly grins.

He puts a big hand to his jaw.

"I don't have a pattern for Montana," he tells me. He unties my ropes with a few quick jerks, sneering at the clumsiness of the knots. Then he sits back in his chair again, and watches me get my bearings.

"I never wanted anything tattooed on me, Mr. Kashpaw, not that I have anything against a tattoo," I say, so as not to hurt his professional feelings. "It was a kind of revenge plot though."

He sits in silence, a waiting quiet, hands folded and face composed. By now I know I am safe, but I have nowhere to go and so I sit down on a pile of magazines. He asks what revenge, and I tell him the story, the whole thing right from the beginning. I tell him how my mother came to me, and go farther back, past the bingo, from when I entered the winter powwow. I leave out the personal details about Shawnee and me but he gets the picture. I mention all about the van.

"That's an unusual piece of good fortune."

"Have you ever had any? Good fortune?"

"All the time. Those guys paid plenty. Maybe they'll want it back, but then again, why don't you just look sore—you know, kind of rub your ass the next time you see them. Keep them off my back too."

He opens a book on the table, a notebook with plastic pages that clip in and out, and hands it over to me.

"You can pick a design out," he says.

I pretend interest—I don't want to disappoint him—and leaf through the dragons and the hearts, thinking how to refuse. Then suddenly I see the star. It is the same one that scattered my luck in the sky after my mother left me alone that night, it is the sight that came into my head as I sat in the woods. Now here it is. The star falls, shedding rays, reaching for the edge of the page. My luck's uneven, but it's coming back. I have a wild, uncanny hope. I get a thought in my head, clear and vital, that this little star will bring my touch back and convince Shawnee I am serious about her.

"This one. Put it here on my hand."

Russell nods, gives me a rag to bite, and plugs in his needle.

Now my hand won't let me rest. It throbs and aches as if it came alive again after a hard frost. I know I'm going somewhere, taking this hand to Shawnee Ray. Even walking down the road in a pair of big-waisted green pants belonging to Russell Kashpaw, toward the bingo palace, where I keep everything I own in life, I'm going forward. My hand is a ball of pins, but when I look down I see the little star shooting across the sky.

I'm ready for what will come next. That's why I don't fall on the ground and I don't yell when I come across the van parked in a field. At first, I think it is the dream van, the way I always see it in my vision. Then I notice it's the real vehicle. Totaled.

My bingo van is dented on the sides, kicked and scratched, and the insides are scattered. Ripped pieces of carpet, stereo wires, glass, are spread here and there in the new sprouts of wheat. I force open a door that is bent inward. I wedge myself behind the wheel, tipped over at a crazy angle, and I look out. The windshield is shattered in a sunlight burst, a web through which the world is more complicated than I thought, and more peaceful.

I've been up all night and the day stretches long before me, so I decide to sleep where I am. Part of the seat is still wonderfully upholstered, thick and plush, and it reclines now—permanently, but so what? I relax to the softness, my body warm as an animal, my thoughts drifting. It makes no sense, but at this moment I feel rich. Sinking away, it seems like everything worth having is within my grasp. All I have to do is reach my hand into the emptiness.

# JOSEPH BRUCHAC

## Bears (1992)

*Among strange things under the sun, the destruction of children and the incarceration of our "animal" relatives are the strangest. Not that it is common for the captives to be overtly abused, as are those in the story that follows, but their suffering in alien surroundings is evident. Many Native traditions emphasize the necessity of respect for all that lives, and many stories emphasize the point, which can be summed up in the ideas of balance, respect, harmony, and integrity. Tradition teaches that our elder relations— the so-called animals and plants—are willing to help us survive by serving as food sources if we are willing in turn to give to the planet more than we take. They require that we share all we gain from them with others so that all might live; that we approach their deaths and lives with great respect, care, self-sacrifice, and danger to ourselves when hunting, fishing, whaling, and the like; and that we honor them by way of dances, prayers, and tangible tokens of our respect and gratitude.*

*Abnaki writer and publisher Joseph Bruchac's "Bears" is concerned with right relation of humans to the Animal People. "Bears" is a contemporary treatment of old Huron stories about Iouskeha, who freed the animals from a huge cavern where they were held captive, using characters and details of setting similar to those in the original narrative while rendering them in terms suited to our times. According to the Huron, Iouskeha was the grandson of Aatantsic, the mother of all humankind. Creator of the lakes and rivers, Iouskeha freed all the animals from a great cave, made corn grow, gave the Huron fire, and was responsible for good weather.*

*In "Bears," the animal's cages are backed up against the hill, and the bear's jail has a cave within it, a setting that reflects the setting of the original myth. So Iouskeha's example is followed by Peter and Foxie, and more than that, the original act of freeing our relatives is repeated, even in geo-graphical particulars. The suggestion is that the power which protects the liberators is the same power that Iouskeha wielded. "Bears" informs readers that certain Laws and certain Powers endure.*

Somebody asked me once why we Indians are so funny about bears, how come we think they are so special. I didn't know quite how to answer that question then. I just grunted and kept working on fletching an arrow. And it wouldn't have been polite to ask why white people *don't* think bears are special?

I've done some thinking about it since. A bear is a lot like a person. Or maybe it's the other way around, seeing as how the stories tell us that some of us are descended from bears. You take the skin off a bear, it looks pretty much like a human being, and according to one of the tales bears used to be able to do that on their own. They could take their skins off, put on human clothes and then act just like a regular human being—except maybe a little more polite. They'd usually do it because they had the hots for some village maiden they'd seen out berry-picking and they wanted to marry her. And then there are the stories—not so old, now—about the bearmen, the medicine men who can put on a bearskin and then turn into a bear, walk like a bear. They have a lot of power like that, but if you're brave enough to wait up at night and hide near the place where one of those bearwalkers is going and then jump out and grab them, they have to give you all you want. Money, power, you name it. Problem is, you got to make sure it is a bearwalker and not a real bear. You grab a real bear when it is walking at night and it will give you all you want—but it won't be money or power. Grab and take your chance.

There's only one road through Sullivan Park, even though you might think there were more from the way it circles and dips around and over the two big hills. The road begins at a pair of stone gates—like those of a prison or an exclusive school. You pass through them and find yourself rising up that first hill that seems to end at the top, going right up into the sky. But when you reach that crest you come down fast and the first thing you see—or smell—is the duck pond of the zoo. Its stagnant water fills the night, even a clear autumn one like this. I could smell that there would be rime on the grass at dawn, that the scummy surface of the small fenced-in pond would be white with ice, patterns as delicate as those of a bird's feathers brushed across its surface by Hatho, the frost spirit. One of the few places in the city limits where there still was an expanse of water for him to work his old magic. Like most Indians today he has had to adapt to new times, do his art work on windows as ponds and streams become less frequent. But at

Swenoga he still walks through the woods on winter days. You may not see him, but if you walk back in a ways you'll hear him on a cold day, striking the trees with his stone ax, making them crack in the old way.

As I sat next to Peter in the front seat of his red van I thought about grabbing a bear and about what we were about to try to do. Try to do. Neither of us was talking, but I could still hear his voice as he told me about the bear while we sat in my lodge. Then, the rain falling, the familiar bark walls around us, it all seemed so logical.

"It's dying, Foxy," Peter said. "Or it's going to die if it stays there. It just walks back and forth, back and forth in that cage. It doesn't look like it is looking at anything. But when it stops you can see that its eyes are always looking toward the hills. Toward Swenoga. I've watched it so often that I feel like I'm in that cage with it. I can see it when I dream. I keep dreaming about it. Nights the kids from the projects climb over the fences and get into the zoo. I've seen what they do. They vandalize the place, spray-paint their names, kill the ducks—knock their heads off with grass whips—and they do things to the animals in open cages, like the bear. I spent a long time looking in that bear's eyes, Foxy, and I swear it was trying to tell me something. It just stopped and looked at me for a long time. Stopped pacing back and forth and looked at me. And as soon as I started thinking there was nothing I could do to help it started moaning and pacing again. So I decided to do something and I decided to ask if you could help me. You know why I want you to help me."

Yup, I knew why. It was because of all the stories I'd told him about bears. But now it wasn't a story. It was very late at night and we were heading for the zoo in a panel truck planning to liberate a bear. I sighed and shook my head. How did I get into this? Well, I'd agreed to come along and I was stuck with it. But at least I knew Peter had to have a good plan. Lawyers always have good plans. He probably had a tranquilizer gun or nets in the back of the van and knew exactly what he was going to do.

Peter heard my sigh and looked over at me, my face illuminated for a moment by the stoplight on Sullivan Boulevard. Pretty soon we'd reach that statue of the old Indian fighter, heroic burner of cornfields and girdler of fruit trees.

"I know," Peter said, "it makes me sigh, too, whenever I think about that zoo."

"Hmmm," I said. What else could I say? We rode along in silence a while longer as the streets grew darker. We were getting close to Sullivan Park. I wondered what sort of plan Peter *did* have.

"Foxy?"

"Yep?"

"How the hell are we going to do this?"

I closed my eyes and put my hand over my mouth like I was thinking. Actually I was holding my mouth shut to keep it from saying *Let Me*

*Out of Here!* I thought, too, about accidentally leaning too hard against the door handle so the door would swing open and I'd fall out. We weren't going too fast, and if I was lucky I'd end up with a couple of broken bones. That'd be better than ending up in jail. But I didn't do it. I knew why. Peter was right. Now that we had said it, now that we had realized it, that bear was like our brother. It was like an Indian. It was a part of Creation as much as we were and we'd promised to do something and now we had to do it. Something.

During the war I saw that sometimes the best plan is to have no plan at all. There was one general who made it all the way across North Africa, confusing the hell out of Rommel, by never having a plan. That general was always making mistakes, too. He'd take a wrong turn and attack at places no sane man would dream of attacking. The Germans always figured he had some master plan they couldn't understand and so they would retreat or get so confused they would make even bigger mistakes themselves and then lose. Sometimes you just have to get into things and then work it out from there. And I was in it now.

"Peter," I said, "that road there goes to the Sphinx Mall, don't it?"

Ten minutes later I came out of the Fatz Stationery Store with a bundle under my arm. We'd made it just five minutes before closing time. I opened the door of the van with my left hand and heaved the bundle up on the seat in front of me.

"Stencils and fast-drying spray paint," I said. "I ever tell you about the time I worked as a sign painter, Peter?"

Half an hour later a van pulls through the gates of the zoo, allowed in by a bored night watchman who pays little attention to it, or to its driver (long hair stuffed under a cap), or to the fact that the letters that spell out ATTICA UNIVERSITY ZOOLOGY DEPARTMENT waver a bit out of a straight line.

Sullivan Park is not quiet at night. It might seem that way to someone who doesn't listen or know how to listen, but not to me. There's a small wind in the trees, but that isn't the sound I'm hearing. Animals make noises at night. In the woods those noises are natural. Here they aren't. They're like the sounds children make when they are about to drift off into a sleep that they know is going to be full of nightmares. Bad dreams about teenage kids carrying long sticks with razor blades embedded in the end. Sticks just long enough to reach into cages. Long enough to slash the heads off the ducks or geese unwary enough to bed down near the edge of their pond where they are still within reach. Whimpering sounds. Sounds that will make me dream bad when I remember them in years to come. Nightmares, but nightmares acted out by kids whose own lives are too often like nightmares when they are awake. The kids like those found OD'd on cocaine or black heroin. They found two of them last week near the west fence to the park. Now the guards watch the fences more carefully. Let them die in their own neighborhoods but not here. Here only animals are supposed to be dying.

I shake my head. This place fills my head with the wrong kind of thoughts.

"You think we should wait a little, Foxy?" Peter says.

"Drive around a little more."

Peter glances at his watch. 10:30 PM.


"You think we ought to do it now, Foxy?"

This time when he asks me I groan. It is the fourth time he's asked, looking at his watch each time. The second time he asked I asked him what he had in the back to keep the bear under control. You need something? he asked. I don't answer him. It is my own damn fault for letting him think I can talk to animals. Well, I can talk to animals. But that doesn't mean they are going to listen to me. The third time he asked I just grunted and shook my head. Part of me was hoping that a night watchman would wonder why we were parked in front of the empty administration building. That same part of me that was weighing whether it was better to go to jail for unsuccessfully attempting to get a bear out of its cage or to end up in the hospital after getting it out successfully and finding myself between it and freedom. Talk to animals. What do you say to a four-hundred-pound black bear? It is like what you say to a four hundred-pound-gorilla. You say "Sir!"

So when Peter asks me I groan. "Oh my oh my," a little moan escaping my lips. "Oh oh oh oh." But as I moan I see Peter starting to tap his hand on the wheel. Somehow my moaning is coming out like a song. I moan a little louder and by gosh I am singing. Somehow. It doesn't even sound too bad and as I listen to my own voice I begin to feel better. An old Swenoga social dance song. A Bear dance, by gosh!

When I've finished the song I feel real good. "What time is it, Peter?"

"Midnight."

"Okay. It's time."


Bears are funny animals. Like people. You never know what to expect from a bear. That's like people, too. Friend of mine, Choctaw guy, traveled for years with the circus and he learned what the most dangerous job was. Not lion tamer or tightrope walker. Nope, bear trainer. Working with those big, clumsy-looking lovable Russian brown bears. Like big teddy bears wearing funny hats and riding bicycles. But you never knew what they were thinking, my Choctaw friend said. You could tell when another animal was getting bad, but a bear might be good one minute and bad the next. Moody. Like to do things their own way. Carry grudges, he said.

He'd feed 'em but he was damned if he was ever going to be talked into working with them in the shows. Saw one big Russian brown swipe the face right off his trainer then get back on his little bicycle and pedal around the ring while they were carrying the trainer off and looking for a gun or a net. After hundreds of years of being trained, being clowns and captives and star attractions in little shows all over the world, deep down inside bears have never accepted that as their place, never accepted belonging to anyone but themselves and the Creator. Like Indian people. And if you think you own a bear, then don't expect it to be your friend.

We're parked right behind the hill that the bear cages are placed against. Right next to the cage where the one remaining black bear is kept. There's a tree stump next to us. As I get out of Peter's truck I place my hand on top of that stump. The tree has been cut down only a few days before and little ridges of ice have formed from the bleeding rings. I think about what each of those rings means, each one a full cycle of the seasons. Together they span all the generations since the white people claimed this part of the continent. It was an old tree, though not as old as some. But still old enough to have been here longer than any single human life. The rings are thinner on this stump near the outside, thinner as they came closer to the present. Tree rings are not all the same thickness. In good years, years good for trees and other living things, the rings are thick. Peter is looking at me in the half-darkness created by the light diffused through the bars from a carbon arc streetlamp fifty yards away.

"This one," I say, "lived a long time. Back when it was young our people used its bark to make longhouses, canoes, bowls. They burned its wood for their cooking fires. I know people say now that elm don't burn good. It's tough wood, all right, tough to split, hard to cut. But we used it and we didn't complain. Wherever there were elm trees, we were there, too. Then they came. They brought the disease with them. The trees got sick—their tops died away first, their branches began to fall. Like this tree, they died. All the elm trees are dying. You know, Peter, when all the elms are finally dead, I want to be dead."

Peter reaches out and puts his hand next to mine on the stump. The ice is melting from the warmth of our hands. "Do you feel it?" he says.

"What?" I say, but I think I already know.

"Like somebody—or something—is watching us."

"Yes," I say.

"I think what we are going to do is right," he says.

I stand there, feeling that the life isn't all gone out of that elm tree, feeling as if its sap is flowing up through my fingers into my arms. I'm thinking the words of the old thanksgiving speech, the one my people always used to say at the start of any ceremony, any great undertaking. I find myself remembering all the living things, greeting them and thanking them. The earth, the trees, the running streams, all those things which give us life. Then I am no longer just thinking them, I am saying them and Peter is speaking with me. Our voices aren't loud, but I can feel everything around us that is not human has begun to listen. Listen. Listen. When I finish and take my hand away from the stump it seems as if the air is clean around us. I feel young and strong. And I'm thinking that getting a bear out of a locked cage is no big thing to do at all. Just bend open the bars and carry it away like you'd pick up a puppy. That strong feeling only lasts a moment and I can feel myself growing weak and small and old again. But this time it is different. I may be weak and small and old, but I'm not alone.

"What's that little building over there?" I say. There's a small shed that is painted a dark color, so dark we hadn't seen it before, even though it is less than thirty feet away. Its door is held closed by a sliding bolt. Unlocked. I slide it back, swing open the door. Peter flicks his pocket lighter and we both smile at what I pick up from the floor. I hand it to Peter.

"Ever use a bolt cutter before?"

I close the door to the shed, feeling once again the presence of approving watchers. "If things keep going this way," I say, "I'm going to start saving my fingernails again for you people."

"Who?" Peter says. "Fingernails?"

"I'll explain it later." We've reached the walkway in front of the cages and I'm looking around.

"Entrance door's back there."

"Just lookin'," I say. A row of a dozen cages is built into the hillside. North American animals. Farther up the hill are the compounds where a single elk and a single buffalo try to roam. I think of setting them free, but it wouldn't do much good unless I had a horse van for them. Those who wear horns are the first ones to get shot. Three years ago the elk wasn't alone in her yard. There was a bull and three cows. A dead limb fell in a storm and knocked down the fence and the four of them got out. The bull was shot within an hour. It got close to the edge of the park and someone shot it with a telescopic rifle from one of the apartment buildings. A sportsman. By then the local police were on the scene and trying to herd the three cows back. One of them got too close to a cop who panicked and unloaded his gun into its neck. Another was hit by a city bus. The third one got back to its pen on its own. A fox or a coyote might still be able to run wild and survive in Sullivan Park, but not an animal with horns.

The Rodioners, the men chosen to be leaders by the Iroquois, they wore horns on their heads as a mark of the honor of that office. When Champlain came down the big lake into our land hundreds of years ago he fired his arquebus into a crowd of Iroquois people standing on the shore, watching his progress. Of those who were killed, several were men who wore horns. One of the reasons why we Swenogas stopped choosing chiefs—publicly, at least—was because of that. Because the ones who wear the horns get shot first. In the mid-1800s three Swenoga head chiefs in a row were shot by person or persons unknown right after they took office. But Coyote doesn't wear horns and Coyote survives. We Swenogas usually learn by the third try. We stopped publicizing who our chiefs were.

"Okay, let's go around here."

"This isn't the bear cage."

"Have to start somewhere."

Peter opens the bolt cutter and grasps the padlock with it. He presses the handles toward each other and the metal shears like butter.

He whistles. "Nice!"

I swing the door open. A pair of small red shapes leap out and dart up the hill, their feet scrabbling the leaves.

"Good luck, Foxes," I say.

Peter is already cutting the lock on the next cage. He stands aside and I swing the door open. Nothing comes out.

"Coyote," I say. "You wouldn't trust your own grandfather, would you?" I can see him, a gray shape in the corner behind a papier mâché log. I leave the door open. If we look back in five minutes, I know this cage, too, will be empty.

Between each cage and the next is a narrow walkway. The one that leads to the door to the bear den dead-ends against the hillside. The end has been built against the rock cliff so that there is a cave in the rock itself, a place where a bear might hide. But the entrance to that cave is blocked off by a door that hasn't been opened in so long it's rusted shut. People who come to the zoo want to see the animals. The lock on the bear cage is twice as large as the others. From the rust on it you can see it hasn't been opened for a long time. It takes Peter three tries to cut through it and even then the two of us have to wrestle with the lock to wedge it out.

My heart is beating fast and my arms feel weak. I'm about to turn the handle on the door to swing it open when I realize what I've been forgetting to remember. How are we going to get a four-hundred-pound black bear from a cage into a van a hundred yards away. Maybe, I think, if we back the van up to the alley between the cages, push the latch open with a long stick? I start to turn around to ask Peter what he thinks.

"You know—" I start to say, raising my hand as I turn. But my sleeve is caught on something. I jerk it hard and realize, just as I hear the click, that what my sleeve was caught on was the handle on the door. The door swings open then, slowly, as if something is pushing it. For a split second as I look up I see only darkness. My nose is filled with the heavy odor of a huge animal's piss and wet fur. I don't hear anything—not a growl or a roar—but then a heavy shape comes rolling out of the cage, right on top of me, crushing me to the ground.

## 2

You know, there's this theory I've got. Well, it isn't exactly mine. It's sort of one that Deskaheh had. He was the Cayuga who went to Europe to talk to the League of Nations about our people. He said the Little People were on good terms with us Iroquois because we got the Dark Dance. Whenever that ceremony takes place, the little ones come and dance with us. We hear their voices join in the singing and they feel real good about it, being thanked and included like that. That's what Deskaheh thought and I think so, too. The Cherokees and some of the others, they're scared of the Little People. In all their stories about them, the Little People can't be trusted. Folks do something that gets the little folks angry and then they get hurt. The Cherokees' Little People are sort of treacherous from what I've heard. But us Long House People, we have the Dark Dance, and so the Little People are friendly. That's what I believe.

There are places where we know they still live. You might not see as much of them as you did many years ago. I don't think they like the pollution any more than us Indians like it. They don't like all that noise that goes with the cities and the four-lane highways. So they make themselves scarce. You'd hardly know they were around most of the time—just like us Indians. But they haven't died off. Not by a long shot. I could show you this cave. And there's one ravine down by the creek where people who want to show the little folks that they're thinking about them still go and throw little bundles of fingernail clippings. The Little People like to use those clippings. I think it's that the scent of the human fingernails covers up their own scent when they go out hunting—or maybe it's to scare certain things off. Whatever it is, they like those nail clippings.

There's different tribes of them, you know. There's the Stone Throwers, they live on the cliffs and they aren't so friendly. You get too close to their territory and a rock will come whizzing at you and you'd better just turn around. Then there's the Underwater People. They have stone canoes that can come to the surface and then go underwater and they eat fish. Their faces are about as thin as a knife blade and they keep away from people. Sometimes you see little rolls and mounds of clay by the water's edge where they've been working making things. I've traveled out west some and Indian people there talk about water babies and I wonder if they might not be related.

Those Little People who live by the streams, they don't like to have folks see them. There was this one place by the St. Ambrose river where they used to come—I heard this story from a Micmac—way up north. Anyhow, this one man decided he was going to watch them when they came out in the evening. He knew they wouldn't come out if they saw him, so he took his canoe down by the water, turned it over and hid underneath. He told the people in the village he'd come back and tell them about what he saw. It came time for breakfast the next day and that man didn't come back. Then it was time for lunch and he still wasn't back. That was unusual, because that man really liked his meals. When it came time for supper and he still wasn't back, his friends thought maybe he was staying to see the show for a second time. But when the next morning came and he didn't show up for breakfast, they got a little worried. And when he wasn't there for lunch, they figured maybe they'd better go and look. They went down to the place where his canoe was by the water, but that canoe was turned right side up now. There was no sign of the man. There by the water, though, the clay had been piled up into a sort of a mound. They looked at that mound and saw it was shaped like a man. There were the arms and the legs and there, just in the middle of the head where the mouth would be, there was a little hole. The clay was all hard. They leaned close and they thought they could hear something like breathing come through that hole. So they broke the clay open and there was the man inside. He was just barely alive. They gave him water and got him up and he seemed to be okay, but he wouldn't talk about what happened to him. Not until he got back to the village. He told them that just when it got dark he was watching and watching. All of a sudden his canoe was turned over and he felt little hands all over him, pulling and pushing him. He didn't see anything, but the next thing he knew he was all covered over with clay and he couldn't move. So he never did see those Little People, but he wasn't about to try again.

My favorites are the Little People who are in charge of the dew. They make sure that it gets on the flowers and the food plants. They especially love strawberries and during the season when the strawberries are getting ripe they're the ones who turn the berries so that they ripen the same on all sides. Those are the Little People who keep a real close watch on things. One thing they do is see that stories aren't told during the summer. You start telling one of the old stories in the summer and a bee might fly right up and sting you to remind you it's the wrong time. That bee is one of the little ones in disguise. Or they might send snakes into your house. Storytelling time is after the first frost. They keep a close watch. On a lot of things. And I think they're keeping an even closer watch these days. Now that some people are finally waking up. That's what I believe.

There's also Little People whose job it is to guard the entrance to the underworld places where the really evil creatures are. Back when the world was new there were two boys, twins, born to the first woman who was born on earth. One of those twins was bad-minded and he made all kinds of dangerous creatures, monsters that would destroy the people. So his brother penned them up in caves under the earth and told the Little People to guard those places. Sometimes some of those evil things get out and the Little People have to round them up. It's a difficult job, protecting the world from evil things, you know that? And these days, those evil things are coming in all sorts of new shapes. But they still come from that same place. That's what I believe.

It took me a while to catch my breath. You'd take a while, too, if you were a man in his sixties who had four hundred pounds of black bear sprawled on top of you.

"Peter," I squeaked, "get me out from under this bear!"

From somewhere on the other side of the mountain of dark furry flesh that had rolled out onto me I heard Peter's voice.

"I'm trying, Foxy. He weighs a goddam ton!"

It took a bunch of pulling and pushing and prying, but somehow we got that bear rolled over enough for me to squeeze out from between it and the hillside. I had a few bruises, but that was all.

"What the hell did you do, Foxy? Hypnotize it?"

"You know as much as I do," I said. I leaned over and held my hand next to the bear's nose. "He's still breathing, but he's out cold. I guess he's knocked out from something those kids fed him, some kind of drugs."

"Is he dying?"

"I don't think so. Something tells me he's okay. But even if he's not, I think getting him out to the woods is the best thing. If he comes to, he'll be able to doctor himself out there."

We scouted around a little and found another toolshed with a heavy-duty garden cart in it. The two of us managed to prop the bear up and roll him back into it. Lying on his back with his feet dangling, he looked like a kid out for a ride. We put down the ramp at the back of the van, rolled him up and dumped him in. While I put the garden cart back, Peter busied himself by the doors of the cages we'd opened. I came over to see what he was doing. With the awl point blade of his Swiss Army knife he was scratching a design into each of the doors. The shape of a bear paw. Not a bad idea. We checked to make sure the back of the van was closed up tight, started it up, and drove out of Hiawatha Park.

# MARTIN CRUZ SMITH

## The Russian Duck (1992)

*Martin Cruz Smith has written a number of novels, including a couple of best-sellers, and three of his novels have been adapted for the screen. The best known is* Gorky Park. *However, Smith has written several novels with more Native themes, the best of which is* Stallion Gate, *a novel about building the bomb so close to Pueblo country. Two others that center on Native American thought or character are* The Indians Won *and* Nightwing. *In the range of his subject matter, characters, and themes, Smith is another of the Native writers whose work draws from the international nature of contemporary Native American life and centers on the interlocking themes of international conflict and mystery.*

    Red Square, *from which this story is excerpted, is the third in the* Gorky Park *series, following* Polar Star. *The hero is a Russian detective, Arkady; his lady love is also Russian, now an ex-patriate, Irina. The first and second books of the trilogy were written before the collapse of the Soviet Union, while* Red Square *was written after. In the wake of the collapse Arkady has been freed from the sentence he was given following his solving a homicide he, as a Moscow city detective, was assigned. In the course of that investigation he met and fell in love with Irina and, after they found the killer, secured the Soviet government's agreement to her emigration. She has moved to Munich and spent much time with other émigrés such as Max and Stas. Arkady has resumed his position as a detective in Moscow and has come to Munich to carry out an investigation, and to find Irina. Like an Indian in the contemporary world, Arkady is a duck out of water. Even so, love, beauty, and honor propel him as they propelled Native "chiefs." And while he is out of his element, he remains fully aware of his responsibility and the purpose of his quest.*

*     *     *

In the morning a heavy fog brought out headlights. Bicycles appeared and disappeared as wraiths.

Irina lived a block from the park, on a street that mixed town houses, artists' studios and boutiques. All the buildings were dressed in fey *Jugendstil* except hers, which was plain and modern. Though her windows were set back, Arkady located her balcony, a chrome rail before a wall of vines, lush and bright in the wet. He stood at a bus stop at the end of the street, the most logical and least conspicuous place to wait.

Did the balcony lead directly to the kitchen? He could imagine the warmth of lights, the smell of coffee. He could also imagine Max having an extra cup, but he had to eliminate Max from the picture in his mind or slide into crippling jealousy. Irina might drive to the station. Worse, she might leave with Max. He focused on the hope that she was alone, was drying a cup and saucer, was putting on her raincoat, would take the bus.

A delivery truck parked in the middle of the block. The driver climbed down from the cab, opened the rear doors, brought racks down to street level with a hydraulic lift and rolled them into a dress shop. The truck's windshield wipers kept time, though rain wasn't falling so much as hanging in the air in fine droplets. Traffic had a sheen. Arkady stepped off the curb for a better view of Irina's house when a bus arrived and chased him back. Passengers boarded and canceled their own tickets in an automatic punch box. Every single one of them—that was the amazing thing.

The bus pulled away and the delivery truck drove off. It took Arkady a minute to notice that the vine-covered wall on Irina's balcony was a darker green, which meant that the lights of her apartment were off. He watched the door for another minute before he realized that she had left while the truck had been blocking his view. He had expected her to use the bus in this weather; instead she'd gone in the other direction toward the park and he'd missed her.

Arkady ran the length of the street to the park. In the foreshortened view that accompanies emotion, umbrellas bobbed on either side. A Turk wearing a conical hat of newspaper biked between the bumpers of limousines. Across the street the Englischer Garten began as a wall of giant beeches. Farther down the street, a woman in a white raincoat entered a park gate.

He darted between cars. The radio station lay diagonally across the park. Where he entered the gate, paths twisted left and right. The Englischer Garten was called the "green lung" of Munich. It had a river, streams, forests, lakes—all veiled now by mist, giving the park a cold, close breath that made Arkady gather his jacket at his neck.

He could hear her, though; at least, he heard someone walking. Did he remember how she walked? Long strides, always sure of herself. She hated umbrellas, she hated crowds. He hurried after the echo, aware that any hesitation put her farther ahead. If she was ahead. The path kept trying to turn away. Overhead, beeches were monkey bars in a cloud. Oaks were shorter, as bent as beggars. Where the path crossed a streambed, steam rose from the water, a ghostly flood tide. A creature resembling a large caterpillar sniffed around wet leaves. Closer, it became a wire-haired dachshund. Its owner crept behind, a yellow slicker with a scoop and bag.

Beyond, Irina had disappeared—if it was Irina. Over the years, at a distance, how many women had he dressed in her features? This was the illusion of his life, the nightmare.

Arkady had the park to himself. He heard the slow condensation of mist on leaves, the thud of nuts from the beeches onto sodden earth, the dash of unseen birds. Where shadows faded, he found he had reached the edge of a wide meadow, completely lost in a circle of green. For a moment on the far side he saw a flash of white.

Running over the grass, he had the labored breath and heavy feet of a farm horse. When he reached the spot where the brief sight of white had been, she was gone again. Now, though, he knew the direction. A path led along a russet screen of maples and the languid vapor of another stream. He heard steps again and, where the maples ended, saw her, a bag over her shoulder. Her coat was actually more silver than white, with a reflective quality. Her hair was uncovered, darker in the rain. She looked back and then continued walking, faster than before.

They walked at the same pace, ten meters apart, down a dark avenue of firs. Where the path narrowed to a strip that threaded a stand of birches, she slowed, then stopped and leaned against the white, papery column of a birch for him to catch up.

They walked on together in silence. Arkady felt like a man who had approached a deer. The single wrong word, he thought, and she would bolt for good. When she glanced at him he didn't dare try to hold her eyes or read them. At least they were walking side by side. In itself, that was a victory.

He was sorry that he looked so bad. His shoes were flecked with grass, his clothes damp and molded to his back. His body was too thin, and probably his eyes had the glower of the chronically starved.

They came to the edge of a lake. The water was black and still. Irina looked down at their reflections, at the man and woman looking up from the water, and said, "That's the saddest thing I ever saw."

"Me?" Arkady asked.

"Us."


Birds collected. The park was rich in them: velvet-headed mallards, wood ducks, wigeons and teal appeared out of the mist, breaking the surface of the water into spoons of light. Shearwaters flew as acrobatically as signatures, geese dropped like sacks.

They sat on a bench.

She said, "There are people who come here every day to feed the birds. They bring pretzels the size of wheels."

It was cool enough for their breath to condense.

"I sympathize with these birds," she said. "The difference is that you never came. I will never forgive you."

"I can tell."

"And now that you're here, I feel like a refugee all over again. I don't like that feeling."

"No one does."

"But I've been in the West for years. I've earned the right to be here. Arkady, go home. Leave me alone."

"No. I won't go."

He half-expected her to rise and leave the bench. He would follow her; what else could he do? She stayed. She let him light another cigarette for her. "A bad habit," she said. "Like you."

Despair saturated the air. Cold penetrated his thin jacket. He heard his heart echo across the water. A walking collection of bad habits was what he was. Ignorance, insubordination, lack of exercise, dull razors.

So many birds arrived, some dropping wholesale in flocks, others wheeling individually out of the mist, that Arkady was put in mind of the factory ship he had spent part of his exile on, and how gulls had mobbed the air above the stern for the overflow and refuse from the nets. He remembered standing in the breeze above the stern ramp fieldstripping a cigarette and a gull snatching the paper from the air and carrying it away as its prize. "Find the Russian duck," he said.

"Where?"

"The one with dirty feathers and a crooked bill smoking a cigarette."

"There is no such thing."

"But you looked, I saw you. Imagine when Russian ducks really do hear about this lake, a lake with pretzels, they'll come here by the millions."

"The swans too?"

A line of swans glided imperiously through the ducks. When a mallard resisted, the lead swan stretched out its long and creamy neck, opened its bright, yellow bill and snorted like a pig.

"Russian. He's already infiltrated," Arkady said.

Irina sat back to study him. "You do look terrible."

"I can't say the same for you."

She bent the light her way. Mist sat on her hair like jewels. "I heard you were doing so well in Moscow," she said.

"Who did you hear that from?"

She hesitated. "You're not what I expected. You're what I remembered."


They walked slowly. Arkady was aware that she walked a critical millimeter closer and that their shoulders occasionally grazed.

"Stas was always curious about you. I'm not surprised you're friends. Max says you're both artifacts of the cold war."

"We are. I'm like a piece of marble you find in an ancient ruin. You pick it up, turn it around in your hand and ask, 'What was this? Part of a horse trough or part of a noble statue?' I want to show you something." He took out an envelope, opened it and showed her the paper and the one word scribbled inside.

"My name," she said.

"It's my father's writing. I hadn't heard from him in years. This must have been almost the last thing he did before he died. You actually talked to him?"

"I wanted to reach you without causing trouble so I tried your father."

Arkady tried to imagine this. It sounded like a dove flying into a furnace, though his father had been a fairly cold furnace in his last years.

"He told me what a hero you were, how they tried to break you but that you forced the prosecutor's office to take you back, that they gave you the most difficult cases and that you never lost. He was proud. He went on and on. He said he saw you often and that you'd write me."

"What else?"

"That you were too busy for women, but women were always chasing you."

"None of this rang a false note?"

"He said the only problem with you was that you were a fanatic and that sometimes you put yourself in God's place. That some things only God could judge."

"If I were General Kiril Renko, I wouldn't have been so eager to see the face of God."

"He said he thought about you more and more. Did you have women?"

"No. I was in psychiatric cells for a while, then I was in Siberia on the move, and then I was fishing. There was limited opportunity."

She stopped him. "Please, I remember Russia. There's always opportunity. And when you got back to Moscow, you must have had a woman there."

"I was in love. I wasn't looking for women."

"In love with me?"

"Yes."

"You *are* a fanatic."

They walked along a pond that bore snowy down and fine drops of rain like pearls. Was it the same lake as before?

"Arkasha, what are we going to do?"

They left the park for a university café that had stainless-steel machines hissing into pots of milk and posters of Italy—ski slopes of the Dolomites, colorful tenements in Naples—on the walls. The other patrons were students with open books and bowl-sized cups of coffee. They took a table by the window.

Arkady talked about working his way across Siberia, from Irkutsk to Norilsk to Kamchatka to the sea.

Irina talked about New York, London, Berlin. "Theater work in New York was good, but I couldn't join the union. They're like Soviet unions—worse. I waited on tables. In New York, waitresses are fantastic. So hard and so old you think they waited on Alexander the Great or the pharaohs. Hard workers. An art gallery. They wanted someone with a European accent. I was part of the gallery ambience, and I started getting involved in art again. What no one was interested in then was the Russian avant-garde. You know, you expected to see me in Russia and I expected to see you walk into an art gallery on Madison Avenue, dressed in a proper suit, good shoes, tie."

"Next time we should coordinate dreams."

"Anyway, Max was visiting the Liberty office in New York. He produced a show on Russian art and happened to interview me and said if I was ever in Munich and needed work to call him. A year later I did. I still do some work for Berlin galleries. They're always looking for pieces of Revolutionary art because now the prices are phenomenally high."

"You mean the art of our defunct and discredited Revolution?"

"Is auctioned at Sotheby's and Christie's. Collectors can't get enough. You're in trouble, aren't you?"

"I *was* in trouble. Not now."

"I mean with your work."

"Work has its difficult moments. The good people die and the wrong people walk away with the spoils. My career seems to be in a shadow, but I'm thinking of taking a holiday, a vacation from professional pursuits."

"And do what?"

"I could become a German. Transitionally, of course. First I'd turn into a Pole, then an East German, finally a fully mature Bavarian."

"Seriously."

"Seriously, I will wear different clothes every day and walk into your life until you say, 'This is just what Arkady Renko should look like; this is the proper suit.'"

"You wouldn't let go?"
"Not now."


Arkady described how the breath of a reindeer herd crystallized and fell like snow. He talked about salmon runs on Sakhalin, the white-headed eagles of the Aleutians and waterspouts that danced around the Bering Sea. He'd never thought before of what a catalog of experiences his exile had brought to him, how unique and beautiful they were, what clear evidence that on no day could a man be sure he should not open his eyes.

They had a lunch of microwaved pizza. Delicious.

He told her how the first wind of the day approaching through the taiga made the million trees shiver like black birds taking flight. He talked about oil field fires that burned year-round, beacons that could be seen from the moon. He described walking from trawler to trawler across the Arctic ice. Sounds and sights not afforded most investigators.

They had red wine.

He talked about workers on the "slime line," the dark hold where fish were gutted in a factory ship, and how each individual was a separate mind with a fantasy unconfined by gunwales or decks—a defender of the Party who had taken to the sea in search of romance, a botanist who dreamed of Siberian orchids, each person a lamp on a separate world.

After finishing the wine, they had brandy.

He described the Moscow he had found on his return. Center stage, a dramatic battlefield of warlords and entrepreneurs; behind it, as still as a painted backdrop, eight million people standing in line. Yet there were moments, the occasional dawn when the sun was low enough to find a golden river and blue domes, and the entire city seemed redeemable.

# MICHAEL DORRIS

## Groom Service (1991)

*"Groom Service" is a Dorris triumph. It belongs right next to "Zuma Chowt's Cave," being as funny a story as I've read. As in Popkes' story, the humor in "Groom Service" rests primarily in its trickster-nature rather than in joking characters or narrative asides. The humor is as much in the double-voiced nature of the story as in its actual development. The story is about a youthful Native who must become a man. That he does so in this particularly traditional manner rather than in ways popularized by a trendy if eerie combination of Robert Bly and Hollywood is the true source of the humor of the tale.*

*Bernard comes to the threshold of manhood in a female-dominant community. Among the people of this community a young man must be accepted by his mother-in-law-to-be, her female siblings, and, of course, his intended. But the courtship is prescribed by the women—his mother and hers—rather than the children, and he must follow custom, however painful or foolish he finds it, if he desires to be counted among the adult men of his community. In part the tradition compels him to develop adult habits of mind and demeanor. It also provides the youth and the young woman who are to marry plenty of time to decide if they truly desire the match.*

*There is a bit being written about gynocentric Native societies in the last quarter of the twentieth century, all of it by Native women and one very talented, hilarious man. Dorris is as skillful a storymaker as any Native writing today.*

I

"She's a piece of pure quartz," Bernard's mother, Martha, said to Marie's mother, Blanche. "A one-in-a-million that you find after walking the beach for half your life with your eyes on the ground. If I had a child like that I would keep her in a safe place."

Blanche paused her blade midway down the side of the fish she was scaling. Her face betrayed no expression except exertion, and even in this intermission her teeth remained set, flexing her jaw. The trader steel reflected what little light filtered through the planks of the smokehouse, and the confined air still smelled green. Blanche had hewn the boards with a mallet and chisel in May, as soon as the ground firmed from the spring runoff, and it took a while before the scent of fire crowded that of drying wood. With her broad thumb she flicked a piece of fin off the carved knife handle, then continued her motion.

Martha waited. She had all the time it took.

"You don't know," said Blanche. She shook her head as if its secrets rolled like line-weights from side to side. She drew a heavy breath. "You can't imagine. You with such a boy."

Martha sat straighter, all ears, while her hands continued to explore, repairing the tears on the net that lay across her lap and hid her pants and boots. Her fingers moved automatically, finding holes, locating the ends of broken cord and twisting them into square knots. She kept her nails sharp and jagged, and when they weren't enough, she bowed her head and bit off any useless pieces. This was mindless work, the labor of ten thousand days, and could be done as easily in the dark as in the light. It required no involvement. Her thoughts were elsewhere.

"You mean Bernard?" Her voice was wary. She had three sons and needed to be sure she knew the one Blanche had in mind.

"Ber-*nard*," Blanche nodded, giving the knife a last run, then inspecting the fish closely before tossing it into the large basket at her feet. The water slopped onto the floor and, from there, leaked to the shale ground inches below. Blanche arched her back and massaged her spine with her fist. With her other hand she reached for the cup of cooled tea that she had nursed for the past half-hour. Martha let the net rest and joined her.

"People talk about him, you know," Blanche said. "His looks, that goes without saying, but the other things too. The respect he pays the old folks. His singing. His calmness. His hunting skill. You must be proud."

Martha closed her eyes as if in great pain. "He is my punishment," she confessed, "but I don't know what I could have done so terrible as to deserve him. He stays out until morning. His hair is always tangled. I sometimes think that the game he brings home has died before he found it, the meat is so tough. You must have him confused with another boy. Or perhaps, with a girl like Marie, you find it hard to think ill of any child."

"Now you make fun of me," Blanche said. "It is well known that Marie has turned out badly. She is lazy and disrespectful, conceited and stubborn. I try my best to teach her, and so do my sisters and even my mother, but she folds her arms and stares at nothing. Hopeless. And she will never find a husband. A boy's mother would have to be desperate to send her son courting at my house."

"But not as desperate as the mother who could tolerate the thought of Bernard as a son-in-law," Martha said. "That would be true desperation. I will never be free of him. I will grow old with him at my side, and with no granddaughters or grandsons to comfort me."

"If only someone like your Bernard would find an interest in Marie," Blanche said as if she had not heard Martha. "If only some young man exactly like him would consent to live in my house, how I would welcome him. I would treat him as my own blood."

The two women met each other's gaze at last. Each held a cup to her lips, and after a few seconds, each drank. Each replaced her cup on the table between them. Each held her mouth firm. Blanche found her knife and reached for a new fish, cool and slippery as a stone over which much water has rushed. Martha shifted the net in her lap, moving a new section to the center. The smell of salt rose like steam as her hands went to work.

"I will speak to him," Martha said.

"And I to her," Blanche replied. "But I know her answer already. I have seen how she regards him."

"She will not be disappointed." Martha allowed one wave of pride to crest. "He's not so bad."

Blanche glanced up at Martha, then looked quickly back to her work. Bernard must be good indeed, she thought, if Martha could not better contain herself.

## 2

Bernard was drawing with charcoal on a piece of driftwood when his mother returned home. He was twenty-two, lean, and had large teeth. His eyes were dark beneath unusually thick brows, and his hands were long and broad. At the sound of Martha's step, he jumped to his feet and assumed the air of a person about to do something important. His fingers curved as if to hold a tool or a weapon and his eyes narrowed as if to see something far away. He was busy at nothing, his energy humming, ready for a focus. But for once she made no comment about his sloth. She did not despair at the time he wasted scratching on any smooth surface. She did not inspect his sketch and then toss it into the cooking fire. In fact, this afternoon she dealt with him rather mildly.

"Well, it's arranged," she announced. "I spent an endless morning with your future mother-in-law and before I left she had agreed to let you come to see Marie. Don't think it was easy."

Bernard's eyes followed his mother's movements as she crossed the floor and sat in exhaustion on the bed. She pushed off her boots, still caked with beach mud, and rubbed her feet together. She wore no socks.

"Marie?" he said at last. "She's too young. You should have asked me first."

Martha's glare clapped a hand over his mouth. In a moment, Bernard tried again.

"I know they're a good family. I know you want to do right for me. But you could . . . *we* could have discussed this. I mean, I think of her as a little girl, not a *wife*." The word, a stranger on Bernard's tongue, vibrated in the air.

"Stop whining." Martha lost patience. "Who do you 'think of' as a wife? *Doris?*"

Bernard blushed. He wasn't surprised that his mother knew about him and Doris, but it did not seem fair for her to mention it. Doris was a widow whose name brought nervous laughs to teenage boys and smiles of disapproval to everyone else. She was a woman almost twice Bernard's age with a missing front tooth and eyes that sparked in his memory, a woman who had summoned him for an errand six months ago and whom he now loved better than he would have thought possible. But it was true: he had never thought of Doris as a wife.

"You should see yourself," Martha said. "Keep that face and you won't have to worry about marrying anyone. But don't expect me to support you forever." She noticed the driftwood, still on the floor, and nudged it with her toe to get a better view. Bernard had outlined the mountain across the bay from the village, and tucked a large sun behind its peak. When he drew it he thought it was his best work, but now its lines looked smudged and shaky. Martha leaned forward to pick it up and turn it over, as if expecting another illustration on the back. Finding none, she held it out for Bernard to take.

"Give this to your Doris," she said. "It looks like her under the blanket where she spends her time."

Bernard didn't move, but he watched the wood until his mother let it fall to the floor. He was angry at the shame he felt. He was angry that he knew it was just a matter of time until he would have to call on Marie. He was angry that his mother was right: his mountain *did* look like Doris, turned on her side.

3

When Blanche went into the house and told Marie that their problems were over, that Bernard, the catch of the village, would be courting, she expected some reaction, but her daughter simply folded her arms and stared at the fire.

"Don't you hear me?" Blanche demanded. "Bernard. Coming to see you. Can't you be happy? Can't you say something?"

Marie, however, only rolled her eyes and drummed her fingers against the pine bench upon which she sat. She wore a close-knit woven cap that, in combination with her unfortunately weak chin, made her head resemble an acorn. She was fifteen, just out of her confinement, trained for adulthood to the limits of Blanche and her sister's patience, but still a sulking child. At length she drew up her knees, circled them with her arms, and watched her mother from the corner of her eye.

Blanche stood across the long room, talking to her older sister Bonnie. She was not hard to overhear.

"Does she say 'thank you'? Does she appreciate what it means to her, to all of us, to get that damn Martha to agree? Does she care that Bernard could have any girl, from any family?"

Bonnie shook her head sadly. Her surviving children had all been boys and had long since moved to the houses of their wives' families, so she had no experience with reluctant girls, unless, she thought, she counted her memories of Blanche. But that would not do to say, especially not in earshot of Marie, who sat with her head cocked in their direction. Blanche's daughter was the hope of the next generation, the one who had to bring in a husband and produce more daughters than her mother or aunt, if the family was to regain its position. For a moment Bonnie thought of suggesting to Blanche that they present that information to Marie directly, to drop the shadows and point out both her responsibility and her power, but then she rejected the idea. The girl was impressed enough with herself as it was. Instead, Bonnie sympathized with her sister and cast occasional looks at her niece in hopes of catching on Marie's face a secret, a streak of pleasure.

4

"What am I supposed to do?" Bernard asked the next time his uncle visited. Bernard had waited for a private moment, and it came when, just before sleep, Theodore had stepped outside to relieve himself. The trees around the village seemed closer at night, taller, like the sides of a box.

From the darkness came rattling sounds of strangulation that Bernard eventually identified as the older man's yawn. When it, and the noise of splashing water, had abated, Theodore spoke. It was clear that he understood Bernard's problem.

"You do whatever they tell you and you hope they're not as bad as they could be," Theodore said. "You don't complain. You don't assume anything. You stay out of the way, because you never know what they're going to find to dislike. You be what they want."

"It's not fair." Bernard leaned against the side of the house and searched the sky. Thin clouds, silver as wet spiderwebs, passed in the night wind.

"That's true, but there are other things in the world besides owning real estate. Your true home will remain here at your mother's, just as it has been for me, but you can't *live* here forever. You need independence, distance, the chance to be a man in a place where you were never a boy. Once you get yourself established, you'll understand what I mean. Your life is not all indoors. You'll hang around with your brothers-in-law, your uncles, your friends. Spend time at the men's house. Go to the sweat bath and gripe, or listen to the complaints of others and make jokes. In a year all your wife's family will care about is whether or not you bring in your share. By then you'll know what's what."

"But what if I don't get along with Marie?"

"*Do* get along with her. Get along with her mother. Get along with her auntie. But on your own time do what you want. It's not a big price to pay. It's a daughter-poor clan and the one they've picked out for you is going to control everything someday: rich fishing sites, a big house. Behave yourself now and you'll get your reward. It's not like you're marrying a youngest sister with no prospects."

Which was, Bernard knew, what had happened to Theodore. No wonder he was not more sympathetic.

"How do I tell Doris?" Bernard asked. This was something he had struggled with for days.

"Doris! She could have told *you*. It's good news to her. She gets a younger guy, fresh the way she likes them, and no hard feelings between you." Theodore laughed, and put an arm around Bernard's shoulders. "Listen to some advice, from your great-uncle through me to you," he said. "Groom service is the worst part, so make it as short as possible. Convince her family you won't be a pain in the ass to live with. Rule number one: appreciate everything they do. Compliment, compliment, compliment."

"Did you do that?" Bernard asked. "Did my mother's husband do that?"

"Do fish fry in hot grease? But don't take my word for it. Ask Pete. He's your father."

"I'd be embarrassed," Bernard said. "He and I never talk about serious matters. He's not of the clan."

"A man's a man," Theodore said.

### 5

"This is what you do," Martha instructed.

It was not yet light and she had awakened Bernard from a sound sleep. He blew into a cup of hot tea as he listened, let the darkness hide the resentment in his face.

"You go hunting and you catch something *good*, I don't care what. Something a little unusual. A beaver, maybe, or a goose. *Not* something small and easy. *Not* a squirrel. *Not* fish. You bring it home and I'll help you clean it. You leave a portion for me as if that's what you always do, to help provide for your family, but you take the best part and you set yourself in front of Blanche's door. You only speak if you're spoken to. You wait for *them* to ask *you*. And if they don't, which they won't right away, you act unconcerned. You do this every day until they invite you in, and then I'll tell you what to do next. This is your chance, so don't ruin it. Now move."

Bernard stepped out into the chill morning grayness, thought briefly of visiting Doris before he went hunting, but then abandoned the idea. He had heard through his mother's husband that Doris had made friends with a seventeen-year-old boy named James.

The dew from high grass had soaked through to Bernard's feet before he reached the edge of the woods. He realized his mother had forgotten to feed him breakfast, forgotten to make him a lunch. He heard a duck call from the lake and paused, but then continued on. He could hear his mother in his mind, and she said a duck wouldn't do.

6

"He's *there*!" Bonnie dropped the firewood she was carrying and rushed to Blanche's side.

Her sister was stirring a pot on the fire, as if what it contained were all that concerned her. "I have eyes," Blanche said. "Keep your voice down. He'll hear you."

"Did you see what he had?" Bonnie asked. "I got a glimpse of something flat and dark, but I didn't want him to catch me looking."

"I think it was a beaver tail. Would you believe, he had the nerve to hold it up to me and smile the first time I passed."

"No!"

"I thought he was better trained. It simply means he'll have to wait longer."

"Did Marie see him yet?"

"She won't go outside." Both sisters turned to the gloom in the rear of the room where Marie crouched, her head lowered over a stick game. Her long hair was loose and covered her shoulders like a shawl, her back to the doorway.

## 7

"Well, what happened?" Martha demanded when Bernard returned home late in the evening.

"Nothing happened," Bernard said, and threw himself down on his blankets. He raised an arm to cover his eyes, then turned to face the wall.

Martha spotted the sack her son had dropped on the floor and looked inside. The beaver tail and quarters were exactly as she had cleaned them that afternoon, and she took them out to add to the broth she had prepared.

"At least we'll eat well for a while," she said.

"I'm not hungry," Bernard replied, but his mother ignored him.

"Tell me everything."

"There's nothing to tell. I walked over there, dressed like I was going to a feast, carrying that beaver. I trapped it clean, surprised it so completely, there wasn't even adrenaline in its flesh. I thought they'd taste it, invite me to supper, but they walked by me like I wasn't there, their noses in the air."

"Whose noses?" Martha wanted to know.

"The mother and the aunt."

"Not the girl?"

"I saw no girl. I heard no girl."

"Ah," said Martha. "So she's shy. Good."

"Why good?"

"Because then she won't bully you at first, stupid boy. I've seen what happens to the husbands of the bold ones."

The smell of stewing meat filled the room, warm, rich, brown. Martha's husband Pete came into the house at the scent, tipped his head in his son's direction, and asked, "Hard day?"

## 8

For a week, then two weeks, the same pattern was repeated. Only the animals changed: they ranged from a porcupine to a hind quarter of caribou, from a fat grouse on a bad day to a string of matched silver salmon on a good one. Once Bernard thought he saw a black bear dive into the brush at the side of a stream, but he was momentarily afraid to investigate, and later berated himself. With a bear skin, he thought too late, he would have been irresistible and his long afternoons and evenings at Blanche's closed door would have been over.

As a month passed, Bernard gave up hope. He lost the alertness he had once felt when Blanche or Bonnie or Marie, the most unsympathetic of them all, approached, and he soon tired of the commiseration that Blanche's and Bonnie's husbands cast in his direction as they went about their business. They could remember, their expressions said, what it was like to wait outside this house, but there was nothing they could do. A word from them might slow the process rather than speed it up, might do more damage than good. If boredom was patience, Bernard achieved patience. If learning to exist without expectation of fulfillment was maturity, Bernard matured. At first he used his time to remember Doris, to wonder what she was doing and to regret not doing it with her. Later he thought about hunting, how he could have succeeded the times he had failed, how the animals behaved, how they smelled and sounded. Finally he found himself thinking about Pete, his father, in different ways than he ever had before. In Bernard's mind Pete became more than just his mother's husband; he became another man, an earlier version of Bernard, a fellow sufferer. It had not previously occurred to Bernard how hard it was to be forever a stranger in the house where you lived, to be always a half-visitor. He wondered how Pete stayed so cheerful, and wondered if his grandmother had kept his father waiting long at the doorway before inviting him inside. On an afternoon late in the second week, Bernard had a thought so profound, so unprecedented, that it straightened his back. What if, he wondered, his grandmother had not let Pete in at all? What if Pete had been judged inadequate? Where would that have left Bernard?

The next morning when he went hunting, Bernard returned to the place where he had seen the bear, hid himself behind a log, and waited.

9

"Did you hear?" Pete asked Theodore as they walked the trail from the sweat bath to their wives' houses.

"About Bernard's bear?"

"It must have weighed three hundred pounds. I didn't know Bernard had it in him."

"Have you forgotten what sitting in front of a house will drive you to? What did you catch to get inside Blanche's?"

"Nothing," Pete said. "It was me she couldn't resist."

"You forget," Theodore replied. "I was still a boy in that house. I recall their words of you. Let me see . . . I seem to remember some mention of the small size of certain of your parts."

"Poor brother-in-law," Pete said. "You still don't realize the lengths to which they went to avoid hurting your feelings! And how *is* your wife? How is the health of her many elder sisters? Is it true that they become stronger and more robust with every year?"

## 10

On the second day of the fifth week, just as she passed through the door, Blanche reached down her right hand and snagged one of the bear claws that rested in the basket by Bernard's leg. So quick was her movement, so apparently disconnected to the intent of her mind, so complete her distraction, that Bernard had to look twice to make sure it was gone. All the same, he felt a warm flush spread beneath the skin of his neck, and a feeling of inordinate pride suffused him so thoroughly that he had difficulty remaining still. He had been found worthy, and now it was only a matter of time.

Every day, with more pause and deliberation, Blanche browsed through his offerings and always selected some choice token. Her expression betrayed no gratitude, yet Bernard was sure that occasionally she was pleasantly surprised. Afraid to unbalance their precarious arrangement, he sat still as a listening hare in her presence. He kept his eyes lowered and held his breath until she had departed, but remained ever watchful for any cue that his probation had progressed. At last it came.

"Bernard!" Blanche said one day. She stood in the doorway, her hands on her hips, her head cocked to the side in amazement. "Is that you crouching there so quietly? Please, come in and share our supper, poor as it is. What a pleasure to see you."

Bernard rose slowly, stiff in his joints and half-skeptical that this was some joke, some new test, but when he entered the house, Blanche's hospitality continued and was joined by that of Bonnie, who sat by the fire trimming her husband's hair with a squeaking scissors. "Sit, sit," she motioned to a bench near the door. "What a shy boy you are. Luckily we have some nice moose to feed you."

Indeed they did. Bernard recognized the remains of the foreleg he had offered yesterday. Bonnie passed him a plate with a small portion of tough gristle, gray and cooled. He knew what to say.

"This is wonderful," he exclaimed. "The best I've ever tasted. What cooks you are. But you are too generous. Let me put some back in the pot."

When they refused, politely and with many denials of his compliments, Bernard made a great show of eating. The act of digestion absorbed his total concentration. He rubbed his stomach and cast his eyes to the ceiling in delight. With great subtlety he periodically raised his hand to his mouth, as if to wipe some grease, and used that motion to conceal the small bits of undigestible food he removed from his cheeks and tucked secretly into his pockets.

When he finished, Bernard sat nervously, breathless with anxiety. From the corner of the room he detected a space so devoid of movement that it attracted his attention. He looked, then quickly looked away. Yet his eyes still registered the image of Marie, her hair oiled and braided, wearing a new dress and a necklace made of bear claws, sitting as composed and shaded as a perfect charcoal sketch.

## 11

"You know, Pete," Martha said as she lay by her husband's side under a robe, "watching Bernard lately brings back memories."

"To me too. Your mother was a terror."

"I notice you still whisper such words, even though she's more than four years gone."

Pete shifted his position and propped on an elbow. In the moonlight Martha's face was seamless and young. A beam like the hottest part of a coal danced off her dark eye. He ran his fingers along her cheek and she turned her head in comfort. "You look the same as then," he said.

Martha caught his hand and brought it to her mouth, let it feel the smile.

"I pestered her, you know, to let you in," she said.

"You didn't care."

"I didn't care the day you found the eagle feathers? I didn't care the day you came an hour later than always?"

"It was raining," Pete said. "The ground was soft and I kept sinking to my knees. I couldn't arrive at your door covered in mud."

"I thought you weren't coming. I confronted my mother and told her that her slowness had cost me . . ."

"Cost you what?" Pete asked, when Martha's silence persisted.

"Enough talk."

## 12

Marie watched the back of Bernard's head and admired the sleek sheen of his long hair, the play of muscles in his arms at his every movement. During the last month she had studied every part of him so completely that she could create him in her imagination whenever she chose, and lately she chose often. She had to fight not to laugh when they gave him the worst meat and he had to spit into his hand and act as though it were delicious. She watched the way his fingers held the plate, the way he sat so compact and attentive. She waited for the sound of his soft voice and wondered what he would say when he could speak in private. She made a game of observing his eyes until just the second before they turned to her, and believed she had been discovered only once.

## 13

Bernard ate almost all of his meals at Blanche's house now, and gradually became more relaxed. For one thing, his distribution increased in both quality and quantity, and he could now expect a reasonable piece of meat or salmon. For another, Blanche's and Bonnie's husbands had begun to join him on his hunts, to show him places to fish that only members of this household knew. He found he liked these men and began to call them "uncle."

Blanche herself still frightened him, but not all the time. There were moments when he found approval in her gaze, times when some word of hers sounded almost like a joke. Bonnie was warmer, more solicitous of his needs, more delighted at the food he brought, and Bernard regarded her as an ally.

As far as Marie was concerned, he still had no clue to her feelings. Even Pete and Theodore observed that this game was lasting longer than the usual and debated whether something might be wrong. They were full of advice for Bernard, full of ideas of how to please Marie, full of reminders that it was her agreement, more than anyone's, that was necessary. But no matter what Bernard did, Marie would not look at him or give him any sign of encouragement. He grew despondent, lost his appetite, found himself thinking once again of Doris and the ease of their association. Marie seemed totally beyond his reach, the focus of mystery and impossible desire. And so he was unprepared on the night, just before the first frost of winter, when, with shaking hands, Marie herself passed him a plate of food.

"This is for you," she said so softly he could barely hear, and she sat beside him while, slowly and with great emotion, he ate.

## 14

A year later, while waiting for the birth of Marie's first child, Blanche and Martha passed the time by nibbling strips of dried eel. Martha, who had no love for the oily skin, threw hers into the fire, where it sizzled briefly.

"The midwife predicts a girl," Blanche said. "When she spun the charm above Marie's stomach, it revolved to the left."

"A girl is most rewarding," Martha nodded. "But there is a special satisfaction in raising boys. So often I think of times when Bernard was young, so often I miss him around the house."

Blanche reached for another stick of *baleek* and did not answer. Her silence was immediately noticed, as she knew it would be.

"How is he doing?" Martha asked at last.

"He will learn," Blanche said. "He has potential. It is clear he cares greatly for Marie, and she is patient."

"That is one word for it." Martha tossed a handful of scraps into the flame and watched the light flare and dance. "Of course, Bernard was used to . . ." She shifted her weight, cleared her throat. "He had such a *happy* home that I'm sure it has taken some adjusting on his part in new surroundings."

"Yes, he *was* somewhat spoiled. But I think he has a good heart."

"As well he must, to remain loyal to such a chinless girl."

"One only hopes their child will inherit the mother's disposition and not be sulky and resentful of every request."

"One can but pray it will have the father's looks and personality."

A single rope of eel remained on the plate. Both women extended a hand toward it, hesitated, and withdrew. It rested between them as they cleaned their teeth with fine bone picks, carefully wiped their fingers, and when, at the sound of Marie's first muffled protest, they rose together and rushed to her side, it remained behind.

# SHERMAN ALEXIE

## Somebody Kept Saying Powwow (1993)

*Alexie's powwow story is a trickster narrative though it does not feature Old Man Coyote. Like many Native stories, it tricks readers by inverting expectations and playing on unspoken assumptions. The narrator, Junior Polatkin, is talking about "Indian belly laughter, the kind of laughter that made Indians squeeze their eyes up so tight they looked Chinese. . . . Maybe some of us Indians just laughed our way over to China 25,000 years ago and jumpstarted that civilization." In that brief passage Alexie constructs a model of double-voiced discourse, playing on the Anglo-European belief that everyone immigrated from the eastern hemisphere to the western, on the supposed physical resemblance between Native Americans and peoples of east Asia, and, finally, on the whole "myth" of Indian migration, turning assumptions and expectations on their heads. "[W]henever I started in on my crazy theories . . . ," Junior continues, inverting the agent of "crazy theories" from the earlier reference to Anglo-European theories to the speaker, an Indian. As the train of thought is embedded in a passage about laughter and wisdom, drunkenness, despair, and Indian humor, its layered edges of meaning shoot out in all directions, a multifaceted pun. An Indian joke of the first water.*

*"Somebody Kept Saying Powwow" captures both tone and substance of contemporary Native dialogue—a feat this brash young man from the Northwest has alone accomplished. His perspective, at once funny and brutal, exposes the many layers of meaning upon which contemporary Native society rests.*

*For example, there's a comment about tipi-creeping and another about buffalo feet—neither particularly relevant to Indians from western Washington but both entirely fitted to a contemporary pan-Indian frame of*

*reference. Then there's the ubiquitous fry bread and powwow—neither tra-*
*ditional to Alexie's part of the woods; indeed fry bread became a Native*
*food only after whites brought wheat over here, and it became an "Indian"*
*ethnic food only recently, when American-pop Indian became the context in*
*which young skins socialized.*

*Gamely, gently, fiercely, Alexie compels us to question what is false,*
*what is true, what constitutes Native life and what constitutes white fan-*
*tasies about Native life somehow internalized by modern Indians. It is a*
*hard story he writes, one that pierces disguise and reveals a truthfulness that*
*words alone cannot contain.*

I knew Norma before she ever met her husband-to-be, James Many Horses. I knew her back when there was good fry bread to be eaten at the powwow, before the old women died and took their recipes with them. That's how it's going. Sometimes it feels like our tribe is dying a piece of bread at a time. But Norma, she was always trying to save it, she was a cultural lifeguard, watching out for those of us that were so close to drowning.

She was really young, too, not all that much older than me, but everybody called her grandmother anyway, as a sign of respect.

"Hey, grandmother," I said when she walked by me as I sat at another terrible fry bread stand.

"Hi, Junior," she said and walked over to me. She shook my hand, loosely, like Indians do, using only her fingers. Not like those tight grips that white people use to prove something. She touched my hand like she was glad to see me, not like she wanted to break bones.

"Are you dancing this year?" I asked.

"Of course. Haven't you been down to the dance hall?"

"Not yet."

"Well, you should go watch the dancing. It's important."

We talked for a while longer, told some stories, and then she went on about her powwow agenda. Everybody wanted to talk to Norma, to share some time with her. I just liked to sit with her, put my reservation antennas up and adjust my reception. Didn't you know that Indians are born with two antennas that rise up and field emotional signals? Norma always said that Indians are the most sensitive people on the planet. For that matter, Indians are more sensitive than animals, too. We don't just watch things happen. Watching automatically makes the watcher part of the happening. That's what Norma taught me.

"Everything matters," she said. "Even the little things."

But it was more than just some bullshit Native religion, some fodder for the crystal-happy. Norma lived her life like we should all do. She didn't drink or smoke. But she could spend a night in the Powwow Tavern and dance hard. She could dance Indian and white. And that's a mean feat, since the two methods of dancing are mutually exclusive. I've seen Indians who are champion fancydancers trip all over themselves when Paula Abdul is on the jukebox in the bar. And I've seen Indians who could do all this MTV Club dancing, electric slides and shit, all over the place and then look like a white person stumbling through the sawdust of a powwow.

One night I was in the Powwow Tavern and Norma asked me to dance. I'd never danced with her before, hadn't really danced much at all, Indian or white.

"Move your ass," she said. "This ain't Browning, Montana. It's Las Vegas."

So I moved my ass, shook my skinny brown butt until the whole bar was laughing, which was good. Even if I was the one being laughed at. And Norma and I laughed all night long and danced together all night long. Most nights, before James Many Horses showed up, Norma would dance with everybody, not choosing any favorites. She was a diplomat. But she only danced with me that night. Believe me, it was an honor. After the bar closed, she even drove me home since everybody else was headed to parties and I wanted to go to sleep.

"Hey," she said on the way home. "You can't dance very good but you got the heart of a dancer."

"Heart of the dancer," I said. "And feet like the buffalo."

And we laughed.

She dropped me at home, gave me a good night hug, and then drove on to her own HUD house. I went into my house and dreamed about her. Not like you think. I dreamed her a hundred years ago, riding bareback down on Little Falls Flats. Her hair was unbraided and she was yelling something to me as she rode closer to where I stood. I couldn't understand what she was saying, though. But it was a dream and I listen to my dreams.

"I dreamed about you the other night," I said to Norma the next time I saw her. I told her about the dream.

"I don't know what that means," she said. "I hope it's nothing bad."

"Maybe it just means I have a crush on you."

"No way," she said and laughed. "I've seen you hanging around with that Nadine Moses woman. You must have been dreaming about her."

"Nadine don't know how to ride a horse," I said.

"Who said anything about horses?" Norma said, and we both laughed for a good long time.

Norma could ride horses like she did live one hundred years ago. She was a rodeo queen, but not one of those rhinestone women. She was a roper, a breaker of wild ponies. She wrestled steers down to the ground and did that goofy old three-legged knot dance. Norma just wasn't quite as fast as some of the other Indian cowboys, though. I think, in the end, she was just having a good time. She'd hang with the cowboys and they'd sing songs for her, 49er songs that echoed beyond the evening's last campfire.

*Norma, I want to marry you*
*Norma, I want to make you mine*
*And we'll go dancing, dancing, dancing*
*until the sun starts to shine.*
*Way yah hi yo, Way yah hi yo!*

Some nights Norma took an Indian cowboy or a cowboy Indian back to her tipi. And that was good. Some people would have you believe it's wrong, but it was two people sharing some body medicine. It wasn't like Norma was out snagging for men all the time. Most nights she just went home alone and sang herself to sleep.

Some people said that Norma took a woman home with her once in a while, too. Years ago, homosexuals were given special status within the tribe. They had powerful medicine. I think it's even more true today, even though our tribe has assimilated into homophobia. I mean, a person has to have magic to assert their identity without regard to all the bullshit, right?

Anyhow, or as we say around here, anyhoo, Norma held on to her status within the tribe despite all the rumors, the stories, the lies and jealous gossip. Even after she married that James Many Horses, who told so many jokes that he even made other Indians get tired of his joking.

The funny thing is that I always thought Norma would end up marrying Victor since she was so good at saving people and Victor needed more saving than most anybody besides Lester FallsApart. But she and Victor never got along, much. Victor was kind of a bully in his younger days, and I don't think Norma ever forgave him. I doubt Victor ever forgave himself for it. I think he said *I'm sorry* more than any other human being alive.

I remember once when Norma and I were sitting in the Powwow Tavern and Victor walked in, drunker than drunk.

"Where's the powwow?" Victor yelled.

"You're in the Powwow," somebody yelled back.

"No, I don't mean this goddamn bar. I mean, where's the powwow?"

"In your pants," somebody else yelled and we all laughed.

Victor staggered up to our table.

"Junior," he asked. "Where's the powwow?"

"There ain't no powwow going on," I said.

"Well," Victor said. "Somebody out in the parking lot kept saying powwow. And you know I love a good goddamn powwow."

"We all love a good powwow," Norma said.

Victor smiled a drunk smile at her, one of those smiles only possible through intoxication. The lips fall at odd angles, the left side of the face is slightly paralyzed, and skin shines with alcohol sweat. Nothing remotely approaching beauty.

"I'm going to go find the goddamn powwow," Victor said then and

staggered out the door. He's on the wagon now bu
drunk.

"Good luck," Norma said. That's one of the stra
the tribal ties that still exists. A sober Indian has infin
drunk Indian, even most of the Indians who have comple
There ain't many who do stay sober. Most spend til
Anonymous meetings, and everybody gets to know the
them on all occasions, not just at A.A. meetings.

"Hi, my name is Junior," I usually say when I walk into a bar or
party where Indians have congregated.

"Hi, Junior," all the others shout in an ironic unison.

A few of the really smart-asses about the whole A.A. thing carry
around little medals indicating how long they've been continuously drunk.

"Hi, my name is Lester FallsApart, and I've been drunk for twenty-
seven straight years."

Norma didn't much go for that kind of humor, though. She laughed
when it was funny but she didn't start anything up. Norma, she knew all
about Indian belly laughter, the kind of laughter that made Indians squeeze
their eyes up so tight they looked Chinese. Maybe that's where those rumors about crossing the Bering Bridge started. Maybe some of us Indians
just laughed our way over to China 25,000 years ago and jumpstarted that
civilization. But whenever I started in on my crazy theories, Norma would
put her finger to my lips really gently.

"Junior," she would say with gentleness and patience. "Shut the
fuck up."

Norma always was a genius with words. She used to write stories for
the tribal newspaper. She was even their sports reporter for a while. I still
got the news clipping of a story she wrote about the basketball game I won
back in high school. In fact, I keep it tucked in my wallet and if I get drunk
enough, I'll pull it out and read from it aloud, like it was a goddamn poem
or something. But the way Norma wrote, I guess it was something close to
a poem:

### Junior's Jumpshot Just Enough for Redskin Win

With three seconds left on the clock last Saturday night
and the Springdale Chargers in possession of the ball, it looked
like even the Wellpinit Redskins might have to call in the
United States Cavalry to help them win the first game of this
just-a-baby basketball season.

But Junior Polatkin tipi-creeped the Chargers by stealing
the inbounds pass and then stealing the game away when he hit
a three-thousand-foot jumper at the buzzer.

"I doubt we'll be filing any charges against Junior for theft," Tribal Chief of Police David WalksAlong said. "This was certainly a case of self-defense."

People were gossiping all around the rez about Junior's true identity.

"I think he was Crazy Horse for just a second," said an anonymous and maybe-just-a-little-crazy-themselves source.

This reporter thinks Junior happened to be a little lucky so his new Indian name will be Lucky Shot. Still, luck or not, Junior has earned a couple points more on the Warrior Scale.

Whenever I pull that clipping out with Norma around, she always threatens to tear it up. But she never does. She's proud of it, I can tell. I'd be proud, too. I mean, I'm proud I won that game. It was the only game we won that year. In fact, it was the only game the Wellpinit Redskins won in three years. It wasn't like we had bad teams. We always had two or three of the best players in the league, but winning wasn't always as important as getting drunk after the game for some and for going to the winter pow-wows for others. Some games, we'd only have five players.

I always wished we could have suited Norma up. She was taller than all of us and a better player than most of us. I don't really remember her playing in high school, but people say she could have played college ball if she would've gone to college. Same old story. But the reservation people who say things like that have never been off the reservation.

"What's it like out there?" Norma asked me when I came back from college, from the city, from cable television and delivered pizza.

"It's like a bad dream you never wake up from," I said, and it's true. Sometimes I still feel like half of me is lost in the city, with its foot wedged into a steam grate or something. Stuck in one of those revolving doors, going round and round while all the white people are laughing. Standing completely still on an escalator that will not move, but I didn't have the courage to climb the stairs by myself. Stuck in an elevator between floors with a white woman who keeps wanting to touch my hair.

There are some things that Indians would've never invented if given the chance.

"But the city gave you a son," Norma said, and that was true enough. Sometimes, though, it felt like half a son because the city had him during the week and every other weekend. The reservation only got him for six days a month. Visitation rights. That's how the court defined them. Visitation rights.

"Do you ever want kids?" I asked Norma.

"Yeah, of course," she said. "I want a dozen. I want my own tribe."

"You're kidding."

"Kind of. Don't know if I want to raise kids in this world. It's getting uglier by the second. And not just on the reservation."

"I know what you mean," I said. "You see where two people got shot in the bus station in Spokane last week? In Spokane! It's getting to be like New York City."

"New York City enough."

Norma was the kind of person who made you honest. She was so completely honest herself that you couldn't help it. Pretty soon I'd be telling her all my secrets, the bad and good.

"What's the worst thing you ever did?" she asked me.

"Probably that time I watched Victor beat the shit out of Thomas Builds-the-Fire."

"I remember that. I'm the one who broke it up. But you were just a kid. Must be something worse than that."

I thought about it awhile, but it didn't take me long to figure out what the worst thing I ever did was.

It was at a basketball game when I was in college. I was with a bunch of guys from my dormitory, all white guys, and we were drunk, really drunk. The other team had this player who just got out of prison. I mean, this guy was about twenty-eight and had a tough life. Grew up in inner-city Los Angeles and finally made it out, made it to college and was playing and studying hard. If you think about it, he and I had a whole lot in common. Much more in common than I had with those white boys I was drunk with.

Anyway, when that player comes out, I don't even remember his name or maybe I don't want to remember it, we all start chanting at him. Really awful shit. Hateful. We all had these big cards we made to look like those GET OUT OF JAIL FREE cards in Monopoly. One guy was running around in a black-and-white convict shirt with a fake ball-and-chain. It was a really bad scene. The local newspaper had a big write-up. We even made it into a *People* Magazine article. It was about that player and how much he'd gone through and how he still had to fight so much ignorance and hate. When they asked him how it felt during that game where we all went crazy, he said, *It hurt.*

After I told Norma that story, she was quiet for a long time. A long time.

"If I drank," she said, "I would be getting drunk right about now because of that one."

"I've gotten drunk on it a few times."

"And if it still bothers you this much now," Norma said, "then think how bad that guy feels about it."

"I think about him all the time."

After I told Norma that story, she treated me differently for about a year. She wasn't mean or distant. Just different. But I understood. People can do things completely against their nature, completely. It's like some tiny earthquake comes roaring through your body and soul, and it's the only earthquake you'll ever feel. But it damages so much, cracks the foundations of your life forever.

So I just figured Norma wouldn't ever forgive me. She was like that. She was probably the most compassionate person on the reservation but she was also the most passionate. Then one day in the Trading Post she walked up to me and smiled.

"Pete Rose," she said.

"What?" I asked, completely confused.

"Pete Rose," she repeated.

"What?" I asked again, even more confused.

"That's your new Indian name," she said. "Pete Rose."

"Why?"

"Because you two got a whole lot in common."

"How?"

"Listen," Norma said. "Pete Rose played major league baseball in four different decades, has more hits than anybody in history. Hell, think about it. Going back to Little League and high school and all that, he's probably been smacking the ball around forever. Noah probably pitched him a few on the Ark. But after all that, all that greatness, he's only remembered for the bad stuff."

"Gambling," I said.

"That ain't right," she said.

"Not at all."

After that, Norma treated me the same as she did before she found out what I did in college. She made me try to find that basketball player, but I didn't have any luck. What would I have told him if I did find him? Would I just tell him that I was Pete Rose? Would he have understood that?

Then, on one strange, strange day when a plane had to emergency land on the reservation highway, and the cooler in the Trading Post broke down and they were giving away ice cream because it would've been wasted, and a bear fell asleep on the roof of the Catholic church, Norma ran up to me, nearly breathless.

"Pete Rose," she said. "They just voted to keep you out of the Hall of Fame. I'm sorry. But I still love you."

"Yeah, I know, Norma. I love you, too."

# DAN L. CRANK

## Neon Powwow (1993)

*There is an Indian joke about a Hopi, a Navajo, and an Apache who are sitting around in a bar. They begin to exchange stories about their respective traditions. The Hopi man says "We dance for rain. Sometimes it rains, and sometimes it doesn't." The men sit silently for several minutes, contemplating the truth of his remark. Eventually, the Navajo man speaks up. "We have a ceremony where we pray for someone to get well." He pauses reflectively. "Sometimes they get well, sometimes they don't," he concludes. After some minutes the Apache man speaks up. "We have a dance where we pray for the sun to rise." He pauses significantly, gazing steadily at his two companions. "And the sun always rises."*

*In "Neon Powwow" several Native Indian students are gathered at their favorite bar in another kind of intertribal gathering. The non-Navajo man sitting at their table seems to be a stranger to them. He is a Hopi among Diné—their own name for themselves—who never say his name. The idea of an Indian being nameless and faceless in the white world is not new to Native fiction, but the idea of a Native of the Southwest, a Hopi, being nameless and faceless among other Natives of the Southwest, Navajo students, is a remarkable twist on an old theme.*

*It must be said that relations between Hopi and Navajo are troubled, and have been for eight hundred years or so. The struggle over the Joint Use Area lands that lie between Hopi and surrounding Navajo lands in the 1980s and 1990s has caused shots to be fired by Hopi ranchers who felt they had been given no recourse by Diné (Navajo people) cutting Hopi fences, causing the dreadfully expensive loss of Hopi livestock. The Navajo Nation's public relations efforts aimed at white American, African American, and European social activists have resulted in busloads arriving on the Res* to demonstrate against Hopi claims and hear poignant speeches by Diné elders bewailing their forced removal from their homes, and articles in American papers across the country focusing on the Navajo Nation's valiant efforts to retain its lands and culture.

That long history of conflict between the two nations, and other Pueblos and other people who have lived in the American Southwest "since time immemorial," informs Crank's short narrative, as does the equally long history of intermarriage between Hopi and Navajo, strong family and religious ties, and an informal socializing among Pueblos, of whom the Hopi are one kind, and the Diné another. The ambiguous position of the stranger reflects both strains, and the resolution is as telling as it is tragic.

"Neon Powwow" bears other subtexts and resonances: The reference to neon means city life—there's little neon in Hopiland or on the Res—and the loss of self signified by the students' regularity at the bar, and the falseness of neon, its allure. The powwow reference is aimed at intertribal Native life and ambiance; one of the major institutions Native people of all nations engage in and share are the powwows held all over North America. Hundreds of Indian people from a variety of tribes regularly participate in several such gatherings each year, traveling between places as distant as the California Bay Area, southern Wisconsin, Denver, Albuquerque, Montana, and around Canada.

One last feature of Crank's story bears mention: "Neon Powwow" works exactly the way stories from the oral tradition work; it is brief, direct, and to the point. It is not embellished with plot twists and artful details in setting and characterization. Within its frame no one changes, no one learns anything, no one is saved—or damned. The story tells us something significant, something from which we can learn—not by observing how a character with whom we identify changes, but by contemplating the story itself and its connection to our own life and circumstances.

Stories in the oral narrative tradition function in similar bare-bones ways. The setting is barely sketched in because the audience is familiar with the locale; it is equally familiar with the characters, and attempts to plumb the depths of interactions or psyches would add little to what it already knows. Crank's story is written in accordance with the ancient tradition of narration as practiced among the Native Indian peoples, whether Diné, Hopi, Lakota, or urban pan-Indian.

In the dark interior of the side street bar, and along the wall in the narrow drinking place, there were dark forms sitting sluggishly or hunched over whatever they were nursing. Empty beer bottles and cans and food crumbs littered the tables. Afternoon light flooded in the open doorway and glints of passing automobiles reflected into the dark room. An Indian guy who chain smoked nonfiltered Camels sat in a booth near the bright entrance.

His cigarette smoke played in the sunbeams. Joe Bluesky sat with a college crowd in the last booth. The barkeep stood behind an old wooden bar made vintage by beer stains, elbows, and greasy food. It was polished to a high gloss with constant rubbings of arms and elbows of numerous past patrons. The bar had supported countless drunk Indians and Mexicans, and occasionally a drunk white man with Indian friends. A red and blue neon Coors sign flickered a little and buzzed and fizzled when it did not flash.

At Bluesky's table were two Navajo college girls, Joe's buddy who only drank canned Coors, and a Hopi guy who attended the same college. The Hopi was bent over, a bottle of longnecked Bud pressed to his cheek. He had held that posture for some time now. He stirred and raised his arm for the last gulp from his bottle.

"Damn," he said. "I think I'm getting wasted," he said to Darlene, one of the Navajo girls. She ignored his bloodshot stare and his crazy grin.

"I think he is dead drunk," Joe commented.

"He was already that way when I met him back on campus," said the other Navajo guy.

The Hopi stirred again, looked up, and laughed. He said, "Now I am *more* drunk. I drank more than you guys, you don't drink fast enough. What kind of Navajos are you?"

"Don't worry," said Joe's buddy. "I only drink fast when I am on a reservation. I'd rather be caught with the liquor in my stomach than in my hands."

"Bull," said the Hopi.

Joe and his buddy laughed out loud.

The chain smoker at the front booth looked around and then lit another cigarette. The early afternoon crowd was thin.

Darlene and Laura looked at the Hopi, then at each other. Laura especially didn't want to waste another Saturday evening, like last weekend. They had drunk stale beer in their apartment while studying for some exams. By the time they got to an Indian bar, their friends had left and gone elsewhere. The girls had sat and endured bleary-eyed drunks and other individuals who had gone over the edge and barely hung on.

Today it might be different. This old place was actually nicer than the other bars lining the front and main side streets. The crowd could drink well and if they got hungry and couldn't walk, they could order microwaved pizza. The barkeep also kept some old-fashioned dilled eggs in large jars on the bar. Serious drinking was accomplished here. In dorms and apartments, everybody drank to get drunk quickly and what subsequently followed was rowdiness. Laura liked this bar. At all the bars, men were always trying to engage in a conversation with the girls or get dates with them. Usually a game ensued where they pretended they were waiting for someone, or that they were their male friends' wives. Joe's Navajo buddy was one of Laura's regular make-believe husbands.

Like the Hopi guy, he was nice and intelligent when he wasn't in his present condition. Laura liked Joe Bluesky, too. She knew Joe from a previous party when he was a student. One day Joe quit attending classes and went back to the reservation. Or someone had said that Joe had gone back to herd sheep. He had kept in touch, though. Now here he was—back for a visit, and he was buying. . . . He also looked good and fit in long hair and faded Levi clothing. The Hopi guy was ragged and wasted compared to Joe. Now Darlene and Laura were the Hopi's only audience as he slowly drank himself into oblivion. When he finally slumped over, perhaps they might celebrate.

Joe said, "I have known some great Indian drinkers with great outlooks on life but they are usually the worst drinkers."

"The quiet ones are the best," Darlene said as she looked at Joe.

Laura then squealed with laughter. She said, "You mean sexually, or as conversationalists?"

"No, you idiot," Darlene replied. "I mean that the quiet Indian guys are the ones that get deep and meaningful."

"You're still talking about sex, aren't you?' Laura again asked. She laughed even louder.

Joe's buddy took a deep drink. He grinned at Laura and Darlene. He then said, "Darlene is talking about both. Either way it's a f—-ing shame some of us don't get pissing philosophical when we're f—-ing sober."

"You're getting real vulgar," Laura said.

He retorted, "Vulgarity breaks the ice and drives home the point, and it breaks the stereotype of the non-swearing quiet Indian."

"He's getting philosophical now, and you're touching a nerve, Laura," said Joe.

The Hopi then raised his head and said, "I want to get deep and meaningful, and I want to be touched." He laughed in a silly high voice, and pushed his point further. "First I want to get philosophical, and then I want to see if I can get laid."

The group looked at each other. The Hopi seemed to be getting a second life. It was an event to drink to. Joe's buddy ordered another round. Their table was littered with bottles and cans.

The barkeep was an old Mexican guy with thinning hair and he had the skin coloring of someone who had lived in a cave or a dark interior for years. He spoke several basic Indian greetings and looked like someone's Navajo grandfather. He spoke good Navajo and exchanged jokes with some of the regulars. He placed the tray of drinks on the table and passed a beer to everyone at Joe's table. He then cleaned up a little and took the empties with him. On his way back he checked each patron's beer level or mental state for later reference. The early Saturday afternoon was not busy. Some patrons stopped only for one drink, then they were off to other beer joints. It was still cruising time; the Indians were looking for a good Coors crowd, and the white college students wanted cheap Mexican food to eat with their trendy Tecates.

The drinks to celebrate the Hopi's revival were drained. Silence again set in. The Hopi excused himself and left the table with a slight stagger. He ran his hand along the wooden bar and walked up to the doorway. He stood there and shaded his eyes against the bright afternoon light. Then he walked back toward their table and passed it. The restroom's door slammed loudly.

"He's okay now," said Joe's buddy. "He was ready to go out. It saves us the trouble of baby-sitting him."

Darlene took a cigarette out of a crumpled pack on the table. She lit it and inhaled deeply. Laura watched the smoke curl and remain in the air. The smoke took the stale odor of the bar away momentarily.

Laura then took Darlene's cigarette and took a drag on it.

"Well, I guess we can cruise on, then," Joe Bluesky said.

"Where to?" asked Laura.

"Anyone hungry?" Joe asked. "We could check out that old Chinese cafe on Aspen Street; the one where there are old photographs of Navajo railroad workers."

"That was some history and they were some drinkers," his buddy said. "I read someplace where these guys worked six days a week, then came into town on Saturday nights to have a wild time. Then they stayed wasted until it was time to go back to work Monday mornings."

The chain smoker in the front of the bar got up and moved about, then he took one of his cigarettes and went out the door.

"Now you have become a historian," Laura said to the Navajo guy.

"I was only giving you some unsubstantiated fiction," he replied.

"It sounds good, like real history," added Darlene.

"Watch out for him; he is the quiet type." Laura commented. She looked at the Navajo guy. "He might become a deep historian and a meaningful philosopher."

He said, "Someday, maybe someday."

The Hopi took a long time to relieve or revive himself. Joe and his buddy became concerned. Joe Bluesky stood up, and stepped over Laura's right leg and foot, the one that Laura had been brushing against him most of the afternoon. He made his way to the bathroom.

Bluesky opened the rough door and stepped into the silent room. One of the faucets dripped slowly, the moist air was slowly sucked outside through the stained vents. A fly buzzed in front of the mirror, darting at its own image. Joe dropped to one knee and looked under the stalls. He saw the Hopi's legs in the last one. His pants were down around the ankles, and the contents of his pockets were spilled out on the floor. It was too quiet. Joe started sweating. All of a sudden, the beer-contaminated blood rushed to his head and awakened him. The faucet dripped louder into the worn and chipped basin, and it reverberated in Joe's head.

# JOY HARJO

## The Woman Who Fell from the Sky (1994)

*In the bleakness of loss and grief that characterizes much of contemporary Native life and literature, especially as the younger and newer writers enter the narrative stream, there are signs of continuance and of hope. "The Woman Who Fell from the Sky" is one such sign. Beginning from a place of anguish, it invokes old visions, old stories, old ways, to show the way to healing that is beyond survival.*

*The plot is taken from a myth of the Haudenoshonee and other Northeast First Nations people and combined with another plot taken from an all too common feature of modern American life. Sky Woman fell from the sky, cast out or jumping out of another world. As a consequence of her fall, Earth was created, and all the beings—supernaturals, animals, humans, everything here—came into being. The falling, fallen woman is a creative force, the old myth informs us, and Harjo takes this concept and creates a story in which that force operates within the dreadful confines of modern urban life. In a number of ways, "The Woman Who Fell from the Sky" is a response to the bitterness of "indigenous irony," "Neon Powwow," and "Crazy Horse Dreams." All of those were written by writers under thirty years of age, while Harjo, a more seasoned writer, is in her forties. Perhaps bitterness and rage decrease with age, as experience and knowledge combine to provide us with greater patience and the barest beginnings of wisdom.*

Once a woman fell from the sky. The woman who fell from the sky was neither a murderer nor a saint. She was rather ordinary, though beautiful in her walk, like one who has experienced freedom from earth's gravity. When I see her I think of an antelope grazing the alpine meadows in mountains whose names are as ancient as the sound that created the first world.

Saint Coincidence thought he recognized her as she began falling toward him from the sky in a slow spin, like the spiral of events marking an ascension of grace. There was something in the curve of her shoulder, a familiar slope that led him into the lightest moment of his life.

He could not bear it and turned to ask a woman in high heels for a quarter. She was of the family of myths who would give everything if asked. She looked like all the wives he'd lost. And he had nothing to lose anymore in this city of terrible paradox where a woman was falling toward him from the sky.

The strange beauty in heels disappeared from the path of Saint Coincidence, with all her money held tightly in her purse, into the glass of advertisements. Saint Coincidence shuffled back onto the ice to watch the woman falling and falling.

Saint Coincidence, who was not a saint—perhaps a murderer if you count the people he shot without knowing during the stint that took his mind in Vietnam or Cambodia—remembered the girl he yearned to love when they were kids at Indian boarding school.

He could still see her on the dusty playground, off in the distance, years to the west past the icy parking lot of the Safeway. She was a blurred vision of the bittersweet and this memory had forced him to live through the violence of fire.

There they stood witness together to strange acts of cruelty by strangers, as well as the surprise of rare kindnesses.

The woman who was to fall from the sky was the girl with skinned knees whose spirit knew how to climb to the stars. Once she told him the stars spoke a language akin to the plains of her home, a language like rocks.

He watched her once make the ascent, after a severe beating. No one could touch the soul masked by name, age and tribal affiliation. Myth was as real as a scalp being scraped for lice.

Lila also dreamed of a love not disturbed by the wreck of culture she was forced to attend. It sprang up here and there like miraculous flowers in the cracks of the collision. It was there she found Johnny, who didn't have a saint's name when he showed up for school. He understood the journey and didn't make fun of her for her peculiar ways, despite the risks.

Johnny was named Johnny by the priests because his Indian name was foreign to their European tongues. He named himself Saint Coincidence many years later after he lost himself in drink in a city he'd been sent to to learn a trade. Maybe you needed English to know how to pray in the city. He could speak a fractured English. His own language had become a baby language to him, made of the comforting voice of his grandmother as she taught him to be a human.

Johnny had been praying for years and had finally given up on a god who appeared to give up on him. Then one night as he tossed pennies on the sidewalk with his cousin and another lost traveler, he prayed to Coincidence and won. The event demanded a new name. He gave himself the name Saint Coincidence.

His ragged life gleamed with possibility until a ghost-priest brushed by him as he walked the sidewalk looking for a job to add to his stack of new luck. The priest appeared to look through to the boy in him. He despaired. He would always be a boy on his knees, the burden of shame rooting him.

Saint Coincidence went back to wandering without a home in the maze of asphalt. Asphalt could be a pathway toward God, he reasoned, though he'd always imagined the road he took with his brothers when they raised sheep as children. Asphalt had led him here to the Safeway where a woman was falling from the sky.

The memory of all time relative to Lila and Johnny was seen by an abandoned cat washing herself next to the aluminum-can bin of the grocery story.

These humans set off strange phenomena, she thought and made no attachment to the thought. It was what it was, this event, shimmering there between the frozen parking lot of the store and the sky, something unusual and yet quite ordinary.

Like the sun falling fast in the west, this event carried particles of light through the trees.

Some say God is a murderer for letting children and saints slip through his or her hands. Some call God a father of saints or a mother of demons. Lila had seen God and could tell you God was neither male nor female and made of absolutely everything of beauty, of wordlessness.

This unnameable thing of beauty is what shapes a flock of birds who know exactly when to turn together in flight in the winds used to make words. Everyone turns together though we may not see each other stacked in the invisible dimensions.

This is what Lila saw, she told Johnny once. The sisters called it blasphemy.

Johnny ran away from boarding school the first winter with his two brothers, who'd run away before. His brothers wrapped Johnny Boy, as they called him, with their bodies to keep him warm. They froze and became part of the stars.

Johnny didn't make it home either. The school officials took him back the next day. To mourn his brothers would be to admit an unspeakable pain, so he became an athlete who ran faster than any record ever made in the history of the school, faster than the tears.

Lila never forgot about Johnny, who left school to join the army, and a few years later as she walked home from her job at Dairy Queen she made a turn in the road.

Call it destiny or coincidence—but the urge to fly was as strong as the need to push when at the precipice of any birth. It was what led her into the story told before she'd grown ears to hear, as she turned from stone to fish to human in her mother's belly.

Once, the stars made their way down stairs of ice to the earth to find mates. Some of the women were angry at their inattentive husbands, bored, or frustrated with the cycle of living and dying. They ran off with the stars, as did a few who saw their chance for travel and enlightenment.

They weren't heard from for years, until one of the women returned. She dared to look back and fell. Fell through centuries, through the beauty of the night sky, made a hole in a rock near the place Lila's mother had been born. She took up where she had left off, with her children from the stars. She was remembered.

This story was Lila's refuge those nights she'd prayed on her knees with the other children in the school dorms. It was too painful to miss her mother.

A year after she'd graduated and worked cleaning house during the day, and evenings at the Dairy Queen, she laughed to think of herself wearing her uniform spotted with sweets and milk, as she left on the arms of one of the stars. Surely she could find love in a place that did not know the disturbance of death.

While Lila lived in the sky she gave birth to three children and they made her happy. Though she had lost conscious memory of the place before, a song climbed up her legs from far away, to the rooms of her heart.

Later she would tell Johnny it was the sound of destiny, which is similar to a prayer reaching out to claim her.

You can't ignore these things, she would tell him, and it led her to the place her husband had warned her was too sacred for women.

She carried the twins in her arms as her daughter grabbed her skirt in her small fists. She looked into the forbidden place and leaped.

She fell and was still falling when Saint Coincidence caught her in his arms in front of the Safeway as he made a turn from borrowing spare change from strangers.

The children crawled safely from their mother. The cat stalked a bit of flying trash set into motion by the wave of falling—or the converse wave of gathering together.


*I traveled far above the earth for a different perspective. It is possible to travel this way without the complications of NASA. This beloved planet we call home was covered with an elastic web of light. I watched in awe as it shimmered, stretched, dimmed and shined, shaped by the collective effort of all life within it. Dissonance attracted more dissonance. Harmony attracted harmony. I saw revolutions, droughts, famines and the births of new nations. The most humble kindnesses made the brightest lights. Nothing was wasted.*

*I understood love to be the very gravity holding each leaf, each cell, this earthy star together.*

☆

# SUSAN POWER

## Christianity Comes to the Sioux (1994)

*There are many boundaries to cross, many rivers whose source must be located, many origin myths to remember if not recount, many transformation tales—whether they are formally known in White America as history, literature, or myth—to learn from. Native children must know all those that come to bear on their minds and consciousnesses so they will know how to assess their experiences, others' behavior, and their own relation to the All-that-is.*

*In "Christianity Comes to the Sioux," an excerpt from* The Grass Dancer, *Susan Power weaves a skillful tale in which boundaries are drawn and may not be crossed by those who cannot understand them. In the story a young man learns the nature of those boundaries, not in his mind, but in his experience. He discovers how he must shape himself and his understanding to accommodate the complexities of modern Native life.*

*In the contemporary world, Native life has two sides that preoccupy Native writers: the Native world as white people—friend or foe—perceive it, and how they therefore interact with Native people; and the Native world that Indian people live in, and how they therefore interact with white or with Native people.*

*Jeannette McVay, the teacher, is Rousseauvian in her approach to her young charges. They are, in her eyes, noble savages, exotic, precious, above her. In their own eyes they are children, Native children, and she's the teacher—a not very good teacher at that. Or is she? Certainly her willingness to be beaten by a lover because he is Indian is properly repellent to Harley Wind Soldier, and her attitude toward her students ill befits the classroom situation they are, after all, in. But her technique is not without its brilliance, however clumsy: She is determined to learn, and her young charges must, perforce, learn at her side.*

*Perhaps they withhold their stories from her, but they remember them for themselves and for one another. In her awkward way Jeannette McVay strengthens what she finds best and truest in their tradition: the power of story to shape experience and provide value to life that without it would be bereft of meaning.*

## (1977)

Harley Wind Soldier was seated in a rigid metal chair that held him like a torture device. He leaned his elbows on the slim board bolted to his chair, which formed a makeshift writing table. Harley and his classmates were arranged in a circle, their eyes trained on the teacher, who sat cross-legged on her desk.

Jeannette McVay—the eighth-grade social studies teacher at Saint Mary's School—was the fairest person in the room, though she had spent the summer baking in the sun on a foil sheet. She addressed her Dakota students with what she hoped was cheerful compassion. "You're probably wondering why I moved your desks," she said. "I thought it only fitting to form a circle, because I know your people have a cyclic worldview. And since this is a give-and-take situation, where I plan to learn from you as much as I hope to share my own knowledge, I want to look at the world through your eyes for a change. Don't you think that's refreshing?"

Harley Wind Soldier shuffled his feet and stared at the big toe emerging from a hole in one of his high-top sneakers. He was only thirteen years old, but he grasped the woman's meaning. He thought she was *unšika*. Pitiful. He could see purple crescents blossoming beneath a wash of liquid makeup, fresh bruises on his teacher's face no doubt stamped there by her boyfriend, Virgil Ribs. There was a tiny cut below her right eye, which Jeannette was attempting to cover by resting her chin in her hand, fingers striping her face. But Harley glimpsed the scabbed seam. He hoped she fought back.

*I bet she feels so sorry for Virgil, just because he's Indian, she cries over his split knuckles,* Harley thought.

Jeannette McVay faced a room of sullen children, admiring their bronze complexions and straight black hair, although the girls had ruined their tresses, in Jeannette's opinion, by getting feathered cuts that framed their faces like black wings, in a Sioux version of the Farrah Fawcett look. She dyed her own hair a flat black, attempting to match her students' shade, despite Virgil's complaints that she looked ready for Halloween.

Jeannette often wondered what kept her in this isolated territory, where she feared she would always be a stranger. The answer that surfaced most often was: *The children. Who better than an outsider can make them understand the wealth within their poverty?* Jeannette doted on her pupils, considering them royalty in exile. On a little shelf built into the wall behind her desk, Jeannette had placed a set of the complete works of James Fenimore Cooper. She shared the books with her students, reading aloud, and didn't notice when they rolled their eyes at one another.

One day, after reading a particularly lengthy passage from *The Prairie*, Jeannette looked up to find Frank Pipe standing before her. He licked his lips and drew empty circles across the smooth surface of her desk.

"Yes?" she prompted.

Frank cleared his throat. "We were wondering." He looked behind him, seemed to find what he needed, and turned back to face his teacher. "Instead of this stuff, could you read some of that Vine Deloria?"

Jeannette picked up her pen and wrote the name on a tablet. "Now who is that?" she asked sweetly.

Frank looked directly into her eyes for the first time. "He's our cousin," he told her.

Since that day Jeannette McVay had plunged into a study of Native American literature, and the James Fenimore Cooper texts were taken to a Bismarck thrift shop. Jeannette became more Sioux than her Dakota students, no longer addressing them by name, which she read had not been common practice in previous generations. When she heard the children call to each other, carelessly spilling names off their tongues, she scolded them.

"Your ancestors didn't do that sort of thing. You should go back to the old ways. They're so beautiful."

Finally she organized the students into the circle of chairs to get their thoughts moving in the right direction. Perhaps her scheme was working, for Harley Wind Soldier no longer noticed Jeannette's injured face or the dim classroom. Harley's mind traveled to the muddy yellow Missouri River. He sat at the top of a steep embankment, settled in new grass. He closed his ears to the voice of his teacher, ignored her long eastern vowels, and listened instead to the song of sliding water.

Harley was remembering a walk he'd taken with his friend Frank Pipe and the boy's grandfather Herod Small War just a week earlier. Herod had led them to the river and pointed downstream.

"That's where Christianity came from," he'd told the boys. Harley squinted at the water, imagining Jesus poling upstream on a raft, His sandaled feet wet from the churning spray, or, if He was traveling when the river was low, stepping across the sandbars without leaving footprints.

"What do you mean?" Frank Pipe had asked.

"Well, I see it this way." The old man put his hands together and scraped his palms absentmindedly. Harley heard a dry rasp: the noise of crisp leaves. "A steamboat finally made it up the Missouri, using stilts to get over the sandbars. It brought the first piano to this area, the first one our people ever heard. They took to that music, I think, because it's dramatic, and you know how we are, always ready for a big show. That sound made them believe about heaven better than any priest's words. They could *hear* it, couldn't they? After that piano and all the church music hit this tribe, there were a lot of converts. A lot of new singers translating those hymns into Dakota."

Herod approached the water, said a few words too quietly for the boys to hear, and dropped a pinch of tobacco into the Missouri.

"What was that?" his grandson questioned when he returned.

"I was just saying to Wakan Tanka that I haven't forgotten Him. I didn't go the way of the steamer and the great piano. I listen for His voice and the music He makes in the water and through the wind."

Harley had stepped away from Herod and his friend so he would see nothing but the river. He watched and watched, looking for the steamboat, certain he would glimpse the piano on its deck and hear the rousing chords produced by a restless passenger. But the water flowed without traffic, and Herod Small War told Harley it was time to go.

"I think we should share a few stories." The voice of Harley's teacher drew him from the river. He returned to stale air and boredom.

Jeannette McVay presented her plan: "I'd like to hear from everyone over the course of the next two days. Each student in this room is the receptacle of ancient wisdom. I know it's there, in the deepest part of you. All the stories you've heard, prayers you've learned, customs you may take for granted. So what we're going to do is pull them out."

Jeannette punched the air with her soft fist, then yanked it back. To Harley she looked like someone working a toilet plunger.

"We're going to tell our extraordinary stories and confirm our way of looking at the world. Your voices are valid." She painted circles in the air. "Valid and necessary and, I'm sure, compelling. So here we go. You." Jeannette pointed to Frank, since she could not call his name.

Frank Pipe fussed with his long braids, poked his fingers through the interlocking strands and tugged, then twisted the loose ends around and around his index finger.

Jeannette made him stand in the center of their communal circle because, she said, "this is the way your people's old-time council worked."

Frank could see that his classmates commiserated and dreaded their own turns. He took a deep breath and launched into a story about Iktomi, the tricky spider who was both clever and imprudent and whose misadventures served to instruct. Frank thought of it as a baby story but knew his friends would understand how inappropriate it would be for him to speak publicly of his grandfather's ceremonies or reveal his heart for everyone to see. As he spoke, he was remembering a different story, which he might tell Harley someday after a savage basketball game, when they had both collapsed on the ground and were counting the rafters on the gymnasium ceiling.

It was a memory from his childhood, one of the first times he attended a Yuwipi ceremony conducted by his grandfather. Herod had been asked to solve a local mystery. Someone was killing the reservation dogs, an animal a week, strangling them and leaving their limp bodies in the owners' yards. The killer was also shooting coyotes, whose corpses had been turning up in sheds and root cellars. The Dakota people loved their dogs and had respect for the tough coyotes; they wanted the criminal found.

The ceremony excited Frank, although he was quaking against his mother for its duration. The lights were extinguished for much of the evening, as if in a blackout, and heavy blankets covered the windows. The spirits were noisy when they came, and mischievous: pulling someone's hair, shaking a rattle in another's ear, so close the person started.

Frank Pipe would never forget the sound of glass exploding in the dark room. Something had burst through the window behind him, and he was lucky for a hanging quilt, which stopped most of the spinning glass that flew through the air like shrapnel. In the sudden moonlight, Frank identified the creature as the largest coyote he had ever seen, tall as a pony. It lunged for one of the participants, and though hands stretched to hold him, the man was carried off like a bone, his head cracking against the window frame as the coyote leapt into the night with its victim. Leo Mitchell's body was found the next day at the foot of Angry Butte, punctured by incisors thick as pencils.

Herod said: "The spirits weren't satisfied with just identifying the person who did those terrible things. They wanted justice."

Frank never discovered why Leo Mitchell, a soft-spoken young man who was skilled at hoop dancing, had hunted the dog population, but he learned something about the swift retribution spirits were capable of working. He wondered what Jeannette would make of the story. Would she accuse him of dreaming? Would she consider him crazy?

Frank finished his tale about Iktomi and returned to his seat.

"Thank you for that fascinating parable!" his teacher enthused. And for a moment Frank wondered whether she was referring to the spider or the coyote.

"Who shall we call upon next?" Jeannette's eyes scanned the group and focused on Charlene Thunder, who was squeezed into a fussy old-lady's dress her grandmother had made. Tiny print daffodils were scattered across Charlene's chunky figure, a field of flowers straining against her abdomen. She thrust her hands into the deep patch pockets to hide her fingers; just a few moments earlier she'd been gnawing her cuticles so much they bled.

"Take your time," Jeannette encouraged the girl. "Just start when you're ready."

Charlene stood in the circle with her back to Harley Wind Soldier because he was her favorite. She couldn't bear to have him watch her, notice the scratches on her short legs, which came from walking through open country in skirts and no stockings, and see the battered slippers with heels worn down unevenly.

Charlene's voice was nearly a whisper. She told the class a simple story she remembered about a Dakota woman who was so unhappy when her husband brought a second wife into their household that she pouted until she turned to stone. Charlene imagined that the other students were smirking; they already knew her stories, too many of them—the numerous legends recounting Mercury Thunder's spells and conquests. These were events Charlene found difficult to discuss, so she murmured her tale of the punished woman, thinking all the while about her grandmother and how *she* would freeze someone *else* into rock, keeping her own flesh pliable.

Charlene was pulled into the memory of a winter three years past, when Mercury Thunder decided she would light her house so that it shimmered on the plains like an earthbound constellation. A crust of ice lacquered her complicated two-story hipped roof, but Mercury was adamant, she wanted lights. After a serving of her delectable corn soup sprinkled with dried parsley from the garden, a young man named Luther Faribault could be cajoled into just about anything. He scaled Mercury's roof, the set of outdoor Christmas lights the old woman had purchased at a Bismarck dime store looped across his shoulder. Charlene watched in horror as his feet slipped and he clung to the surface by his fingers; then, at another step, his hands lost their precarious hold and only his well-placed toes, gouging ice, kept him from plunging to the ground.

Luther had gained the treacherous peak and was fastening the lights, when a slight miscalculation in the distribution of his weight sent him falling. He landed on his back and couldn't breathe for several moments. Mercury stood over him, her eyes blinking with curiosity, while Charlene knelt beside him in the snow, tears streaming down her cold face.

"I'm pretty lucky," Luther finally said.

"What?" The girl leaned closer.

"The snow saved my neck pretty good." Luther struggled to his feet and stamped snow off his boots. He looked unhurt except for his left shoulder, which was dislocated.

"You better go to Indian Health," Charlene told him.

Luther shook his head. "No, I'm going to give this one more shot."

Charlene appealed to her grandmother because she could see that Luther Faribault was lost somewhere behind his eyes, guided only by Mercury's desires. "Don't let him!" she begged.

The old woman placed her heavy hand on the crown of Charlene's head. "But it will be so nice," she said.

Once again Luther climbed Mercury Thunder's house, this time with the use of only one arm. *The spirits must pity him,* Charlene thought, when he somehow managed to complete the job.

"I think this legend's going to require some discussion," Jeannette told her class, startling Charlene.

Charlene wandered back to her chair. The image of her grandmother's twinkling roof burned her eyes.

"This is great," Jeannette continued. "The perfect material for a serious discussion." She slid off her desk and leaned against it, staring at her pointy boots. "I'd like to hear what the girls think about the woman's plight. What were her options with a second wife moving in?"

Jeannette tried valiantly to lead her class into a debate about the old Dakota practice of taking plural wives. But getting the students to express themselves was like heaving a thrashing lake trout out of the water. Some of them didn't care one way or the other, hadn't the slightest interest in what they considered the minutiae of history. Others felt their teacher would never understand the intricacies of tribal relationships, how a woman could seem downtrodden, at the mercy of her husband's whims, yet turn around and join him in battle if she desired, tell him to vacate the lodge, which belonged solely to her.

*It's complicated,* Harley Wind Soldier was thinking, unwilling to explain.

*Things aren't always what they seem,* Frank Pipe thought to himself.

And Charlene Thunder could see only her grandmother—a plump, majestic sage grouse, a robber fly, a towering hill—wrapping her long arms around the earth and squeezing firmly, her enemies whirling into lost space.


The next day Jeannette called on Harley to speak. He was the tallest of his classmates and stood in their midst like a stiff red cedar. He watched the floor and tried to generate some moisture in his mouth. Harley didn't know what to say. He hadn't been raised in a house of conversation; he couldn't produce stories his mother had told him. What Harley did surprised him. He made up a story. It was all about a lonely warrior who was an outcast from his tribe because of his penchant for telling lies. In the warrior's mind they were tales, but his delivery was so compelling that his listeners were taken in, time and again, only to discover at the end of the narrative that it had been fabricated. Soon no one would listen to him, and he wandered the prairies alone, telling his stories to the wind and the grass. The creatures who were not human, and didn't chase after the truth, appreciated his anecdotes and would follow him at a discreet distance so they wouldn't miss anything. They decided to thank him for the many hours of pleasure he had given them, and each night one of their species served as a guide and led him through their world. He scratched his back against trees with the bears, tunneled into the ground with the prairie dogs, coasted in the air with hawks, and raced the mule deer across flat stretches of grass. Finally he returned to his tribe and shared his experiences. The people laughed—his neighbors, even his cousins. His uncles told him: *You are em-*

*barrassing us.* The warrior was ridiculed until the creatures who were not human emerged from the countryside to surround him. An eagle landed on his shoulder and glared at the people, grasshoppers rode the arches of his feet, a gray kit fox lectured the gathering of humans with his short barks. The menagerie claimed the warrior and accepted him into their society. He left then and never returned, although some said he followed his own kind on occasion, lonesome for conversation.

Harley shrugged at the end and dropped back in his seat.

"How wonderful." Jeannette sighed. "How sad. Where does that come from?"

Harley scraped at a hardened wad of gum stuck beneath the seat of his chair. He shrugged again.

"Just heard it somewhere?" Jeannette asked.

He nodded in response because, in truth, he felt so empty he believed it must have come from outside him.

"So that teacher's been telling you stories?" Herod Small War asked.

"No, she's been making *us* say them," Frank Pipe answered.

Herod, his grandson, and Harley were cleaning the yard in front of the old man's cabin. When Herod's wife, Alberta, brought them lemonade, they took a break, lounging near the back door.

"I want to tell you something," Herod said to Harley. "I've been thinking about one of your ancestors nearly every day. He's probably tired of waiting for me to speak out, so now he's pestering my thoughts."

Harley sat on the ground, his back against the cabin wall.

"The one I'm referring to is your uncle, Ghost Horse. Actually, he is the brother of your great-great-grandfather. That's how far back he goes."

Harley nodded; he had heard the name before.

"This uncle of yours had a powerful dream, where the thunderbirds appeared to him. You know what that means?"

"Yes," said the boy.

"Sure. He had to become *heyo'ka.* And that is hard." Herod ran his thumb in jagged lines across his arm. "He painted the lightning on his arms and legs and his face too. He did everything the opposite of the way it's usually done, and he said what he didn't mean."

Harley looked up. "He lied, then?"

"No." The old man shook his head. "He just said things in reverse. But everyone understood that, so they got the drift."

Harley trailed his fingers in the dirt, etching parallel streaks of lightning.

"That one was fearless and took many risks on the battlefield. Your father was that way too. You come from a long line of soldiers."

Harley's breath caught at the mention of his father, the man in a photograph who had never held him. "He fought?" Harley asked, unable to say "my father."

"Oh, yes. In Korea. And, some would say, right here." The old man coughed into his hand and stood up with difficulty. "Ghost Horse, you leave me alone now," he scolded. "I said your name to this nephew."

As far as Frank Pipe was concerned, his friend Harley Wind Soldier had become insufferable. He was copying his ancestor's contrary behavior. Frank resented not only the aberrant conduct but also the fact that Harley wasn't properly respectful, acting as if he were playing a game. It was the end of September and still quite warm, yet Harley went around in a windbreaker, shivering and blowing on his hands.

"So cold," he insisted. "Gonna freeze to death." He'd taken a ballpoint pen to his limbs, tracing lightning bolts that marked his flesh like blue tattoos, and now when he shot hoops, Harley aimed for the rim of the basket rather than the net, and cursed when the ball dropped cleanly through the hole.

"Play right" Frank said, annoyed. But Harley didn't seem to hear.

Finally, in the vast parking lot of a Bismarck movie theater, Frank lost his temper. The boys had come with the rest of their class to see *Star Wars*—a Saturday outing planned by Jeannette McVay and funded from her own pocket. The students were so transported by the film that they persuaded their teacher to sit through it twice. She observed their eager faces in the flickering light and wondered what they were thinking. She watched her class rather than the movie.

Harley Wind Soldier stared at the screen with great intensity, imagining himself in that other time and other galaxy, a world where the forces of good and evil were clearly separate, no murky territory of ambiguity. He was currently obsessed with order, maintaining a psychic balance by discovering the opposites of his desires and voicing them. Harley was so uncertain of the positive space he took up in the world that he was investigating the negative. Although, when he thought about his changed behavior, it was in terms of ancestry. Harley imagined himself in a long line of men, erect soldiers who followed one another in perfect order. He wanted to stand behind them in his own allocated slot, looking straight ahead, confident, his eyes focused rather than flitting from side to side.

He charged from his seat when *Star Wars* ended for the second time, and hit the parking lot before everyone else. Frank soon joined him, awed by what he had seen. He chattered about hyperspace and light-speed and a world with two suns.

"Wasn't that cool?" he asked Harley. He was frustrated by his friend's silence.

"No," the boy breathed, meaning yes. "It was the dumbest thing I ever saw."

Frank Pipe's fist shot straight out from his shoulder, surprising him even as it landed squarely on Harley's nose, breaking it.

The next Saturday, Harley Wind Soldier left his house early in the morning to visit the sluggish Missouri. He was no longer mimicking the contrary life-style of his predecessor Ghost Horse. He walked against the flow of water, in the direction of its source, soothed by its lush voice. He squatted on his heels, wondering what his tribesmen thought when they saw a steamboat for the first time. It must have seemed like a monster, chewing up their trees to power its journey. And then it must have struck them as a powerful spirit because of the wondrous music it introduced.

The water was full of dark chords, which Harley struggled to hear. *Would my father have enjoyed that music?* he wondered.

Harley Wind Soldier squinted at the Missouri, his eyes nearly closed. Within that strained vision he could see the figures emerge, stepping from the past to line the present river. His ancestors in their smooth buckskins streamed by him in a dignified parade. They were followed by their children and cavorting dogs, whole villages turning out to watch the eventful passage.

A ripple went through the crowd, which pulsed forward for a better view. Harley was the last to see it, gliding toward him. The flat-bottomed steamer rolled across the water, spun forward by its great wheel. The boy searched the deck, and there it was, an elegant upright piano inlaid with mother-of-pearl. The pedals glinted in the sun, and the ivory keys were arranged in such perfect symmetry that Harley was reminded of the spine of a fish.

A young man in a bowler hat seated himself at the instrument and pumped the pedals as if to test them. His fingers drifted to the keys, and then the young man teased music from the wood-and-ivory table, his eyes closed and torso rocking: so intent on his performance he didn't notice the dense crowd along the shore and never guessed that he was ushering in a new religion.

# BETTY LOUISE BELL

## Beat the Drum Slowly...don't...stop...too...fast (1994)

*In the hearts and minds of Native people live strong women, shy women, women who will not ask and will not take, women who will stand on their own and defend those they love to the death, who will also abuse those they love to death, or banish them, or subject them to emotional neglect. Such have lived in our minds for centuries, and in our narrative tradition— women just like their modern counterparts, whom Bell recalls for us, shapes before our consciousness so we can understand in some small measure; come to terms with their pain, rage, and grief; and forgive.*

*"Beat the Drum Slowly" is part of a novel,* Faces in the Moon. *It is a story of women—mothers, grandmothers, and aunties—and of the modern forms the ancient traditions have taken. "Beat the Drum Slowly" is set in that most womanly of spaces, the kitchen: the table, the older women, the child. They are telling her who she is by telling her who they have been. That is the way the old traditions have been transmitted, generation by generation. The oral tradition is more of the kitchen than of the audience-hall, and its purpose is only partly to educate. It is mainly to bond a child to her family, her community, her cosmos, and herself.*

"Your grandma was a full-blooded Cherokee," my mother said again and again, as far as I can remember. It was the beginning of a story, the beginning of a confidence, and I lean forward, knowing that in the next few minutes no cheek will be pinched, no broom handle swung, no screams or tears wasted. I listen and watch, grateful to be part of the circle. Her words come slow, a chant filling her sunken face and smoothing her wrinkles. Across the kitchen table, I never take my eyes off her.

I did not hate her, then. It was easy to believe in the photograph on Lizzie's bureau: a dark-eyed beauty with olive skin and black hair to her waist, shapely in a cotton housedress and holding a newborn baby. She stood forward in a new field, the baby close to her cheek, the woods far behind her. As a child I called the woman "Momma," slipping close to the photograph and tracing her outline with my fingers, whenever I passed through Lizzie's parlor. After my great aunt's death, it was harder and harder to put the pretty girl with the child together with the fat, beat-up woman who cursed and drank, pushed into her only threat, "Maybe I'll just run away and leave y'all to yourself."

Some tension had given, some spirit snapped in the space of ten years, and the pretty girl had swollen into fatigue and repetition. In her last years a big cozy mother appeared, in short housedresses with snaps down the front and letters sticking out of her pockets, letters written to me on scraps of paper, backs of envelopes, and carried around for weeks, even months, before she dropped them in the mail. Her running scrawl refused time, pushing ahead of it the events of her day and health, always confessing her secret love and pride in me, and arriving months after the fact.

But, long before the letters began to arrive, long before she knew she had something to say, she already lost me to her stories. And there, I loved and forgave her.

"You was always her favorite. She was crazy 'bout you. I never seen her take to nobody the way she took to you. Ain't that right, Rozella? She was always too good for the likes a us. Uppity Indian. Her nose so turned up, her own shit don't stink."

"What did she look like?" I ask.

"Don't y'all member Lizzie?"

I shrug, my palms turned wide and open. I remember but I'm not supposed to remember. And I want to hear it again. I listen for Lizzie's name, watching as she moves before me in a calico apron and a tight face. She never smiles. Even as Momma and Auney move from laughter to tears, Lizzie stands silent and unamused.

"She was an Indian," Momma says. "She looked a lot like our momma, the same black hair and black eyes."

"Like us?"

"Y'all carry the Indian blood, that's for sure. Your black hair and Rozella's quiet ways, ain't no mistaking y'all. I ended up with the Scotch blood. Don't look like there were a drop left for y'all. Member that woman ask me if I'm Irish? Black Irish, she says. I'm a thinking she means nigger, and I almost give her a beating right in front of the chicken shack. I just look her in the eye and say, as cool as you please, 'There ain't no nigger in my woodpile.' But Lizzie and momma, they looked Indian."

"Indian," Auney says with a nod and a blow of smoke.

She was my spinster aunt, a survivor of four marriages, and my mother's chorus since birth. When one of her marriages broke up or she was looking for a new start, she came to us. And there, she was my mother's constant companion and an angel to me: silent and placid, she told no tales and didn't hit. And she gave me everything, except her bingo money. She drank and married hard-drinking no-good men. They almost killed her, more than once, but the closest she came to fighting back was to refuse to forget.

"I can forgive," she explained, "but I can't forget."

When she had had enough she came to us, put on her hairnet and went to work in the cafeteria with my mother, giving her slow attention to portions of corn and mashed potatoes. She never bothered with divorce, she simply lived in one married name until the opportunity for another came along. And like my mother, she just as easily switched from married to maiden name without consistency or legal considerations.

They were Evers, sometimes more, sometimes less, but always Evers. The daughters of Helen Evers and some no-account traveling Scotch preacher who never married their mother, turning up only to impregnate her a second time, and leaving them, finally, on the side of the road. The young Indian mother walked, carrying one baby and coaxing the other, until she came to a junkyard. There, she made a home for them in an abandoned car. There, until the rent money was saved, she left Gracie in the back seat to look after the baby, Rozella, while she walked into town and looked for work.


"You member, Rozella," my mother's mind fluttering from one story to the next, "the time I locked you in the outhouse?"

"I member."

Momma lit her cigarette from Auney's and spoke to me. "Your grandma used to have to go to work in town. Five miles there and back, she walked. Ever day, even Sundays. She was afraid someone would steal us, so she always locked us up in the house." Her eyes darted across mine, and she blushed with shame. "It was just an old shack, tar paper and cold in the winter."

"Cold."

"We was always up to no good." Her face lit up. "Still are, eh Rozella?"

"Yep. Sure was. Your momma was always the ringleader."

My mother took the compliment with a laugh.

"As soon as your grandma was down the road, we scrambled right out the window and back 'fore she got home that night. More coffee, Rozella?"

Auney was a strong coffee drinker. She'd been waiting for the offer for some time but instead of saying "yes," she looked down into her empty cup, took a drag on her cigarette, and came as close as she allowed herself to expressing want. "I believe so," she said in a slow and uncommitted drawl. She lived with us, on and off, for most of her life, but she never asked nor took without multiple invitations and assurances of plenty. That, my mother said, was the Indian in her.

Momma brought a new cup and the coffeepot to the table. She filled their cups and poured me half a cup. I wanted to smoke too but knew better than to ask.

"One day, you member Rozella?"

"I member."

"You went to the bathroom and I locked the door from the outside." Momma laughed, Auney blushed. "You didn't so much as raise a yell. I heard you try to open the door. But then you got real quiet."

"How did Auney get out?" I was the audience, and I held the story's cues.

"She did the durnest thing. I'm waiting out front, wandering when she's gonna start yelling, and here she comes around the corner of that outhouse. What a sight you was, Rozella. I thought I was seeing things when you come around that corner." Momma turned to me. "She was covered with shit and piss from head to toe. She crawled right out of that damn hole! And she stunk! Lord have mercy."

"Amen."

"Momma came home that night and whupped the living daylights out of me. She whupped Rozella too."

"She did. Yes, she did."

"She said the county'd come and get us if we didn't behave. They woulda, too. A young Indian woman with two little girls and no man around."

"No man."

"But she kept us together. I wander how she did it, Rozella?" The kitchen curtain flapped. Momma went to close the window and found it shut tight. "Witches, Rozella. You member them witches down there in old man Jeeter's river?"

"Sh-h-h," Auney said. "Y'all gotta watch who y'all call up."

Momma laughed and turned to me. "Your Auney were always afeared a them witches. Long afore our momma died, she'd a shiver and shake anytime she come near that water."

"Now, Grace, I weren't the onliest one afeared."

"That's true," Momma admitted, "true enough. Momma used to say only fools don't know what to be afeared of. And the good Lord save us from them. Eh, Rozella?"

"Ain't nothing scarier'n fool. The God's truth."

*In the dream I'm being chased. Through city streets, down
alleys, only a few slippery feet ahead of the monster behind me. I
feel his reaching darkness, gaining and gaining, almost in grabbing distance. I watch the horror of running without moving,
screaming without noise, the terror striking and missing, striking
and missing, and I pull myself treading to the surface. Sweating
and shaking, I lie still in my corner of the room. "Shoo," I whisper, "go on."*

"Those was tough times," Momma said. "The Depression and the
wind blowing the topsoil clean outta Oklahoma. Times was rough all over.
There was no welfare, no nothing for an Indian woman with two little girls
to feed. Even ifn there was, she had that Indian pride, don't take nothing
from nobody."

"Member she beat me fer askin Mz. Wilkins for that apple?"

"I thought she was gonna kill you."

"Almost did."

"Why'd Grandma do that? It was just a apple." The words slipped
out of my mouth. I knew better. "I mean," I tried to explain as I watched
the humor drain from Momma's face, "why'd she have to be so mean?"

"What ya know 'bout it? It ain't ever just a apple. Things ain't never
that simple. 'Cept you, sometime." Auney dropped her laughing eyes, and
Momma commenced shaking her finger at me. "Missy, ya ain't but ten
years old and you think ya know it all. Ya'll don't know donkey shit."

"I know something," I mumbled and pushed my shoulders back.

"Horse manure."

Auney laughed and gagged on her smoke. Through a fit of coughing
she tried to say, "Grace ... we ... was ... the same way."

"At her age Momma was dead and we was on our own with that old
devil Jeeter. We had to grow up fast, it ain't the same."

I considered the distance from my mother across the table and
gambled, "I can take care of myself."

"I wisht I believed it. I'd a take the first Greyhound bus and leave
youse to yourself. The trouble with you, Missy, is you ain't never knowed
hard times. Ya don't know what it means to spend just as much time *not*
looking hungry as being hungry." She was wrong, but I knew better than
to gamble again. "I wisht I'd a had a mother to look after me. Maybe things
a been different for me."

"Ya did your best, Grace."

"Lord knows I tried. I'd tried and tried till I'm a plumb tired out
from trying."

"Plumb tired out."

"I tried to forget an' go on living. But those was hard times. Don't
seem like there's a way a forgetting 'em. I member Momma like it was yes-

terday. I see her as clear as I see myself. I member her taking off down that road ever morning, walking those five miles to town to clean the Wilkins house and the Davis house . . ."

"And that one with the big white porch. The Johnson house."

"Yep. Those white women worked her to death, and the white men was always touching her up. Sometimes she'd come home crying. You member, Rozella?"

"I member."

"You member how we used to sit on old man Jeeter's back porch and watch for her in the moon?"

"I member."

"The day she died she said she'd be watching for us from the moon. You member?"

"I member."

"Used to be we'd see her. Most every night. All's we had to do was sit on old man Jeeter's back porch and watch for her. Soon those eyes a hers would be looking at us."

"Yep. Plain as day."

"We sit right there and talk to her like she could hear us. About old man Jeeter and the hard life we had without her." Momma laughed and shrugged. "Those eyes a hers would change. Look like she were going to kill somebody."

"You member, Grace, what she used to tell us?" Momma and Auney laughed, and I saw Lizzie turn from her work at the sink and almost smile.

"I sure do." Momma leaned toward me, as if I hadn't heard it a hundred times before, and said slowly, "Don't mess with Indian women."

"Less you're a fool."

"Even a fool got more sense 'n that."

"Grace, you ever see Momma after ya left old man Jeeter's place?"

"Used to be when I ran away with that old man Baptist preacher, I'd see her. Now and again. You see her, Rozella?"

"Now and again."

Momma waited for Auney's words to clear the room. We waited for what Auney would not say. Then Momma laughed and said, "Used to be we believed Indians went to the moon when they passed on." The joke passed through Momma's face before she spoke. "What y'all think? We gonna make it to the moon?"

"I can't see why not."

"Me too?"

Momma lit a cigarette. Auney said low and careful, "I believe so."

"You just tell them you're Helen Evers' grandbaby. She ain't gonna let them turn ya away. They'd have a fight on their hands, sure enough. Wouldn't knowed what hit 'em. Ya member, Rozella?"

"I member."

"I remember."

Momma laughs, Auney stops mid-draw on her cigarette. "You weren't even born. How can you member?"

"I do remember."

My mother looks at me. The kitchen curtain flaps above my head. Finally, she says, "You musta dreamt it."

"Dreamt it."

# KAREN WALLACE

## Mary (1994)

*You know how it is when you're walking between worlds, not yet firm on your feet, how it was when you were learning to walk: a few steps, then plop! then perhaps a whimper of fear, or a yell of rage, then up again, totter a few tiny paces. Well, that's how it is with whoever among us walks between the worlds of the mundane and the arcane. Mary is one of us: a white woman who touched other understandings of the nature of reality long before, in her youth, and never came to terms with what she actually learned. Now, as she grows aged—a state that thins the barriers between materialist logical positivist modes of conceptualizing experience and more holistic modes that allow perception of things outside the factory-model of modern life—her perception moves back and forth between the fearful past and the terrible present, between the solid, material, familiar, and the fragile, immaterial, and equally familiar.*

*Mary's situation is one we all share, whether Native or non-Native, aged or barely born, adolescent or stolidly middle-aged. There are times when the barriers that usually exist between the worlds grow thin and all but disappear, when we move in time and place, in perception and expectation, when we are compelled to question our very foundations. Such times, when the usual barriers are little more than a morning mist, when a liminal state brings people to the brink of other worlds, or catapults them beyond the brink, causing them to journey in strange realms or in the past, the future, or the unknown, are those times which most occupy Native writers' attention.*

Mary can't remember when exactly it happened, but at some point her body and her mind took off in different directions. In her head, she is still an energetic, not-too-cynical social worker with long red-orange hair that falls past her waist, and three small children. What she feels as she walks down the street, with a cheap straw hat tied a little too tight under her double chin, is heaviness. Her joints ache and the knee that was operated on last year still pains her. She is embarrassed, because even though she uses a cane, she can just barely shuffle along. A block seems like miles.

The only time her mind connects with her body is when she berates God for abandoning her.

It is hot outside, and she feels like crying. She won't though. It's important to stick with her daily routine and leave the house under her own power at least once every morning. It's not death she's afraid of exactly, but rather being trapped inside such an old frail body. That's what she says, at least. She worries that one day she'll wake up dead, but no one will notice and she'll have to stay in her house, day after day, waiting for someone to catch on.

As she moves forward, each step a bit slower than the last, Mary can see the heat waves rising off the pavement. How stupid she was to wear her blue polyester pants and the plaid workman's shirt that used to belong to Bill. How hot she is. She worries that she will stumble, so she wrenches her attention away from the sweat soaking her shirt and the fire under her feet and forces herself to see each step before she makes it.

"Why on earth must you go out today?" Faye had asked as Mary reached for the front door, lulled by the air conditioning into a false sense of strength and confidence.

Mary had pulled open the door and almost gasped as the hot afternoon air hit her face. She'd stepped onto the verandah and shut the door on Faye's questions.

If only the old bag hadn't seen her leave, Mary could have sat on the glider, trying to convince herself that this counted as leaving the house. Then she would have been able to go back into the cool air of the sitting room and read her *House & Garden* magazine. Instead, here she was walking down Main Street on what had to be the hottest afternoon in a century, hoping to God that she wouldn't fall.


Mary stopped walking. She looked up from her feet and tried to decide the quickest way to get home. She had only walked four blocks and felt like she had run a marathon. Maybe two. How smug Faye would be. Mary spotted a bus stop and a faded blue bench down the street and thought she would sit there for a while, just long enough to convince Faye that she was as strong as she had said. The sidewalk seemed to stretch ahead of her as she moved—reeling away, propelled by the sound of her steps.

She sometimes saw visions, especially at times like this. She raised her chin and squinted, peering out from under the floppy hat. She saw running ahead of her a small child. He looked like Bill, with long black hair and a ruddy complexion. He looked back for an instant, as if contemplating her, then ran out of sight around the corner. Mary gasped and closed her eyes.

When she looked again, tentatively, tensed to shut her eyes, the boy was gone, had not returned. She took a deep breath and resumed her slow and painful journey toward the bench. All of a sudden she smiled grimly, picturing Faye's wrinkled old face, those bone-white teeth, the metal of her bridge gleaming if the light was just so when she smiled. Bill had gotten one of those, an eerie row of teeth set in a glass on his nightstand. He said that they hurt his mouth, but he kept them for the rare "special occasion." He liked to entertain the smaller children with his toothless grin, telling them incessantly how handsome he had been, women always wanting to talk with him, be seen with him. They would stare adoringly at the tall, gaunt old man, uncomprehending, with beautiful gap-toothed smiles of their own, clapping and giggling every time he parted his lips. Their parents, the other children who Mary sometimes forgot to remember and their mates, would look toward the group dominated by the old man with a long pony-tail, in faded blue jeans and old work boots, his gums pink and wet. They would smile, shaking their heads ever so slightly, glancing one to the other to confirm their sense of the man's infirmity. He's harmless, Mary could see them thinking, making her fume, though she never said anything about it. Bill's hair stayed thick and black 'til late in his life. It wasn't until he started going gray that Mary prepared to lose him.

Mary paused again, clasping her hand over and over on the handle of the cane, trying to get a better grip, her hand slippery now from the sweat coursing down her body. She had been foolish to go out. Faye was right. Mary remembered her mother-in-law saying, long ago, that if the bird was meant to die, it didn't matter when you threw the stone. She had been newly married and felt baffled by this woman's articulated train of thought, her every idea spoken, mumbled into the air regardless of who might be there to hear. Mary recalled her still gray hair, twisted into a bun, but let loose every night, falling below her waist as she brushed and brushed it. Carmelita looked like Bill, but was mysterious, lacking Bill's easy personality and charm, an old Indian woman who Mary had feared from the start.

Carm had been old already when Bill was born and was, to Mary, ancient by the time they married. She would have to sit in front of the old woman, who eventually turned a uniform shade of gray and then died, as she mended or beaded or read the Bible, a burbling laugh erupting from the recesses of her body every so often. Mary would stare, acutely aware of her own head of red hair, washed and set every morning before she would leave the house. She could even remember thinking, the same day that the woman uttered this most strange statement about a bird, that she hoped their children would look like her side of the family. Let them be called Mick, never Chief.

These were Mary's jumbled recollections as she prepared to move on, wondering too how difficult it would be to call a cab and how much of Faye's pettiness she would then be forced to endure. The sound of a bird's wings echoed briefly for a moment close to her ear and she saw, vaguely and out of the corner of her eye, the same small boy walking through the parking lot as she passed. She imagined that he held a cherry-red lollipop in his hand and that his lips and tongue had been stained the same bright color. He could have been her son.

Carm had been delighted when Mary announced her pregnancy, but was disappointed when they decided to name the baby James. She had expected that Bill would insist upon her own father's name. Tlanuwa, a name to be proud of. But Mary had insisted instead. No Indian names for her son, no tags of umpteen syllables to be attached to her firstborn in particular, marking him for life. That would be the point, said Carm in a quiet fury. Mary had responded with an equally fierce silence. The boy had been christened James Arthur at the Church of the Holy Cross. Carm had stayed home that day.

Mary had been so pleased with James. But, unlike her other children, he had inherited a measure of his grandmother's character. He was often silent, and saw the world in rather odd ways. Carm, ignoring Mary's distress, called him Yona Us'di, his Indian name, refusing until the last day of her life to call him James. Bill never interfered. He would stroke his wife's hair, smiling all the while at his mother and son as they played, the name of the bear resonating pleasantly through his memories.

Mary hadn't been thoroughly horrified, though, until she came to understand James' perception of God. He had been staring up into the sky, standing on Main Street next to the greengrocer's, old women with shopping bags looped over their arms as they pawed through piles of rotting fruit. Is that where Granny went? he had innocently asked, referring, Mary thought, to last Sunday's sermon on heaven and hell, too sophisticated, she had thought, for even this peculiar, barely five years old, less than two feet tall boy. She in turn lifted her eyes to the sky and said that yes, Granny had gone to heaven, grinning suddenly despite herself as her gaze drifted inexorably down toward its alternative. James continued to stare up at the sky, rapt, until Mary had shaken him, lightly, by the shoulder, bony and sharp under his thin woolen shirt. But, he said, his eyes turned still to the sky, why would Granny want to live in the black ropes when she could live in a tree or swim in the lake?

Mary had listened, a scowl on her face as she tried to decipher his words, screened as they were by her own sacrilege. He was still crying when they got home, his skin bruised and sore from the pressure of her fingers, locking around his skinny arm as she dragged him down the street. What, Bill had asked, what did he do? Mary had been too shocked to tell him at first, sure that somehow the child's mind had been tainted by the old woman, the gray and somehow inviolate Carmelita. Bill was eventually able to understand that Mary's outrage came from the fact that James, looking up toward the sky, has assumed that God and heaven were located in the thick black power lines over his head. Mary had never seen Bill laugh so hard and wouldn't talk to him for almost a week after.

Standing in the hot sun, listening to the sound of her heartbeat and the fading whisper of a bird's wings, Mary chuckled, surprised at her own memory and the still palpable strength of her unreasonable anger. She had given up on James then, allowing him to believe in his strange ideas, images and constructions peculiarly suited to the boy, who so resembled his grandmother.

As she stepped again toward the blue bench, its edges blurred by the heat emanating from the pavement, Mary became aware of the boy. He was sitting on the bench, his skinny legs swinging back and forth in a regular rhythm. As she moved slowly toward him, faltering now and again as the rubber on the bottom of her cane slid unhappily over the sidewalk, she looked intently into his eyes, a clear hazel like her own. He stared at her without blinking, his legs moving incessantly, his hands clasping the edges of the bench.

She tried to keep the boy in focus, searching her memory to understand why he seemed so familiar, forgetting about Bill and James, only the figure of Carmelita flitting along the edges of her thoughts. Mary felt tears running down her cheeks as she panted and held on to her cane as though for dear life. The heat was unbearable. She tried to recall why she was standing on Main Street in the middle of the day, looking down at the small and silent boy who wouldn't keep still.

She thought she heard Faye's voice behind her, shrill and high, chastising her for walking so far in the heat. Mary turned to face the disembodied voice, at which point it faded, blown away it seemed by the barely perceptible breeze that was as warm as the still air through which it passed, becoming instead the wrinkled face of her best friend. Faye hurried to the woman's side and helped her into the waiting car, concern softening her expression. Mary looked through the dirty window toward the bench, a mere spot of color. She thought she saw a pair of legs swinging as the car sped away, but she would never be sure.

•   •   •

Sitting in the car, the cool air from the air-conditioning restoring her fragile sense of well-being, Mary was overwhelmed by a vision of Carmelita. A grayness permeated Mary's very sense of self, she felt a need to confirm her dislike of the dead woman, while simultaneously suffering remorse for her treatment of her son. If the bird is meant to die, she thought, it doesn't matter when you throw the stone.

When Mary woke, her limbs were stiff and sore. She felt she might never leave her bed. She heard Faye's voice from outside, coming through the window, as Faye told the gardener in piercing tones about Mary's ill-fated walk toward town. Mary slipped gratefully back into sleep, the clock next to her bed ticking softly in the darkening afternoon.

The dream seemed so real later that she dared even to tell Faye. She spoke hesitantly at first about the boy, the small restless boy with the black hair and hazel eyes who Faye claimed not to have seen, sitting at the bus stop swinging his legs. With a growing disregard for Faye's opinion, Mary spoke more freely about the sequence of events, mirroring, she thought, her progress down the sidewalk the previous afternoon. It was Carmelita, she said, a little louder than she meant to. I was young and Carm was braiding my hair, mumbling as she did about the color that seemed to her so unnatural. James was there, sitting on Carm's old embroidered couch swinging his legs. There were thick black power lines over my head, she said, nodding for emphasis. James was right. God was there. Bill said so.

Faye nodded, a grim smile on her face as she guided Mary from the chair to her door and on beyond it to the bed. Sleep, she told the old woman, try not to dream. Mary laughed at this admonition. She looked out the window, lying on the bedspread, her head propped up by so many pillows. As she watched, a hummingbird came to her window, hovering as it contemplated the feeder with red sugar-water that she had sitting on the sill. It drank, she presumed, then flew away, a blur of wings. The whirring of a tiny and miraculous machine, Mary thought unexpectedly, the work of God in his infinite wisdom and goodness. She looked up toward the ceiling then, sad suddenly as the sense of her mother-in-law again overwhelmed her. She made an effort to recall, if not a picture of her son, whose face she could not see beyond his ninth year, then at least of her husband, whose passing, she thought, should have been more abrupt, a burst of red rather than the seeping grayness that seemed to overcome him even as she watched.

•   •   •

She tried and tried, but in the end it was Carm who won. The woman sat in the center of Mary's imagination, creaking back and forth in her old redwood rocking chair with a string of green and yellow beads in her gnarled hands, her shank of thick, practically colorless hair loose now and hanging over her shoulder. Mary sighed and gave up. If the bird is meant to die, sang James in a quiet, toneless voice from the darkest corner of her memory, it doesn't matter when you throw the stone.

# D. RENVILLE

## Siobhan La Rue in Color (1994)

*Abduction and quest stories in the traditional narrative cycle generally contain a segment concerned with the return of the abducted one, or seeker, though he or she may not return permanently. In some Yellow Woman stories from the Keres Pueblos, for example, Yellow Woman is returning home with her child after living beyond the sky in the clutches of a Sky Kachina. He has instructed her family to make no sound of greeting until Yellow Woman has climbed all the way down the ladder into her family home. But one of her sisters, unable to contain her joy at the sight of her, gives a cry of greeting, and Yellow Woman vanishes, her child with her.*

*In Renville's "Siobhan La Rue in Color" the story begins near the point where the hero will escape his captor with the help of his loyal female relative. He has, like many contemporary Native people, been abducted by the city: by college, by sophistication, by the glamour of urban and suburban America. Finding the way home is difficult, and many are unable to do so.*

*Because death itself produces a liminal state not only in those who have died but in those closest to them, Tim enters a transformational period, amnesiac, ungrounded. He almost loses his sense of self, finding himself estranged from himself in two directions. But as the transformation proceeds he regains his balance: He's "a new man," in a sacred rather than clichéd way. He goes through fire and death, and communication with the world he left behind is as impossible for him as it is for his parents and grandparents. They can't talk to him, directly, and he can't talk to Siobhan La Rue.*

•　　•　　•

Siobhan La Rue has called me three times now, and though I've listened to her messages scores of times, I've not returned her calls. I can't even stay in the same room in which they're playing: They are, for the most part, a soundtrack to a blank TV screen in my dead grandparents' living room. Every day the messages echo a bit more severely, as every day the house they sound in becomes emptier. For the past month, I've been removing my grandparents' belongings, and storing them in the garage of the Old House, up on the hill. The excess things I've been burning, and so lately I've been walking around smelling like a fire.

I've also been filling in cracks in the walls and re-weatherproofing the windows; for the first time in my life, I'm leaving my grandparents' house better than I found it. Each time I finish a crack or a window, I imagine the house to be that much more airtight. I find this concept very appealing these days, and often I've glared out into the stormy flatland I've exiled myself to, waiting for the world to fill up with water to test my handiwork.

I've done all this largely on my own, though this last weekend my cousin Caitlin arrived with a case of beer and a pair of smiley face buttons and pulled me temporarily out of my grief-driven asceticism. By midnight, we'd laid ourselves out on the kitchen floor and were trading stories of our kunsi and tunkansina, and by two, I was addled enough to play Siobhan La Rue's messages for Caitlin. She ambled out of the back room afterward, plopped down in front of me, and said; "Why don't you just call her?"

Yes, I thought. Yes, well, it's like this . . . .

Shortly before I drove through fire to reach what turned out to be my grandparents' deathbeds, I called Siobhan La Rue from Roundup, Montana. It was her birthday, and she was depressed because, from now on, more of her cells would be dying than reproducing.

"The tortoise and the hare is being played out inside me at a cellular level," she said. "The tortoise is now winning."

"Well, happy birthday, anyway," I said. "It's your silver anniversary as a person, you know. A quarter of a century on earth."

"When you coming back?"

"As soon as possible," I said, believing it.

"Sure," said Siobhan La Rue, who didn't.

The next night my grandparents died within an hour of each other in a hospital in Great Falls. My grandfather died while I was in a downstairs restroom, shaving two days driving worth of fuzz off my face, wanting, as always, to impress him. I arrived in his room to the cacophony of Caitlin's and my Aunt Renata's grief. A bearded doctor, hands frozen in the air, looking both ineffectual and false, stared at me from beside my grandfather's bed. My grandfather lay with his head cocked toward me, eyes closed, unimpressed.

Later, while I sat in a waiting room dialing the numbers of relatives, Caitlin's wail came through the door from down the hall.

"Kunsi's dead," I said into the phone.

"Oh, Tim," my Uncle Simon said from South Dakota.

I put down the phone and cursed myself for not being there a second time.


It's never been clear how my grandparents' car came to rest in a ravine a few miles outside of Great Falls, Montana; they had traveled there from South Dakota to visit relatives. (Though my grandparents were Assiniboines from Montana, they had moved to South Dakota to be next to my parents when I was born. My parents were there because my mother was Dakota from the Lake Traverse Reservation and couldn't bear to live away from her family for very long.) Their car had rolled several times, but my grandfather had not braked before leaving the road, which led some at their wake, held in a gym at their home reservation, Fort Belknap, to speculate that it hadn't been an accident. Kunsi was dying of pancreatic cancer, after all, and who could imagine them not together? I rejected this when I heard it, and angrily swept out of the wake. I stood in bitter October cold, and blew smoke at the full moon.

The next morning, a team of horses pulled a wagon carrying my grandparents' bodies away from the gym. A pickup trailed behind, a drum group in the bed. Somewhere up front, Caitlin was among those leading us on horseback to a small cemetery on a rise.

I was sitting in the backseat of a station wagon, holding my three-year-old niece Lisa, who was pressing her face into my shoulder. As I patted her back and sang softly to her, "Ah, boo," I wondered what she would remember of all this.

My parents had died in 1977 in South Dakota under similar circumstances: Their car, too, had been found in a ravine, and officially, their deaths were listed as accidents. Sometime later, my Aunt Renata, who was to take in my twelve-year-old self, largely against my kunsi's wishes, obtained through the Freedom of Information Act a copy of my parents' autopsies. In addition to the injuries incurred when the car had plunged into the ravine, my mother and father each had a bullet in the back of their heads.

Their funeral had been a loud, crowded business: I remember scores of men and women, some familiar and some strange, many dressed in khaki green jackets and jeans and wearing bandannas and black armbands, the men singing and the women trilling. I remember Aunt Renata lopping off most of her hair over my parents' graves. And I remember that when we returned to visit, red, blue, yellow, and white flags flew at all corners of the mounds.

"Ah, boo," I sang to my niece.

Later, as I stood above my grandparents' graves with a shovelful of dirt, I glanced up and saw my niece watching me, troubled by the sight. I threw the dirt into my grandfather's grave and then handed the shovel to one of my cousins. Lisa's eyes never left me. She will remember this, I thought. And later, when Lisa turned away from me at the feed, I thought, She is remembering *now*.

When I finally made it back to Berkeley, I found Siobhan La Rue sleeping in my bed. I sat at my writing table and watched her for the better part of an hour, trying to imagine myself back into the world where we had both lived. I ran through my friends' names—Ollie, Patti, Lyle, Brett—hoping they would fix me in place, but after a while I stopped, and wandered into the kitchen. I checked the buzzing refrigerator and found a stray beer. I settled into a creaky metal chair and drank it at our dining table with the worn Formica floral pattern. I sat there quietly, next to an ashtray badly in need of emptying. After a few moments, my roommate Stefan surprised me, emerging out of the room he had so seldom occupied in the past six months.

"Tim," he said, smiling a groggy smile. "You're back."

He further surprised me by giving me an affectionate hug.

Eyeing my beer, he said, "Want some celebratory scotch? Couldn't hurt . . ."

"Well . . ."

"Might help."

"Sure."

He returned from his room with the scotch and some pink metallic tumblers. . . . Then he was playing the guitar I hadn't seen for some time, and we were singing, badly for my part. . . . And then Siobhan La Rue appeared, her light blonde hair, shot through with black streaks, no longer bound tightly against her head, but loose at her shoulders. I spoke her entire name, as I usually do, because it has always sounded like some sort of magic incantation coming out of my mouth.

"Why didn't you wake me up?" she said, voice hoarse from sleep. She blinked her deep brown saucer eyes rapidly a few times, trying to squeeze the weariness out of them.

"I was giving peace a chance," I said.

She smiled, and sat next to me.

"Can I kiss you?" she asked.

I nodded. And through her mouth passed into mine the world we had both shared, and by dawn, I was already denying I had lived in any other world.

•   •   •

After we left Roundup on the way to the hospital in Great Falls to see our stricken grandparents, Caitlin and I drove up towards Grassrange on Hwy 87, a fairly lonely stretch of road that I've never actually seen during the day. I've had to imagine the dark terrain, and that particular night I was imagining endless nuclear warheads lurking just off the road: I had recently heard that were a nuclear war to break out, Montana would be one of the worst hit, owing to the scores of missile silos dotting the countryside. I kept seeing in the shadows strange lights and the outlines of chain-link fences and the occasional glint of surveillance cameras, all far more frightening and starkly treacherous than any living things that might bound out in front of me.

Caitlin saw the dark red stain on the horizon first, but she kept it to herself. I did much the same, but when it became clear that we were both seeing the same thing, I stopped the car:

"What the hell is that?" we both said together.

I shut off the lights in the car to be sure that it wasn't some sort of reflection on the windshield. That established, we began to speculate.

"It's a fire," I said. "It's reflecting on the smoke."

Caitlin nodded. "Maybe a city, too. You know, the lights."

But as we drove on and the red stain loomed larger, we began to abandon our more rational theories.

"What if it's a UFO?" Caitlin said, perhaps inevitably.

"That big?"

"Maybe it's the mothership."

"Maybe it's a cici."*

"Don't say that."

"Maybe Hell's opened up and we're driving right into it," I said.

She chastised me in Assiniboine, but we were both spooked and felt a creeping dread that grew stronger the closer we came to the dark red stain. We fell into silence, contemplating forthcoming communions with aliens or scary monsters or the Devil himself; the car hummed through a darkness made corporeal by our fears.

We drove into the smoke as the road began to curve toward Grassrange. It was everywhere, like a gray veil pulled over the landscape. Once in town, we pulled into a gas station, filled my car up and asked where the smoke was coming from. The cashier told us there were wildfires all over the state, but none closer than Lewistown, still thirty miles away. We would have to pass through Lewistown.

The smoke got worse the nearer we got to Lewistown, and we came into the fierce winds that were fanning the wildfires. The road began to narrow as we drove into a mountain range, and I fought the steering wheel, trying to keep us on the road. We saw the first flames a few miles outside of

---

*a being often invoked by parents to scare their children into obedience

town, leaping above the peaks of the mountains, clawing at the sky. We passed a mountain bright with fire, the flames spilling down its side, unchecked. Finally, the road lowered and the mountains folded over the fires and we were in Lewistown.

We called Great Falls from outside a convenience store, and Aunt Renata told us to stay put: Our grandparents were stabilized, and there would be no point in driving straight through, particularly with the winds blowing the way they were. Come in the morning, she said.

We drove up and down Main Street and finally found a motel room, apparently the last one left in town. Lewistown was filled with evacuees fleeing the fires. The room was oddly placed in back of the motel, the only one like that, and the motel, used to not having it rented, had put up a NO VACANCY sign. We found out about it accidentally, having gone into the motel office to ask how far it was to the next town.

It was an old room, the motel itself having been built back in the fifties, and looking like it. I took to the room immediately, and I described it enthusiastically on the phone to Siobhan La Rue, who had, that day, moved into the house I lived in back in Berkeley.

Caitlin sat, amused, watching me from the bed next to mine. When I was off the phone, she asked me if I had ever dated a Indian woman.

I shook my head: "Not as far as I know."

"You know, I'm pretty sure Auntie told kunsi your girlfriend is Indian."

"She did," I said, considering this. "Well, Siobhan La Rue isn't Indian."

"No Indian princess grandmothers in her family tree?"

I shook my head again: "No. No Cherokee chiefs as far as I know, either."

Caitlin sipped at her beer, thinking of what to say next.

"Well, I think you should date an Indian once. Just to see what it's like."

"You mean, just so I can say?"

"Something like that."

I turned the radio on and a country song came blaring on too loud, though it was soon interrupted by the disc jockey, telling the general populace the latest about the fires, telling them not to panic, that if the winds were to change and the fires change direction, seventy-five firemen gathered in the local high school gym were prepared to respond, and things were under control. Even so, as the night wore on, he endlessly cut into the middle of songs to send out the same message of non-urgency.

"I think I need a beer," Caitlin announced after a time.

There was no discussion: We pulled on our jackets and tramped outside, in search of a store.

As we ambled down Main Street, our eyes drifted up to the mountain that stood above Lewistown: It was dark with shadow, its peak outlined by the dull, pulsing glow of the fires somewhere behind it. My eyes were already drifting away again when a bright yellow flash exploded off the mountain.

"Holy!" Caitlin shouted, and out of what she later termed "some weird maternal impulse," she threw a protective arm in front of me, which hit me across the chest and effectively stopped me in my tracks.

"What the hell is it?" I said.

The flash meanwhile grew more intense and reached higher into the sky, dispelling the darkness there, as if the sun was erupting out of the mountain and was now rising over Lewistown.

I was waiting for the inevitable report, but none was forthcoming, and then, as I was thinking of turning and running, the flash died out, and the mountain fell into a even deeper darkness, the glow of the fires behind it gone.

I turned to Caitlin, who was already looking at me; the outline of the mountain was bouncing around in our eyeballs, sticking and unsticking to our own images.

"What the hell was that?" she said. "You saw that, right?"

We quickly glanced at the street around us: The lights in town were blinking normally; no electromagnetic pulse had passed through Lewistown. Traffic puttered by calmly, and no one we could see was standing at their windows or in their doors staring up at the mountain in disbelief. We were apparently the only ones who had seen it.

We hurried to the nearest store and got our beer and made tracks back to our motel room.

Later, while we sat in our beds, the smell of smoke came drifting into our room, accompanied by hollow-sounding voices. The voices didn't sound close at all, and it was hard to pinpoint where they were coming from. The smell of smoke got stronger, and I thought of those seventy-five firemen, lounging in a gym somewhere in town.

Caitlin, sitting on the floor at the edge of her bed, said, finally, "Cicis."

We spent most of the night drinking our beer and listening to the radio, to music interrupted by nerve-wracking assurances that everything was fine, the both of us waiting to be scuttled out of our room at any moment by firemen with grim smiles, fresh from a gym, smelling of floor polish and dried sweat.

I told Siobhan La Rue about the mountain we'd seen above Lewistown, and how a cousin at Fort Belknap told us it was probably phosphorus being dropped on the fire, but that the explanation hadn't made it any less creepy.

We spent most of the first week I was back in the house in Berkeley trying to talk, about anything, but never any one thing; I tried to tell her that I felt like I was being chased, or that maybe I had been infected by something, a fever, amnesia, when I was out in Montana.

When she would go to work in the mornings, I would stumble around the rooms, carelessly invading the privacy of my roommates. I would rummage through their possessions, as if investigating the mysteries of their lives. I would handle their possessions with my eyes closed, appealing to sense memory in my attempt to ground myself once again in their world. I would lie down on Stefan's or Siobhan La Rue's bed, trying to blink out the flames that kept leaping up behind my eyes. Siobhan La Rue would come back in late afternoon to find me sitting on the covered porch, and she told me later that, coming upon me like that, she always thought I had locked myself out.

"Are you Indian at all?" I asked Siobhan La Rue late one night.

Stefan's James Brown CD was blaring in the other room, but I was perfectly clear.

"I knew you were going to ask me that," she said.

"How come?"

"The way you look at me. I didn't get a haircut, I didn't gain or lose weight, I haven't changed the way I dress. No corrective surgery. Why?"

"What?"

"Why do you ask?"

"Aunt Renata told them you were," I said. "I was just wondering where she got that."

"She told your grandmother that I was Indian?"

"Kunsi wanted me to have only Indian girlfriends . . . Assiniboine girlfriends, especially."

Siobhan La Rue was staring at me.

"Listen," I said, "she wasn't a racist or anything. It was just that . . . our tribal population isn't what it used to be." I smiled. "I'm supposed to help repopulate the race."

Siobhan La Rue smiled now, too.

"And you can't do it with a white girl."

"I didn't say that—I just can't repopulate the race with a white girl."

She jumped up and tackled me in my chair.

"Ambush!" she shouted.

Later, when the night was darker and we were more evenly covered with shadows, she said:

"What tribe? Assiniboine?"

"I'm not sure. . . . Caitlin didn't say. Maybe Assiniboine—that would've made her happy."

"It'd make you happy."

"Yes," I said. "It would. My parents are dead. I have no brothers or sisters. If I married a white woman, it would be the beginning of the end of my mother's line. If we married, our child would be more white than Indian, because I'm not a full-blood. It didn't bother me before, if that's what you're wondering. I'm not sure why it's bothering me now. I don't know—I'm thinking differently these days, like I've been possessed or something."

I tapped my fingers on the carpet like I was tapping ash.

"I know all this talk isn't some sign of maturity," I said. "The only sign of maturity I've managed to show so far is that I've gotten fatter. I mean, really, what's so great about my DNA?"

"I don't think it's your DNA you're worried about."

"Well, don't be so understanding."

"I'm not. . . . At least I know your intentions regarding me are honorable."

I turned to her, dismayed: "I'm being stupid about this, aren't I?"

"No, no," Siobhan La Rue said. "Just confused. I know a thing or two about that."

We left it at that.


I left two months later.

My grandparents' probate came up, and I went to Montana to settle their affairs. I ended up inheriting their house and property in South Dakota, where they had lived out the last years of their lives, having remained even after my parents' deaths. After the probate business was over, I traveled to South Dakota, and stayed.

I'm not sure why I didn't return the first call. I just remember being vaguely angry that she had called, and perhaps in a juvenile way, I was punishing her for pushing me into a decision. The second call, I was standing above the answering machine with my hand on the phone. I had a funny feeling she knew I was there, because she paused after she said "Call me," as if she were giving me a chance to pick up. I don't know that if she had just waited a few more moments, I would've picked up the phone, said her name, and let that world—hers, ours—come into this one. I don't know. I know that when she finally hung up, I was disappointed, but also relieved, as if we had finally come to some sort of a decision.

When Caitlin rescued me, at least for the weekend, I told her about my newly colorized emotions, but underneath the automatic sympathy relatives have for other relatives' plights, I could detect a note of approval.

"Do you love her?" she asked toward the end of the night.

"Yes," I said, though I said it like I was just remembering it, like something drawn out of me in a hypnotic state.

"Then," she began, "then you should act like it." But she added: "I guess."

Caitlin left a few cigarettes behind when she left, and so now I've taken up smoking, if in a half-assed way: I smoke half a cigarette, get over-whelmed by the head rush, and toss away the butt. I always think I want a smoke, but I never really do; even so, I've been carrying a pack, my razor in a case just in case of depression.

I'm smoking now, off the back porch. The phone is ringing be-hind me.

I can see Siobhan La Rue sitting at the end of my bed, with the phone cradled between her chin and neck, maybe lighting up a cigarette herself. She doesn't really expect me to answer right away. . . . She's giving me time to think about it.

I blow smoke at the blank sky. The moon and the stars have dropped out of this particular night, and I am left with darkness. I tap out ash, and from the corner of my eye, it looks like the ash is falling directly out of me.

She is talking now—I can hear her behind me.

I close my eyes and I can see Siobhan La Rue's voice coming through the openings in my grandparents' house, through the cracks and the places I haven't yet sealed up. Her voice is spilling through these openings, cas-cading down the walls like blue sheets of rain.

"Call me," she says now, and she waits. I can hear her. She is waiting. We wait.

# Supplementary Readings

## ANTHOLOGIES

Allen, Paula Gunn, ed. *Grandmothers of the Light: A Medicine Woman's Sourcebook.* Boston: Beacon Press, 1991.

―――*Spider Woman's Granddaughters: Traditional Tales and Contemporary Writing by Native American Women.* New York: Ballantine Books, 1989.

―――*Voice of the Turtle: American Indian Literature 1900–1970.* New York: Ballantine Books, 1994.

Bruchac, Joseph, ed. *Returning the Gift: Poetry and Prose from the First North American Native Writers Festival.* Tucson: University of Arizona Press, 1994.

Cunningham, Keith. *American Indians' Kitchen Table Stories: Contemporary Conversations with Cherokee, Sioux, Hopi, Osage, Navajo, Zuni, and Members of Other Nations.* Little Rock: August House, 1992.

Hobson, Geary, ed. *The Remembered Earth: An Anthology of Contemporary Native American Literature.* Albuquerque: University of New Mexico Press, 1980.

King, Thomas, ed. *All My Relations: An Anthology of Contemporary Canadian Native Fiction.* Norman: University of Oklahoma Press, 1992.

Lesley, Craig, ed. *Talking Leaves: Contemporary Native American Short Stories.* New York: Dell-Delta Books, 1991.

Oritz, Simon J., ed. *Earth Power Coming: Short Fiction in Native American Literature.* Tsaile, Navajo Nation, Arizona, 1983.

Roscoe, Will, and Gay American Indians, eds. *Living the Spirit: A Gay American Indian Anthology.* New York: St. Martin's Press, 1988.

Rosen, Kenneth, ed. *The Man to Send Rain Clouds.* New York: Random House/Seaver Books, 1974.

Trafzer, Clifford E., ed. *Earth Song, Sky Spirit: Short Stories of the Contemporary Native American Experience.* New York: Anchor Books, 1993.

Walters, Anna Lee, ed. *Neon Powwow: New Native American Voices of the Southwest.* Flagstaff, Ariz.: Northland, 1993.

## SINGLE-AUTHOR SHORT FICTION COLLECTIONS

Alexie, Sherman. *The Lone Ranger and Tonto Fistfight in Heaven.* New York: Grove-Atlantic, 1993.

Brant, Beth. *Mohawk Trail.* Ithaca, N.Y.: Firebrand Press, 1985.

Bruchac, Joseph. *Turtle Meat and Other Stories.* Duluth, Minn.: Holy Cow! Press, 1992.

Conley, Robert J. *The Witch of Goingsnake and Other Stories.* Norman: University of Oklahoma Press, 1988.

Cook-Lynn, Elizabeth. *The Power of Horses and Other Stories.* Boston: Little Brown-Arcade, 1990.

Dorris, Michael. *Working Men.* New York: Henry Holt, 1993.

Maracle, Lee. *I Am Woman.* North Vancouver, B.C.: Write-On Publishers (Box 86606, North Vancouver, B.C., V7L 4L2), 1988.

## CRITICISM, BACKGROUND, AND HISTORY

Allen, Paula Gunn. *The Sacred Hoop: Recovering the Feminine in American Indian Traditions.* Boston: Beacon Press, 1986.

Brandon, William. *The Last Americans: The Indian in American Culture.* New York: McGraw-Hill, 1974.

Hirschfelder, Arlene, Mary Lou Byler, and Michael A. Dorris, eds. *A Guide to Research on North American Indians.* Chicago: American Library, 1983.

Krotz, Larry. *Indian Country: Inside Another Canada.* Toronto: McClelland & Stewart, 1992.

Lincoln, Kenneth. *Ind'in Humor: Bicultural Play in Native America.* New York: Oxford University Press, 1993.

Momaday, N. Scott. *The Way to Rainy Mountain.* Albuquerque: University of New Mexico Press, 1969.

Owens, Louis. *Other Destinies: Understanding the American Indian Novel.* Norman: University of Oklahoma Press, 1992.

Ruoff, A. LaVonne Brown. *American Indian Literatures: An Introduction, Bibliographic Review, and Selected Bibliography.* New York: Modern Language Association, 1990.

Welch, James, with Paul Stekler. *Killing Custer: The Battle of the Little Bighorn and the Fate of the Plains Indians.* New York: W.W. Norton, 1994.

# About the Authors

**Sherman Alexie** (Spokane-Coeur d'Alene) lives on the Spokane Reservation in Washington. He has published three books of poetry, *The Business of Fancydancing, I Would Steal Horses, Old Shirts & New Skins,* and two collections of short stories, *First Indian on the Moon* and *The Lone Ranger and Tonto Fistfight in Heaven.* His work has appeared in *The Atlantic.*

**Paula Gunn Allen** (Laguna-Lakota) lives in Albuquerque. She has published a number of books of poetry, fiction, criticism/essays, fiction anthologies, and retold legends from Indian Women's Country, including *Shadow Country, Skins and Bones, The Sacred Hoop, The Woman Who Owned the Shadows, Spider Women's Granddaughters, Grandmothers of the Light,* and *Voice of the Turtle: American Indian Literature 1900–1970.* Allen is a professor of English and American Indian studies and women's studies at UCLA. She received the Native American Prize for Literature in 1991, and the Wise Woman Award from the Center for Policy on Women, Washington, D.C., in 1994.

**Esther Belin** (Navajo) is involved in film writing and production and has written several short stories. Her work appeared in *Neon Powwow: New Native American Voices of the Southwest.* Belin lives in Berkeley.

**Betty Louise Bell** (Cherokee) teaches literature at the University of Michigan, Ann Arbor. Dr. Bell taught the first American Indian literature course at Harvard University.

**Beth Brant** (Bay Quinte Mohawk) lives in Melvinville, a suburb of Detroit, near the Canadian reserve of her branch of the Mohawk. Brant has published two collections, *Mohawk Trail* and *Food & Spirits*, and edited *A Gathering of Spirit*, a collection of Native women's writings.

**Joseph Bruchac** (Abnaki) lives in New York State in the house that he was raised in by his mother's parents. He and his wife Carol have edited and published the Greenfield Review Press and run the Greenfield Literary Center for a number of years. He is widely anthologized and has published several books, including *Turtle Meat and Other Stories, Survival This Way: Interviews with American Indian Poets,* and, with Michael Caduto, *Keepers of the Earth* and *Keepers of the Animals*. Bruchac has edited fifteen anthologies of poetry and fiction and is one of the organizers and guiding spirits of the American Indian Writers Association.

**Michelle T. Clinton** (Cherokee-African) has published a book of poetry, *Good Sense & the Faithless*. She lives in Los Angeles.

**Robert J. Conley** (Cherokee) has published several collections and novels, including *The Witch of Goingsnake and Other Stories, Killing Time, Colfax, Nickajack, Go-Ahead Rider, The Saga of Henry Starr,* and a series of novels about his Cherokee heritage (*The Way of the Priests, The Dark Way, The White Path,* and *The Way South*) and a collection of poetry, *The Rattlesnake Band and Other Poems*. His work has been published widely in anthologies and journals. He lives in Talequah, Oklahoma, the capital of the Cherokee Nation.

**Dan L. Crank** (Navajo) lives in Dennehotso, Arizona Navajo Nation. He is of the Bitahni clan and born for the Kinlichiiini clan. His work has appeared in *Neon Powwow: New Native American Voices of the Southwest* and several journals.

**Michael Dorris** (Modoc) has published several nonfiction books, including *The Broken Cord*, which received the National Book Critics Circle Award; two novels, *A Yellow Raft in Blue Water,* and, with Louise Erdrich, *The Crown of Columbus*; and a collection of his short stories, *Working Men*.

**Debra Earling** (Flathead) is enrolled in the M.F.A./Ph.D. program at Cornell University. Her stories have been published in several collections, including *The Last Best Place: A Montana Anthology, Dancing on the Rim of the World,* and *Talking Leaves*. Her home is in Polson, Montana.

**Louise Erdrich** (Turtle Mountain Chippewa) won the Literary Circle Book Award for *Love Medicine*. Erdrich has published several novels, including *Love Medicine*, *The Beet Queen*, *Tracks*, *The Bingo Palace*, and, with Michael Dorris, *The Crown of Columbus*; and two books of poetry.

**Diane Glancy** (Cherokee) has published several volumes of poetry, including *Lone Dog's Winter Count* and *Iron Woman*, and *Claiming Breath* and *Trigger Dance*, collections of short fiction. Glancy lives in Minnesota.

**Roxy Gordon** (Chocktaw) lives in Dallas, Texas, where he writes poetry, performance art pieces, block-busting journalistic articles on news from Indian Country that is not always the standard opinion in same, draws, and survives. His stories and poetry have been published in anthologies and journals and he has published two books: *I Saw*, poetry, and *Some Things I Did*, an autobiography.

**Joy Harjo** (Creek) was born in Oklahoma and lives in Albuquerque, where she teaches at the University of New Mexico. Her publications include poetry and prose in numerous anthologies and journals; collections of poetry such as *In Mad Love and War*, *She Had Some Horses*, and *What Moon Drove Me to This?*; and (with photographer Stephen Strom) *Secrets from the Center of the World*. She also writes screenplays.

**Linda Hogan** (Chickasaw) lives in Idledale, Colorado, on the eastern face of the Rockies. She is widely anthologized and has published several books, including *Calling Myself Home*, *Eclipse*, *Seeing Through the Sun*, *Daughters, I Love You*, and *Savings*, poetry; *Red Clay: Poems and Stories*; and *Mean Spirit*, a novel.

**Dean Ing** (Cherokee) is a well-published writer. He mostly publishes science fiction, and his stories appear frequently in journals. His books include *Anasazi*, *Butcher Bird*, *Systemic Shock*, and *The Ransom of Black Stealth One*. Ing lives in Ashland, Oregon.

**Thomas King** (Cherokee-German-Irish) is associate professor and chair of American Indian studies at the University of Minnesota. King has published several books, including *Medicine River*, which was made into a film starring Graham Green. He has edited a volume of fiction by Canadian Native writers, *All My Relations*, and coedited *The Native in Literature*, a collection of essays.

**N. Scott Momaday** (Kiowa), born in Oklahoma, was raised at Jemez Pueblo in New Mexico. He received a Pulitzer Prize in 1969 for his novel *House*

*Made of Dawn*. He lives in Tucson, where he serves on the English faculty at the University of Arizona, writes, and paints. His books include *The Way to Rainy Mountain*, *Gourd Dancer*, *The Names*, *The Ancient Child*, and *In the Presence of the Sun: Stories and Poems*. Momaday received the Native American Prize for Literature in 1990.

**Louis Owens** (Chocktaw-Cherokee) lives in Albuquerque and is a professor of English at the University of New Mexico. His books include the novels *The Sharpest Sight* and *Wolfsong* and the critical studies *American Indian Novelists: An Annotated Critical Biography* (coauthored) and *The Grapes of Wrath: Trouble in the Promised Land*.

**Opal Lee Popkes** (Chocktaw), raised near Roswell, New Mexico, has written poetry as well as fiction and has taught at the college level.

**Susan Power** (Standing Rock Sioux) is currently a Bunting Institute Fellow in Cambridge, Massachusetts. Her short fiction has been published in the *Atlantic Monthly*, the *Paris Review*, *Story*, and *The Best American Short Stories of 1993*. *Grass Dancer* is her first novel.

**D. Renville** (Dakota-Assiniboine-Gros Ventre) is a writer who lives on the Lake Traverse Reservation. The story included here is an excerpt from a novel, *Siobhan La Rue*, that he is completing while attending Sisseton-Wahpeton Community College.

**Ralph Salisbury** (Cherokee) was born on a farm in Iowa and lives in Eugene, Oregon, where he recently retired from his position at the University of Oregon. Salisbury's work has appeared in collections such as *I Tell You Now*, *The Clouds Threw This Light*, and *Songs of This Earth on Turtle's Back* and in magazines and journals such as *Chariton Review*, *The New Yorker*, and *Transatlantic Review*. He served as editor of the *Northwest Review* for a number of years. His collections of poetry include *Going to the Water: Poems of a Cherokee Heritage*, *Ghost Grapefruit and Other Poems*, *Spirit Beast Chant*, and *Pointing at the Rainbow*.

**Leslie Marmon Silko** (Laguna Pueblo) lives on a ranch near Tucson, Arizona. She has published two novels, *Ceremony* and *Almanac of the Dead*; a book of poetry, *Laguna Woman*; and a multigenre collection, *Storyteller*.

**Patricia Clark Smith** (Micmac-Canuck) was born in Maine and lives in Albuquerque, where she is associate professor of English and creative writing at the University of New Mexico. Her books include *Talking to the Land* and

*Changing Your Story.* Smith was one of the editors for the recently published anthology *Western Literature in a World Context.*

**Martin Cruz Smith** (Senecu-Yaqui-Isleta Pueblo) has authored novels including *The Indians Won, Gypsy in Amber, Canto for a Gypsy, Nightwing, Stallion Gate,* and the trilogy *Gorky Park, Polar Star,* and *Red Square.*

**Mary Randle TallMountain** (Koyukon) was born in Nulato, Alaska. She was the first Koyukon from Nulato to come "outside," which she did as a child in the custody of her white adoptive parents. They eventually settled in California, where Mary lived and worked, taking up writing poetry in the 1960s and fiction in the 1970s. Her work has been published in a number of anthologies and journals. TallMountain's books include *There Is No Word for Goodbye* and *The Light on the Tent Wall.*

**Luci Tapahonso** (Dine) lives in Lawrence, Kansas, where she teaches on the English faculty at the University of Kansas. Her publications include poetry in magazines and anthologies such as *A Gathering of Spirit, Ch'iyaan 'iil'ini binaaltsoos* (a traditional cookbook), and *Conceptions Southwest.* She has published four books of poetry: *One More Shiprock Night, Seasonal Woman, A Breeze Swept Through,* and *Saanii Dahataal: The Women Are Singing.*

**Karen Wallace** (Cherokee-Osage) lives in Los Angeles, where she is enrolled in the Ph.D. program in English at UCLA. This is her first publication.

**Anna Lee Walters** (Otoe Pawnee) lives in the Navajo Nation and teaches English at Navajo Community College in Tsaile, Navajo Nation, Arizona. Her work has been published widely in journals and anthologies since the 1970s, and she has authored or edited several books, including *Neon Powwow: New Native American Voices of the Southwest; The Sacred: Ways of Knowledge, Sources of Life* (with Peggy Beck); *The Spirit of Native America: Beauty and Mysticism in American Indian Art; Talking Indian: Reflections on Writing and Survival;* and *The Ghost Singer,* a novel.

**Emma Lee Warrior** (Piegan) is a poet and short-story writer whose work has been included in several anthologies. She currently lives in Washington state.

**James Welch** (Blackfeet/Gros Ventre) is primarily a novelist, who has also written one book of poetry, *Riding the Earthboy 40,* and one history (with Paul Stekler), *Killing Custer: The Battle of Little Bighorn and the Fate* *of the Plains Indians*. His novels represent some of the most significant native-authored fiction of the 1970s and 1980s. He has written *Winter in the Blood*, *The Death of Jim Loney*, and *Fools Crow*, a historical novel. His most recent novel is *Indian Lawyer*.

# Permission Acknowledgments

Grateful acknowledgment is made for permission to reprint previously published material by the following authors:

Sherman Alexie, "Somebody Kept Saying Powwow" from *The Lone Ranger and Tonto Fist Fight in Heaven*. Copyright © 1993 by Sherman Alexie. Reprinted with the permission of Grove/Atlantic, Inc.

Paula Gunn Allen, "Charlie." Copyright © 1987 by Paula Gunn Allen. Reprinted with the permission of the author.

Esther G. Belin, "indigenous irony." Copyright © 1991 by Esther G. Belin. Reprinted with the permission of the author.

Beth Brant, "Coyote Learns a New Trick" from *Mohawk Trail*. Copyright © 1985 by Beth Brant. Reprinted with the permission of Firebrand Books, Ithaca, New York.

Joseph Bruchac, "Bears" from *Turtle Meat and Other Stories*. Copyright © 1992 by Joseph Bruchac. Reprinted with the permission of Holy Cow! Press.

Michelle T. Clinton, "Humiliation of the Boy." Copyright © 1991 by Michelle T. Clinton. Reprinted with the permission of the author.

Robert J. Conley, "Wili Woyi" from *The Witch of Goingsnake and Other Stories* (Stillwater: University of Oklahoma Press, 1987). Originally published in *The Remembered Earth* (Albuquerque: Red Earth Press, 1979). Copyright © 1979 by Robert J. Conley. Reprinted with the permission of the author, c/o The Peekner Literary Agency, Inc.

Dan L. Crank, "Neon Powwow" from *Neon Powwow: New Native American Voices of the Southwest*, edited by Anna L. Walters, Northland Publishing, Flagstaff, Arizona. Copyright © 1993 by Dan L. Crank. Reprinted with the permission of the author.

Michael Dorris, "Groom Service" from *Working Men*. Copyright © 1993 by Michael Dorris. Originally published in *Louder Than Words*, 1989. Reprinted with the permission of Henry Holt and Company, Inc.

Debra Earling, "Jules Bart, Giving Too Much—August 1946." Reprinted with the permission of the author.

Louise Erdrich, "Lipshaw's Luck" from *The Bingo Palace*. Copyright © 1994 by Louise Erdrich. Reprinted with the permission of HarperCollins Publishers, Inc.